DOUBLE HAPPINESS

A Novel

HEATHER ENG

An imprint of Penguin Random House LLC
1745 Broadway, New York, NY 10019
penguinrandomhouse.com

Book design by Alissa Theodor

LIBRARY OF CONGRESS CATALOGING-IN-PUBLICATION DATA
Names: Eng, Heather, author
Title: Double happiness: a novel / Heather Eng.
Description: New York, NY : Tiny Reparations Books, [2026]
Identifiers: LCCN 2025040603 (print) | LCCN 2025040604 (ebook) |
ISBN 9798217046980 trade paperback | ISBN 9798217046997 ebook
Subjects: LCGFT: Romance fiction | Novels
Classification: LCC PS3605.N427 D68 2026 (print) | LCC PS3605.N427 (ebook)
LC record available at https://lccn.loc.gov/2025040603
LC ebook record available at https://lccn.loc.gov/2025040604

Printed in the United States of America
1st Printing

The authorized representative in the EU for product safety and compliance is Penguin Random House Ireland, Morrison Chambers, 32 Nassau Street, Dublin D02 YH68, Ireland, https://eu-contact.penguin.ie.

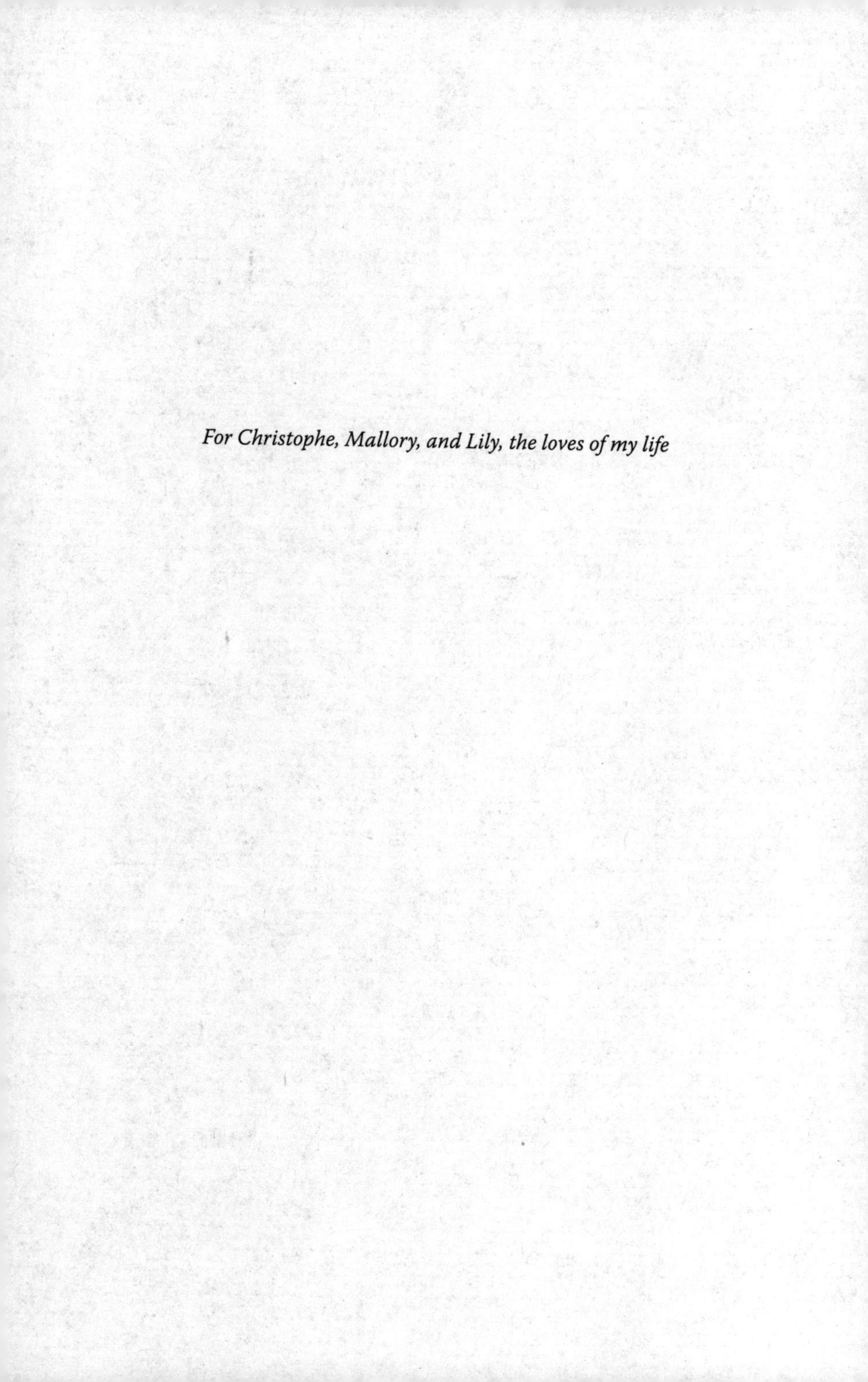

For Christophe, Mallory, and Lily, the loves of my life

DOUBLE HAPPINESS

CHAPTER ONE

Mei glanced at the clock and saw that it was go time. Before she could overthink, she snapped her laptop shut with a decisive thump.

"All right. I'm packing it in."

Her teammates looked up in shock.

"No way," said Bryce. "It's only six."

"Right?" quipped Ayanna. "There could be blizzards, hurricanes, or holiday weekends. But I've never seen the great Mei leave work this early."

"Oh please." Mei grabbed the yellow water bottle she'd gotten two years ago on her first day at the buzzy startup. "You all work as much as I do, if not more."

"If you say so," Ayanna replied nonchalantly, though Mei saw the pride glinting in her eyes. "You and the fiancé have big plans tonight?"

Mei shrugged but couldn't contain the smile pulling at her lips. "Something like that."

"Good for you!" Tamiko chimed in.

"You lovebirds enjoy," Ayanna agreed. "See you on Monday."

Mei shouldered her tote as she walked off. "Ping me if you need anything!"

Sunlight streamed through the windows of Livin's global headquarters, highlighting the poured concrete floors, colorful furniture, and silver Airstream trailer retrofitted as a bar. Thanks to a massive influx of cash from the latest round of funding, the experiential lifestyle company had recently doubled in size. Now Livin had twelve thousand employees, boasted offices in twenty countries, and offered stylish long- and short-term apartment rentals on every continent except Antarctica—though rumors swirled about a forthcoming site there.

Diana, Mei's manager and the VP of brand marketing, perched on a sleek leather couch in a common area. A street art mural behind her proclaimed, "Livin the Dream!"

"Heading out, Mei?" Diana asked, glancing up from her laptop.

"Just this once." Mei's stomach tightened with guilt. "I'll be on Slack if you need me, and online all day Sunday."

"Won't we all?"

Mei smiled gratefully. "I'll send you the latest campaign deck then."

"Thanks, Mei. You deserve an early Friday!"

Mei rode the elevator to the ground floor, then burst out the revolving door. Park Avenue South teemed with New Yorkers eager to start a perfect July weekend.

She hightailed it south, threading between commuters and darting across streets. On another day, she might have tilted her head up to savor the sun on her face, the warm concrete beneath her feet. But not today. She had no time for that.

At Twenty-Third Street, she dashed past the entrance to the

southbound 6 train, then doubled back and ran down the stairs. A familiar rumble signaled an approaching train. *Yes!* Mei hurried onto the platform and jumped into a car just before the doors closed.

At Astor Place, she was the first one out. She trotted east on the crowded sidewalks until she approached her destination: a hand-pulled noodle shop with white walls and imposing wooden doors. Mei's heart leapt when she spotted her fiancé's broad shoulders and gelled black hair, the sun glinting off his silver-rimmed glasses.

"Joey!" She closed the gap between them with a few steps and wrapped her arms around him.

"Happy anniversary," he said, bending down to meet her lips. "This has been the best year of my life."

Mei's stomach fluttered. "Mine too."

Hand in hand, they walked into the restaurant.

"Reservation for two at six fifteen," Joey said.

The host led them past the neat rows of tables to a long wooden bar. He gestured to the two seats at the end.

Joey winked. "A table might be more comfortable, but I want to sit in the same seats where it all began."

Mei laughed. "Of course."

Exactly one year ago, Mei had stopped into this noodle place for a late dinner. She'd just wrapped up a twelve-hour offsite with her team. All she wanted was a big bowl of soup in a quiet setting. She'd just given the waiter her order when the man beside her struck up a conversation.

Excuse me, he'd asked. *Are you on a date?*

Mei had raised an eyebrow. She shook her head no.

Well, you are now! the man replied.

An incredulous laugh escaped Mei's throat. She had stared at the stranger in disbelief. Normally, she'd have shut him down, but something about this guy felt familiar. With his outer-borough accent, olive complexion, and day-old scruff, he reminded Mei of a grown-up version of the boys who'd gone to her Queens public schools. They'd been rowdy, self-assured, and never remotely interested in her.

This guy clearly was, though. As they ate their noodle soup, his easy manner and lopsided smile drew Mei in. Her hunch had been right; the man next to her was named Joey DiGiacomo, and he was a proud Queens native. While Mei had fled to Manhattan as soon as she could, Joey never left. He knew the borough's rich food scene, and by the time they finished eating, Mei had agreed to meet him for dim sum in Flushing that Sunday.

Now, as they placed their order, Joey reached for Mei's hand. "Sorry I couldn't get a later reservation. I know it's not easy for you to leave work this early."

"I'll have to work this weekend, but I wasn't going to miss this." She squeezed his hand reassuringly. "Thanks for always being my number one supporter."

"Of course, my baby. I know how much Livin means to you."

Gratitude filled Mei's chest. Whenever they were with others, Joey always bragged about her role as Livin's senior director of brand marketing. He told everyone she was the brains behind the splashy ads, buzzy brand collaborations, and headline-grabbing events that made Livin a household name all over the world. Joey had no insecurities about her outearning him—her salary was nearly twice his. And he never complained about her eighty-hour workweeks or the pressure she put on herself to maintain her standing as the highest-ranked marketing employee.

Mei sipped her water, then chuckled. "Do most people celebrate the anniversary of the day they met?"

"Who cares? We are! I want to celebrate everything about us. Our first official date—this Sunday, by the way. Our first kiss. The first time I went to your place. The very first time we—"

"Joey!" Mei swatted his arm.

"What? I was going to say the very first time we went away together. To that frou-frou B and B upstate."

"Ha, okay." Mei rolled her eyes but couldn't help smiling. "We'll see about all those anniversaries. I can't always escape Livin this early."

"I know, my baby. Every day is special. I still can't believe how lucky we are. What if we hadn't sat next to each other that night?"

"Or if my team had gone out to dinner after our offsite?"

"Or if I'd gone straight home to work on my music files instead of picking up those hard drives from that place down the block?" Joey's eyes lit up just talking about music. Mei didn't quite get his hobby of identifying, labeling, and organizing thousands of unnamed music files he'd bulk-downloaded years ago. But she appreciated his dedication to his craft.

"We never would have met." She touched his scruffy cheek.

"And you never would've moved back to Queens."

"Nope! I needed my Queens guy to bring me home."

In their first months together, Mei ate her way through neighborhoods she hadn't seen in decades. With Joey, she braved mouth-numbing Thai food in Elmhurst and went on a quest to find the best spanakopita in Astoria. They whiled away summer afternoons in the Rockaways, then chowed down on burgers and fries on the boardwalk. Every Friday, they picked up plump Nepalese momos and ate dinner holding hands in Joey's Jackson Heights apartment.

Joey commuted to Midtown for his IT job at a document-shredding company, but he never spent time in Manhattan. He knew nothing about the Upper West Side, where Mei lived, and threw himself into exploring her world. Mei had to stifle a giggle whenever Joey arrived at her local wine bar, clad in one of his signature graphic tees. (Mei's favorite had a cartoon beaver declaring "Best Dam T-shirt!") Sometimes, when they strolled through Central Park, he'd stop to show her an epic fail video—someone falling off a ladder while hanging holiday decorations, or face-planting into a birthday cake. Whenever she suggested they try something new, like seeing the opera or ballet at Lincoln Center, Joey sent her into gales of laughter, ribbing her about how far she'd come from her humble roots and how those snooty places would never let in a ruffian like him.

When both of their leases were up, moving in together was a no-brainer. They already spent every night with each other. The only question was where. Joey was open to Manhattan, but he preferred Queens. Mei was intrigued about returning to the borough where she'd grown up—just not the neighborhood where the worst years of her life had unfolded.

They decided on Long Island City. With their combined salaries, they could afford an apartment in a newer high-rise right across the river from Manhattan. Neither of them had ever lived somewhere with large windows, central air-conditioning, and stainless steel appliances; it felt like the perfect place to start their life together.

On their first night in that shiny new apartment, ten months after that fateful dinner at the noodle shop, Joey had gotten down on one knee amid the half-unpacked moving boxes. As Mei wiped tears from her eyes, she'd said *Yes* and kissed Joey with certainty.

Now Joey held up his pint of beer. "To us, my baby."

Mei clinked her glass against his. "Happy anniversary."

The waiter arrived with their bowls of dumpling noodle soup.

"Do we have any plans tomorrow?" Joey asked as he sipped a spoonful of broth.

"We're going to Ali's, remember?" Ali and Luc, her little sister and brother-in-law, were hosting a barbecue.

"Oh right. I texted Ali the other day and said we'd bring egg tarts and red bean buns."

Mei grinned. "I love how you and Ali text."

"Your sister is my sister."

Mei happily bit into a dumpling. Joey knew Ali would always hold the largest place in her heart. She and Ali had taken care of each other during their parents' horrific divorce, their father's unexpected death, and the years of financial strife that followed—all the events that led Mei to leave Queens and never return. Until she met Joey.

"So what's Luc's brother's name?" Joey asked. "The dude we're celebrating tomorrow?" Ali and Luc's barbecue was in honor of Luc's older brother, who had just moved back to New York after many years away.

"Alexandre."

"Alexandre," Joey repeated, enunciating every syllable. "What's he like? An older, grayer version of Luc?"

Mei laughed. "He's only forty-two." She and Joey were both thirty-six. "And he and Luc don't really look alike."

That had always surprised Mei. At two years apart, she and Ali were often mistaken for twins. They were both five-one with long, dark brown hair and big brown eyes. Luc and Alexandre were both lean and athletic with chestnut hair. But while Luc was clean-shaven and six feet tall, Alexandre was several inches shorter, had a more wiry build, and sported long hair and a beard.

"I don't really know what he's like, either." Mei swirled a dumpling in chili oil. "From what I remember, he's quiet. A little intense. And smart. He has a PhD and was doing some kind of biology research at the University of Oregon."

Joey ate a spoonful of noodles. "I don't get it. Luc's your brother from another mother—"

"That is true." Ali and Luc had been together for sixteen years, since their freshman year at Fordham University. In that time, Luc had become like a sibling to her.

"How do you not know *his* brother?"

"Alexandre's always lived in Oregon. He only came home for some holidays, and not in a while."

"Got it. Guess we'll get to know him soon enough."

They finished dinner, then ambled to the subway, savoring the warm evening. Mei rested her head against Joey's chest as the 7 train trundled through the tunnel between Manhattan and Queens.

At Vernon-Jackson, they exited the subway and walked west toward the water, until they reached their building's glassy entrance. Joey greeted Julio, the evening doorman, with a hearty hello, while Mei flashed her warmest smile. As usual, her megawatt grin didn't extinguish her discomfort about him being paid to open the door for her.

The elevator whooshed them up ten floors. Once inside their apartment, Mei sighed with contentment at her living room's creamy white walls and new finishes.

"I never thought I'd live anywhere so beautiful."

"Me neither," Joey agreed. "But here we are."

Mei stood before the large glass picture window, drinking in the view. Manhattan sprawled out before her in all its intoxicating glory.

Joey slipped behind her, his arms encircling her waist. Together, they admired the blazing orange sunset backlighting the city skyline. Mei leaned into Joey, relishing the feel of his strong chest against her back. She tilted her head up. He leaned down to meet her lips. *Here we are.*

• • •

The next morning, Mei and Joey hopped into his trusty white Corolla. As they drove north, Mei settled back in the worn passenger seat and admired how fine her fiancé looked behind the wheel. Joey's black hair was neatly slicked back, his eyes intent behind his silver-rimmed glasses as he concentrated on the road. To their left, the Hudson River glinted in the hazy July sun.

An hour later, they arrived at Ali and Luc's cozy, low-slung ranch home in the lower Hudson Valley.

Mei rang the bell, then swung open the door before anyone could answer. "We're here!"

Little footsteps sounded from inside the house. A moment later, Kaia, her niece, came running toward her, jubilant in a violet sundress, her light brown ponytail streaming behind her.

Mei crouched down to hug her. "Who's my favorite three-year-old?"

Kaia giggled. "I am."

"You got that right!"

Joey patted Kaia affectionately on the head. "She's a Li woman. Of course she's the smartest one in the room."

"Mei! Joey!" Ali and Luc appeared in the hallway.

Mei embraced her sister tightly. "Nice outfit," she said with a laugh. She and Ali were both wearing V-neck sundresses, hers in yellow, Ali's in teal. "Hey, Luc!" She gave her brother-in-law a squeeze, while Joey pulled Ali into a bear hug. Mei grinned at the sight of all her favorite people together.

"Thanks for coming early," Ali said as she led them through the house. "Can you take Kaia out back?" she asked Luc and Joey. She turned to Mei. "We can plate your pastries."

Mei smiled. She always loved getting a few minutes alone with her sister.

"How's the wedding planning?" Ali asked once they reached the kitchen. "Have you made any progress?"

"We just finalized our menu!" In three months, she and Joey were tying the knot at their favorite neighborhood bistro, then celebrating with a family-style lunch. Initially, Joey had wanted a traditional church wedding, followed by an all-night dance party at a catering hall, while Mei's preference was to say "I do" at city hall, followed by dim sum with their immediate families. For some reason, she had no problems giving big presentations at work. But elaborate celebrations that were all about her made her want to run and hide.

"That's so exciting!" Ali passed Mei a platter. "Did you schedule your hair and makeup trials?"

"Not yet." Mei removed egg tarts from their wax-paper bags. "I was hoping to do that this week, but I've been so slammed."

Ali smiled sympathetically. "Is Livin insane, as usual?"

Mei groaned, even as a familiar fiery rush ignited her veins. "Always. But it's exciting. I'm presenting my three-year brand vision to the leadership team on Wednesday."

"That's right! You'll wow them." Ali picked up a plate of chips and guacamole. "Seriously, if you need help with wedding stuff, just let me know."

"I will." Mei grabbed the platter of Chinese pastries and followed her sister through the sliding glass door. "It looks great out here!"

Ali and Luc had decorated the patio with round paper lanterns in tropical shades of pink, orange, and yellow. Wildflowers in bud vases adorned the tables.

"Shouldn't there be a 'Welcome back, Alexandre' sign?" Mei asked.

"I was going to put one up. But then Alexandre told Luc that if we made this an obvious welcome home party, he would, I quote, 'hop in my car and drive straight back to Oregon.'"

Mei laughed. "I totally get it."

Guests began arriving. Mei poured herself a glass of rosé. One of Luc's neighbors chatted with her and Joey about a new breakfast café in town. With the sun shining on her face and a tingly wine buzz going, Mei luxuriated in the feel of Joey's hand on her back.

She finished her last sip of wine. "I'll get us a refill."

On the now-crowded patio, Mei topped off her rosé and found another beer for Joey. As she turned to rejoin her fiancé, she nearly bumped into Luc's parents, Clarisse and Jean-Germain Brodeur. They were retired French history professors, and Mei always thought they looked the part, with their wire-rimmed glasses, earth-toned clothing, and silver hair.

"Are you glad Alexandre's back?" she asked them.

"We are," Clarisse said as she and Jean-Germain exchanged rueful smiles. "Though I wish the circumstances were different."

What did *that* mean? Before Mei could ask, she spotted her mom and stepfather talking to Joey. She excused herself, then made her way to her parents.

Mei embraced her mom, taking in her cheerful floral blouse and long-layered bob. She was still thrown, at times, at her mother's relaxed demeanor. For most of Mei's life, her mom had been a stressed-out single mother who toiled long hours to pay rent on their dreary one-bedroom apartment. But over the years, Vivian had worked her way up from a receptionist to an office manager at a manufacturing company. After she met Henry, a kind accountant, ten years ago, their joint income finally let her save enough to retire.

"How are you two doing?" Vivian asked.

"We just celebrated the one-year anniversary of the day we met!" Joey slung an arm around Mei and kissed her temple.

Mei turned pink as her parents congratulated them. "I'm giving a big C-suite presentation on Wednesday. And I'm leading a major initiative with my best work friend, Ayanna. We're refreshing the Livin brand so it's more inclusive, with language and imagery guidelines for every region. That way, anyone, anywhere in the world, will see they belong at Livin, no matter their race, ethnicity, gender identity, age, religion, or ability."

"That's a lot," Vivian said.

"A very worthy project," Henry added.

Mei knew her parents understood the gravity of her undertaking. They'd both been people of color in the workforce. Mei could only imagine what Henry had faced as a Black man in corporate America.

"I'm excited about it," she said. "Oh, and we're going away soon! Joey and I are renting a house on Long Beach Island with Ali, Luc, and Kaia."

"How nice!" Vivian placed a hand on Joey's arm. "We took the girls there for a week every summer when they were kids."

Joey smiled. "My folks took me there, too. The Jersey Shore gets a bad rap, but I love it."

"I do, too." Mei took his hand. She was glad Joey was a Jersey Shore guy, not a Hamptons one. Once, after hearing colleagues talk about their Sagaponack summer homes, Mei ran a search on Zillow. She'd pictured little cottages with weathered wood shingles, but the palatial estates and eight-figure price tags made her jaw drop. Mei had never understood generational wealth until then. Even if she and Joey quadrupled their salaries, they'd never be able to afford a home like that.

As Joey, Vivian, and Henry traded Jersey Shore stories, Mei excused herself to refresh the appetizers. After replenishing the chips and guacamole, and adding more Chinese pastries to the platter, Mei stood on the patio to take in the scene. A few people played cornhole. Kaia ran barefoot on the grass. Where was the guest of honor? Mei couldn't spot Alexandre, but she saw Joey chatting with Luc and one of his friends by the grill. As Luc stacked vegetable skewers on a tray, he nodded politely, his eyes glazed over. That could only mean one thing: Joey was telling them about his music files. Mei hurried toward them.

"I've been trying out new song identification programs," Joey was saying. "You'd think AI would've made them better, but most are still shit."

"Ooh, those steaks look delicious!" Mei said. Luc shot her a grateful look.

"Hey, babe," Joey said. "I was just telling Luc and Alexandre about that old hard drive I found mixed up with my work stuff."

Mei did a double take. Joey and Luc were, in fact, talking to Alexandre. She hadn't recognized him without the thick brown beard and shaggy hair. Now Alexandre was clean-shaven. His chestnut hair was shorter and stylishly tousled, giving him a slightly rakish look. His hazel eyes were bright with intelligence; when he turned to Mei, she blinked at their intensity.

"Alexandre! I didn't recognize you without the—" Mei mimed a billowing beard.

Alexandre chuckled wryly. "Some days, I have a hard time recognizing myself."

"We're trying not to give him too much grief about his 'new life, new look.'" Luc jostled his brother playfully.

"Well, I'm digging it. You look good." Mei studied Alexandre's face. She had always thought of Luc as the more attractive brother. But without all the hair covering his cheeks and hanging in his eyes, Alexandre was handsome, too. Maybe even better-looking. The angles of his face were well-defined. Mei could make out his lean shoulder muscles beneath his white summer button-down, his taut forearms under his rolled-up sleeves.

"Thanks," Alexandre replied. "You look great, too."

Mei's cheeks warmed. Why did compliments make her so awkward? "How's being back? You got here when?"

"Last week. Not going to lie. It's a little weird."

"Why'd you move back?" Joey asked.

Alexandre's eyes flickered. "Tenure wasn't happening."

"Oh yikes," Mei said. So that's what his mother was referring to. "I'm sorry." Should she pat his shoulder? Hug him? She looked away and sipped her drink.

"It's okay. Twenty years of research to not achieve the ultimate goal. But it's fine. Everyone wants to start from scratch in their forties, right?"

Mei smiled uncomfortably.

"Well, you're not starting from scratch." Luc turned the steaks on the grill. "You'll be doing what you're good at, and what you enjoy, without all the stress of tenure."

"What's your new job?" Mei asked.

"Teaching at SUNY New Paltz. Genetics, microbiology, and molecular biology."

"Whoa." Mei's eyebrows shot up. A disbelieving laugh escaped her throat.

"What's so funny?" Alexandre asked.

The fierce glint in his eyes startled Mei. She coughed to compose herself. "I'm laughing at what you call starting from scratch: teaching classes like that at the university level." Mei saw a hint of surprise on Alexandre's face. "That sounds so prestigious."

A begrudging half smile formed on Alexandre's lips.

"Yeah, man, it's not like you're bagging groceries now," Joey agreed. "No disrespect to supermarket workers, of course. I put myself through community college while working at ShopRite."

"You did," Mei said proudly. "We both went to SUNYs," she told Alexandre. "Joey got his associate's from Nassau. I went to Binghamton but never took anything like what you're about to teach. That was Ali's realm." Her sister had aced every science class on her way to becoming a physical therapist. "Your new job sounds amazing."

"Thanks." Alexandre fiddled with the label on his beer bottle. "But in academia, all anyone cares about is research. There's a big difference between being a tenured professor doing research and a professor who's only teaching. Which is what I will be. It's considered a huge step down."

Luc set the grilling tongs aside. "No one thinks that except some academic a-holes. It's not even true."

Mei nodded vehemently. "What's more important than teaching the next generation?"

Alexandre shrugged. "I'm trying to focus on that, and not what my former colleagues think. Or my parents."

"They dreamed of us carrying on the Brodeur family academic tradition," Luc explained. "They were devastated when I went into tech without getting a PhD, or even a master's. And they were horrified when I quit tech to start my company." Luc had worked as a software engineer at a major tech company for a decade before opening a custom carpentry and furniture business. "But at least they had Alexandre. He was always their great hope."

"Clarisse and Jean-Germain were history professors at Fordham," Mei told Joey. She turned to Luc and Alexandre. "I didn't know they wanted you to be academics, too."

"Oh yeah." Luc nodded gravely.

"That's a story for another day," Alexandre added.

Mei spied Clarisse and Jean-Germain on the patio and narrowed her eyes. *What snobs!*

She glanced back at Alexandre. He was sipping his beer, but Mei could see the tension in his shoulders, the unease in his eyes.

"Are you teaching this summer?" she asked.

"Not until the fall. I'm going to spend the next few weeks settling in and working on lesson plans. Maybe check out some of the local hiking and running trails."

"You probably already know this, but the Hudson Valley is great for outdoor activities. There's tons of biking, rock climbing, and skiing."

"That was a big draw for moving back. That, and spending more time with this guy." Alexandre shook Luc by the shoulders as he smiled at Mei.

Alexandre's mischievous grin took Mei by surprise. She beamed back at him.

"I don't know if you're into the beach, but we're renting a house on Long Beach Island the second week of August," Joey said. "There's an extra bedroom if you want to come."

Alexandre raised his eyebrows. "Yeah? I'd like that."

"I'll send you the info," Luc said.

The four of them clinked their drinks.

"What'd I miss?" Ali ran over and added her wineglass to the circle. "What am I cheers-ing?"

"Alexandre is coming to the beach house. Joey invited him." Mei rubbed her fiancé's arm.

"Perfect!" Ali cheered. "Alexandre, we're so glad you're back. I hope you're ready to make up for lost time. These two"—she angled her head at Mei and Joey—"are always up here, so you'll be seeing lots of them, too."

Alexandre nodded politely. "I can't wait."

Luc set the steaks on the platter. "The food's ready. I'm going to bring everything to the table."

"I'll help you." Alexandre grabbed the tray of vegetable skewers.

"I should get Kaia ready to eat." Ali headed across the lawn to her daughter.

Mei smiled up at Joey. "That was nice of you to invite Alexandre to the beach house."

Joey shrugged. "He seems like a good guy." He glanced at Alexandre on the patio and lowered his voice. "I feel kind of bad for him. He's single, right?"

Mei followed Joey's gaze. "I think so."

"Wonder what his deal is."

"He probably never found the right person." She watched Alexandre place his tray on the table, then bend down to talk to Kaia. Alexandre's eyes met hers, catching her mid-stare. Mei flushed and turned back to Joey. "Dating in New York was rough. It's probably much worse in an Oregon college town."

"Yeah." Joey wrapped his arms around her. "I'm so glad we found each other."

Mei breathed in his spicy scent. "I am, too."

When they drew apart, Mei spotted Alexandre laughing with Luc, his smile lighting up his face. She nodded to herself. *He'll find someone soon, too.*

CHAPTER TWO

The doorbell rang, making Alexandre jump. The sharp buzz was jarring, compared to the melodic chimes of his old doorbell back in Oregon.

Alexandre padded to the entryway to greet his visitor. "Fancy seeing you again," he said jokingly to Luc.

"You'd better get used to it. We've got years to catch up on." Luc shook his head and grinned. "Sorry. I'm still getting used to the new you."

Alexandre ran a hand self-consciously through his hair. During his drive east, he'd detoured into Chicago. He was set on devouring a deep-dish pizza but had surprised himself by walking into the first barbershop he spotted. *Cut it all off*, he'd said. The symbolism of shedding his Oregon look was painfully obvious. Alexandre still couldn't believe he'd done something so melodramatic.

Luc surveyed the compact living room. "Looks like you're nearly unpacked."

"It helps that I didn't have much to begin with."

Alexandre had always lived frugally on his meager academic salary, and the cost of a cross-country move ticked up with every piece of furniture. In the end, he'd brought the bare minimum to the small apartment he was renting in a townhouse complex near the university. His bed and dresser just fit in the snug bedroom. His tidy collection of pots, pans, and dishes filled the wooden cabinets in the narrow galley kitchen. His desk and bookcase sat by the living room window. His bike, skis, and camping equipment lined another wall—a reminder to get out and use them. Alexandre still needed a sofa, coffee table, dining set, and some kind of artwork for the walls. But, as he kept reminding himself, starting a new life took time.

Luc picked up a two-foot-long crocheted zebrafish from the bookcase. "I wasn't sure old Danio would make it. I figured he'd end up in some Pacific Northwest thrift shop."

Alexandre motioned for Luc to toss him the fish. "I have nothing against zebrafish. Plus, he's from you."

"Damn straight. And he's custom-made. You should've seen all the craftspeople I messaged on Etsy, asking if they'd crochet a giant zebrafish."

Alexandre turned the striped fish in his hands. Luc had given it to him when he landed his tenure-track position researching genetics in zebrafish, an aptly named "model organism" with a gene structure similar to that of humans. Alexandre had named it Danio after the zebrafish genus. For years, Danio sat proudly in his lab, witnessing as he achieved one breakthrough after another and tenure seemed inevitable.

Until it hadn't.

Alexandre set the fish back on the bookcase. "I'll always have a place in my heart for zebrafish."

"As long as you're not planning to go back and study them."

"No way." In the three weeks since Alexandre had cleaned out his office at the University of Oregon, he'd had fewer nightmares that jolted him awake in a cold sweat, fewer moments of despair. He couldn't say he was done with research forever, though. Funny how his brother seemed to sense his lingering interest.

Luc eyed him sympathetically. "How are you doing with everything?"

"That's a loaded question."

Alexandre never imagined he'd be back in New York. Twenty years ago, when he was finishing undergrad at Columbia and looking at PhD programs, the University of Oregon had flown him out to Eugene. They'd spent days wooing him with their extensive research facilities and storied history: UO was the birthplace of zebrafish research. Alexandre would be conducting his own studies on the same campus where George Streisinger cloned the first vertebrate: a zebrafish. As Alexandre strolled the picturesque campus, admiring the giant trees, he saw his life unfolding there. Beyond UO's research program, Eugene was an outdoor lover's paradise, teeming with hiking, biking, and nature trails, and just an hour's drive from Oregon's scenic coast. The city was known as "TrackTown USA" for producing scores of elite runners and hosting Olympic track-and-field trials—a big draw for a lifelong runner like Alexandre.

When he moved to Eugene, Alexandre thought it would be forever. He'd made that dream a reality, earning his PhD, then a coveted professorship at UO while he continued his research.

And then it all ended.

Alexandre drew a breath. "Part of me will always miss Oregon. But I'm also kind of glad to leave it behind."

"Yeah, and once you start classes and get into a routine, you'll feel even better."

"As long as I avoid Mom and Dad. 'Those who can, do. Those who can't, teach.'"

Luc rolled his eyes. "Do me a favor and never say that again."

Alexandre couldn't count how many times he'd heard his parents quote that George Bernard Shaw line. Despite their history professor titles, Clarisse and Jean-Germain believed their life's work was to advance their fields through research, not teaching. They had little respect for academics who didn't make tenure or left research for other opportunities.

"If only they'd known their firstborn would be among those who can't."

"Please. Mom and Dad might think they're 'carrying the torch of humanity'"—Luc shuddered at another of their parents' favorite sayings—"by studying obscure topics no one's ever heard of. But you'll be passing the torch to future scientists. You won't even miss spending all day in a closet full of fish tanks, crunching numbers on an ancient laptop."

Alexandre couldn't help but laugh at his brother's exaggerated but accurate description of academic life.

"I know it's shocking, but outside of academia, people make career changes and end up better off. I did."

Alexandre had never expected Luc to quit his lucrative tech job to turn his lifelong woodworking hobby into a business. But his brother did seem happier now. More at ease.

Alexandre stifled a sigh. Now that he thought about it, Luc had never followed the blueprint their parents had laid out for them. Sure, he'd gone to Fordham, where their parents worked, and taken advantage of the nearly free tuition. But then Luc had eschewed the hallowed halls of academia for the fast-paced tech world, earning an eye-popping salary. Once he'd amassed a comfortable nest egg, he'd quit software engineering to pursue his real dream: carpentry. Look where Luc was now: happily married and financially sound, with time to spend with his family.

Maybe his brother was onto something. Alexandre's eyes strayed to the outdoor gear lining his wall.

"With teaching, I won't be tied to experiments and conferences. We should plan some camping and skiing trips. Or just drive up to Vermont when conditions are good."

"For sure. It'll be easier to get away if Ali and Kaia come. If it's just the two of us, I'll have to figure that out with Ali, but it's doable."

Alexandre deflated. Of course Luc couldn't just take off on a whim. The few friends Alexandre had in New York were married with kids, too.

Then he remembered something. "What about Mei and Joey?"

"Mei doesn't ski, but she'd be into hiking and weekend trips. Joey too."

Alexandre nodded. The few times he'd spoken to Mei on his past visits to New York, she seemed much younger. She was working in advertising, trying to figure out her life and career, while he was deeply entrenched in his research.

Talking to Mei at the barbecue was like meeting a new woman. She radiated confidence, filling him with a warm glow and making him slightly flustered when she complimented his new look. She'd talked up his teaching job with genuine respect. Until that moment, Alexandre had never even considered that his new gig might be impressive.

Alexandre replayed how Mei's brown eyes lit up when she spoke. A faint lemon-coconut scent had tickled his nose every time she threw her head back in laughter.

"Mei seems different," he said.

"A few years ago, she got a job she loves." Luc shot him a pointed look.

"Okay, got it. Career changes are good."

"And she met Joey."

The tall, broad-shouldered dude who'd draped his arm around Mei popped into Alexandre's mind. "What do you think of him?"

Luc shrugged. "He's a good guy. He makes Mei happy."

Alexandre sensed there was more than Luc was saying, but he didn't want to pry. He personally found Joey a bit odd. The guy was wearing a T-shirt that said "OverKOALAfied," with an illustration of the marsupial. *Overqualified for what?* Alexandre had wondered. Then Joey made Alexandre watch videos of dogs trying to skateboard, then rambled about some old music files he kept on hard drives. Hadn't he ever heard of streaming? Or cloud storage?

Still, Joey had invited him to the beach house. He couldn't be that bad.

Alexandre checked the time. "Do you have to run? Or can we grab a bite?"

"Let's get lunch. We just have to stop at my van."

Alexandre fixed Luc with a look. "Don't tell me—"

"It was nothing."

In the parking lot, Luc opened the back doors to his van. A small sofa and coffee table sat side by side.

"Ali and I figured this could help you while you're getting settled. The sofa is ours, from when we lived in the city. The coffee table is new."

Alexandre climbed in for a better look. The table was made of smooth reclaimed wood. The clean lines bore Luc's aesthetic touch.

A lump rose in Alexandre's throat. "It's beautiful."

They carried both pieces inside. The canary-yellow midcentury modern sofa was clearly meant to be a pop of color in a stylishly decorated apartment. Alexandre never would have picked it out, but he was glad it was now his. The yellow lit up his living room and the handsome coffee table paired perfectly.

Brighter. Just like my new life, Alexandre thought drolly.

As if reading his mind, Luc clapped him on the shoulder. "So glad you're back."

CHAPTER THREE

Hey, queen," Ayanna called, stopping by Mei's desk. "Ready for your big moment?"

Mei looked up from her presentation and smoothed the white blazer she wore over a silky cami in Livin's bright yellow. "You know it."

"I can't wait." Ayanna started down the hallway. "You're going to crush it, as usual."

Mei turned back to the slide deck with her three-year brand vision. She had revised it countless times, and now it was perfect.

Her phone buzzed. Mei clicked on a new text from Joey.

Go get 'em, babe!

He'd attached a gif of an animated spatula saying, "You're *flipping* awesome!"

Mei laughed. Spirits high, she gave her slides a final read.

Ten minutes later, she stood at the head of the executive boardroom. Oversized prints of Livin's marquee buildings hung on the wall: a stately Haussmann with wrought iron balconies on the Champs-Élysées, a beachfront Miami art deco. The leadership team and senior stakeholders sat around the conference table. Raucous male chatter filled the air, though a hush fell when Julian Fredericks, Livin's CEO, strode in.

Tall and imposing with flowing golden locks, piercing green eyes, and a neat goatee, Julian resembled a gracefully aging pop star more than the head of New York's highest-valued private company. He took a seat and acknowledged Mei with a dip of his head.

Diana shot Mei a confident smile. Ayanna gave her a steely nod that said: *You. Got. This.*

Mei clasped her shaking hands, then lifted her chin and addressed the room. "As you all know, in three years, Livin will be in more than one hundred cities on every continent. This brand strategy will ensure we continue our unprecedented growth while letting the world know about us in a big way."

For the next hour, Mei outlined the global brand campaigns they'd run, plus targeted campaigns for Livin's key offerings: *Livin the Life* (beautifully furnished rentals, from big-city apartments to rustic-chic homes in stunning rural settings), *Livin Like a Boss* (hip business travel accommodations), and *Livin It Up* (stylish apartments full of amenities, like gourmet meal plans and luxe fitness centers). Mei highlighted projected year-over-year growth and detailed how the company would break into new markets and expand in existing ones.

"By upleveling our brand, localizing our campaigns, making our storytelling and imagery more inclusive, and streamlining processes with AI-driven solutions, we'll transform Livin into the world's hottest brand—with the revenue to match."

She faced Julian expectantly. The CEO was sitting with his

hands folded against his lips. Mei's heart thudded as she awaited his reaction.

Finally, Julian lowered his hands. "What more can I say? We're on a mission to revolutionize the way people live, work, and play. Right now, Livin impacts millions of people every day. In two years, it'll be billions. This brand strategy is exactly what we need as we're transforming the world. That, and your leadership." Julian flashed her his rock-star grin, the one that had made him an overnight media darling and pop culture phenom.

Mei grinned back. "I'm thrilled to be on this journey with you."

When she returned to her desk, Mei opened her laptop to a slew of Slack messages.

You killed it!

That presentation was 🔥!!!

Word on the street is that you slayed. Get it, girl!

Mei closed her eyes and smiled. She needed to get back to work, but this moment was worth savoring.

● ● ●

"My presentation went so well!" Mei spooned papaya salad onto her plate, then passed the dish to Joey. She'd picked up dinner from her favorite Thai place to celebrate. "The head of finance asked tough questions but was fine with my answers. James, our new chief marketing officer, was there, too. He signed off on my strategy over email, but he's never seen me present. I bet I wowed him." She bit into a spring roll with gusto. "I still can't believe Julian praised *my* leadership! This makes me want to keep rising through the ranks. There are so few women or people of color at the top."

Joey clinked his water glass against hers. "I'm so proud of you. There's no doubt in my mind that you'll be running Livin soon."

Mei laughed. "I don't know if I want to *run* Livin. But VP of marketing would be nice."

"You'll get there, babe. I know it."

"Me too." She filled her plate with pad see ew. "I still can't believe this is our life. Who would've thought two kids from Queens would go and make something of themselves?"

"Well, *you* have. I'm still just a schlub in IT," Joey said with a chuckle.

"Oh please. You only manage everyone's access to every system in your company. And you're moving up!" Earlier this year, a larger paper-shredding company had acquired the one Joey worked for. The new head of IT had met with Joey and saw his potential. She'd arranged for him to take a network security certification exam at a national testing center to position him for a promotion.

"Your test is Monday, right? Have you studied?" Last night, when Mei was reviewing her presentation, Joey had been lounging on the couch, laughing at videos of people falling off trampolines. The previous night, he'd been at his desk, playing obscure songs and cursing when music identification apps failed to recognize them.

"Not too much."

"Why not?"

Joey shrugged. "I'm not sure I want the gig."

"Why? It's more money and a step up. And you'll be learning something new."

"It's also more responsibility. I like being a systems admin. I'm already making good money."

"Yeah, but a raise could always help." Their combined income was several tax brackets higher than where their parents had been, but now wasn't the time to be complacent about their finances. Mei gestured to their kitchen's glass tile backsplash. "This apartment is as much as our separate places combined, so we're not saving extra money. And, yeah, our wedding's small, but it's still costing several thousand. What if there's an emergency?"

Mei's mind flashed back to her preteen years. Her family never had much to begin with, but their situation became dire after her parents divorced and her father died. Mei recalled winter afternoons with Ali, shivering under blankets as they tried to do homework in their frigid apartment. She could still smell the twenty-five-cent packaged ramen they cooked for dinner every night as their mom worked late.

Joey chewed his lower lip. After a moment, he scooched his chair closer to hers. "I get it, my baby."

Mei rested her head against his chest. Joey understood. When he was a teenager, his father injured his back and lost his job at an auto repair shop. Joey had worked full-time slicing cold cuts at the ShopRite deli counter to support his family, while finishing high school and going to community college.

He kissed her cheek. "Don't you worry. I'll study and pass my test."

"And work toward that promotion?"

"Yup. You and me, baby. Moving up in the world."

Mei's heart swelled. She brushed Joey's cheek with the back of her hand.

He leaned into her touch, his lopsided smile turning devilish. "Now, how about we get to bed early and really celebrate your presentation?"

Familiar heat spread through Mei. She nuzzled her face against Joey's neck, relishing the scratch of his facial hair. "I like the way you think."

• • •

On Sunday morning, Mei kissed Joey goodbye outside their building as he set off for Virginia.

"I got this, my baby. Gonna ace this exam."

"You will." Joey had studied every night for the last few days, and all day Saturday. Mei had kept an eye on him, even as she reminded herself not to micromanage his career. Hopefully he'd crammed well enough to pass.

Mei watched Joey's Corolla drive out of sight. Then she rode the subway to Grand Central and boarded a train north. An hour later, she met Ali at the station, and they drove to join Luc, Kaia, and Alexandre at a summer festival on the Hudson.

They perused vintage furniture in the antiques tent, then strolled down rows of farm stands laden with homemade pies, cakes, and preserves. A local cover band played on a small stage, filling the air with rootsy music.

After a lunch of assorted tacos, Ali turned to Mei and

Alexandre. "Luc and I are going to take Kaia to the playground over there. We'll meet up with you in a bit."

Mei glanced at Alexandre. It was a little weird to be stuck with him. "What do you feel like doing?"

He scanned the scene. "How about the beer garden?"

They ordered pilsners from the taps, then found seats across from each other at a long wooden table beneath a tree. The sun highlighted a few strands of gray in Alexandre's hair. They suited him, Mei decided.

"How's your new place?" she asked.

"Not bad. It's right across from campus, but it's kind of generic, with beige carpets and an amazing view of the parking lot."

"You should've considered a Livin," Mei said teasingly. "We have Hudson Valley rentals."

Alexandre raised an eyebrow. "Livin? That startup with the ridiculous valuation?"

"Yup. I'm kidding, though. I work there, so I couldn't resist."

"I didn't know you worked there. Livin came to Oregon last year and it was big news. Everyone in my lab was talking about it."

"I like to think that's due to our *incredible* marketing." Mei smoothed her hair facetiously.

Alexandre laughed. "That would be you?"

"Me and my teammates." She tilted her face up to the sun.

"Well, it's working. I can't go a day without seeing an ad or a news story about your company. I saw photos of the Portland factory that Livin turned into apartments."

Mei nodded knowingly. Pride flowed through her, though she attempted to play it cool.

"I also read how they're building a wilderness compound outside Salem, with glamping and tiny houses."

"Our CEO actually wanted to build that on Crater Lake, along with a massive lodge and helipads. You can imagine how conversations with the National Park Service went."

"So there are some things that billions can't buy."

"Apparently."

Alexandre shook his head. "I've read so many crazy stories about your CEO—Julian Fredericks, right? I'm sure some are exaggerated, but others have to be true."

"Try me." Mei arched an eyebrow in challenge. "I might be able to spill some dirt."

"Ha. Okay." Alexandre brought his hand to his chin and looked away pensively. Mei couldn't help but notice his handsome profile.

Alexandre turned back to her. "Fact or fiction: Livin only serves vegan food in the office because Julian is all about sustainability and saving the world."

"Fact. I only eat vegan at work because I'm not saying no to free food. So now I have very strong opinions about fake meat."

Alexandre chuckled and sipped his pint. "What about Julian's office? Does he really have a cryotherapy chamber and a space devoted to sound baths?"

Mei smiled slyly. "I'm not confirming or denying, but let's just say that Julian is *very* into rich-person wellness."

"Ha! Next question: Even though he's so passionate about the environment, Julian flies around the world on a private jet he bought with VC funds."

Mei groaned. "You're not making this easy for me! I shouldn't say this, but it's true, though obviously Livin tries to keep that under wraps."

"The hypocrisy of those people."

Mei caught the distaste in Alexandre's voice. She stifled an eye roll and looked at Alexandre squarely. "I get it. I don't agree with everything Julian does, but that would be the case with any CEO at any company. I'm at Livin because it works for *me*. Before, I was at Daisyland Dairy, where I had no creative freedom or growth opportunities. At Livin, I manage a big team and a multimillion-dollar budget." She saw Alexandre's eyes widen, sending a satisfied thrill through her. "Yeah, I work crazy hours—"

"Like what?"

"About eighty a week."

"Oof, that used to be me."

"But I love what I do, so I don't mind. I'm climbing the ladder at a company where there are no women or people of color in leadership positions." Mei paused to let Alexandre absorb her words. "And while I can't control *everything* Julian does, I can fix some things."

"Like what?"

"When I started, our ads had slogans like 'Livin La Vida Loca,' with photos of drunk people doing keg stands."

Alexandre smothered a laugh. The corners of Mei's lips turned up, too.

"We've evolved our brand, and now I'm giving it a total refresh to make it more inclusive so people from all walks of life, all over the world, will see they're welcome at Livin." Flushed, Mei took a sip of beer.

"That's huge," Alexandre said. "The world needs more of that."

Mei smiled from behind her beer.

"Hearing you speak about your job gives me hope as I'm about to start my new one."

"What exactly happened in Oregon?" Mei ventured. "Only if you want to tell me."

Alexandre winced. It was nearly imperceptible, but Mei noticed.

"I was studying neuromuscular degeneration and aging in zebrafish, a model organism that shares many genes with humans. Basically, my research was in service of helping people stay mobile longer in life."

"That's important. How could there be a problem with that?"

"All research is high-risk, high-reward. I had some big findings early in my career. But in the last few years, all my studies were inconclusive. I couldn't get publications or funding, and you can't make tenure without both."

"That doesn't make sense. Couldn't people still see what you tried and learned?"

"Yeah, but that means nothing in academia."

"The hypocrisy of those people," Mei deadpanned.

Alexandre let out a sharp laugh. His eyes shone with appreciation. "Touché."

Mei made herself shrug nonchalantly, though her cheeks warmed at Alexandre's attention. "So are you excited to teach?"

"I think so. I've taught since grad school. It was just hard to abandon research before I was done with it."

The wind rustled the tree branches above them.

Mei turned her pint glass on the table. "Your scientific career isn't ending. It's just—" She racked her brain for a biology-type word. "*Metamorphosing.* Is that a real scientific term?"

Alexandre laughed. "It is."

"It's never too late to carve out a new path for yourself. I am." She considered herself a late bloomer but didn't want to say so, since that would make Alexandre an even later bloomer.

"I like that." Alexandre lifted his pint. "To carving out a new path for yourself."

Green flecks shone in Alexandre's hazel eyes. Mei hadn't noticed them before.

Joey's brown eyes suddenly appeared in her mind. She hadn't thought of him this entire time.

Mei swallowed her guilt. She tapped her glass against Alexandre's. "To carving out a new path."

CHAPTER FOUR

Evening approached and Kaia showed no signs of fatigue. Alexandre watched as she walked up Luc's legs and flipped over, nonstop.

"Hey, Kaia, want to give your dad a break? I can flip you," Alexandre offered.

Kaia looked at him hesitantly, still gripping Luc's hand. Alexandre held out his arms. Inside, he berated himself. *No wonder Kaia's timid around you. You only saw her once before moving back and only because you happened to be on the East Coast for a zebrafish conference.*

Finally, Kaia took his hands. Alexandre grinned as Kaia walked up his legs and flipped over.

"I think it's time to get this one home," Ali said.

Alexandre reddened upon seeing Ali and Mei watching him. "Mei, can I give you a ride to the train?"

A look of surprise crossed her face. She glanced at Ali, then shrugged. "Sure, if you don't mind."

"Of course not. It's on my way." Alexandre wasn't sure where the train station was, but he'd enjoyed chatting with Mei and wanted to be helpful.

They walked to his car, the compact blue SUV that had hauled his gear on countless camping and skiing trips and had ferried him from Oregon to New York. Alexandre opened the door for Mei, then went around to the driver's side.

"This was a nice break from the city," she said as they pulled out of the parking lot.

Something about her words made Alexandre think of Joey. He hadn't come up once in their conversation.

"Where's Joey today?" he asked.

"Driving to Virginia. He's taking a certification exam there. It's an IT thing."

Maybe Alexandre was imagining it, but he heard a hint of worry in Mei's breezy tone. "How did you two meet?"

Mei chuckled. "When I was out to dinner by myself one night, Joey sat down next to me and said, 'Are you on a date? Well, you are now!'"

"Wow." Alexandre grimaced. "Kudos to Joey for pulling that off." A goofy guy like Joey could get away with a line like that. "If I ever said that, I'd sound like a sociopath."

"Right? Before Joey, all the guys I met were so polished with their fancy upbringings and finance careers. Joey's dad was a mechanic. His mom was a kindergarten assistant. Joey went to public school in Queens, just like me."

"I grew up in the Bronx and went to public school, too." Alexandre hadn't lived there since he was a teenager, but he was still proud of his NYC roots.

"You did?"

Alexandre caught the interest in Mei's voice. "Yup. My parents mostly taught at Fordham Rose Hill, so we lived nearby. They moved to Westchester with Luc when I went to college."

"So you know what it's like to be a New York City kid."

"Sure do." A laugh escaped his nose. "Believe it or not, my first word was 'bagel.'"

"Stop! Are you serious?"

"Swear to god, that's what my parents said."

"That's some real New York cred there! So what was your usual bagel order?"

"Cinnamon raisin with cream cheese. Though, this might be sacrilege, my absolute favorite was"—Alexandre dropped his voice to a hush—"a bialy."

Mei burst into giggles. "No way! Mine too. You hardly ever meet someone else on Team Bialy. What about pizza? Did you have a favorite slice shop?"

"Of course. Tony's, just around the corner from my apartment. I ate there at least once a week when I was growing up." Alexandre could practically smell the rich tomato sauce. "I always got a baked ziti slice and a side of garlic knots."

"Yes! The garlickier, the better!"

They grinned at each other.

"I haven't thought about any of that in ages." Talk about being shortsighted. Alexandre had been so busy mourning the West Coast, he hadn't even considered everything awaiting him back in New York. Now he pictured himself checking out the latest museum exhibits, getting lost in the stacks of his favorite used bookstores, and going for long runs in Central Park. "Now all I want to do is rediscover New York."

A content smile appeared on Mei's face. "I felt the same way when I met Joey. I hadn't been to Queens in years, but he reminded me of everything I was missing."

The mention of Joey knocked Alexandre out of his nostalgia. "That's great you found someone who gets where you came from."

"I know. I feel really lucky."

Alexandre drove in silence. Was dating in New York going to be miserable? He wouldn't be in the city, but he'd read all those news stories about how the Hudson Valley was the new Brooklyn. For years, New Yorkers had relocated upstate or purchased weekend homes there.

Alexandre frowned. He'd never wanted for anything growing up. But as he got older, he realized how prudently his parents had raised him, and how modestly he still lived. From sealing drafty windows to patching sweaters, Alexandre knew how to fix nearly everything around the house. He made all of his lunches from leftover dinners. He gladly accepted hand-me-down gifts, like Luc and Ali's sofa.

A flash of panic seized Alexandre. What would dates think when they learned he'd purchased most of his clothing years ago? And all his furniture was secondhand? Alexandre's eyes darted toward Mei. What would *she* think?

His worry must have shown on his face, because Mei looked at him with concern. "You okay?"

"Just thinking about dating again."

"Are you planning to?"

"At some point."

"You sound thrilled."

"I'm dying to download the latest app."

Mei laughed, making Alexandre's lips curve up.

"I never liked dating, either," she said. "I just wanted to meet the right person."

"Same." Alexandre pulled into a spot at the train station. "So I guess I'll see you . . ."

"In two weeks! At the beach house."

"That's right!" Alexandre was ready for a week at the beach. He was also glad he'd be seeing Mei again, a thought he didn't know what to do with as he leaned over and gave her a light hug.

• • •

The next morning, Alexandre strolled across the SUNY New Paltz campus, taking in the unfamiliar surroundings. The summer term was in session. He passed groups of chatty students sipping large iced coffees.

As he walked, Alexandre attempted to silence the critical voice in his head. SUNY New Paltz was a third the size of the University of Oregon but felt much smaller. Though well-kept, the buildings appeared a bit worn. The blocky Brutalist architecture felt as heavy as his spirit. Even the craggy Shawangunk Mountains, visible in the distance from anywhere on campus, failed to lift Alexandre's mood.

He tried not to think of the beautiful trees he walked by daily on UO's campus: fragrant pines and firs, towering cedars, a massive redwood. He willed himself not to picture Hayward Field, the world-class track-and-field stadium with flags from dozens of countries waving around the perimeter. Alexandre wasn't a big team sports guy, but SUNY New Paltz's provincial vibe had him missing the fervent school spirit around UO's Division I football and basketball teams: the yellow O's adorning dorm windows, the sound of the marching band warming up before games, and even the Duck, UO's mascot, whose likeness was everywhere on campus, from bronze statues to hoodies.

Alexandre stared at the student union's triangular glass atrium at the heart of the campus. Its sleek elegance only made the concrete buildings around it look shabbier.

What have I done? Alexandre lowered himself onto a bench. The summer sun beat down on his back. A few students shuffled by, oblivious to his plight.

He forced himself to take deep breaths.

I made the right decision.

I'll be passing on my hard-won knowledge to the next generation.

I'm carving out a new path for myself.

The words shook Alexandre out of his spiral. Where had he heard them?

Oh right. From Mei. At the beer garden.

Alexandre replayed in his mind how Mei had shrugged as if it was no big deal to make such a major life change.

He squinted up at the Shawangunk Mountains. The low ridge had a stark beauty. Even with the summer greenery in full bloom, Alexandre could make out the horizontal striations of gray and brown rock.

He inhaled through his nose and resumed the short walk to the science building, repeating his new mantra: *I'm carving out a new path. I'm carving out a new path.*

• • •

At noon, Alexandre met with Dr. Andrea Johnson, his new boss and the head of the biology department. At a nearby Moroccan restaurant, they exchanged pleasantries about his cross-country move and placed their orders: vegetarian couscous for her, a merguez platter for him.

Dr. Johnson had a regal presence with perfect posture and graceful movements. As Alexandre watched her hand her menu to the waiter, he realized he couldn't think of a single other Black woman leading a university's biology department. Mei popped into his head again, her brown eyes flashing with determination when she spoke about being a woman-of-color leader in a company where there were few. Alexandre snuck another glance at his new boss. Clearly, the academic world suffered from the same lack of diversity.

"I can't tell you how happy we are to have you," Dr. Johnson said.

Alexandre snapped to attention.

"We had more applicants than ever, but you stood out," she continued.

Wow, praise. It had been so long, Alexandre had forgotten what it sounded like. "Thank you. I'm glad to be here."

"Your teaching philosophy is right in line with where I'm moving our department. I'm striving to create an inclusive environment where every student can thrive, no matter their background or career goal. Here at New Paltz, my department is focused on grounding lessons in practical applications and bringing in the latest research findings." A waiter arrived with their food. "You'll find complementary teaching styles among your colleagues. My more recent hires also spent years in research, though not as many as you."

Is that a good or bad thing? Alexandre wondered as he ate a piece of merguez.

"SUNY New Paltz may not be a research university, but we give our students the knowledge and confidence to shape their scientific futures, whether in healthcare, industry, or research. I hope you'll take some creative liberties in this position."

"I'm planning to." Alexandre told Dr. Johnson about his favorite interactive teaching methods, like having students make TikTok-style videos about a topic, holding real-time quizzes (that he ran in the style of bar trivia, though he omitted that detail), and hosting "Yes, and" improv sessions where he'd name a scientific concept and ask each student to build upon it with a new piece of information.

"I'll also ask students for ongoing, anonymous feedback," he added. "I'm still growing as a teacher. I want to know how I can improve so students get the most out of every class." As soon as the words left his mouth, Alexandre realized he meant them.

Dr. Johnson didn't bother tamping down her smile. "You'll be a great addition here, Alexandre. I can't wait to see what you'll do."

CHAPTER FIVE

On Monday evening, Joey was already seated at their neighborhood trattoria when Mei arrived. She kissed him warmly, then slid into the chair across from him.

"Have you ordered?"

"Yup. I got our usuals: spaghetti bolognese for me, rigatoni with eggplant and fresh mozzarella for you."

"I love how well you know me."

"It's because I love everything about you."

Mei nudged his foot affectionately and bit into a piece of focaccia. "So," she said as the waiter arrived with their dishes, "how was your test?"

Joey grimaced. "Not good. I failed."

"I'm sorry." Mei reached for his hand. She couldn't remember the last time he looked so defeated.

"Yeah. It sucks."

"Did you need more time to study?"

Joey nodded, his eyes regretful.

Mei speared a rigatoni, trying to suppress the little voice that threatened to blurt out, *Maybe you should've started earlier!* "So what happens now?"

"I can retake it."

"Oh good! When?"

"I have to see." Joey twirled spaghetti around his fork. "Honestly, I don't even want to think about it for a while."

They ate in silence. Mei peeked at her fiancé. How was he not jumping at the opportunity?

Joey finally looked up, his lopsided smile rueful. "I'm sorry, my baby. I know you're disappointed in me."

Mei squeezed his hand. "I'm not disappointed in *you*. I just don't get why you're not going for this. Do you know how lucky you are to have a manager who cares about you and is trying to get you promoted?" Until Mei reported to Diana, her current manager, none of her bosses had looked out for her career.

"I know. But I like my job how it is. I make a good living. I have time for you and my files. If I get promoted, I'll have to manage people. I don't know if I'm up for that." He rubbed his thumb against the back of Mei's hand. "I'm not like you. I don't need to go full throttle at work. I'm already doing more than anyone ever thought I would."

Mei studied his face. Behind his glasses, Joey's eyes looked tired. Defeated. And a little scared. Understanding dawned on Mei. She leaned forward in her seat. "Joey, I think you're suffering from imposter syndrome. Just because you didn't go to a four-year college doesn't mean you can't be an IT leader. You're so good at what you do."

She had never met anyone who loved IT as much as Joey. He was thrilled to figure out the best Wi-Fi setup for their apartment. He often got sucked into watching hours of DIY IT videos on YouTube. Even his music file hobby, which sometimes drove

Mei crazy, was a form of IT geekery. "You deserve more responsibility. You'd be a great manager, too."

"You think so?"

"Yes." Mei eyed his "Romaine Calm" T-shirt with a cartoon head of lettuce. *Maybe we can update his wardrobe before he starts leading a team.*

"I don't know."

"I do. This will be good for you. And us."

"Okay." Joey nodded slowly, then with more resolve. "Think you can help me study? Encourage me when I need it?"

"Of course." That familiar fiery rush flowed through her veins.

"Thanks, my baby. I don't have your big brains. Or your confidence." The candlelight threw shadows on Joey's scruffy face, making him even more ruggedly handsome. His lopsided smile made Mei's heart flutter.

She tugged him toward her. "Well, I believe in you. And that's all that matters."

• • •

The next afternoon, Mei hurried to the London conference room. The working red phone booth and photo wallpaper of the Thames always made her smile. She composed herself, then slid into the seat across from her manager.

"Is everything okay?" Mei asked. Diana had scheduled this one-on-one just an hour ago.

"Yes, but I have some news. I'm leaving. Next Friday is my last day."

"Wow." Mei's eyes widened. "Where are you going?"

"Revolution. I'm going to be their CMO."

"Congratulations!" The chief marketing officer position was the pinnacle of any marketer's career, and Revolution was the hottest streaming platform and film studio. "Revolution is lucky to have you."

"And Livin is lucky to have *you*." Diana raised her eyebrows emphatically. "You're the reason Livin is a global brand. I've made the leadership team aware of your talent. The call is theirs, but I've strongly recommended you to fill my role."

"Thank you!" Mei struggled to speak. She might be Livin's new VP of brand marketing! She'd never dreamed of reaching that level so soon. It was just an abstract idea in her mind when she mentioned it to Joey last week. "What are the next steps? I'm happy to take on anything."

"I'll create my transition plan, but I won't give you too much. You're already overloaded. Oh, and after I leave, you'll report to James."

Mei frowned. James Smith was Livin's new CMO. Julian had scooped him up from a telecommunications company as part of a new slate of executives he was hiring as Livin prepared to go public.

Livin's marketing team wasn't thrilled. *The dude is as bland as his name*, Tamiko had griped after googling James. *He has no creative credits or leadership awards*, Ayanna agreed. *He never speaks at conferences or gets profiled in the trades.*

Mei was trying to keep an open mind, but so far, she wasn't impressed. In the marketing all-hands where he introduced himself, James was a confident speaker, but his cool demeanor and soft voice were like a humid fog. When he'd signed off on her three-year vision, he'd only written "Approved" in his email.

"Huh, James. I haven't met him one-on-one yet. What's he like?"

Diana's mouth twisted. "He's an old-school corporate marketer who cares more about managing up than driving innovation. But if anyone can win him over, it's you. You're creative, data-driven, and personable."

Mei sat up straighter. She and Diana talked through more logistics, then wrapped up.

"You're the best manager," Mei said. "I'm going to miss working together. You didn't want to wait until after we went public?"

Diana gave her a meaningful look. "We're still deep in the red and years from turning a profit. Who knows when the IPO will happen? It came down to this: I could keep chasing the dream. Or I could work at a company where I can live it."

• • •

Two weekends later, in the passenger seat of Joey's car, Mei stifled a yawn.

"How you doing, babe?" Joey reached for her hand.

"Tired." She fumbled for her iced coffee and took a long sip. "But good, now that we're on vacation." A tree-lined stretch of the Garden State Parkway whizzed by.

"Were you working all night?"

"I got a few hours of sleep." Before leaving, Diana had transferred several responsibilities to Mei, including managing the agency of record and sending the leadership team a weekly performance update. Mei had been working past midnight, then waking up at five every morning to pick up where she'd left off. "I'm in good shape now. I should be able to unplug this week."

They approached the causeway leading to Long Beach Island. A warm sea breeze blew through the open windows. Mei closed her eyes and inhaled the salty air.

Long Beach Island was two hours outside the city, and the one place where Mei had vacationed as a kid. For her and Ali, LBI was paradise. They'd spend hours jumping in the waves, building sand castles, and eating creamy clam chowder for lunch.

Those vacations had stopped when Mei was ten and their parents separated. The trip was no longer possible on a single parent's income. Still, Mei had only good memories of LBI. It was a place where she was a kid with childlike concerns, like whether to get chocolate or rainbow sprinkles on her soft serve, not whether or not her mom could afford to pay rent.

As she and Joey drove down the main drag, Mei exclaimed over the familiar sights. There was the surf shop where she and Ali had pooled their allowance to buy an inflatable whale float. And that was the old-fashioned fudge place where they always got slabs of vanilla chip.

Joey turned onto a side street abutting the beach. Ali and Luc's black SUV was in the driveway next to the two-story rental. Alexandre's compact SUV was parked on the street, leaving her and Joey the other driveway spot.

Mei threw the front door open, then let out a contented sigh. The living room had a nautical vibe with crisp whites and navy accents. Framed photos of waves hung on the walls. Sliding glass doors opened onto a wide porch facing the beach.

"You're here!" Ali and Kaia descended the staircase, both in pink sundresses with bathing suit straps peeking out. Luc and Alexandre followed.

Mei greeted each of them with a hug. She caught a whiff of pine and sunscreen when she leaned into Alexandre. "So good to see you." He looked relaxed and tan in a soft green T-shirt and gray swim trunks.

"You too," Alexandre said, his eyes warm. He held out his hand to Joey. "Thanks again for inviting me."

"Anytime, bro." Joey gave Alexandre a back-slapping handshake. "Glad you could join."

They changed into their swimsuits, and everyone headed to the beach. As they emerged from the grassy dunes onto the sand, Mei's heart swelled with joy. Wispy white clouds drifted across the blue sky. The ocean sparkled in the late morning sun.

They claimed a spot on the edge of the tide. Ali and Luc waded into the surf. Mei watched Alexandre point out different types of seabirds to Kaia.

"Want to go for a walk?" Joey asked, suddenly at her shoulder.

Hand in hand, they strolled by the water. With the ocean lapping over her feet, the stress Mei hadn't realized she was carrying began to melt away. Diana's departure, her ballooning workload—everything seemed to roll out with the waves.

Mei kissed Joey's hand. "This week will be good for me."

CHAPTER SIX

The next morning, Alexandre was heading to the porch to read, when Mei intercepted him.

"Joey and I are going mini golfing. Want to come?"

"Sure." Alexandre noted Mei's short navy skirt, sleeveless white polo shirt, and yellow Livin visor. She looked cute in her preppy getup. "Let me guess. That's your special golf outfit."

"Yes!" Mei rolled her eyes. "Joey hates mini golf, so I wanted to make it more fun."

"How could anyone hate mini golf?"

"It's a long story."

Mei's tone made it clear that she wasn't getting into the details. Alexandre nodded. "All right. Let me get changed. Glad to be in on this."

He ran upstairs and pulled on a blue polo, a lightweight pair of gray athletic pants, and a white baseball cap. When he returned to the living room, he noticed how nicely he and Mei matched. Joey was wearing his usual baggy cargo shorts with the pockets hanging open and a T-shirt with a camel on Rollerblades.

"Are Ali, Luc, and Kaia coming?" Alexandre asked.

"No. Ali said mini golfing with a three-year-old wouldn't be fun for anyone."

They piled into Joey's car. When they arrived at Shipwreck Island Mini Golf, Joey pulled into a parking spot but left the ignition on.

"Okay, you kids out."

Mei turned to him in surprise. "You're not coming?"

"Nope." Joey unlocked the doors. "I just remembered those big box stores right off the island. I can get a hot spot there. The connectivity on the beach blows."

"Connectivity?" Alexandre asked.

"For my music files. The Wi-Fi on the beach is too weak to power my song identification programs."

"Ah." Alexandre bit back an incredulous laugh. Then he noticed Mei frowning.

"You said you'd play."

"I said I'd *drive* you to mini golf." Joey glanced at the road, clearly itching to leave. "I want to check out wireless speakers to use on the beach. You can play your music. I won't make everyone listen to mine."

"Okay," Mei relented. "See you in a bit."

Alexandre stepped out of the car. He didn't need to sit there and watch Mei kiss Joey goodbye.

They waved as Joey drove off, then walked to Shipwreck Island's welcome hut. Alexandre breathed in the scent of damp turf and chlorine. Ahead of him, giant sandstone rocks, waterfalls, and beach grass created a wonderland of caverns. The golf course had just opened at ten, but already small groups of players puttered around the greens.

Mei flashed him a little smile, but her lowered eyes told Alexandre she was disappointed about Joey's absence.

"Sorry he left you with me," Alexandre said. "I'm probably not as funny as Joey, but if you give me a few minutes, I might be able to think up some obscure music facts."

Mei laughed, sending a pleasant zing through Alexandre.

"Between you and me, I'm okay not hearing about Joey's music files."

A six-foot pirate statue with a peg leg greeted them at the first hole. Alexandre gestured for Mei to go first. They played through, both sinking their balls in three strokes.

A pile of rum barrels lay in the middle of the second green. The most direct route to the cup was through a tunnel carved into one barrel.

Alexandre lined up his putter and aimed for the tunnel. His ball just missed the opening, bouncing off the barrel and rolling to a stop.

With a firm *thwack*, Mei hit her ball right through the tunnel. She sprinted to the end of the green, then squealed with glee. "A hole in one!"

"Nice!" Alexandre gave her a goofy high five. "I should've gotten that on video."

Mei let out a wry laugh. "Joey probably wouldn't even watch it."

"What's his deal with mini golf?" Alexandre glanced at the oversized treasure chest in the middle of the third green.

Mei knocked her ball down the turf. "He hates all sports."

"Why?" Alexandre tapped his ball in the direction of the cup.

"Joey's super unathletic—according to him, that is. I've never seen him play anything. He didn't have a lot of friends growing up because he couldn't throw, catch, or kick. None of the kids on his block would play with him, and his classmates never wanted him on their team." Mei shook her head sympathetically, then chuckled. "Unironically, he told me that even all the girls got picked before him."

Alexandre laughed. "Poor Joey." He wouldn't have guessed Joey had a sports phobia. The guy was tall and solidly built, with broad shoulders. Alexandre couldn't help but gloat. He didn't have the best free throw or pitch, but he'd always been a fast runner and a decent all-around athlete.

Mei set her ball down at the fifth hole. "Joey was a lonely kid. He's an only child, too. I think that's why he likes hanging out with Ali and Luc. He's getting the siblings he never had."

Alexandre caught the fondness in her voice. The idea of Mei, Joey, Ali, and his brother as a neat foursome rendered him an outsider. Alexandre nodded and knocked his ball past an iron anchor.

At the seventh hole, a Jolly Roger flag flapped overhead.

"This place hasn't changed," Mei said. "Ali and I used to come here back in the day. It was our favorite mini golf course."

Now that Mei mentioned it, the place was a bit worn. All the pirate statues looked like they'd been painted several times over. Some rock formations were chipped. Still, the course retained a sense of whimsy.

"I can see why," Alexandre said. "It feels a world away from New York."

"Exactly. Ali and I would wear matching outfits because we loved being mistaken for twins."

"So you always dressed up for mini golf," Alexandre said playfully. They walked into a cave with a waterfall rushing down one side. Alexandre noted the light sheen of sweat on Mei's shapely neck. "And you and Ali were tight, even as kids."

"We were. Even before—" Mei hesitated, then continued. "Even before our parents got divorced and our dad died. Ali and I had to look after each other."

Alexandre stopped mid-putt. "That's right. I'm sorry." He knew Mei and Ali's father had passed away, but he didn't know when or why. "How old were you?"

"Twelve."

"That's a terrible thing to go through at any age, but especially so young." No wonder the sisters had such a tight bond.

Mei looked like she was about to say more when cheerful voices approached. "We should keep moving."

She took the first shot at the ninth hole. "I can't imagine having a sibling who's so much younger, but you and Luc seem close."

Alexandre sent his ball down the turf, past an oversized parrot with an eye patch. "Not as close as you and Ali. But Luc's the biggest reason I'm back."

"So you could spend time with him?"

"Yeah, but it's more than that. He was the one who pushed me to leave tenure track."

Mei paused at the cave leading to the tenth hole. "Why did he do that?"

Alexandre laughed dryly. "In retrospect, it was obvious, but I couldn't see it at the time. I was working nonstop. I wasn't eating or sleeping well. I had that crazy hair and beard because I stopped taking care of myself. I was always nauseous." Alexandre set down his ball. "Luc flew to Eugene for my fortieth birthday. He planned for us to go hiking, biking, and visiting breweries. But I refused to see him."

"What? Why?"

"I had so much work to do, and he expected me to drop everything to spend time with him. I pushed him off, saying I'd meet him in an hour or two, but I never did." Alexandre knocked his ball down the green. He felt Mei watching him. "Luc went home pissed. We didn't speak for weeks. Then he started calling and texting, trying to get me to talk to him. Eventually, I told him my tenure was in danger. He spent the next few months trying to get me to leave my job. I didn't. Finally, he flew back and basically held an intervention."

"What did he do?"

"He dragged me, kicking and screaming, to go skiing."

"Skiing?"

Alexandre caught the skepticism in Mei's voice. "That trip saved me."

She softened. "How?"

"It woke me up to how depressed I was." Alexandre recalled racing Luc down snow-covered mountains under a pale blue sky. How exhilarating the icy wind had felt after years holed up in a lab. "For the first time in ages, I remembered I used to have a life outside of research. I saw that maybe I could be happy at a different job, in another state. It took me two years to leave. But I started updating my CV after that."

"I had no idea." Empathy emanated from Mei's eyes.

"Well, I don't exactly go around broadcasting it." Besides Luc, and probably Ali, no one knew the full details of his final years in

Oregon. Something about being in the darkened mini golf cave made Alexandre open up to Mei.

"I'm sorry," she said. "If your dream starts ruining your health and relationships, it's not worth it."

"It's not." A grinning skeleton met them at the next hole. "This is quite the conversation for mini golf."

"I'm glad you're here. You saved me from a solo game, since Joey clearly had no intention of playing." Mei shook her head good-naturedly.

Joey. Alexandre had completely forgotten about him. He arranged his face neutrally. "Well, glad I could be your golf buddy."

They finished the course, then sat on a bench to tally their scores.

"You beat me by three!" Alexandre leaned over to show Mei the card, just as she moved in for a better look. Their shoulders brushed, sending tingles down Alexandre's arm. He glanced down at Mei, his eyes meeting hers.

She jumped up from the bench. "Let's see if Joey's back."

In the parking lot, they spotted Joey's car and walked toward the atmospheric swells of eighties power ballads.

"Did you get your hot spot?" Mei asked.

"Fuck yeah!" Joey pumped his fist. "Look at how fast everything is."

Alexandre climbed into the back seat without bothering to comment. At least he didn't have to feign interest in Joey's inane hobby.

Joey pulled out of the parking lot. "Where to now?"

"Want to get a snack?" Mei suggested. "Maybe an outdoor place with peel-and-eat shrimp?"

"Sounds good, because *I are hungry!*" Joey exclaimed.

Alexandre looked at Joey, confused.

"Joey, what?" Mei was staring at him, just as bewildered.

Joey laughed. "*I are hungry!* Bao and Miguel always said shit like that when they were learning English."

Mei let out a huff of disbelief. "You can't say that!"

"It's our inside joke. They're my best friends! We've had it forever."

Alexandre stared at Joey. For most of his life, he had never thought about race—which, he'd eventually learned, was the ultimate privilege. But even before that, he knew there were topics you never joked about as a straight white guy. He leaned forward in his seat. "Hey, Joey—that's not how jokes work. Saying stuff like that is not okay."

Joey glared at him through the rearview mirror. "Thanks, *professor,* but no one asked you."

"Alexandre is right," Mei shot back. "It's kind of racist and not funny. Forget the snack. Let's just go to the house."

Joey's neck turned crimson. He hunched over the wheel.

Alexandre tried to catch Mei's eye. A few weeks ago, she'd told him her rationale for working at Livin. Sure, she was getting financial stability and professional challenges. But she was beholden to leaders with some unsavory morals.

Was she making similar trade-offs in her love life?

Alexandre tried to ignore the attraction simmering beneath his skin. Mei didn't need to settle for Joey. Had she ever considered that?

CHAPTER SEVEN

For the rest of the car ride, Mei burned with embarrassment. She stared out the passenger-side window, not looking at Joey. Good thing Alexandre was in the back seat so she didn't have to face him. And really good thing Ali and Luc weren't there. Then she'd be beyond humiliated.

Ugh. Joey's sense of humor was a little immature. She *knew* that. Sometimes she cringed when he told her friends corny jokes, or when he made Ali and Luc watch too many epic fail videos. But he never made off-color remarks. Until that moment, Mei had never heard Joey say anything remotely like *I are hungry!*

After dinner, in their room, Joey reached for Mei's arm. "Hey, can we talk?"

Mei sat stiffly beside him on the bed. "About what?"

"About what?" Joey parroted. "Cheeseburgers aren't as tasty when your fiancée looks like she wants to throw you on the grill!"

Mei cracked a smile. "Okay. Let's chat."

"I know you're upset about the car ride. I just wanted to make you guys laugh. I'm sure as hell not racist! You know that."

Mei inhaled through her nose. This couldn't be happening. She was having the "I'm not racist" conversation with her fiancé.

"My best friends are Mexican and Chinese. They're coming to our wedding! You're Chinese, too, and you're the love of my life."

"Well, I'm Chinese American." She and her parents had all been born in New York. None of them had ever been to China.

"You know what I mean." Joey took her hand. "I'm sorry. I didn't want to offend you. It's just that I've had this joke with Bao and Miguel forever. We say it all the time."

Mei studied their entwined hands. She hadn't spent much time with Bao and Miguel, but she *could* see them saying stuff like that. Bao was an Asian bro. The last time she and Joey had gone to dinner with him and his girlfriend, Chloe, Bao had talked them into doing shots and staying out until two in the morning. Miguel and his partner, Ivan, tended to be more reserved, but they always loosened up after a few drinks.

"How about you keep that joke between you, Bao, and Miguel?" Mei finally said. "I don't ever want to hear it again."

Joey kissed her temple. "Okay, my baby. Anything to make you happy."

• • •

They went to bed early. As soon as they shut the lights, Joey sidled up to Mei and cupped his hands around her breasts. "Makeup sex?"

Heat kindled between Mei's legs. The feeling of Joey's strong, solid body always put her in an amorous mood. But this evening, her mind wasn't there.

"Let's just cuddle." She nestled against him.

Joey kissed her ear. "All right."

Moments later, he was snoring. Mei tried to match her breathing to his. Twenty minutes later, she was still wide awake. She wriggled out from under Joey's arm and pulled on a sweatshirt.

Mei tiptoed into the hallway. As she headed to the bathroom, a gust of wind blew through the window, brushing her arm. She turned, then padded down the stairs.

The porch door was ajar. Alexandre sat in a lounge chair reading. He looked up and gave a little wave. Mei hesitated. Then she slid the door open.

"I hope I'm not disturbing you," she said as she walked to the wooden railing.

"Not at all." Alexandre set down his book and flashlight. He rose to join her.

His scent pricked Mei's nose. Fresh soap and pine, mingling with the salty air. As her eyes adjusted to the dark, Mei could make out the whitecaps on the thundering surf. She let the sound of waves wash over her.

"I love the beach," she said. "It's such an escape from the everyday."

"I love it, too. I need more beach time in my life."

"Did you go a lot in Oregon? I've never been there, but I've seen pictures of Cannon Beach. So beautiful." Mei recalled a photo of the massive Haystack Rock rising out of the sea.

"That was farther north from where I lived, but the whole Oregon coast is spectacular. The beaches are bigger and wilder than here, especially when the fog rolls in. You can go hiking along the cliffs, through towering fir trees, and end up on the sand."

Mei nodded, envisioning a vast expanse of glittering sand, hazy sunshine reflecting off the waves. She could practically feel the cool Pacific mist against her face. "That sounds amazing. Think you'll go back sometime?"

"No."

The finality in Alexandre's voice was clear. Mei stared out at the water. Why had she brought up Oregon? Between that and the car ride, Alexandre probably thought she was socially inept. Mei steeled herself to apologize. "By the way—"

"I just wanted to say—"

They laughed.

"You first," Alexandre said.

"I'm sorry for mentioning Oregon. And I'm sorry Joey and I fought in front of you, and that he was rude." Mei winced, remembering Joey's "professor" comment.

Alexandre let out a sad little laugh. "You don't have to apologize about Oregon. I did love it out there. I should be okay talking about it without having a total meltdown."

Alexandre's tone was self-deprecating, but given what he'd told her earlier, Mei suspected he might be serious.

"You don't have to apologize for this afternoon, either," Alexandre continued. "I'm sorry for butting in."

Mei waved her hand. "It's fine," she said lightly. "Sometimes I need a little help with Joey." As soon as the words left her mouth, they felt a little too real. Why didn't Joey know not to say things like *I are hungry*? Why wasn't he more proactive about his career? *Why does he only ever wear silly graphic T-shirts?* Mei gnawed guiltily on her thumbnail.

She felt Alexandre watching her. Mei glanced up. The intensity of his gaze made her breath catch. *He'd never need hand-holding like Joey.* During mini golf, she'd noticed how Alexandre eyed the hole intently, then tapped the ball with a sure hand. Mei could see his careful focus extending into all areas of his life—in teaching, in research, with women. She pictured Alexandre in a darkened lab, his hands gentle yet firm on the shadowy figure of a woman, kissing her as zebrafish swam in glowing tanks.

In the distance, a seagull cried, bringing Mei back to the present. "In all seriousness, Joey's great. He helps me remember where I'm from. He's always up for anything. He doesn't take life too seriously, and I need that."

Alexandre was silent for a moment. "Yeah, but is that enough?"

The clouds parted. Under the moonlight, Mei could see the angles of Alexandre's jaw. She felt a wild urge to grab his face and kiss him deeply, roughly, her hands clawing at his hair. She looked away, her cheeks aflame.

"I don't mean to upset you." Alexandre's shoulders dropped. "Now I'm overstepping again," he mumbled, seemingly to himself.

Mei stared at him. Was Alexandre giving her relationship advice? She knew nothing about his love life, other than that he was forty-two and single.

"It's just that sometimes," Alexandre began hesitantly, "when you talk—not just about Joey, but Livin, too—you remind me of me. And I don't want what happened to me to happen to you."

Irritation flitted through Mei. Yes, what Alexandre told her at mini golf was terrible. She couldn't see herself deteriorating the same way, though. The American Dream was a myth, but her family was one of the lucky few who'd achieved it. Her grandparents had come to the United States and toiled twelve-hour days at their hand laundry. Her mom had raised her and Ali on a receptionist's salary. During high school, she and Ali worked thirty hours a week at a local café to pay for college. Work hard, save money, create a better life. That survival instinct ran through her blood.

Sure, Alexandre was a public school kid, too. But his parents were happily married, tenured professors who expected him to get a PhD.

Mei barely suppressed an eye roll. She and Alexandre were nothing alike. *I'm killing it at work. I'm getting married.* She wasn't depressed and stagnated like he had been.

She turned to go. "I should get back inside."

"Wait." Alexandre touched her arm.

A charged current shot through her. Mei froze. Alexandre dropped his hand. *He felt it, too.*

He took a step away from her and swallowed. "Just look out for yourself."

Mei opened her mouth to object. Then she caught the concern in Alexandre's eyes. Something in her heart clenched. "I will."

Alexandre nodded.

Mei forced herself not to glance back at him as she slipped into the house and headed up the stairs.

• • •

The next morning, a light rain fell. Everyone ate banana pancakes at the kitchen table. Though she sat between Joey and Kaia, Mei was uncomfortably aware of Alexandre's presence a few seats away. The questions he'd asked last night echoed above the breakfast din.

After they cleared the table, Mei returned with her laptop and a full French press. "Wedding planning calls for lots of coffee."

Ali opened her own laptop. “Luc and Alexandre are taking Kaia to the grocery store and the doughnut shop. We should have two hours. Is Joey joining us?”

“No, he’s working on his files.” Part of Mei wanted to ask Joey to help. The other part of her just wanted a bride-to-be/matron-of-honor planning session with her sister. “I’ll share my spreadsheet with you.”

For the next hour, they worked through the task list. Mei added photos and event details to their wedding website. Then she purchased the digital invitation template she and Joey had chosen. Ali organized the guest list with everyone’s email addresses.

“Okay, so we have you and Joey, obviously.” She paused, consulting her spreadsheet. “Me, Luc, Kaia, Mom, Henry, and Joey’s parents. Aunt Rose, Uncle Arthur, and Evie.” Their cousin, Evie, was several years younger than they were.

Mei nodded along as Ali named Joey’s extended family members. Should she invite Alexandre? No, she didn’t know him well, and they could only invite thirty guests.

“Kathy and Luis,” Ali said.

Mei smiled at the mention of her best friend, who lived in Chicago. At the advertising agency where they’d worked years ago, colleagues always mixed them up, even though Kathy was Korean, five inches taller, and sported a pixie cut. In addition to commiserating over the ongoing slights, Mei and Kathy were always the first ones in the kitchen after meetings, scrounging leftover bagels to stretch their minuscule salaries.

“They’ve met Joey, right?”

“Once, when they were here in February.” She and Joey had

just decided to move in together. Kathy and Luis were over the moon for them.

"Oh right! Are you inviting any other friends?"

"No, given the space. But Joey's inviting his best friends, Bao and Miguel. Bao is bringing his girlfriend, Chloe, and Miguel is coming with his partner, Ivan."

"Should I invite them to the bachelor/bachelorette?" A smile tugged at Ali's lips.

Mei groaned. "Yes."

"I love how Joey's set on having one."

"He won't take no for an answer! You'd better plan something low-key."

"I already booked the pink Hummer limo. And ordered shirts with your faces on them."

Mei threw a balled-up napkin at her sister. "Very funny!"

Ali cackled, then attempted to pull a straight face. "We'll have a fun night out. And I have a surprise for you." She paused dramatically. "I made an appointment for you at the Little White Dress."

Mei gasped. "How'd you know I wanted to get my dress there?" The Little White Dress wedding boutique in Tribeca carried ready-to-wear dresses geared toward city hall elopements and smaller, casual ceremonies.

"It's so your type! Mom and Kaia are coming, too. We'll get brunch after." Ali clicked on her laptop. "Just sent you the confirmation. The appointment's two weeks after we get back."

The front door opened, unleashing Kaia, who came running in toward Ali. Luc and Alexandre followed.

"What've you been up to?" Alexandre asked.

"Just some wedding planning." Mei shut her laptop before he could see the bridal email.

Joey bounded down the stairs. "Success! I finally identified a bunch of Mongolian metal songs that were stumping the programs!"

Alexandre stared at Joey. "That's what you've been doing while Mei and Ali plan your wedding?"

Mei shot him a look. Why was he asking that?

Joey's eyes narrowed. "What are you implying? That I'm not helping? I actually came down to tell you all my brilliant idea." He took the seat beside Mei. "I know you're always so busy with work, and it's hard to find time for wedding planning. How about we set aside one night a week to bang out whatever we need to do?"

Mei raised her eyebrows. "I like that."

"We'll put it on our calendars. I know how much you like calendars."

Mei laughed. "I can never resist a good calendar invite."

Joey snapped his fingers. "I got it. Wedding Wednesdays. We'll order in something yummy, too, like Egyptian from Astoria or dosas from Jackson Heights."

"I love it." Mei hugged Joey's arm. She tried not to notice how Alexandre forced a smile, then quietly retreated upstairs.

CHAPTER EIGHT

Alexandre bit into his crab cake sandwich and tried to enjoy the salty air on his face. For the first time all week, he was alone. Tonight had turned into an unofficial date night. Mei and Joey were at an Italian restaurant. Ali and Luc had found a seafood place with a nice kids' menu for Kaia. Both couples had invited him along, but Alexandre declined. He figured they all wanted some time to themselves.

Since he'd always lived a bachelor lifestyle, Alexandre expected the solitude to feel normal, or even welcome after so many days in a house full of people. Instead, loneliness lingered around him like a cloud.

To shake himself out of self-pity, Alexandre opened his latest fantasy novel. Ever since he left Oregon, he'd devoured one series after another. The escape into otherworldly realms was exactly what he needed—along with tales of good people embarking on epic quests against impossible odds.

He was so lost in his book that he jumped sometime later when the porch door creaked open behind him.

Ali stepped onto the porch, rubbing her sweatshirt-clad arms. "Sorry, Alexandre. Didn't mean to scare you."

"No worries." His shoulders dropped. He hadn't realized he'd been hoping Mei would walk through the door.

"Luc's giving Kaia her bath." Ali sat beside him at the picnic table so they both faced the beach. Streaks of pink, purple, and orange lit up the feathery clouds. "You've got the right idea being out here."

"I'm having a great time. Thanks for letting me be the fifth wheel on your vacation."

"Oh stop! No one's a wheel. We're Legos. We break apart and form new combinations, and they all work."

Ali's description was accurate. Alexandre enjoyed spending time with each permutation of people, except for Joey. As much as he tried, he couldn't see him as anything but an overgrown child. Alexandre grimaced, remembering how he'd challenged Joey to help Mei with wedding planning. That was none of his business.

"Who knows?" Ali said. "Maybe you'll have a girlfriend or fiancée next time we're here."

Alexandre raised his eyebrows. Usually, speculation about his love life irked him. If he compiled all the unsolicited advice, pep talks, and questions he'd received in his forty-two years, that volume would be thicker than his academic publications.

But Ali's casual directness made Alexandre consider her words. Mei's face popped into his mind before he could stop it.

"Maybe."

"You'll be dating at a good age."

Alexandre let out an incredulous laugh. "Why's that?" What did Ali know about dating? Her last date was when Luc asked her out sixteen years ago. She'd never downloaded a dating app, been set up by friends, or mingled at parties hoping to meet the one.

"People are more fully formed in their thirties and forties. You know what you want, and you have your life together."

Mei was completely different from the twenty-something he'd met all those years ago. But his big scientific accomplishments, grants, and publications had been in his early thirties. Even his prestigious *Nature* publication, which should have made him untouchable, hadn't been enough to save him when everything had gone so spectacularly downhill. Alexandre snorted.

"I know what you're thinking." Ali eyed him. "You don't feel fully formed."

"How'd you guess?"

"But you will be. Because you'll be doing what you love."

"Why do you say that?"

"Whenever you talk about teaching, you're relaxed. You give off a sense of calm." Ali shrugged. "You were always passionate about research, but it stressed you out."

"My research wasn't exactly going well."

Ali bumped her shoulder against his. "I'm not just talking about the last few years. We've been in-laws for a long time."

"You're right." Agreeing that his new job was good for him had become like a script. Alexandre just had to follow it. "Teaching will be good for me. And who knows? Maybe I'll have my own Joey soon."

Ali's grin wavered for less than a second. Before Alexandre could determine whether it was a trick of his imagination, a moment of wishful thinking manifested, Ali's smile was as vibrant as ever.

"Oh, you will." She patted his hand, then stood up. "I'm going to put Kaia to bed."

After Ali left, Alexandre watched the daylight fade from the sky. His thoughts drifted to Mei. Her spirit had captivated him—her stubborn determination and somewhat delusional optimism. Alexandre could already read her mannerisms: The way Mei cocked her head and shot him a challenging stare when he asked a question she didn't want to answer. How she'd flick and smooth her hair when she was pleased with something he'd said. Her begrudging smile that blossomed into a brilliant grin. Alexandre's internal compass drew him toward Mei whenever she was around.

He dragged his hand over his face. Great. The first woman to catch his attention in years was his sister-in-law's sister. Who was already engaged.

A car door slammed in the driveway. The breeze carried Mei's and Joey's voices toward him. Alexandre grabbed his book and headed upstairs. It was better for everyone if he didn't see them now.

CHAPTER NINE

The last days of vacation passed in a blur of sunshine, sand, and salt water. On the final evening, Mei and Ali concocted a simple broth with lots of Old Bay, then dropped in blue crabs, potatoes, and corn. Luc and Alexandre laid the food out on the newspaper-covered picnic table. Everyone cracked open the succulent seafood as the sun dipped and the sky turned pink.

A full moon was out by the time they'd cleaned up. Mei pulled on a yellow "Livin the Dream" hoodie. She took Joey's hand and walked onto the beach. The salty breeze whipped her hair. Waves fizzled on the sand, brushing her feet. The night on the porch with Alexandre flitted into her mind.

"This week was dope, but I can't wait for our honeymoon," Joey said. "You and me. Stuffing ourselves on pasta. Ravishing you every night and being as loud as we want."

Mei elbowed him but smiled. They were going to Italy. Neither of them had been there before. Joey's dream was to visit the country where his family was from, and Mei had been won over by photos of the Amalfi Coast and Venice's canals.

"An Italian honeymoon to match your new name. Mei DiGiacomo."

Mei's stomach dropped. She had never been sure about changing her name, but with the wedding drawing closer, she was realizing that she didn't want to. "Actually, I want to keep my name." She forced a smile.

Joey stopped walking. "You never mentioned that."

"I've been torn. It's a lot to ask of someone, especially when they're established in their career, like I am. My whole network knows me as Mei Li. Plus, Li is clearly Chinese. I want everyone to know me as Mei Li as I rise through the ranks."

Joey shoved his hands into the pocket of his gray hoodie. "I always thought you'd take my name. It's tradition."

Mei touched the soft fabric of his shirt, searching his eyes in the low light. "What if it were the other way around? Would you become Joey Li?"

Joey was silent for a moment. Then he sighed. "I get it. I wouldn't want to lose my family name, either."

They resumed walking. The distance between them closed. Mei reached for Joey's hand. He brought her fingers to his lips, the familiar scruff on his chin brushing her skin.

"Thanks for spending this week with my family," she said.

"I love Ali, Luc, and Kaia. I'm still getting used to the professor, though. Dude barely says two words, except to lecture me in my car and give me shit about wedding planning."

Mei's face grew hot. "Come on. Alexandre is a good guy. You said so yourself."

They started up the sandy pathway to the house.

"Speaking of Le Prof." Joey nodded to where Alexandre stood on the porch gazing at the ocean, his arms resting on the wooden railing.

Mei looked up at the same moment Alexandre noticed them. She lifted her hand to wave, when Joey wrapped her in a tight embrace, kissing her greedily. Mei tried to pull back, but Joey pressed his lips against her harder, his tongue rough in her mouth, his facial hair scraping her chin. Mei gave in, returned the kiss, then extracted herself. She snuck a glance at the porch. Alexandre was gone.

• • •

Back at Livin, long days at the beach became a distant memory. Mei stifled a sigh. Her new manager was ten minutes late for their first one-on-one.

"Thanks for waiting." James finally strode into the O'ahu conference room, his white button-down crisply starched, his light blond hair slicked back. He grimaced at the tropical plants and oceanic wallpaper, then gave Mei an appraising once-over. "Before she left, Diana spoke highly of you. Said you're her pick to fill the VP role."

"That's very kind of her." Mei already missed Diana and her warm, empowering leadership style. "I'm interested in the job and would love to talk to you about it, once you're familiar with my work." Mei launched into an overview of her projects, wrapping up with her upcoming campaign. "We're kicking off the *Livin the Dream* campaign with a global media plan, inclusive new imagery, holiday pop-ups in twenty cities, hundreds of videos and pieces of content on our owned channels, ten brand partnerships, ten executive op-eds, and major features in outlets like *The New York Times*."

James pursed his lips. "Decent. What are your goals?"

Mei swallowed her shock. Her team was one of Livin's most productive. "We run one global brand campaign annually, highlighting one key message a month through seventy videos, forty blog posts, twenty podcast episodes, dozens of pieces of sponsored content, five executive op-eds, and a global media buy that spans digital and out-of-home. We also write fifty event scripts a year and run one experiential activation in at least twenty markets every quarter."

"Double that."

"Double that?" Mei choked. "Everything?"

"You can think bigger. That's what leaders do."

Mei smiled sweetly. "I'm well aware of that. The Livin pop-ups in airport lounges? Our billboard takeovers in Times Square? Getting Julian keynotes at South by Southwest and Cannes Lions? All my ideas."

"Good for you."

Mei flinched. "And I'm planning a lot more activations on that scale."

"'More' is the operative word." James leaned forward in his seat. "You're probably not aware, but we're preparing to file with the Securities and Exchange Commission. This could be our last few months to go big with our marketing before the quiet period."

"Thanks for the context." So Livin was planning to go public soon. "I can commit to more. But rather than just doubling our output, let's focus on areas that'll drive the most return."

"No. We need to show numbers. Big numbers. Julian won't

understand impressions and click-throughs. He'll get quantity. All the other teams have committed to more. If you don't step up, your team will sink in the rankings." James let out a low whistle as he moved his hand on a downward trajectory. "Is that what you want?"

Mei looked away. Livin fired employees who landed in the bottom ten percent three months in a row. If James was telling the truth and her team's rankings plummeted, everyone could lose their jobs. Tamiko was caring for her ailing mother. Bryce's son had special needs that insurance didn't cover. And she had a wedding and honeymoon that were about to eat a huge chunk of her savings.

"Fine." She'd see what her teammates could take on, then do the rest. "We'll need to ramp up through the end of the quarter. That's also when I'm getting married."

"Oh? Are you taking time off?"

"Two and a half weeks at the end of September and early October."

"That's a long time, but I suppose it's reasonable, given the occasion. Tell you what. I'll give you September to ramp up. If you hit your numbers, we'll talk about the VP job."

"You won't be disappointed." Mei smiled confidently, despite her growing panic.

"Good." James stood up to leave. "Oh, and, Mei?"

She looked up expectantly.

"Book another room for our one-on-ones, will you? I really don't like plants." He shuddered at the tropical greenery, then walked out the door.

• • •

"I have no idea how I'll do everything." Mei shoved her laptop aside on the couch and curled up in the fetal position.

Joey rubbed her leg. "That's way too much, babe. Even for you. Think it's time to find a new job?"

"No way!" Mei bolted upright. "Not before we go public. I'm not losing my shares."

"We'd be okay without that money. Our parents raised us on much less."

Mei was quiet. Joey was right. But for the first time, she could pay rent without checking her bank account. In the winter, she turned up the heat without worrying about the cost. If something broke, she dealt with a friendly management company, not a shady landlord who never fixed anything. For the first time ever, she'd saved six months of living expenses, creating a little financial cushion.

"True. I just don't want to live like that again."

"I get it." Joey wrapped his arms around her. "I don't miss those lean times, either."

Mei rested her cheek on his shoulder. Her eyes roamed their living room, noting Joey's new MacBook Pro, noise-canceling headphones, high-end monitors, and a gaming chair that somehow cost more than their sofa. *Maybe I wouldn't worry if you got a raise and spent less on your hobby!* But that wasn't fair. Joey lived within his means. He wasn't saving much, but he wasn't running up debt, either.

"Can I help with anything?" Joey asked.

The words she'd spoken to Alexandre that night on the porch surfaced in her mind. *Sometimes I need a little help with Joey.*

"How are you doing with your exam?" she ventured.

A flicker of annoyance crossed Joey's face.

"Think you can study without me?"

Joey opened his mouth like he was about to argue, then nodded with resignation. "Yes."

"Thanks, Joey." She couldn't wait to delete the corporate firewall study guide from her laptop. "I know it'll take time, but can you make a plan with your boss and work toward it? For the promotion?"

Joey scrunched up his face, a red flush creeping up his neck. "Why are you so fixated on *my* promotion?"

Mei bit her lip. Joey never got annoyed at her. "Because it'll help *us*. Once we've saved more, I can think about other jobs."

Joey sighed. "Okay. I'll do it. For you."

"And yourself. We're a team now. Remember?" Mei's eyes searched his until he finally relented.

"All riiiiiiight. Okay, my baby."

Mei exhaled with relief as Joey ruffled her hair.

"I'll get cracking on my exam and you keep kicking ass at work. We'll do our first Wedding Wednesday tomorrow, too. I'll send you that calendar invite."

A moment later, it arrived in her inbox. Mei chuckled at his over-the-top title: "WEDDING WEDNESDAY!!! 👰🤵💍💒💐🍾🥂❤️💋" When she glanced up, Joey was watching her, pleased.

"You know, I was just thinking I can take on more of the planning, too."

Mei started to object, but Joey continued.

"You need to focus on Livin. My exam's not for another few weeks. I can do wedding stuff outside of Wedding Wednesdays."

Mei raised her eyebrows. "Really?"

"Yes. I want to. Because it'll help *you*."

Mei was speechless. Behind his silver-rimmed glasses, Joey's eyes shone with determination. His lopsided smile filled Mei with hope. Joey was an underdog, just like her.

He was *her* underdog.

That familiar fiery rush flooded Mei's veins. She traced Joey's scruffy cheek.

As if sensing her thoughts, he pulled her onto his lap, pressing his forehead against hers. "Like you always say, my baby, we're moving on up, together."

CHAPTER TEN

On Monday morning, Alexandre stood before his empty classroom. His heart raced from an emotional cocktail of nerves and excitement.

The first class of the fall semester was about to begin, officially ending his life as a research scientist.

Students trickled in, filling the empty desks. The sight of them shook Alexandre out of his rumination. He smiled whenever he made eye contact with someone.

He connected his laptop to the overhead projector. Then giggles filled the room. The notes in his presentation slides were in full view, including his "Hi, I'm Professor Alexandre Brodeur!" introduction. Alexandre turned red, then laughed along with his students.

"Welcome to General Microbiology," Alexandre said once the titters died down. "I'm Professor Alexandre Brodeur—as you clearly saw on the screen. This is my first semester at SUNY New Paltz. I recently joined the faculty from the University of Oregon. We're going to have a fascinating time exploring the world of microorganisms."

Alexandre's nerves vanished as he spoke. Muscle memory

kicked in. He no longer needed the notes he'd painstakingly prepared. Sure, a few students looked like they were still waking up. But most nodded along, buzzing with the excitement of the new term.

"I promise to make every class as interesting as possible," Alexandre continued. "Ask me anything. There are no dumb questions. As scientists, it's our job to challenge accepted beliefs and find new ways to look at the world."

As he wrapped up, Alexandre held up a stack of notecards. "I take your feedback seriously. At the end of each class, please write down one thing you liked, one thing you didn't, and any questions or comments. Everything is anonymous, so don't go easy on me. If I bored you to sleep or explained something terribly, tell me. I'll improve. For today, please include why you're taking this class and what you hope to get from it."

His students bent over their desks. The sound of pens scratching paper filled the air.

Back in his office, Alexandre read every card. A few students hoped to go into cancer research. Several planned to be doctors or nurses. Others mentioned pursuing advanced degrees.

Some students wrote that they were the first in their families to go to college. Others noted the lack of people who looked like them in their chosen career paths, and their desire to change that reality. Their words echoed what Mei had told him.

Alexandre could barely remember being as young and optimistic as his students. Still, the small but potentially formative time he'd have with them imbued him with pride.

He was organizing the notecards into a neat pile when another thought hit him: If these undergrads were the future of biology, then he belonged to its past.

• • •

Alexandre drove south with the windows down, the hot summer air rushing through the car. His first week of classes had gone better than he'd expected.

In Tarrytown, Alexandre parked outside his parents' aging but well-kept two-story home. He drew a breath as he approached the door. Why was he dreading a simple lunch?

"Alexandre!" Clarisse embraced him. "I still can't believe you're here. Come in."

Alexandre trailed his mother through the living room, past the overstuffed bookcases and worn armchairs. He smiled at the framed watercolor of Saint-Malo, a fortified city in Brittany, the region of France where both sets of his grandparents were from.

Clarisse led him to the kitchen table. His parents had prepared a green salad with a mustardy vinaigrette, a rustic vegetable soup, and sliced sourdough bread with salted butter. Alexandre loved his parents' humble yet hearty cooking, served on mismatched plates.

"How's the semester going?" Jean-Germain asked.

"Really well." Alexandre helped himself to a slice of sourdough. "My students are enthusiastic. I've met most of my colleagues, too."

"That's wonderful." Clarisse passed him the butter. "You can learn how they advanced their field before becoming teachers."

Alexandre bristled. Was his mother implying that his colleagues no longer contributed to science because they were full-time teachers and not researchers?

"Is your schedule nice and easy?" Jean-Germain asked. "Now that you're just teaching?"

There it was. *Just teaching.*

"Not really. I have a full course load." Alexandre tried to keep his tone light. "Are you still in touch with your old colleagues?" His parents had both retired two years ago.

"We are." Clarisse nodded. "We're seeing the Goldfarbs for lunch next week." Seth and Sylvie Goldfarb were another husband-and-wife professor couple from Fordham.

"How's Bradley and his malaria research?" Over the years, Alexandre had heard about the Goldfarbs' son, who was also a research scientist.

"Bradley recently made tenure. At Brown." Clarisse quickly sipped her soup.

Bradley was five years younger than Alexandre. The news gut-punched him. "That's great!" Alexandre made himself grin. "Tell the Goldfarbs I say congratulations."

Clarisse smiled, relief evident on her face. "I will."

"And, Mom? You can talk about other people's tenure with me. I'm not going to spontaneously combust." At least he hoped not.

"It's a darn shame, though." Jean-Germain set down his fork. "You're such a gifted scientist. You deserve everything Bradley Goldfarb has. Are you sure about leaving research?"

Alexandre gritted his teeth. "I made my decision."

"Have you explored every option? Spend a year at New Paltz, then find a new lab. Think of this as a sabbatical."

"Dad. No." Alexandre scrunched the floral napkin in his lap.

"Just look at what the New Paltz students are gaining." Clarisse shot her husband a look. "A professor with Alexandre's talent and experience. We've had a few colleagues who decided to just teach, too."

There it was again.

"Mom. Dad." Alexandre struggled to keep his voice even. "In the last few minutes, you both referred to my new career as 'just teaching.' Do you know how that sounds?"

Jean-Germain looked down. Clarisse's face fell.

"I'm sorry," she said. "I never meant to make you feel bad."

"I didn't even realize I'd said that," Jean-Germain said.

"Thanks. I don't need to feel like a failure every time I see you."

For a few moments, everyone ate in silence.

"Looks like you got some sun," Clarisse said. "How was your vacation?"

Alexandre recalled the long days on the beach and evenings on the porch. Mei's face materialized in his mind. "Just what I needed."

Jean-Germain finished his soup. "I'm glad you got a week away with Luc and the girls."

"And Joey." Alexandre bit back his distaste. "Mei's fiancé was there."

"I keep forgetting she's engaged." Clarisse gave her husband a knowing look. "So does your father. He was joking that maybe you and Mei would hit it off."

"You never know," Jean-Germain said. "Stranger things have happened."

Alexandre chuckled. His neck reddened.

Clarisse clapped her hands together. "I just remembered! I did know a pair of sisters who married a pair of brothers."

"See, Alexandre?" Jean-Germain grinned.

Clarisse swatted his arm. "But Mei's engaged, honey."

"Oh right."

"How about dessert?" Alexandre jumped up from the table. He'd rather discuss Bradley Goldfarb's tenure in excruciating detail than carry on with this topic.

Clarisse stacked their dishes. "We're only teasing. Your father and I are so glad you're back. You can't blame us for being a little silly."

Alexandre began plating the chocolate-dipped butter cookies he'd brought. Sure, his parents were happy to see him. But would they ever accept his new career?

And when would he stop caring if they didn't?

CHAPTER ELEVEN

The door to the bridal boutique swung open, revealing a cheerful brunette with a red-lipsticked smile. "Welcome to the Little White Dress! I'm Gabby and I'll be taking care of you. Now, who is our bride?"

"I am." Mei grinned at Ali, her mom, and Kaia. She wasn't used to calling herself a bride.

"Congratulations!" Gabby ushered them into a reception area with blush-pink sofas. "We'll get started in a minute."

"Do you know what you're looking for?" Vivian asked, giving Mei's arm a squeeze.

"Kind of." Mei held out her phone so her mom could see the photos she'd saved. The brides wore tailored jumpsuits with asymmetrical necklines or lace details. Others donned red jersey dresses. "Lucky red," she said, citing the Chinese tradition.

"I like the red," Kaia said.

"I do, too." Mei patted her niece's cheek. "Joey's worried his parents won't approve of any of those outfits. He doesn't want to upset them even more."

"Since you're not getting married at their church?" Ali asked.

"Yeah." Mr. and Mrs. DiGiacomo were practicing Roman

Catholics. They were disappointed when Mei and Joey had told them they were having a small civil ceremony at a restaurant, instead of a traditional religious ceremony at the DiGiacomos' parish church.

"It's your day, not theirs!" Ali said. "Wear whatever you want."

Mei chewed her lip. Joey had held firm about their wedding venue choice, shielding Mei from his parents' chilly treatment. She didn't need to rock the boat again. "I'll find a nice white dress. Something my style."

Gabby reappeared and led them to the showroom. As Mei sifted through the racks of soft white fabric, her spirits rose. Everything the Little White Dress carried was elegant, yet understated—just what she wanted for her big day.

Under the changing room's flattering light, Mei stepped into a simple maxi dress with cap sleeves. When she looked in the mirror, her eyes widened. The dress elongated her petite figure. The deep V neckline accentuated her shoulders. Mei swept her hair into a loose bun, then turned from side to side, taking in her reflection from every angle. She was the picture of a beautiful bride, nearly unrecognizable to herself.

"Do you need help?" Ali called.

"Nope!" Mei took a deep breath and smiled at the mirror. Then she drew back the curtain.

Ali and Vivian gasped.

"You look amazing!" Vivian dabbed her eyes with a tissue.

"Mom, you're going to make me cry," Ali said as she snapped photos.

Mei laughed at the lump in her throat. "You're both making me teary! I think that's my cue to try on another dress."

The next hour passed in a flurry of lace and silk. Mei tried on dress after dress, but none came close to the first. "That's the one."

"Okay, great." Ali and Vivian exchanged impish smiles. "We're buying your dress! We're not taking no for an answer!"

Mei's jaw dropped. "No way."

"It's Chinese tradition." Vivian gripped her arm. "You'll have bad luck if you don't let us pay."

Mei burst out laughing. "Nice try! You're making that up."

"I told you she'd never fall for that." Ali flashed a determined grin. "Can you watch Kaia while we talk to Gabby? We're getting your dress. End of story."

"Fine." Mei rolled her eyes with exaggerated irritation. "But you really shouldn't." She pulled her mother and sister into a hug.

As she was putting on her shoes, Kaia ran in.

"Aunt Mei!" Kaia grabbed Mei's hand. "I found your dress!" She led her to the boutique's small collection of colorful frocks. Mei hadn't even looked at them.

"Here." Kaia nudged the edge of a red gown.

Mei pulled out the dress. Her breath caught. The top was a simple cheongsam, the bottom a soft tulle skirt, all brilliant red. The effect was sophisticated and romantic. Chinese and American.

"Are you going to get it?" Kaia asked.

"Maybe for my next wedding."

Kaia's eyes went round. "You're having *two* weddings?"

Mei snapped back to attention. "No, I was only kidding."

She trailed her hand over the mandarin collar and delicate red buttons. A scene unfolded in her mind. She was stepping into the sunlight on a small roof deck. Her vibrant red dress reflected the joy and certainty in her heart. Sunshine obscured her husband-to-be's face, but she could feel the delicious warmth radiating from him, his grin mirroring hers. He didn't have Joey's height. Nor his broad shoulders. He was shorter and trimmer, with tousled brown hair. As Mei approached, he turned toward her, his intelligent eyes shining with happiness.

Mei dropped the hanger.

She scrambled and caught the dress before it hit the floor.

"There you are! Oh wow." Ali came up behind her, followed by Vivian and Gabby. "That dress! It's gorgeous."

"It's a beauty," Gabby agreed. "Willow Wu is the designer. She's a local, born and raised on the Lower East Side. Her line reflects her Chinese American heritage."

"She sounds like us!" Ali turned to Mei. "Are you going to get it? Or at least try it on?"

Mei ran her hands over the silky fabric. She took a breath, then shook her head. "I'll stick with my original pick."

"Yay!" Ali wrapped her arms around her. "You have your dress!"

Vivian hugged the two of them, then pulled Kaia in.

"Congratulations," Gabby chimed in over their laughter.

As they walked out, Mei ignored the tiny pang in her chest as she bid the beautiful red dress goodbye.

• • •

At a popular New American brunch spot down the block, Mei scanned the oversized menu. "It's not too early for a cocktail, right?" She couldn't shake the scene she'd envisioned at the bridal boutique.

"You just found your wedding dress. That calls for a toast," Ali said.

When their beverages arrived, they clinked their drinks together. Mei gulped her mimosa with relief.

"Mommy." Kaia shook Ali's arm. "How many weddings did you have?"

"One. I had one wedding to Daddy."

"Aunt Mei is having two!" Kaia announced, looking at Mei, then Ali.

Mei coughed. "At the shop, I told Kaia I was going to wear that red dress to my second wedding. I was just kidding."

"Aunt Mei is having one wedding to Joey," Ali told Kaia. "She was joking about two."

"Oh." Kaia turned to Vivian. "How many weddings did you have, Grandma?"

"I actually had two. One, a long time ago, to your grandfather, who is no longer with us. And one, just before you were born, to Grandpa Henry."

Kaia covered her mouth with glee. "Wow, two weddings!"

Mei stared at her menu. She'd never asked how her mother had felt about marrying their father. Had she gone into her first wedding full of misgivings but hoping for the best? Or head-over-heels in love, blissfully unaware of how her marriage would devolve? As much as Mei tried, she couldn't remember her parents ever being happy. A suffocating tension had filled the room anytime they were together, her father drunk on whiskey and anger, her mother fearful of igniting his temper.

"What's everyone getting?" Mei asked. "I'm debating between the spinach Benedict and the lemon ricotta pancakes."

"Let's split them," Ali suggested.

"Do you need any help with the wedding?" Vivian asked after they placed their orders. "I can send you favor ideas or make menu cards. Whatever you need."

"Thanks, Mom, but we're actually in good shape."

Ali raised an eyebrow. "Wedding Wednesdays?"

"Yes! Joey chose a place for the rehearsal dinner and made a lunch playlist. I had to remove some songs that were too weird, but still." Mei smoothed the napkin on her lap. "He's even been co-ordinating with all the vendors outside of Wedding Wednesdays."

"Wow, good job, Joey!"

A swell of pride ran through Mei as she smiled at her sister and mother. Joey was stepping up, just like he said he would.

• • •

After the delicious brunch, Mei and Ali hugged Vivian goodbye, then walked to a nearby park to wait for Luc. They found a bench in the shade with a good view of Kaia on the playground.

"What was Luc doing today?" Mei asked.

"He and Alexandre were in Brooklyn. They stopped by two boutiques that carry his furniture, then got pizza."

"Alexandre?"

"Yeah, he came along."

Mei eyed Ali. Maybe now was her chance to confide in her. But what would she say? *I love Joey, but I'm having weird thoughts about your husband's brother.*

"The guys are here." Ali waved toward the entrance.

Mei looked up. Luc and Alexandre were walking over. Alexandre's eyes were bright. He looked relaxed in navy shorts and a sage button-down with the sleeves rolled up. He was more handsome than Mei remembered. The scene from the wedding shop played through her mind.

It was just a ridiculous thought. It doesn't mean anything.

Still, her heart thumped and her mouth felt dry as she raised her hand in greeting.

CHAPTER TWELVE

Alexandre knew he'd probably see Mei today, but he was surprised at his nerves when he entered the park. A flush rose to his cheeks when he spotted her looking summery in a cute green minidress, her hair partially swept back from her face. Alexandre hugged her hello, hoping she couldn't tell how flustered he suddenly felt, and took a seat beside her on the wooden bench.

"How was shopping?" Luc asked.

"Good! I found my dress."

"She looked amazing in everything," Ali added proudly.

Alexandre tamped down the twinge he felt picturing Mei resplendent in her wedding dress as she said her vows to Joey. He gestured toward Mei, Ali, and Luc. "Is this the last time you three will be seeing each other before the wedding?"

Mei laughed. "No. Livinpalooza's in two weeks."

"That music festival?" Alexandre asked. "You're going?"

"Not Lollapalooza," Luc replied. "*Livin*palooza."

"As in, my company," Mei said. "I'm the only one going, but Ali's picking me up at the end, because Joey will be back in Virginia for his exam."

"What exactly is Livinpalooza?" Alexandre asked. "I still have no idea what you're all talking about."

"Sorry. It's a mandatory Livin event that's a cross between adult summer camp and Coachella. Livin flies in every employee from around the world and makes us camp for four days. Last year, it was outside London. This year, it's in the Hudson Valley. Julian calls it a celebration of togetherness, but it's really his excuse to throw his own music festival with nonstop booze."

"No way." Alexandre shook his head. "At my lab, our big holiday rager was pizza in a conference room."

"You need to show him photos," Luc said.

Children's voices rang out from the playground.

"I'm going to check on Kaia," Ali said. She walked toward the slides. Luc followed her.

Mei scooched closer to Alexandre on the bench. "This was last year." She handed him her phone.

Alexandre swiped through the pictures. One showed rows of flimsy tents in a scraggly field littered with paper cups. In the next, hordes of ravenous people mobbed a tater tot truck. In another, inebriated young people in various states of undress mugged for the camera. Alexandre tried to tamp down his disgust. This was a work event?

"Wow. I can practically smell the booze." He passed the phone back to Mei.

She laughed uncertainly. "Not feeling Livinpalooza?"

"Not really."

The sounds of birds chirping filled the silence. Alexandre felt Mei studying him.

"Why are you so annoyed?" she asked. "I'm the one who has to go."

Alexandre tried to make sense of his thoughts. Why was he such a grump? "In academia, I wrote countless grant proposals to fund my research—research that would've improved people's lives as they got older. I didn't get all the grants I applied for, but even if I did, they would've been a tiny fraction of the cost of an event like that."

"I get it." Mei wrinkled her nose. "It's not fair."

"It's capitalism at its worst. Why do you go along with it?"

Mei huffed, clearly displeased with his moral grandstanding. "You know why. Livinpalooza is just one event I have to deal with. I hate camping, and being forced to do it with twelve thousand coworkers is the worst."

Alexandre shuddered. "I love camping, but Livinpalooza would be my nightmare, too."

"Last year was cold and miserable. I was freezing the whole time. And sleeping outside is creepy. I'm always afraid of an ax murderer breaking into my tent."

"You don't have to worry about that, City Girl." Alexandre playfully nudged her shoulder. "There won't be any ax murderers at Livinpalooza. Just lots of drunk people."

Mei laughed. Alexandre's chest filled with warmth. The midday sun filtered through the trees. A soft breeze blew the loose strands of Mei's hair.

Alexandre pictured the outdoor equipment lining his living room wall. He could only imagine what percentage of the Livinpalooza budget went to alcohol and what went to keeping employees comfortable. There was a twisted logic to the breakdown, as much as he hated to admit it.

"Do you need any camping gear?" he asked.

"You have some recommendations for me, Mountain Man?"

"I don't know how you're picturing my life in Oregon, but I actually lived in an apartment, not a log cabin in the woods."

"Aw, you're ruining my fantasy! Please tell me you at least wore flannel shirts. And woolen beanies."

"I may or may not have a few of those." Alexandre took in Mei's shining brown eyes. He felt different around her. Infused with a sense of calm, combined with something else. Something unfamiliar.

"So what kind of camping gear would help?" Mei asked.

Alexandre mentally ran through the essentials he packed for every trip. "Good wool socks that are light enough to wear during the day, but warm enough when the temperature drops at night. A headlamp for walking in the dark and lighting up your tent."

"I could use that."

Alexandre reached for his phone. "I'll send you links."

Mei typed in her number. "We should start a group chat with Ali and Luc. I'll send you Livinpalooza updates in real time."

"And if you need anything before or during, let me know." Alexandre stopped himself from adding, *I'm here for you.*

Still, Mei seemed to understand. She gave a little nod before glancing toward the play area, searching for Kaia and her sister.

Alexandre forced himself to follow her gaze, away from the sunbeams dancing on her hair.

CHAPTER THIRTEEN

All set with the florist?" Mei consulted her spreadsheet and reached for a scallion pancake. The fourth Wedding Wednesday was underway, fueled by a feast of dumplings and sides.

"Yup. They confirmed they'll have the white ranunculus by our date." Joey spooned pork dumplings onto his plate. "Photographer?"

"Just sent the shot list. Car service?"

Joey held out his laptop. "Here's what I chose."

Mei brightened at the sight of the vintage Checker cab. "I love it." She pulled him in for a kiss. "Wedding Wednesdays were your best idea ever."

"Thanks, babe. Wedding planning is fun. Gives me something to do at work."

Mei set down her chopsticks. "What about your test? Have you studied?" In a week and a half, Joey was going back to Virginia to retake his IT exam.

"Not yet. I've been too busy with wedding planning."

"Joey." Guilt threatened to ruin her appetite. If only she weren't so swamped at work, doubling her output to hit the pointless new goals James had set. Then she would've been able to take on more wedding planning and help Joey study, like she'd promised.

"Hey." Joey took her hand. "My exam is my exam. Not yours. I'll deal with it."

Mei's eyes strayed to the chalkboard sign they'd just unwrapped for their welcome table. White script spelled out "Always and forever." In less than a month, Joey was going to be her husband. She had to trust him. "Okay. You got this."

"*We've* got this. It's you and me, my baby." He pointed to the sign. "Always and forever."

The corners of Mei's mouth pulled up, though her stomach flipped. Even with the excitement of starting a new life together, weddings were also nerve-rackingly final. No one ever vowed to live in one place, work at one job, or have the same best friend forever and ever. Why was it normal to commit yourself to one romantic partner?

Behind his silver-rimmed glasses, Joey's eyes shone with tenderness. Certainty. He had no hesitation promising himself to her for the rest of their lives.

His conviction buoyed Mei. She pressed her lips against his, letting Joey's warm kiss wash away her momentary qualms.

• • •

The next evening, Mei settled into the O'ahu conference room with a tumbler of sauvignon blanc. Since moving in with Joey, she'd been taking her monthly video catch-ups with Kathy at Livin, indulging in the after-hours privacy and free wine.

Her laptop chimed with an incoming call. Mei eagerly clicked the answer button.

"Kathy!" Mei grinned at her best friend's wide smile.

"Mei! I'm counting down to seeing you at your wedding! So exciting!"

"It's happening." Mei shivered for effect. "Kind of surreal."

"Girl, I hear you. I felt the same way." Kathy and Luis had gotten married just two years ago.

As Mei regaled Kathy with Wedding Wednesday tales, Luis appeared over her friend's shoulder.

"Hey, Mei!" Luis called. "I'll let you two get back to chatting, but just wanted to say hi."

Mei waved back. "Can't wait to see you!"

Luis touched Kathy's shoulder affectionately. Her eyes followed him as he walked out of the room. When she turned back to the screen, she glowed. A twinge of envy surprised Mei. Did she look like that around Joey?

"You and Luis are so cute," she said. "I can see how happy you are."

"Thanks, Mei. I never thought I'd find anyone like him, as you know."

"Oh, I do." For years, she and Kathy had propped each other up when promising dates went awry and when there seemed to be no appealing men left in New York.

"When we got engaged, one of my aunts was like, 'Are you sure he's the one? You don't think it's too soon?'" Kathy laughed at the memory.

Mei sipped her wine. Kathy and Luis had also gotten engaged after less than a year of dating. "What did you tell her? Did you ever think, 'Oh yikes, maybe it is too soon?'"

Kathy cocked her head. "A few things gave me pause. Luis still has business school loans. He's always debating whether to stay at his job or find a new one. And the man takes forever to order anytime we go out to eat."

"Yes! Joey has some weird hobbies, and I wish he were more ambitious at work—"

"But that's nothing compared to all the upsides of being together."

"Exactly!"

The glowy smile returned to Kathy's face. "I'm so glad you and Joey found each other. When it's right, you just know it."

Mei swallowed. She held her tumbler up to the screen. "When you know, you know."

"Cheers to that."

They took a long sip in unison.

• • •

The following Thursday, Mei disembarked from a motorcoach on the edge of a massive field.

"Welcome to Livinpalooza!" an event staffer yelled into a bullhorn.

A magnificent balloon arch in Livin's yellow and white stretched across the entrance. A famous DJ spun sunny pop remixes. Excitement rippled through the air, infecting Mei as she joined the throngs of people streaming through the gates, across the grassy expanse.

Up ahead, a crowd converged. Mei gasped as she approached the spectacle. Livinpalooza lay in the valley below. Sunshine glinted off the gargantuan main stage. White geodesic domes, food stations, and rows of tents stretched as far as Mei could see.

Around her, colleagues from all over the world chatted in a multitude of languages.

A thirty-minute hike later, Mei dropped off her backpack at Reflection, her assigned campsite. Then she began the trek to the main stage for the opening ceremony. On the trail, she saw three of her direct reports, Kaden, Bryce, and Tamiko, several paces ahead. She ran to catch up with them.

"I'm so glad you found us!" Bryce said. "There are so many people and the cell phone reception is terrible."

"Oof, yeah," Mei agreed. Thousands of Livin employees descending on a rural area had strained the local bandwidth. "Now we can stick together."

The stage loomed before them. Mei found an empty spot where they could sit.

A slow, pulsating beat boomed through the speakers. Three towering screens flashed to life. A Livin employee with long red hair, identified as "Caroline, 26, Dublin," spoke directly to the camera. "At Livin, I'm doing the best work of my life."

Cheers erupted. Mei and her teammates smiled at one another.

Kyoko, twenty-three, from Tokyo, appeared on-screen. "At Livin, I make a difference every day."

The crowd hollered.

"At Livin, I'm not only living my dream. I'm helping others live theirs, too," said Rashad, thirty-three, from Chicago. He chuckled and wiped his eyes.

A lump rose in Mei's throat. She got teary at every Livin event.

The video ran through a hyperspeed montage of Livin employees. Words flashed on-screen: "6 continents. 25 countries. 700 locations. 12,000 employees. 1 epic celebration. Livinpalooza."

The DJ cranked up the music. A euphoric dance track with a thumping bass poured from the speakers. Cannons exploded with yellow and white confetti.

Through the confetti, a tall figure with flowing locks rose from the depths of the stage. Clad in dark jeans and a yellow "Livin the Dream" T-shirt, Julian raised his arms and addressed the crowd: "My Livin family! Welcome to Livinpalooza! Who's ready to celebrate everything we've accomplished—and get fired up for where we're about to go?"

Mei and her teammates cheered. Julian was clearly referring to the IPO.

"One hundred percent," Julian said. "Last year, we hired one hundred percent more employees. We opened one hundred percent more locations. This year, we're going even bigger! Two hundred percent more employees! And locations! Next summer, we're cutting the ribbon on Livin Antarctica. Then we'll be on all seven continents!"

A rendering of sleek glass buildings in a frozen blue and white landscape appeared on-screen. The audience gasped, then roared with approval.

Julian luxuriated in the applause. "I want to acknowledge that even though we're making history, none of this is easy. I see your sacrifices. The late nights. The long weekends. The time away from your loved ones. If you ever feel like giving up, remember that what you're building is bigger than you, me, and everyone here." He held his hands in a prayer position. "Now, think back. When you were a kid, what were your hopes? Your dreams?"

Mei's answer came immediately. She wanted to get the hell

out of Queens and find a good job so she, Ali, and her mom never had to worry about money.

"I bet you didn't have to think hard," Julian said. "I didn't. I grew up dirt-poor in rural Arkansas. Still, I dreamed of dipping my toes in the Pacific and walking the streets of Paris.

"I started Livin for all of us who wanted more than life gave us. Maybe you were the only person of color in your town and everyone treated you differently. Maybe you were a woman whose voice was always silenced. Maybe you weren't free to share your love openly or live as your true self. Despite your hardships, you never gave up."

Tears pricked Mei's eyes. Around her, people sniffled and nodded along.

"Livin lets people find their place in the world and live their best lives. Now." Julian paused. "Who's with me? To the next year of Livin! To two hundred percent growth and beyond!"

Another confetti cannon showered the stage in a blizzard of yellow and white. The DJ blasted a soaring dance track. The crowd hollered and danced along. Mei snapped a selfie with her friends.

Back in her tent that night, she read through the texts she'd received.

Joey: I miss you so much, my baby. I'm counting the minutes until you come home.

Mei laughed and shook her head. *Oh, Joey.* She clicked the unread messages in her group chat with Ali, Luc, and Alexandre.

Ali: Have fun, Mei!

Luc: Send pics! I want to revel in the ridiculousness.

Alexandre: Enjoy the great outdoors! Not gonna lie—it's a perfect night and I kind of wish I were camping, too.

Mei felt a funny flutter in her stomach. Was Alexandre wishing he were camping with her? Not at Livinpalooza, of course, but somewhere beautiful, like the California coast. They could sip hot cocoa and watch the stars come out.

Joey! She and Joey could do that!

Mei quickly replied to her fiancé's message.

Miss you, too! 😘

Then she typed back to the group chat.

Having a great time!

Mei attached the photo of her and her teammates. In it, she was grinning broadly, the setting sun haloing her with a golden glow. With a satisfied nod, Mei hit send.

• • •

The tinkling chimes of Mei's alarm roused her at eight the next morning. She reached for her phone and opened the weather app. A red banner slowly appeared: "A HURRICANE WARNING is in effect for this area." Overnight, a tropical storm had gained strength and speed and was heading inland. Hurricane Theo was approaching the Carolina coasts and would travel north, hitting the Hudson Valley the next evening.

Mei checked her email and Slack. No word from Livin. A few texts arrived, though.

Alexandre: I just saw the hurricane alert. Are they calling off Livinpalooza?

Ali: Should we come get you? Luc is picking up Kaia at 3 and I have a staff meeting, but we'll figure it out.

Alexandre: I'm around, if that helps. My last class ends at 1.

Joey: Babe! I saw the hurricane alert! That means you're coming home, right? The apartment isn't the same without you.

Mei frowned at Joey's text. Why was it all about him? She replied to Ali and Alexandre.

No news from Livin yet. I'll let you know as soon as I hear. Thank you for offering to get me!

Mei threw on a T-shirt and leggings, then hurried to the main grounds to meet her teammates.

"Mei!" Kaden called. "Do you know what they're planning to do?"

"No. Let's hope Julian says something now."

They settled on the lawn in front of the stage. Around them, everyone speculated about the hurricane.

"My ex was named Theo. If the storm is anything like him, we're screwed."

"I kind of hope a hurricane hits. It would bring some excitement to this Snoozapalooza."

"If they don't cancel this, I'ma break outta here. I'd rather be fired than dead."

After a slick hype video, Julian took the stage. "Welcome to day two of Livinpalooza!" He smiled his trademark grin, then launched into an inspirational speech about how employees could harness their superpowers to reshape humanity.

Restless chatter rippled through the crowd. Julian kept talking. The crowd rumbled louder.

Finally, Julian paused. "My friends. My Livin family. I know many of you saw a hurricane warning. Rest assured that we're monitoring the situation. All of today's festivities will go on as planned. Attendance is still mandatory, like our commitment to changing the world."

"That's all?" Tamiko exclaimed. "Do they not understand that a hurricane is coming tomorrow?"

Mei struggled to concentrate as Livin's chief sustainability officer took the stage and detailed the great lengths he'd taken to make Livinpalooza a green event.

"We have bamboo utensils instead of plastic," he said. "Boxed water instead of bottled. Our vegan menu cuts down on greenhouse gas emissions, and we're donating all your camping gear to the homeless."

Mei swallowed her discomfort. She pictured the skepticism on Alexandre's face when he'd questioned Livin's sustainability claims.

After the morning session, Mei got barbecue jackfruit sandwiches with Kaden, Bryce, and Tamiko, then split off. She did a round of gentle yoga and made a flower crown at a craft station. As the hours passed, Livin remained silent about the hurricane.

Mei was walking to a ukulele painting session when she ran into Ayanna.

"How are you doing?" Mei asked. "Do you have any hurricane intel?" Ayanna and her team were holed up in the social media trailer, strategically posting and monitoring all content related to the event.

"I'm hanging in there. Trying to make the most of our all-white male speaker lineup. You'd think that in this day and age, they'd have POC and women speaking on topics besides diversity and belonging."

Mei grimaced in agreement.

"As for the hurricane, Julian's been throwing fits all day about how many millions he's spent on Livinpalooza and how he's not calling it off."

"So we're stuck here?"

"No. Julian finally came around. The public affairs team pointed out that it would be a PR nightmare if employees were injured—or worse. We'd never go public."

"*That's* what changed his mind?" Nausea rose in Mei's throat.

"Disgusting, right?" Ayanna checked her phone and sighed. "I need to get back. Julian will announce the change of plans at the evening session. We're all out of here tomorrow."

Mei exhaled with relief. "Thanks, Ayanna. Stay safe."

Ayanna gave her a quick hug. "You too, gal."

• • •

As dusk fell, Julian took the stage with a somber air. "My friends. My Livin family. I have sad news. Livinpalooza will end tomorrow. We made this heartbreaking decision out of an abundance of caution for your safety."

And your IPO, Mei thought.

"For New York employees, we have buses back to the city. For all other employees, we've made hotel accommodations. You can also arrange for your own ride to arrive between nine and eleven tomorrow morning."

Around Mei, everyone whipped out their phones.

"Ending Livinpalooza early only means one thing." Julian's green eyes glinted. "We're going twice as hard tonight! We're not stopping until the drinks run dry."

The DJ turned up the tropical house music. Julian bopped offstage.

Mei texted Ali the update. The clock icon appeared next to her message. Shoot. The network was overloaded with everyone trying to get rides home.

Mei walked away from the main grounds. Up the hill near the entrance, her message finally went through. Text after text appeared.

Joey: What's the latest? You on your way home?

Ali: So glad they finally canceled! But ugh, my car has a flat and Luc's van is in the shop! I'm so sorry! Alexandre, can you give Mei a ride to our place?

Alexandre: Of course! Mei, let me know when to get you.

Mei tapped out a reply but stopped before hitting send. Today was Friday. Joey wouldn't be leaving for Virginia until Sunday. Should she take the bus home to be with him? The thought of riding a cramped bus for hours, surrounded by unwashed co-workers and rah-rah Livin spirit was excruciating, compared to the peace of Alexandre's car. Mei chewed her lip. Luc drove her places all the time. Why did it feel different with his brother?

Her phone buzzed, shaking her out of her thoughts.

Joey: Babe! Have you heard yet? I'm so lonely.

Mei inhaled through her nose. She clicked away from Joey's text and replied to Alexandre.

Thank you so much for the ride! Can you meet me at 9 a.m. tomorrow?

She was sticking to the original plan, just one day earlier. And now she'd get extra bonus time with Ali. Mei hit send. Her message timed out. She walked farther and farther until she reached the chain-link fence surrounding the perimeter. Finally, her text went through.

Alexandre replied a minute later.

Yes! See you at 9 tomorrow.

The tension in Mei's jaw released. She had no doubt Alexandre would be there right on time. She texted him directions, then squared her shoulders and sent Joey an update.

Car doors slammed. Male voices sounded nearby. Mei squinted into the parking lot. James, the chief sustainability officer, and other execs boarded a fleet of glossy black SUVs.

"See you back at Castle Ridge," the CFO called to the others.

"I'm ready for a bourbon and a steak," James replied. Everyone laughed heartily.

Mei's face burned. Of course the execs were staying at Castle Ridge, a luxury mountain resort where rooms started at a thousand dollars a night. Mei pulled out her phone, ready to ask Alexandre to get her now.

Then she paused. Anyone who left Livinpalooza early faced termination. She couldn't risk her job over this.

With a resigned sigh, Mei pocketed her phone and trudged back down the hill.

• • •

Mei's hand splashed into a puddle, jolting her awake. She snapped on the headlamp hanging from the top of her tent, even though she knew what she'd see. Her sleeping bag was submerged in water. She was completely drenched. Rushing rain filled the air.

Mei swiped water from her face and peeked outside. People crawled from tents, equally soaked. Some shouldered backpacks and ran barefoot from the campsite.

Frozen in place, she took in the chaos. If she ran, would she get hit by lightning? If she stayed put, would a tree fall on her? Dying at Livinpalooza was not how she wanted to go.

Her phone chimed, shaking her out of her stupor. Mei fumbled in her backpack for it. Alexandre had texted.

Mei, I'm in the parking lot. Can I meet you in there?

She glanced at the time. Seven a.m. He'd come for her? This early? She drew a shuddering breath and tried to think.

I don't think so. This place is huge and my campsite is so far. There are fences all around.

Alexandre replied a second later.

Got it. Be safe and let me know if you need me. I'm ready to bust in there for you.

Mei exhaled shakily with relief. She pulled on her wet sneakers, grabbed her bag, and ran into the storm.

CHAPTER FOURTEEN

Rain drummed on Alexandre's car. He was comfy and dry, but he couldn't say the same for the half-dressed, waterlogged people emerging from Livinpalooza and being herded onto buses. So this was the startup world.

Alexandre squinted. He could barely make out people's faces in the driving rain. How would he ever find Mei? Then he spotted a familiar petite figure cutting her way through the crowd.

He rolled down the window. "Mei!"

She looked around.

Alexandre got out and ran toward her. "Mei!"

She turned in his direction. When she saw him, she waved wildly. Alexandre broke into a sprint. When he reached her, Mei threw her arms around him. Alexandre held her tightly. They stayed there for a moment as the rain fell and people shouted around them.

Mei looked up and grinned. "Am I glad to see you!"

It took all of Alexandre's willpower not to wipe the water from her cheeks. Mei's sweatshirt was soaked through. He took her bag and pointed to his car. As they jogged over, he held Mei's shoulder, then quickly withdrew his hand when he realized what he was doing.

Inside the car, Alexandre handed Mei a clean bath towel and an insulated tumbler. "Coffee with a splash of oat milk."

Her hair hung limply in her face, and her saturated clothing clung to her skin. Still, she managed a grateful smile. "Just the way I like it."

"I remembered from the beach house." Alexandre started the car and slowly merged into the sea of vehicles crawling to the campground exit.

Mei laughed self-consciously. "Sorry I'm a wreck. I've had quite a morning. My tent flooded. I woke up in a small lake."

"Wait, what?"

"You're probably used to camping in the rain, but I can't deal with this."

"No one is used to camping in a hurricane." Alexandre gestured to the water rushing down the windows. "This is the edge of Theo! When I woke up and heard the storm, I knew Livinpalooza was over. Then I saw that Theo was over New Jersey." Alexandre gripped the steering wheel tighter, remembering the panic he felt when he read the hurricane update.

"I can't believe Livin didn't evacuate us sooner." Mei's eyes widened. "I hope my teammates are okay!" She pulled out her phone and started texting.

Alexandre swallowed his ire. Now was probably not the time to rant about Livin's abysmal leadership.

Mei read something on her phone and shuddered. "My colleague Tamiko was on a bus back to the city, but now they're taking everyone to nearby hotels."

"What a mess."

They finally reached the exit. Alexandre turned slowly onto the main road. Even with the headlights on and the windshield wipers at top speed, he could only see a few feet ahead. His apartment was much closer than Ali and Luc's. Would it be weird if they went to his place? He didn't want to put Mei in an awkward position.

"So," Alexandre began hesitantly, "my apartment is about twenty minutes away. Ali and Luc are almost an hour from here. Do you want to come to my place? Or stick to the original plan?"

Mei stared at the rain battering the windshield. "Maybe head to your place?"

Alexandre caught the uncertainty in her voice. "Are you sure?"

Mei nodded. "Yeah."

"Okay." In his pocket, his phone buzzed.

"Ali just texted us: 'The rain is so bad! Go to Alexandre's. He's way closer.'" Mei leaned back in her seat. "Well, thanks for getting me and dealing with an unexpected houseguest. I'm sure this is the last thing you want to do in a hurricane."

Alexandre frowned at Mei's self-deprecating tone. He hadn't thought twice about coming early to get her. He was more than happy to have her company, he realized with a prick of guilt.

He glanced her way. "I have one request: Stop acting like you're a burden. Like I've been forced to do you a favor. I'm glad you'll be riding out the storm with me."

"Really?"

"Yes."

Mei was quiet for a moment. "I have a hard time letting people help me."

Alexandre let out a wry chuckle. "That makes two of us."

• • •

They sprinted into his apartment as the wind picked up. Alexandre set Mei's bag on the floor and removed his jacket.

Mei shucked off her sopping sneakers. Her eyes roamed her surroundings. "Nice desk! Wow, you do have a lot of outdoor stuff."

Alexandre smiled. Besides Luc, no one had visited his place. Alexandre hadn't realized how much he missed having company. Even with the still-bare walls and lack of furniture, his modest apartment felt warmer and cozier the minute Mei stepped inside.

"I love how that couch is now yours." Mei pointed at the small yellow sofa. "Reminds me of good times when Ali, Luc, and I all lived on the Upper West Side."

"I didn't know you lived there." Alexandre hung up her jacket. "When I was growing up, I went to the Museum of Natural History all the time. Then I lived in Morningside when I was an undergrad. I used to think I'd end up living somewhere in the West Seventies or Eighties." He hadn't thought of that in ages, but now he could see himself renting a studio in an older brownstone and going for daily runs in Central Park.

"I always wanted to live on the Upper West, too, and for a while I did. Now Joey and I are in Queens."

Maybe Alexandre was imagining the note of wistfulness in Mei's voice. Was she not thrilled about living in Queens? Or being with Joey?

He realized they were still in the entryway. He quickly ushered Mei into the living room. "Make yourself at home. Do you want to shower while I cook?"

"I would love a shower."

Another idea popped into his mind. "How about a bath?"

"Seriously?"

Alexandre couldn't tell whether Mei loved or hated his suggestion. He shrugged. "They're great after a long day outside. Or a few long days."

The corners of Mei's lips turned up.

"I usually take baths after skiing. Or a hard run. Or an especially grueling lab."

Now Mei was laughing.

"I even have scented Epsom salts," Alexandre added.

"Okay. That sounds amazing." She lifted her eyes teasingly. "And I'm not going to make a big deal about how you're being too kind."

"Good."

In the bathroom, Alexandre tweaked the taps until he found the perfect temperature. Then he poured in the salts. The fragrant aroma of mint and eucalyptus filled the room. He glanced around. What could make the bath a little special? He reached for his liquid soap and trickled it into the running water. Success! Bubbles floated to the surface. The pine scent mingled nicely.

Alexandre strolled back to the living room. "Your bath is ready."

Mei followed him to the bathroom. She eyed the tub, then pulled him into a side hug. "This looks amazing. No one's ever run me a bath."

Alexandre's body tingled where they touched. He released her reluctantly to retrieve her backpack and fresh towels.

"Take your time," he said. "I don't think we'll be going anywhere."

"That's fine with me."

The wind howled. Mei shivered.

"Well, I'll get the food started." Alexandre stepped into the hallway and closed the bathroom door behind him.

In the kitchen, he chopped mushrooms, red peppers, and herbs for a frittata. Other than trying not to think about taking off his clothes and climbing into the tub with her, cooking while Mei bathed in his apartment felt perfectly normal, as if they'd established this rhythm ages ago.

Alexandre pressed his lips together. Was that a good or bad thing?

CHAPTER FIFTEEN

Alone in the bathroom, Mei closed her eyes and inhaled deeply. The soothing scent of eucalyptus, mint, and pine filled her lungs. There was just one person standing between her and that bath.

She clicked on her latest text from Joey.

I'm glad you're safe, but you really couldn't make it home?

Guilt gnawed at Mei, picturing Joey alone in their apartment, even as she typed the truth.

No. All the buses went to local hotels.

Joey replied a minute later.

Okay, my baby. I just hate that you're with Le Prof and not me. This sucks.

Mei drew a breath.

I know. But we'll be together in two days, or tomorrow,
if your test gets canceled. I'll talk to you in a bit.
My phone's about to die. Love you.

She zipped her phone into her bag. Then she peeled off her wet clothing and stepped into the bath. The hot water enveloped her like a hug. A blissful "Ahhhhh" escaped her throat.

She slid her shoulders under the bubbles. She could get used to this. Had anyone ever taken care of her the way Alexandre did today? She'd always been proud of her self-sufficiency. Now a sinking feeling filled Mei's stomach. Had she asked too little of her past boyfriends? And Joey? Sure, Joey happily complied with everything she asked of him. But when was the last time he'd cleaned the apartment on his own? Or picked up groceries?

Mei bit her lip. Everything with Joey was a team affair—folding the laundry, cleaning the bathroom, going to the store to buy oatmeal. She'd always relished their closeness: Couples who did everything together were enviable. Or so she used to believe. Now their inseparability was starting to feel stifling. Unhealthy. A little codependent.

Mei swirled her hand in the bubbles. The fragrant salts brought her back to the present. The eucalyptus was a healing balm, and the mint cleared her head. The undercurrent of pine sharpened her senses. Alexandre's scent.

She studied her surroundings. Like the rest of Alexandre's apartment, the bathroom was small and a bit dated, with seventies-style beige tiles. But it was cozy and spotless in a homey way. Forest-green towels hung on a rack. A smooth piece of driftwood adorned one shelf. Next to it sat a print of Grand Teton, the fir trees and mountain peaks dramatic against the blue sky.

How was Alexandre still single? He was so kind and thoughtful. *And hot.* Mei's cheeks turned pink thinking of Alexandre's piercing hazel eyes and lean muscles his clothing couldn't quite conceal. In just a few short hours, he'd treated her better than anyone she'd ever been with. *Including Joey.* The thought bubbled up before she could stop it.

The wind roared, vibrating the walls. Mei submerged herself deeper in the toasty water.

• • •

Mei emerged from the bathroom restored. She found Alexandre at his desk in the living room, reading on his laptop. A pair of thin metal glasses perched on his nose. Mei smiled. He looked cute in glasses.

A ferocious gust rattled the windows. Alexandre startled and removed the glasses. His face warmed when he spotted her. "How are you feeling?"

"Like I've washed away weeks of stress and grime. You may have converted me to baths."

Alexandre led her to his couch. He'd set the coffee table with silverware, a pitcher of iced tea, and a plate with bread and butter. "Sorry I don't have a dining table yet."

He looked so chagrined that Mei chuckled. "I love this setup. When I lived alone, I ate every meal on my couch and coffee table, too." A little pang hit her as she pictured her tiny Upper West Side studio.

Alexandre carried over a frittata and a salad. He filled her plate, then his.

"This is so good." Mei inhaled her frittata slice, then cut another. "What were you working on?"

"On my laptop? I wasn't working. I don't work on weekends."

Mei's eyebrows shot up.

Alexandre laughed. "I know. It's weird for me, too. But I decided to commit to my new life, which means setting hard boundaries and not working more than forty-five hours a week."

"Otherwise, you'd just burn out teaching."

"Exactly. And all of this would be for nothing. I was actually researching things to do around here."

Alexandre had a new looseness in his shoulders, an ease with which he moved. Mei regarded him with envy. "Did you find anything good?"

"A few scenic hikes nearby, and some restaurants to check out. There's even a farm that brews their own beer and makes wood-fired pizza in their garden."

Mei had to stop herself from blurting out, *We should go sometime!* The two of them wouldn't be going anywhere together, unless it was with Ali and Luc. *He'll probably take dates there.* Mei snuck a glance at Alexandre. Was he dating? He'd get snatched up right away. Why did she feel like his life was beginning while hers was reaching a very final conclusion?

She forced a smile. "You look really happy."

Alexandre shrugged. "I'm getting there."

Mei softened. "I hear you."

A blast of wind shook the house. She and Alexandre jumped,

then laughed at their skittishness. The lights flickered once, then twice. The apartment plunged into darkness.

• • •

Mei blinked. In the low light, she could just make out Alexandre's profile. Together, they walked to the window. Not a single light shone through the sheets of rain.

Alexandre checked the kitchen sink. "We've got water, at least." He bent over his camping equipment and unearthed a lantern. A soft glow filled the room.

They settled back on the sofa.

"We were talking so much about me. How've you been?" Alexandre's hazel eyes glowed in the lantern light.

Mei warmed under the weight of his attention. "Want to hear about Livinpalooza?"

"I'm curious, but I'd get it if you wanted to talk about anything but that."

"No, I have some good stories." Mei started with the perfect weather and celebratory atmosphere of the first day. She turned somber as she recounted the rest of the event.

Alexandre's expression went from incredulous to incensed. "I can't believe those bastards cared more about their IPO than people dying."

"My job is a disaster, too." Mei told Alexandre about James and her impossible goals. "Livinpalooza revealed all the ugly parts I ignored, or justified, because I finally had a job I loved. I thought I could fix some of the problems."

Alexandre looked her in the eye. "What you just described is appalling. You're one person in a huge company run by a megalomaniac."

This wasn't the first time Mei had heard Julian described that way. In the past, she'd disagreed. Now the word felt accurate.

"I assume Julian is surrounded by enablers who will all cash in when you go public."

Mei recalled the execs as they filed into their SUVs, smug with their special treatment. She nodded.

"I'm sorry, but all those people care about is their big payday. No matter how much you try, you can't change a toxic work culture. Not when it's rotten to the core."

Mei winced. Deep down, she knew he was right. She laughed bitterly. "Great. Just when I thought I'd figured everything out. Work. Life. Love."

Alexandre was quiet for a moment. "You're getting married in a few weeks. That's something, right?"

Mei let out a dry huff. "Sometimes I don't know about Joey, either." She clapped a hand over her mouth, but it was too late.

Alexandre's eyes flickered with surprise. "Do you want to talk about that?"

Now Mei was silent. If Joey still had power, he was probably playing snippets of obscure songs, cursing out loud, and noisily labeling files on his laptop. Mei's heart brimmed with affection, even as it sank with the realization that she wasn't looking forward to leaving Alexandre's place.

"Well, I told you about how Joey helped me rediscover a part of my life I left behind." Heaviness spread through Mei's chest.

"Now I'm seeing that we built our relationship on our shared past. I haven't focused enough on who we are now, and who we'll be in the future."

"Do you love Joey?"

Mei blinked. "Yes."

Alexandre looked away.

"I just don't know if I love him enough, or in the right way, to sustain a lifetime together." Admitting the truth left her breathless. Why was love so complicated?

Alexandre seemed to be wrestling with whether to say something. "I know how you feel. My last relationship was kind of similar."

"What happened?"

"My ex, Julie, and I met soon after I moved to Eugene. She had her own business, a secondhand outdoor gear shop." Alexandre gave her the side-eye. "I know what you're thinking. 'Wow, that's so Oregon.'"

Mei stifled a giggle. "I'm, uh, totally not."

Alexandre laughed. "It's okay. Her shop was very Oregon and she was proud of it. We bonded over our love of the outdoors."

"That must have been nice."

"It was. At first. But it kept us from seeing how we had nothing else in common. Julie's eyes glazed over every time I talked about my research. She nicknamed me 'Aquaman' and told everyone I was a 'zebrafish whisperer' instead of a research scientist."

Mei nodded and tried to keep a straight face.

"Julie was also a hardcore extrovert. We lived together for two years and our apartment was always full of people until two in the morning."

"That's my worst nightmare. What was your breaking point? Or hers?"

"My thirty-seventh birthday. Every year, I wanted a quiet night in, and every year, she threw me a huge party. She didn't get that I hate big events that are all about me."

Mei smiled. "I can relate."

"Exactly. So for this birthday, Julie took me to my favorite restaurant, just the two of us. It was perfect. Then we got home. I opened the door, and fifty people jumped out and yelled, 'Surprise!'"

"Oh no."

"They were all wearing T-shirts that said 'Happy Birthday, Aquaman!' with my face next to zebrafish in party hats."

"Yikes." Mei tried not to snicker.

"It's kind of funny now," Alexandre admitted. "But not at the time. The party went until four a.m. People spilled beer on my laptop and had sex in our bed. At some point during the night, I had an out-of-body experience, looking around and thinking, 'Is this what you want your life to be like?' I broke up with her soon after."

"Do you ever regret it?"

"No." Alexandre didn't hesitate. "There's a specific loneliness that comes from being with the wrong person. Anytime I get down about being single, I remember that. That loneliness never would have gotten better. It was only going to get worse."

Mei chewed her thumbnail. Alexandre's words poked at feelings she'd been avoiding for too long.

"I also didn't want to settle. I want to believe I'm worthy of happiness, even if I'm still working on that." He chuckled self-consciously. "Sorry if this is getting too deep."

"No, I get it. Why wouldn't you be worthy? Because of tenure?"

Alexandre nodded.

"So? You already have an impressive new job. Plus, there's a lot more to life. You deserve happiness in everything."

"Thanks. I try to remind myself every day." He nudged the lantern closer on the table. "What about you?"

Heat rose to Mei's cheeks. "What about me?"

"Don't *you* think you're worthy of more? Of a job that's not a treadmill to death? With leaders who respect you? And marrying someone you're sure about?"

Mei glared at him.

He held her gaze. "I think you're worthy of more."

Mei's heart pounded. Her palms turned clammy. Alexandre's words were dredging up her worst memory. The reason she left Queens so many years ago. She took a breath, trying to quell the light-headedness threatening to roll in.

Alexandre's forehead creased with concern. "Are you okay?"

Mei nodded shakily. "I'm going to tell you something no one knows. Not even Ali. So please don't ever tell her or Luc."

Alexandre's eyes widened in surprise. "I won't. Are you sure you want to tell me?"

"Yes." Mei couldn't say why she trusted Alexandre, but she did. "This goes back to when we were kids. My dad was an alcoholic.

He never hit us, but he had a bad temper and would fly into terrifying rages. My mom divorced him when I was ten. My dad wasn't happy, so his one condition was that Ali and I had to go stay at his place every other day, and every holiday."

"*Every other day?* That's awful."

"It was. He didn't even like spending time with us. His apartment was filthy, and he'd just drink and smoke in front of the TV."

Alexandre shook his head.

"Ali and I kept each other strong, but after two years, we'd had it. We decided to ask our dad if we could live with our mom and visit him on weekends. We planned to ask him after Thanksgiving, when he'd be in a good mood. Then Ali started panicking. She wanted us to drop it, but I said I'd speak to him alone. Eventually, she gave in.

"One afternoon, a few weeks before Thanksgiving, Ali was at a friend's house. I figured I'd get it over with. My dad flipped out. He got so drunk, he couldn't stand. He spent hours slamming his fists on the table and yelling about how stupid and selfish Ali and I were. Finally, he said we could do whatever the fuck we wanted. That night, he crashed his car into a tree. He died instantly. Obviously he was wasted."

"I'm so sorry you went through that. Ali too."

"I don't blame myself now, but I did for years. I never wanted Ali to feel the same. As far as she knows, our dad died before I could speak to him."

"How did you stop blaming yourself? Therapy?"

"Yeah. In my college psych class, I learned about PTSD. I spent months working up the courage to seek counseling. Over time, I realized I didn't cause my dad's death."

"You didn't. Not at all."

"Thanks. I still need to hear that, even today. I dated terrible guys who treated me the way I thought I deserved to be treated, and had so-called friends with benefits who only wanted to sleep with me but not date me."

"Jerks."

"Yeah." Mei wrinkled her nose, disgusted at those men and herself. "When I met Joey, everything felt so magical. He's the only guy who's ever loved me for being me. In his eyes, I'm smart, talented, and beautiful."

"You are."

Mei's cheeks turned pink. She gave an awkward laugh, then pressed on. "For the longest time, I couldn't believe I was lucky enough to find Joey. Now I'm starting to wonder whether I'm worthy of more. And if I'm a horrible, selfish person for thinking that." Mei's vision blurred as tears spilled over.

Alexandre got up from the couch. A moment later, he placed a soft tissue in her hands. Mei dabbed her eyes as he pulled her into a hug. He kept his knees between them, but she was close enough to rest her head on his shoulder.

"You're not selfish for wanting love and happiness," he said into her ear. "You deserve it all."

CHAPTER SIXTEEN

Alexandre rubbed Mei's back until her tears subsided, wishing he could say or do more to comfort her. What a weight she'd been carrying. And was still carrying.

She drew back slowly and wiped her eyes. "Well, now you know my life story."

Before Alexandre could stop himself, he brushed a stray tear from her cheek. "It means a lot that you shared it with me."

Mei let out a dry little laugh. "Now I just have to figure out what to do."

"You don't have to stay in every impossible situation just because you survived worse," Alexandre said carefully.

Mei's eyes welled up. She nodded, then looked away.

Shoot. Alexandre hadn't meant to make her cry more. He touched her shoulder. "Remember what you told me a few weeks ago? About how it's never too late to carve out a new path for yourself? That stayed with me. Maybe it's worth considering."

Mei groaned. "Remind me never to tell you anything." She fiddled with her engagement ring. "Do you think it's possible to be one hundred percent sure about someone? Or anything?"

Alexandre thought through her question. "Scientifically speaking, nothing is one hundred percent certain. And I think that's true about everything in life."

She sighed. "I'm not going to figure out anything today."

"Not after Livinpalooza and a hurricane." Alexandre wasn't going to push her. Mei needed to decide about Joey and Livin herself.

A gust of wind made them jump.

"I should see how Ali's doing," Mei said. "Unless you have an update."

Alexandre peered at his phone. "Nope. Go text her." *And Joey.* The unspoken acknowledgment hung between them.

Mei retrieved her phone without meeting his eyes. "Ali and Luc are fine. They lost power, too, so they're hunkered down like we are." She scrolled through her texts. "Oh god, my colleague Kaden is stuck in a motel room with seven random drunk people." She looked up. "I'm so glad I'm here with you."

Alexandre gave her a don't-mention-it shrug.

"Do you want some downtime?" Mei walked to his bookcase and pulled out a fantasy novel he'd recently finished. "Don't worry about entertaining me."

Alexandre grabbed a flashlight, settled into his desk chair, and opened his own book. For a minute, he felt odd reading while Mei was there, but she looked content curled up on his couch.

A few hours later, Alexandre glanced at the time. "I'll get dinner together."

Mei stood up. "I'll help you."

In the narrow kitchen, they moved with ease, despite the small space. Mei arranged a platter of cheese, salami, crackers, and olives. Alexandre plated the leftover frittata wedges. They settled onto the couch and toasted their cans of seltzer. Rain fell steadily outside. In the soft glow of the lantern light, they laughed and chatted until the food disappeared.

Mei stifled a yawn.

Alexandre stood up. "Ready for bed?"

Mei's eyes widened in alarm. "Where are we sleeping?"

"You're in the bedroom. I'll be out here."

"You're too tall for the couch."

"I'll sleep in my sleeping bag." For a second, Alexandre had thought about them sharing his bed but nixed the idea immediately.

"No way! You're not sleeping on the floor of your own apartment. I can fit on the couch. See?" Mei curled up in the fetal position.

Alexandre smiled. Mei was cute when she was insistent. "Nope. The sofa is too small for you to stretch out comfortably. You were just camping in a hurricane. You get the bed."

Mei looked like she was about to protest, but relented.

Alexandre made his bed with his softest sheets. He fluffed the pillows and stacked them in a welcoming pile. For the first time since moving in, he wished his room were bigger and brighter, and that all four walls weren't bare. But at least his bed was comfortable.

He showed Mei to his room. Her eyes scanned the modest space, lighting up when they landed on the freshly made bed. "This looks heavenly." She pulled him into a side hug.

In an instant, his arms were around her waist. Mei smiled up at him, her lips inches away. Alexandre touched her cheek.

They froze, then jumped apart.

Alexandre stepped back to put more space between them. "Here. You take this." He held out the lantern.

Mei reached for it, her eyes barely meeting his.

"Well, I'll be out there if you need anything." Alexandre pointed to the living room, unsure of what to do with himself.

Mei waved awkwardly. "See you in the morning."

• • •

Alexandre couldn't sleep. And not because he was in a sleeping bag on his living room floor. The scene in his bedroom doorway looped through his mind. Was he going to kiss Mei? Was she going to kiss him? How did his hands get to Mei's waist? It happened so quickly Alexandre couldn't figure it out. Would everything be weird now? Holidays and family get-togethers were going to be a blast. He eventually fell into a fitful sleep.

Sunlight and chipper birdsong roused him the next morning. Alexandre shuffled to the window. Leaves and tree branches littered the parking lot. The grass glistened. Otherwise, Hurricane Theo had left no trace.

The power was still out, so Alexandre showered and shaved in the low light filtering through the bathroom window. He emerged in the same T-shirt and shorts he'd slept in as Mei stepped out of his bedroom.

She gave him a shy smile. "Did you sleep well?" Her wavy brown hair was flattened on one side, and she hid a yawn behind one hand. Still, she looked beautiful.

"I did," Alexandre lied. "How about you?"

"Like a log, even though I felt bad about you sleeping on the floor."

Their exchange felt normal. Alexandre headed to the kitchen, relieved.

As Mei showered, he set out bread, jam, granola, and cold brew on the coffee table. A feeling of melancholy threatened to roll in. This might be his last meal with Mei.

She smiled gratefully when she appeared in the living room and saw the breakfast spread. "I texted Ali," she said as she spooned strawberry preserves onto a slice of bread. "Their power is back, but their yard is a mess." She picked up her phone. "I should check the train schedule."

Alexandre looked away to hide his disappointment.

"The trains aren't running. There's too much storm debris on the tracks. Joey already left for Virginia. His exam is still on."

Alexandre perked up. "I can drive you."

"No way. I'll ask Ali."

"She's cleaning her yard and her car has a flat. I'd just be sitting here with no power."

"Okay." Mei reached over to touch his arm, then seemed to think better of it. "Thank you."

• • •

On the drive down to the city, they stopped at Ali and Luc's. As Alexandre parked, he spotted Ali raking leaves, Luc dragging tree limbs into a pile, and Kaia gathering twigs.

Ali ran over and threw her arms around Mei. "You survived Livinpalooza! And Hurricane Theo."

"With this guy's help." Mei smiled up at Alexandre. He grinned back at her.

The five of them settled onto the patio. Ali and Luc set out chips and salsa.

"Good thing this wasn't two weeks from now," Ali said. "You would've had to postpone your wedding and bachelor/bachelorette."

Now that Alexandre knew about Mei's conflicted feelings, he didn't dare glance her way. "It's a joint bachelor and bachelorette party?" he asked Ali. "What are you planning?"

"Korean barbecue at this amazing place in K-town. Then karaoke."

"Nice." Alexandre hadn't been invited. He wasn't invited to the wedding, either, which was fine with him. But the bachelor/bachelorette actually sounded fun. A wisp of envy snaked into his chest. Mei, Ali, and his brother would be having a big night out while he sat at home.

Everyone seemed to have the same thought.

"You should come!" Mei and Ali exclaimed in unison. They looked at each other and burst out laughing.

"I was going to invite you," Ali said. "I'm sending out the details this week."

"You really should come," Mei said.

Alexandre shot Mei a quizzical look. Had he imagined her saying she had doubts about Joey? Then he saw the hope and trepidation in her eyes. Ah. Until she made up her mind about Joey, she was going along with the plans and praying for the best.

Ali and Luc didn't have a clue about her doubts. He was the only one.

Well, he knew a thing or two about putting on a brave face. Mei's shining eyes told Alexandre she wanted him there, despite the potential awkwardness. He felt the exact same way.

Alexandre smiled. "I wouldn't miss it."

CHAPTER SEVENTEEN

On the drive back to Queens, Mei tried to ignore how her time with Alexandre was drawing to a close.

Last night, alone in his bed, ensconced in his sheets, she'd thrummed with longing. She imagined Alexandre climbing on top of her, kissing her neck and running his hands over her, certain and firm. At one point, she'd reached between her legs to staunch the throbbing. Guilt immediately seized her. She pictured Joey instead, but that also felt wrong. Which was worse, fantasizing about Alexandre or Joey in Alexandre's bed? The debate killed her arousal, letting her drift into a dead sleep.

When they pulled up to her apartment building, Alexandre's eyebrows lifted at the glassy entrance. "Sweet place."

Mei flushed. "I'm still getting used to it." She hesitated. "Want to come up?" Did she even want Alexandre to see the life she shared with Joey?

"Thanks, but I'll get going. Let you settle in."

Out on the sidewalk, Alexandre helped her into her backpack. Before Mei could stop herself, she wrapped him in a hug, burying her face in his neck. Alexandre's arms around her were tentative at first, then tight.

"If you ever want to talk about anything we spoke about, I'm here for you," he said.

Mei drew back so she could see Alexandre's face. Her heart pounded as she took in his caring eyes, the angle of his jaw. She nodded and swallowed hard. Then she let him go.

• • •

Mei walked through her apartment as if for the first time. She ran her hand over the smooth kitchen counter and the blue easy chair where Joey watched his epic fail videos.

Her phone chimed, shaking her from her daze. Maybe she'd left something in Alexandre's car and he was driving back. Mei peered at the screen.

Oh balls! I'm in Virginia now.

Joey had sent her a screenshot of his driving route. The highlighted loop-de-loop for a highway exit resembled a thirteen-year-old's drawing of a penis and testicles.

Mei's breath grew shallow. Not long ago, she would have laughed at Joey's silly joke. Now the sight of it turned her stomach.

In two weeks, she'd be bound to Joey forever. Alexandre's words spun through her mind. *Don't you think you're worthy of marrying someone you're sure about?*

Should she call off their wedding? Break up with Joey now over video chat? But what would she say? *I don't want to get married because you make penis jokes?*

Mei ran to the bathroom. She retched over the toilet, but

nothing came up. She rested her head against the cool seat and tried to take deep breaths until, spent, she slid onto the floor.

Sometime later, her phone chimed. Mei glanced at it wearily. Joey had attached a photo of his study materials spread out on a table.

Gonna make you proud, my baby.

Mei smiled wanly. Another text from Joey appeared.

I already passed two practice exams. Network security promotion, here I come!

Mei's heart lifted. She typed back.

Amazing! I'm so proud of you.

She flopped onto the couch as her phone chimed again. She glanced at it, expecting Joey's "aw shucks" reply. But it was Alexandre.

Just got home! My power's on, too. I hope you're resting up. I meant what I said. I'm here if you ever want to talk.

Mei closed her eyes. This weekend, she'd felt so carefree with Alexandre. No, not carefree. Cared *for*. Safe and secure, like all of life wasn't an uphill battle with no one to rely on but herself. Could she have that forever? With Joey?

Her eyes wandered to the table where they kept their wedding supplies. Joey was coming through now, like he always did. He just needed a little coaching when it came to taking initiative. *We'll get there,* Mei thought with a nod.

Her heart in her throat, Mei replied to Alexandre.

So glad your power's on! Thanks for your offer to chat. Now that I'm back, I'm feeling much better about everything.

She sent it before she could second-guess herself.

Mei reached over to the end table and picked up her favorite framed photo. She and Joey were in Flushing Meadows Park, beaming at the camera, their faces pressed together. The silver Unisphere, the unofficial symbol of Queens, rose proudly behind them.

Mei touched the photo. The sight of Joey's lopsided smile made her lips tug up. *I'm already home.*

• • •

"Happy bachelorette!" Ali popped open a bottle of champagne and poured two glasses.

Mei grinned as they clinked their flutes. "Getting ready together was the best idea." Her wedding weekend was here, and Ali and Luc were staying at a boutique hotel near Park Avenue South. Hair tools, makeup, and snacks covered every surface of the room.

"I'm going to call the guys back," Ali said. "We need to leave for the restaurant soon."

Alexandre was crashing in Ali and Luc's room tonight, though Mei hadn't seen him yet. Just thinking of him made her stomach flip. Anytime she remembered the electric feel of his arms around her waist, she made herself think of Joey, the man she was about to marry.

Luckily, the past two weeks had been full of distractions, like mountains of Livin projects.

"Have you unplugged from work?" Ali asked, as if reading Mei's mind.

"As of four this afternoon." She didn't mention how she'd pulled back-to-back ninety-hour weeks. When she'd finally logged off, she'd collapsed on her bed, shaking and chattering. Her hard work had paid off, though. She'd already exceeded her September goals and was on track to hit October's. James said they could discuss the VP job after her wedding.

"Good! Now you can enjoy your wedding and honeymoon."

Mei wrapped a lock of hair around her curling iron. In two days, she'd officially be Joey's wife. Why did the thought make her heart race? *Pre-wedding nerves*, she reminded herself.

Ali slipped on her olive-green minidress. Mei pulled on her own little black number with ruching on the sides and a plunging neckline. They rode the elevator to the ground floor. Mei scanned the dimly lit lobby lounge for Alexandre and Luc.

"There they are!" Ali said.

Beside a potted plant with massive fronds, Luc was speaking and Alexandre was laughing. They looked handsome in blazers and dark jeans. Mei drank in Alexandre's easy smile. Her body buzzed with attraction.

The brothers looked up and spotted them. Luc grinned at Ali and strolled toward her.

Mei's eyes met Alexandre's. His eyebrows lifted. A smile formed on his face. Mei felt him taking her in. He was clearly enjoying what he saw. She couldn't tamp down the slow smile spreading across her face, conveying the same. When Mei reached him, she wrapped her arms around his neck, grateful for the heels that brought her face closer to his. Ahhh. He smelled divine. Alexandre hugged her back, angling his body to put space between them.

"You look great," he said quietly.

Mei brightened, but noted his use of "great"—a more impersonal term than "gorgeous" or "stunning."

They took a cab to the restaurant, where an elevator whooshed them up to the penthouse. When the doors opened, they gasped. Through the floor-to-ceiling windows, Manhattan shimmered in the twilight. The Empire State Building loomed close enough to touch.

In their private dining area, a waiter passed out flutes of champagne. Ali and Luc excused themselves to speak to the event manager, leaving Mei and Alexandre at the windows.

Mei flushed as he glanced her way. "Quite the view, huh?"

"It's amazing. I've never seen the city from this high up." They took in the sea of lights. "Your big weekend is here. Are you still feeling okay about everything?"

"I am."

"Good."

Their gazes locked. The longer Mei stared into Alexandre's

eyes, the more her resolve melted. *Tell me I'm making the right decision!*

Alexandre seemed to sense her thoughts. He took a step closer. "Mei—"

"There you are!"

Mei spun around. Kathy ran over in a sleek cobalt dress. Luis followed her in a merlot jacket. Her cousin Evie arrived, her slim figure clad in a black jumpsuit.

Mei hugged them in turn, then pulled Alexandre over. She let go quickly when she realized she was holding on to his arm. "This is Alexandre, Luc's brother. He's a biology professor at SUNY New Paltz."

Ali and Luc rejoined the group. As Mei chatted with Kathy and Luis about their flight, she spied Alexandre talking to Evie. Her cousin had always seemed much younger, but at twenty-nine, Evie was no longer a kid. She worked at a nonprofit and was a lifelong dancer. Mei bit her lip. Evie and Alexandre were the only single people at the party. They'd probably get together by the end of the night.

Just then, the air shifted. Joey strode in with Bao, Chloe, Miguel, and Ivan.

"The bachelor's here!" he bellowed. "Where's my bride?"

Mei turned red.

Kathy and Luis laughed generously.

"Go to your man," Kathy said.

Cheeks aflame, Mei pecked Joey on the lips. He would have looked downright dashing in his dark jeans and navy blazer if he weren't so wild-eyed and rumpled.

He gripped Mei's waist and swayed. "Babe. I missed you. So glad we're together now."

Mei coughed as the stench of alcohol hit her. "Let's get you some water." She led Joey to the bar, then put on her most composed smile, not unlike the one she used to make presentations at work.

"Wow, looks like you had quite the pregame," she said to Miguel and Ivan.

"I blame those two." Miguel tilted his head toward Bao and Chloe, who were taking champagne flutes from the waiter.

"They'd done four rounds of shots before we even got there," Ivan added.

Mei blanched. "Joey never drinks that much."

Miguel patted her arm. "We'll keep an eye on him and make sure he's okay. You just enjoy your evening."

"Thank you," Mei said. Joey and Miguel had known each other since elementary school, when they'd gotten into all kinds of mischief. Now Miguel led product design at a booming AI e-commerce startup. He and Ivan, a high school calculus teacher, had met five years ago while volunteering for an LGBTQ+ shelter. They'd recently bought an apartment in Sunnyside and were saving up to start a family. Not for the first time, Mei wondered how much Miguel and Joey still had in common.

She strode over to Bao and Chloe.

"Meiiiiiiiiiiiiiiiiiiiiii." Bao pulled her into a side hug. Mei enthusiastically returned his embrace, charmed by his boisterous greeting.

"I didn't know Joey was such a lightweight!" Chloe gave Mei an air-kiss on the cheek. She was Chinese American, too, and she'd grown up in New Jersey. "Don't worry. We'll make sure he eats well and sobers up."

Mei smiled gratefully. Joey's friends were kinder and more mature than she'd remembered. Maybe she'd judged them too harshly.

Waiters motioned everyone to be seated. Mei took her place between Ali and Joey at the center of the table. Alexandre, she noticed, was diagonally across from her, with Kathy and Luis in between.

The table bore an array of banchan: fiery cabbage kimchi, tart pickled radish, and seasoned spinach. Everyone passed around platters of seafood pajeon and japchae.

Ali stood up and tapped her glass. "I'll keep this short and sweet. Mei and Joey, we wish you a lifetime of love and happiness. May this be the start of a fabulous wedding weekend and your beautiful future together. Cheers!"

"Cheers!" everyone echoed.

Mei leaned in to meet Joey's lips.

Wine and appetizers flowed. As everyone talked, Mei couldn't help but notice how Luis threw his head back in laughter at Kathy's stories. Chloe rested her hand on Bao's, who turned his palm over so they could lace their fingers together. Miguel glowed with pride when Ivan spoke. Ali and Luc finished each other's sentences.

No one looked down in embarrassment or tried to change the subject like Mei did each time Joey opened his mouth. When Evie was telling everyone about an electro-pop concert she'd attended, Joey jumped in with an overly long description of how he'd finally identified a batch of cryptic Moldovan techno songs. When

Miguel and Ivan shared stories from their recent vacation in the Bahamas, Joey recounted how he'd once suffered a massive bout of diarrhea while snorkeling in Florida.

"I didn't tell the other snorkelers why the water got cloudy!" He guffawed.

Mei filled her wineglass to the brim.

The waiters lit the barbecue grills embedded in the table. The rich scent of kalbi filled the air. Alexandre's raised eyebrows asked Mei how she was doing. She tried to smile reassuringly. She guessed Alexandre saw through her act when he glanced at Joey and frowned.

The conversation dipped when everyone started eating.

"This is the best Korean barbecue I've ever had." Chloe licked her lips in delight.

"This is the best meal I've ever had," Luc agreed, drawing enthusiastic murmurs.

"I'm loving tonight." Joey touched his forehead to Mei's. His eyes radiated pure joy.

"Me too." Mei drained her wine, then refilled her glass.

Joey launched into a story about the latest epic fail video compilation he'd found. Mei squeezed his shoulder, then addressed Kathy and Luis. "Want to hear about Livinpalooza?"

Their eyes lit up.

On their other side, Alexandre turned his head. "You mean when I braved a hurricane to come get you?"

Mei giggled as she and Alexandre recounted her escape, her shoulders loosening for the first time that night.

Once the waiters cleared the table, Ali stood up, nearly tripping on her chair. "Who's ready for karaoke?"

• • •

Two buildings away, at Pop Star Karaoke, a hostess showed them into a private room. Smooth leather couches lined the perimeter. A jumbo flat-screen TV hung on one wall. In the middle of the room, a large coffee table bore beer, wine, cocktails, and little paper cups.

"Looks like someone got the works!" Bao shouted.

"It's not every day your sister gets married!" Ali cried.

"Are those Jell-O shots?" Evie grabbed one of the little paper cups.

"Lychee Jell-O shots," Ali confirmed with pride. "We have glow bracelets, too!" She waved a handful of thin fluorescent tubes in pink, orange, green, and blue.

Mei laughed and slid a few onto her wrists. "Anyone want to start a playlist?"

"I got you, Mei." Luc reached for a songbook and remote.

A familiar bass line thumped through the speakers. Everyone laughed and groaned.

"Any takers on '500 Miles'?" Luc asked.

"Right here!" Miguel grabbed a mic and passed one to Ivan.

After "500 Miles," Ali and Kathy sang "I Want It That Way." Everyone screamed along to "Bohemian Rhapsody," "Don't Stop Believin'," and "Party in the U.S.A."

Mei threw back two Jell-O shots. The night now had the glossy quality that only comes from imbibing massive amounts of alcohol.

The title card for "All the Small Things" appeared.

Joey jumped up. "This one's mine!"

Mei beamed. She'd asked Joey to stick to songs that everyone would know. Thank goodness he'd picked a crowd-pleaser. Everyone gleefully joined in.

During the musical interlude, Joey put down the mic. He wove a stack of glow bracelets between his fingers. As the music built to a crescendo and the beat dropped, he started raving, bopping up and down and swirling his hands in wavelike motions. He kick-kicked his feet faster than Mei had ever thought possible, jumping around crisscrossing his legs.

There were not enough Jell-O shots in the room, or on earth, to drown Mei's humiliation. Joey had mentioned he'd been into raving as a teenager, but Mei had never seen him rave and certainly hadn't thought to ask him not to go rave-crazy tonight.

"Whoa, raving!" Kathy exclaimed.

"Yeah, Joey!" Luis called out encouragingly.

Mei looked helplessly at Ali.

She smiled overenthusiastically. "I didn't know Joey raved!"

Luc and Alexandre were deeply engrossed in opening a bottle of wine. Bao, Miguel, Chloe, Ivan, and Evie sipped their drinks and watched Joey dance, their smiles a touch too wide, their eyes faintly pitying.

They're embarrassed for Joey, Mei realized. *And me.*

The final chords of the song faded out. The opening lilt of "Eternal Flame" filled the room. Mei exhaled with relief.

A karaoke employee dropped off food menus. Ali held them up. "Anyone want a look?"

Joey grabbed a menu. "Me! Because *I are hungry!*" His eyes met Mei's, and the grin fell off his face. "Oh shit. Sorry."

Everyone looked at him in confusion.

"*I are hungry*?" Luc repeated. "How drunk are you?"

"Ah, it's nothing. Just an old joke with these two." Joey waved his hand toward Bao and Miguel.

Bao snorted and rolled his eyes.

"Dude, you're still saying that?" Miguel said.

Neither he nor Bao seemed particularly surprised or offended, but Mei suspected this wasn't the hilarious inside joke Joey claimed it was.

"I don't get it," Ivan said to Miguel.

"Yeah, let us in on the joke," Chloe chimed in.

"It's so dumb, it's not even worth explaining," Miguel said. "When Bao and I were kids, we sometimes made mistakes when we were learning English. This clown always gave us shit about it." He cuffed Joey on the back of his head.

Ali wrinkled her nose. Evie arched an eyebrow. Kathy and Luis exchanged a look. Chloe glanced at Bao, then eyed Joey with distaste.

Mei's face burned. She grabbed the remote and flipped to the next song. "Anyone want 'I Got You Babe'?" She shot Ali a desperate look.

Her sister took the mic. Luc grabbed the other.

Mei slipped into the hallway. In the bathroom, she dabbed her forehead with a damp paper towel. Other than the typical signs of drinking—her eye makeup smudged, her hair slightly mussed—one would never know she'd just realized her fiancé was a joke and everyone felt sorry for her.

As Mei started back to the room, Alexandre stepped out.

He'd shed his blazer and rolled up the sleeves of his white button-down. Mei slackened at the sight of him, barely managing to stumble over.

"Remember that out-of-body experience you told me about?" she asked.

Alexandre nodded.

"Well, I just had one, during the epic rave."

Alexandre cracked a smile. Then his expression turned serious.

"I don't know what to do." Mei's voice broke.

Alexandre nudged her chin up with the edge of his finger. He withdrew his hand, but his touch lingered.

"You have a choice," he said. "This is your life. Your decision. You may not always have had choices, but you do now. If this isn't what you want, only you can change that." His hazel eyes seared into her.

"I know." Mei's shoulders dropped. With a shaky inhale, she touched Alexandre's arm, then trudged back to the room.

CHAPTER EIGHTEEN

Alexandre couldn't remember the last time he'd had so much alcohol. During the first hour of karaoke, he'd gone from buzzed to drunk, though he thankfully hadn't entered the sloppy realm. The endless quantity of booze had taken the edge off the weirder elements of the evening, like celebrating a bachelorette he had growing feelings for, and a bachelor he simply didn't like. He had to commend Ali for the drinks. And for getting the party back on track. She and Luc were leading everyone in a rousing rendition of "Mr. Brightside."

Still, an air of forced cheer pervaded the room. Alexandre glared at Joey, making no attempt to hide his disgust.

The final chord of "Mr. Brightside" reverberated into silence.

Ali clapped her hands in front of her chest. "How about we call it a night? We have a big weekend ahead."

Everyone exited the karaoke bar and converged on the sidewalk. Ali, Evie, Kathy, and Luis chatted in one group, while Bao, Chloe, Miguel, and Ivan spoke in another. Alexandre watched Mei converse with Joey. He appeared contrite, his posture sagging, his eyes downcast. She looked sad and embarrassed.

"A bit rocky just now, but otherwise a good night," Alexandre said to Luc.

"Yeah. I think Mei had fun. Joey too." Luc's expression hardened.

Alexandre followed his gaze. Joey was now chatting with Bao and Miguel.

Luc let out a dry laugh. "'Clown' is right."

Alexandre studied his brother. Luc had been drinking all night, but he still had his wits about him. "Have you always thought that about Joey?"

Luc flushed. "Not until now. I mean, Joey's not exactly who I thought Mei would end up with. He's kind of goofy. This sounds terrible, but sometimes I wonder what they even talk about."

"I'm going to guess his music files."

Luc chuckled, then his smile faded. "But I always thought he was a good guy. Before tonight, I never heard him say anything remotely offensive. He clearly adores Mei, and she always seemed so happy. Ali and I thought that was all that mattered."

Alexandre glanced at Mei. She looked beautiful under the lights of K-town's glowing storefronts.

"I guess I chalked up any misgivings to the fact that Mei is like a sister to me." Luc shrugged. "And no dude's ever going to be good enough for your sister."

How about your brother? Alexandre almost laughed out loud. "Maybe you should talk to Mei if you think she's about to make a huge mistake."

"Now? To what end? Get her to call off the wedding?" Luc pinched the bridge of his nose. "I'm in no shape to do that. Plus, it's not really my place."

Alexandre nodded. Deep down, he knew it wouldn't matter if Luc said anything to Mei. Only she could decide whether or not to marry Joey.

Bao, Chloe, Miguel, and Ivan came over to say goodbye. Then Evie hugged him and Luc before hopping into a cab.

Alexandre followed Luc to the remaining group. Joey was talking animatedly to Kathy and Luis. Luc leaned in to ask Ali a question, and then Alexandre was face-to-face with Mei.

"Hi," he said, because he couldn't think of anything better to say.

"Hey." Mei smiled up at him. Streetlights reflected in her pupils, making her eyes dance.

"I had a great time. Despite all that"—he gestured to intimate the messiness at the end—"it was a good party."

"I'm really glad you were here."

"Me too." He was driving back to the Hudson Valley tomorrow morning. Luckily, his only class of the day didn't start until eleven thirty. He wondered if his students would smell booze seeping through his pores and be able to tell he was hungover. *Hey, kids. Your old professor can still party, too.* The thought filled him with dorky pride.

Alexandre debated what to say next. *See you after the wedding? Next time I see you, you'll be married?* Nearby, Joey proclaimed that tonight's songs were just mid and couldn't compete with the ones on his hard drives.

Mei smiled sadly. "I should rescue Kathy and Luis." She looked up at him hesitantly.

Alexandre opened his arms. Mei stepped in.

"You deserve all the love and happiness in the world," he

whispered into her ear. "You know that, right? You're worthy of everything." After a beat, he felt Mei nod against his shoulder.

Alexandre yearned to pull her close and run his hands down her back. Instead, he released her. Mei blinked hard, her eyes searching his. Alexandre held her gaze. Then he shoved his hands in his pockets and made himself look away so she could return to Joey.

CHAPTER NINETEEN

The late morning sun seared through the bedroom window. Mei cracked an eye open, then scrunched it shut. Her head throbbed. The sticky-sweet scent of lychee Jell-O shots lingered on her skin, making her gag.

A blast of fetid air hit her nose. Joey snored directly in her face. Mei narrowed her eyes. She'd never unsee his raving or the looks of barely concealed disgust on their friends' faces when they'd learned what he'd meant by *I are hungry!*

Nausea rose in her throat. Was this her future? Waking up disappointed every day? Alexandre's words flooded her mind. *This is your life. Your decision.* In the harsh light of morning, Mei knew he was right.

Joey snored loudly, jolting himself awake. "Huh? Wha?" He rubbed his eyes, then winced. "Wow. I'm in rough shape. What a night."

"What a night is right." Did he even remember what happened? And did it even matter?

Concern clouded Joey's face. "You okay, babe?"

Could she break up with him now? Mei's stomach lurched. "Just a little queasy."

Joey smoothed her hair. "Want to go to the diner for pancakes and eggs?"

Mei leaned into his familiar touch. She and Joey both loved family-owned Queens diners and their laughably large portions. "I'm getting brunch with Ali."

Joey pulled her against him. "Fine! Hurry back so we can be together." His sour morning breath hit her nose. His arms squeezed her like a vise.

Mei wriggled out from his embrace. "I'm going to get ready."

She ran into the bathroom and locked the door.

• • •

Ali was already seated at the bustling brunch restaurant, sipping a glass of water. "Mei! How are you feeling?"

"Desperately in need of some food. Have you looked at the menu?"

"Want to split the huevos rancheros and the egg and cheese biscuit?"

"Perfect." They gave the waiter their order, then Mei turned to her sister. "I had a great time last night, despite Joey."

"It's fine! I nearly died from his raving. I haven't seen anyone dance like that in—"

"Ali, stop." Her sister blinked at her stern tone. "I'm not talking about Joey's ridiculous dancing. I'm talking about his sad 'joke' of pretending he can't speak English."

Ali grimaced. "Yeah, that was messed up. Have you ever heard him say that before?"

"Once. Obviously, I wasn't thrilled. I asked him to stop and he said he would. I guess he forgot after all the drinking."

"People make mistakes."

Ali was being kind. And generous. More kind and generous than Joey deserved. More than *she* deserved. Mei remembered the pitying looks on her friends' faces last night as they laughed politely at Joey's immature stories and gamely cheered on his dancing while clearly cringing on the inside.

"I don't know if I can do this."

Ali stared at her. "Do what? Get married?"

Mei's vision blurred. One tear slipped down her cheek, then another. "I don't know what to do. I love Joey. I really do. I'm just not sure I want to be with him forever."

"That says a lot," Ali said carefully.

"The problem is, all my doubts are so minor. They don't seem like reasons to give up on us completely."

"Like what?"

"Do you call off your wedding because your fiancé tells dumb jokes? Or has weird hobbies? Or doesn't really care about his career?"

"I thought Joey had a good job."

"He does. But his boss is trying to get him promoted and he's been so blasé about it. I could barely get him to study for his exams. At first, it was about the money—when you grew up the way we did, it seems crazy not to make as much as you can."

Ali nodded and thanked the waiter as he discreetly set down their food.

"Now I think it's more than that. Joey says his priority is

spending time with me—well, me and his music files, which is kind of nice. But it also feels like a burden. Like everything is riding on me."

"You want an equal partner."

"I do." Mei broke off a crumb from her breakfast biscuit.

Ali chewed thoughtfully. "The problems you mentioned aren't nothing. Life is full of decisions, and you and Joey will have to figure out everything together: where to live, how to spend your money, where to send your kids to school—or whether to even have kids. You want to be with someone you relate to. And can talk to."

Mei flushed. "I can talk to Joey." *Kind of.*

"How about I ask you some questions and you tell me the first thing that pops into your head? Do you light up when you see Joey?"

Mei gritted her teeth. "Sometimes."

"How do you feel about marrying him?"

"Um, kind of nervous."

"What do you think about spending the rest of your life with Joey?"

"I don't want to," Mei whispered. Her insides wrenched, releasing a flood of tears.

Ali rubbed her back. "Mei, life is tough. Your relationship should be your salvation. Not one more problem to solve."

"I feel so stupid. I just kept going with everything."

"You were trying to make it work. You and Joey haven't been together that long."

A thought occurred to Mei. "Did you ever have doubts about Joey?"

Ali was quiet for a moment. "I thought you got engaged quickly. But you were thrilled. You both always looked so happy."

Mei rubbed her forehead.

"Plus," Ali continued, "whenever you wanted anything, you went out and did it. Like moving to Manhattan and going all in at Livin. So when you and Joey appeared to be two Queens natives who'd found each other, I believed it."

"I did, too."

"I know it sucks, but it's better to call off your wedding, rather than go through with it, be miserable for years, and then get divorced."

Mei's mind flashed back to her and Ali hiding in a closet, trying to block out the sound of their parents screaming at each other. "And way better to do it before we have kids," she said wryly.

Ali stared at her water glass, a faraway look in her eyes. Mei knew she was also reliving their parents' fights.

Her sister shook her head, as if dislodging the memories. "To go back to your question, I wouldn't say I had doubts about Joey. Well, until last night. He just wasn't who I'd pictured you settling down with. I always saw you with someone more thoughtful. More sophisticated and intellectual."

Mei nodded, unable to speak. Now that Ali had said it, she could admit that was what she wanted, too.

"You deserve more."

Tears sprang to Mei's eyes. Alexandre had whispered the same thing last night. Did she still deserve happiness if she broke Joey's heart?

Her eyes blurred as the tears fell. She pictured the charismatic guy who helped her rediscover a part of herself. The bighearted man who smiled adoringly at her every time they spoke about building their life together.

Ali held her hand until her tears subsided.

Mei inhaled shakily. "Joey deserves more, too."

• • •

I'm doing the right thing, Mei told herself as she steadied her trembling hands and unlocked her front door.

Joey was in his easy chair laughing at something on his phone. He glanced up and rushed over to her. "Babe! I missed you."

The stench of day-old alcohol was gone. Mei breathed in his spicy scent.

"Look what came today!" Joey released her and wheeled a large suitcase from the wall. "Right on time."

Their honeymoon was going to be Joey's first trip outside the United States. *Can I crush his dreams even more?* Mei perched on the edge of the couch. Her vision grew bright around the edges. "Hey, can we talk?"

"You okay?" Joey sat down beside her. Understanding dawned on his face. "It's what I said last night, isn't it? I told you, I'm really sorry. I get why you're upset. I'm embarrassed, too."

Blood roared in Mei's ears. "No, it's not about last night. It is about us, though."

Joey laughed uncertainly. "You're scaring me."

"I know this is the worst timing. But I'm having second thoughts about the wedding." Mei winced. She couldn't even bring herself to say "our wedding."

"About the wedding? What part of it?"

"The whole thing," Mei whispered.

Joey stared at her. "Are you serious? Please tell me you're joking."

"I'm sorry, Joey."

"What does this mean? You don't want to get married?" Joey's voice grew louder. "Is that what you're saying?"

"I don't want to get married." Mei barely choked out the words. But once she did, the tightness in her chest loosened a tiny bit.

"Are you shitting me? Are you fucking shitting me?" Joey slammed his palm on the coffee table, making Mei skitter back. He backhanded a mug, sending it flying across the room. "What the fuck, Mei? What the fuck?"

Mei cowered behind her arms. She'd never seen that hard look in Joey's eyes. Her mind flashed back to her father's drunken rages. How well did she know the man in front of her? "I'm so sorry." Mei covered her face and cried.

Joey was crying, too. "I thought we were happy. I thought you loved me."

"I do love you."

"So why the fuck don't you want to get married?" Joey hollered.

"I'm not sure about us. Getting married won't change that."

"You never said anything about not being sure. Ever. Why didn't you tell me?"

"I wasn't sure how I felt." Mei knew she sounded ridiculous.

Joey's eyes darkened. "Now you're telling me? The day before our fucking wedding? Jesus, Mei. I'm your *fiancé*. You never thought of talking to me about this? That's what people do when they're in a fucking relationship. They *talk*."

Mei's face burned. Shame overwhelmed her ability to speak.

"What are you unsure about anyway? We have a great life. I'm working my ass off because you want me to. I aced that fucking test!"

"I love you, Joey. I really do." God, she should have thought of talking points. "I just don't see us together in the long run."

"Fuck!" Joey jumped up and paced around the room. "There's something you're not telling me. Is there someone else?"

Alexandre's face popped into Mei's mind. "No."

"Then what is it?" Joey flopped into his chair and stared at the floor. When he lifted his head, his eyes blazed with a clarity Mei had never seen before. "You're a liar, Mei. All this time, you've been lying by omission, never giving me a clue you didn't want to get married. Did you ever talk to Ali about this? Kathy?"

"Just Ali. Today."

"Today!" Joey threw his hands up. "Wow, Mei. You're an even bigger liar than I thought. You go through life pretending everything is perfect. You're always like, 'Ali and I are so close, we tell each other everything!'" Joey sang in a high-pitched, mocking voice. "Well, guess what? You don't tell Ali jack shit!"

Hurt washed over Mei. Yet, a tiny part of her was impressed. Joey knew her better than she gave him credit for. Then his eyes narrowed. *Oh no.*

"Luc's brother."

Mei flushed. "What about him?"

Joey slapped the arm of his chair, making her jump. "Did you fuck him?"

"No!"

"You never fucked him? Or kissed him? Not during that cozy hurricane weekend you spent together?"

"No! I swear, nothing happened!"

"But you wish something did."

Mei looked away before she could stop herself.

"Fucking hell." Joey chuckled to himself. "That's why you're doing this."

"Joey, no. That's not true." She still couldn't sort out her feelings for Alexandre, but they weren't at the root of her problems with Joey.

He, however, didn't see it that way. "Fuck! I can't believe you're leaving me for him!"

"I'm not! That's not it at all!"

"Yes, it is! You're ruining everything we have so you can fuck Le fucking Prof!"

Mei watched helplessly as he sobbed.

"How could you do this, Mei? How could you?"

"This has nothing to do with Alexandre." Tears streamed down Mei's face. She reached for Joey's shoulder, but he shook her off.

"I almost feel bad for Le Prof, that pretentious prick. You're going to take him down, too. You and your lies. And how's that going to play out with your dear little sister—your best friend in the whole world—and her perfect family?"

"Joey. Stop. No."

"Maybe my problem was that I loved you too much. I only saw the best in you. That's what happens when you love someone, right? I ignored how you wanted to change me to be more like you. Well, you know what? At least I know who I am. Your whole life is a fucking lie. All you do is hide from the truth. No one knows you, and no one ever will. Not even you, Mei."

Lava-hot shame burned through Mei's body. Was Joey right? Was that who she was? Mei lunged for him, but he walked to the door and shoved his feet into his sneakers. When he looked up, his face was so anguished, Mei's heart ripped in two.

"Well, godspeed to Le Prof." Joey roughly wiped his eyes. "You're going to destroy him. Ali, Luc, and Kaia, too. Just like you've fucking ruined me."

Through her tears, Mei watched, frozen, as her ex-fiancé walked out and slammed the door.

• • •

For the rest of the day, and all through the weekend, Mei holed up in Ali's hotel room. At every moment, someone—Ali, Luc, her mom, or Henry—was by her side, reminding her she'd made the right decision and that the pain would pass. Still, every second was excruciating. A thousand knives ripped her apart as she pictured Joey packing his stuff and moving to his parents' house on what was supposed to be their wedding day.

Meanwhile, her phone buzzed nonstop as friends, family, wedding vendors, and Livin colleagues called, texted, and emailed.

Kathy: Love you, Mei. I'm here anytime you want to talk. Just say the word and I'll fly back to see you.

Beauty by Veronica: Mei, darling, I was so sad to receive the update from your sister. I'll only charge 75% of my wedding makeup fee. You can Venmo me at @beautybyvero.

Evie: Sending you so much love! I don't want to speak out of turn, but I think this is for the best. You'll find the right person and he'll be way better. XOXO.

James: My condolences about your called-off wedding. Given the circumstances, will you still be taking off the next two weeks? PS: We can talk about your possible promotion when you're back.

Alexandre: Mei, I'm thinking of you. This will be a difficult time, but you chose yourself, and you'll be happier. I'm always here, anytime you want to talk.

Mei couldn't bring herself to respond to anyone but James. She sent him a quick email saying she'd update him in a few days.

• • •

Ali tried to talk Mei out of moving—she didn't need that stress on top of everything else. But Mei couldn't imagine staying in that apartment one day longer.

With her savings account hemorrhaging from paying off the entire non-wedding and honeymoon by herself, then breaking her lease, Mei could no longer afford to return to her beloved Upper West Side, or anywhere in Manhattan.

Thanks to an extraordinarily low inventory, all her options were in Queens, and not particularly appealing: a minuscule place in Sunnyside with a cardboard box suspiciously taped to the ceiling. A basement-level Jackson Heights apartment with windows that opened onto the building's dumpster. An Astoria studio with water-stained ceilings, slanted floors, and a parallelogram-shaped living space.

She went with the Astoria studio. Her desperation to move outweighed her distaste of renting an apartment reminiscent of the one she grew up in.

• • •

Mei returned to Livin on Thursday. Going to work beat crying all day in her depressing apartment.

Once her laptop came to life, Mei sighed with relief at her familiar routine. Then her meetings began. In each one, Mei smiled bravely and accepted her colleagues' sympathetic words. Afterward, she ran to the nearest bathroom to pull herself together.

The sheer volume of her goals hit her. The fiery rush that normally fueled her failed to ignite. Fatigue paralyzed her every time she looked at the endless strategy decks, campaign designs, media plans, videos, and event scripts she needed to tackle.

She was operating at a fraction of her normal speed, so she worked more than ever. Ninety-two hours one week. Ninety-four the next. She canceled weekend plans to see Ali and Luc, and her mom and Henry. Instead, they took turns driving to the city and bringing her food from her favorite restaurants: dim sum from Chinatown, bagels and lox from Russ and Daughters. Mei picked at the food while silently willing them to leave. Holding herself together took so much energy. And she had so much work to do.

Despite her efforts, for the first time since she'd started at Livin, Mei wasn't one of the top three marketing employees. The October rankings placed her twelfth. Upon seeing her new standing, Mei had the urge to go home, curl up in bed, and cry. But she didn't. She could edit a strategy deck in that time.

• • •

Every week or two, Alexandre reached out.

How are you feeling? I hope each day is a little better.

Hi Mei. I was remembering what we talked about during the hurricane. You've overcome so much and you'll get through this, too.

He also called three times.

Each time Mei saw Alexandre's name on her phone, she froze. She *could* talk to him. He, more than anyone else, knew what she was going through. Mei longed for Alexandre's calm words, his thoughtful eyes intent on her when she spoke.

Then Joey's face appeared in her mind. *You're ruining everything we have so you can fuck Le fucking Prof!*

Mei let Alexandre's calls go to voicemail. She waited a day or two before texting him back.

Thanks for thinking of me! I'm actually doing pretty well. Just super busy.

• • •

On the Tuesday before Thanksgiving, James called a marketing all-hands. The New York team crammed into Livin's boardroom and video-conferenced the regional teams.

At the front of the room, James was actually smiling as he spoke to a cheerful young woman. *A new exec?* Mei wondered, studying the woman's sleek blowout, cashmere sweater, and tailored trousers. *Nah, too young.* She looked to be in her early thirties, tops.

James called the room to attention. "I'm pleased to introduce Erika Fairchild, our new VP of brand marketing." The woman beside him grinned. "She officially starts in January, but we couldn't wait to share the news. Erika comes to us from Vigor, the at-home workout system you all use and love. I've been trying to woo her away since August, and she finally said yes!"

Mei stared at James. *Since August.* The month they'd first spoken about the job. So he'd never considered her for it. He'd just made her think so to keep her churning out work at an insane pace, despite everything she'd been going through.

Around her, people murmured excitedly. Mei got it. Vigor was a hot brand.

"I'd like to thank Mei Li for keeping the lights on," James said. "Now Mei and her team will report to Erika—and with Erika's leadership, we can finally show the world what real brand marketing is."

Mei smiled tightly as all eyes turned to her.

After the meeting, Mei researched her new boss. Erika Fairchild had been Vigor's director of marketing for a year. Previously, she'd been a brand manager at a once-hot athleisure startup whose cachet had plummeted following revelations of a body-shaming work culture. Before that, she'd been a marketing coordinator at the telecom company where James had worked. She was five years younger than Mei.

• • •

For Thanksgiving, Henry had offered to drive down and pick up Mei from the city. She'd declined. She could work better on the train. Surprise new boss or not, Livin's holiday campaign still launched the day after Thanksgiving, and Mei had to oversee the pop-up experiences in twenty cities, plus the mountain of ads, videos, email campaigns, and partnerships that would roll out through the end of the year.

She'd planned to take the train up after work on Wednesday. But from the moment she opened her laptop, one issue after another appeared. The marketing automation server was down and Mei couldn't review any email proofs. The DJ they'd hired for the Paris event had pulled out. The subtitles in the launch video had a typo. The signage for the Rio event used the wrong shade of yellow.

At six that evening, Mei dashed off a text to her family.

Swamped with Livin emergencies.
I'll come up tomorrow morning.

She tossed her phone in her bag, then worked through the night, only pausing for a quick nap at three a.m.

Mei awoke at five. Luckily, no other country was off for Thanksgiving. Her European colleagues were well into their day. Mei messaged her teammates there and got to work. James's remarks echoed in her head: *With Erika's leadership, we can finally show the world what real brand marketing is.*

Well, I'll show YOU, Mei thought. This *Livin Your Dream* campaign was their biggest one yet. They'd painted shipping containers Livin yellow, turned them into Livin-style common rooms, and dropped them in the middle of major shopping cities, like New York, London, and Hong Kong. Starting tomorrow, people could visit the faux Livins to listen to local DJs, sip free cocktails, eat hors d'oeuvres, and enter to win free stays at Livins around the world. They had special deals for Black Friday, Cyber Monday, and all the winter holidays, plus surprise gifts for Livin members throughout the season.

Real brand marketing, Mei thought with a sniff. She just needed to work through the last-minute issues.

Around nine, her phone started buzzing.

Ali: Hey! What train are you taking?

Vivian: We're planning to have dinner around 4, as usual.

Henry: I can still drive down and give you a ride.

Mei sighed. So many logistics. She opened the Metro-North schedule. There was a train every hour. Mei replied to her family.

I'll prob take the 11:50,
which gets in at 1:20!

That would give her a few hours to wrap everything up.

Her phone buzzed again.

Luc: See you soon! Also, Kaia wants to know if you're bringing your famous cornbread.

Shoot. She'd totally forgotten to make it. Over the years, Mei had honed her cornbread until it was the perfect blend of savory and sweet, with a crisp, golden outside and whole kernels throughout. Everyone adored it, especially Kaia. Mei eyed the ingredients on her counter. Maybe she could still bake if she finished working in the next hour.

Yes! Really need to focus now.
Will text when I'm on my way!

Mei set her phone to "do not disturb." She hopped on a video conference with the French team, then went straight into a call with the Rio team, followed by a lengthy Slack exchange with her Canadian colleagues.

Mei glanced at the clock. How was it already 11:08? Her campaign was in good shape, but she hadn't showered, packed, or made the cornbread. The 11:50 train was out of the question. Maybe she could make the 12:50. She updated her family, then ran into the kitchen.

Just as Mei ripped open the box of cornmeal, her phone buzzed. All the campaign email proofs were in her inbox. Stella, a marketing ops manager, also pinged her on Slack.

Hi Mei! Can you please review the email proofs now? I need to get back to my kids for Thanksgiving.

Mei set down the cornmeal and raced back to her laptop. Forty-five minutes later, she'd approved every email.

It would be tight, but the 12:50 train was still doable if she skipped the cornbread. Her heart twisted as she pictured Kaia's disappointed face.

Mei dashed into the shower. When she emerged at 12:05, her phone brimmed with notifications. The creative agency had updated the launch videos. They needed her to sign off on them ASAP. Kaden, Bryce, and Tamiko also wanted to touch base before logging off for the holiday.

Mei sucked in a breath. The 12:50 was out. The 1:50 would get her there right in time for dinner. She texted her family. Everyone wrote back immediately.

Ali: Is everything okay?!

Luc: Want a ride so you don't have to deal with the train? I can leave now to get you.

Vivian: Should we move dinner back an hour or two?

Mei slammed her phone down. How did they expect her to finish working if they kept asking questions? She picked up her phone and pounded out a reply.

I'm fine! PLEASE just let me wrap up. I'll be on the 1:50. I PROMISE!!!!

She silenced her family's texts. Enough was enough.

At 12:58, Mei snapped her laptop shut. She'd finished the urgent tasks. She'd deal with everything else on the train. Mei ran through her apartment, stuffing clothing into her backpack.

As she laced up her sneakers, her phone buzzed.

James: I'm preparing an update for Julian. I need an overview of the upcoming campaign.

Mei sighed. She'd already given James her strategy deck three times. She re-sent it.

Here you go! All the key points are in there.

James replied.

I need an executive summary. Can you get that to me ASAP?

Mei stifled a scream. It was 1:12. She'd never make the 1:50 train. Her phone buzzed.

James: Hello? Are you there?

Rage surged through Mei's veins. *Do it yourself, asshole!* But it was her responsibility to send him that summary.

Mei drew a shaky breath and replied.

I'll send it to you in a few.

Fifteen minutes later, she sent him the summary.

James wrote back.

> Thx. Your overview looks good, but strategy means nothing if the execution fails.

Mei rolled her eyes. Her campaign was good to go. She started replying to James when another message from him appeared.

> We can't afford any mistakes. Not one. Julian and Erika's eyes will be on this. I'm paying close attention, too. Given your recent performance, this campaign will be a deciding factor in your November, December, and end-of-year rankings.

Her rankings. This was her chance to claw her way back to the top. The end-of-year rankings determined everyone's annual bonus. God, she needed the money. Her savings account was terrifyingly low.

Mei ran through every campaign element in her head. Was every video perfect? Every ad? Every piece of signage in every language?

If they weren't already, they would be. She'd double-check everything. Triple-check.

That fire she'd been missing these last few weeks roared back to life. Mei replied to James.

> This campaign will be perfect.
> You have my word.

She settled onto the couch and triumphantly opened her laptop. Then she remembered.

Thanksgiving.

Celebrating was out of the question.

Mei video-called Ali.

Her sister's eyebrows shot up when she answered. "You're still at home?"

"Yeah." Mei plastered on a cheerful smile. "I have a major campaign launching tomorrow and so many things to do for it. I won't be able to make Thanksgiving."

"Seriously? Not even for a little? We can wait—"

"No. You all enjoy."

"You're not coming, Mei?" Vivian appeared at Ali's shoulder.

"Sorry, Mom. Too many work emergencies."

"I can still give you a ride," Luc called from behind Ali and Vivian.

"No! It's just one holiday. I'll see you all soon. Please have Thanksgiving without me."

Ali and Vivian protested. Luc and Henry kept offering to drive her.

Mei cut them off. "I'll come up tomorrow. I promise. If I'm not on a train by six tomorrow night, Luc and Henry, you can both come get me."

Her family reluctantly agreed. Mei hung up with relief.

She began checking every detail of her campaign. After forty minutes, her fiery adrenaline sputtered. Her European colleagues were no longer online. Occasionally, Mei received messages from coworkers in Canada and Latin America, but most of her American teammates had shut down for the holiday.

Meanwhile, she'd yet to find a single mistake. *Is this even necessary?* she wondered. Still, she kept checking. Her eyes blurred from the tedium. Her mind wandered. Her family was probably sitting down to dinner, their plates full of turkey, cranberry sauce, and mac and cheese. Thanksgiving was her favorite holiday. In addition to cornbread, she usually cooked a showstopping dish, like sourdough stuffing with a white wine sauce, or crispy Hasselback potatoes with garlic butter.

Mei's heart sank as she pictured the room. Evie and her aunt Rose and uncle Arthur were also at Thanksgiving. So was her ninety-year-old grandmother, who lived with her aunt and uncle. Grandma spoke little English and had dementia. Still, she lit up every time she saw Mei and Ali together. How many holidays did Grandma have left?

Mei forced herself to eat a handful of dry cereal. Then she turned back to the ad banners she was reviewing.

• • •

At nine the next morning, Mei clicked through all the campaign components that were now live. She hadn't found a single error. Her head throbbed from lack of sleep. Her jaw ached from clenching. But she'd done it. Her campaign was perfect.

The doorbell buzzed. Mei jumped. She padded warily to the door.

"It's me!" Ali called from the other side. "Open up!"

Mei yanked back the door. "Why are you here? Is everyone okay?"

"Everyone's fine." Ali stepped out of her boots. "You're the one we're worried about!"

"Me? Why?"

Ali searched for a place to hang her coat. Mei bit her lip as she saw her apartment through her sister's eyes. Half-unpacked moving boxes lined the walls. Cornbread ingredients, crusty coffee mugs, and empty takeout containers littered the kitchen counter. Piles of dirty clothing covered the dining table.

Ali gingerly placed her coat on the back of a chair. "How about we chat?"

Mei led her to the couch. "What do you want to talk about?"

"What do you think? Mei, you're not okay. Stop pretending. You completely bailed on Thanksgiving and you're not taking care of yourself. Are you just working all the time?"

Mei's eyes slid to her laptop. "No."

"Yeah, right. What the hell are you working on that's so important?"

"Just a massive global campaign that went live this morning."

"You launch a global campaign every holiday season! And you run campaigns all the time. What's so special about this one?" Fear glistened in her sister's eyes. Despite her harsh tone, Ali looked close to tears.

James played me, Mei realized. *Just like he did with the VP job.* She'd worked herself into a frenzy for no reason. Again.

Mei slumped down. "Nothing. It's all so stupid." She told Ali about James, her impossible workload, the false promise of a promotion, and her soon-to-be new boss.

"Quit." Ali's eyes blazed. "They don't deserve you."

"I can't. I need the money."

"Get a new job. You'll make as much or even more somewhere else."

"No. I need my bonus. And I want to be there when we go public."

"When's that?"

"Sometime next year."

"You need to leave now."

Mei glared at her sister. "Easy for you to say! You have a husband and a second income. If I quit, I'll have nothing!" How was it that just a few months ago, she'd been a top performer at Livin, with a beautiful apartment, a healthy savings account, and an adoring fiancé? "I already have nothing."

Ali rubbed her shoulder. "That's not true. You have us. And your friends."

Mei nodded begrudgingly.

"You'll get a better job, too."

"I don't want another job."

"Mei," Ali said gently. "Are you seeing a therapist?"

"No." She needed to. But finding a therapist took time and energy, and she had neither.

"How about we find you one? Then clean and unpack?"

Mei glanced at her laptop. Several new emails had come in. Then she remembered James's smug face when he introduced Erika as the VP of brand marketing. "All right."

Ali lit up. Her excitement was contagious. Mei couldn't help but smile. Her first genuine smile since the bachelor/bachelorette. She opened the browser on her laptop. Ali typed on her phone. A minute later, she yelped with excitement.

"Look what I found." Ali thrust her phone at her. "A mental health network for Asian Americans, founded by therapists our age."

Mei perused the site. All her therapists had been white men and women in their sixties. She'd never considered finding an Asian American therapist, let alone one who'd be her peer. "I'm going to email them."

Ali grinned. "Good. I'll tackle the boxes."

• • •

On Monday, replies from therapists collected in Mei's inbox. They either weren't accepting new patients or her insurance. *Good thing I don't have rejection issues,* Mei thought.

Late in the afternoon, Mei received a reply from Violet Chu, the last therapist she'd emailed, asking if she'd like to meet. Mei wrote back immediately. The next day, she took an introductory call from the O'ahu conference room.

Even through the laptop screen, Violet exuded compassion and knowledge. Her warm smile put Mei at ease. She nodded empathetically when Mei spoke. With her cozy white sweater and long hair with bangs, Violet looked like someone Mei would befriend. Mei now had a therapy session every Wednesday evening.

She sank back in her chair. She would heal. Day by day. Month by month. Year by year. For the first time since the breakup, Mei believed it.

Maybe she'd even peek at job listings.

Mei opened LinkedIn's job search. Then an email notification caught her eye. Livin's November rankings were up. Mei held her breath as she clicked to the leaderboard.

She was still twelfth.

Mei closed out of LinkedIn. She had one month to climb back to the top. She needed the maximum annual bonus. And she sure as hell wasn't going to look like anything less than a star when Erika started in January.

• • •

When Ali rang her doorbell on Saturday morning, Mei was expecting her.

"Ho ho ho!" Ali burst in wearing an oversized red sweater belted at the waist.

"Ali, what the . . . ?" A cackle escaped Mei's lips. "Nice Santa outfit."

Wow, laughter. It felt strange, but good.

"I'm wearing it for a reason! I have a surprise." Ali paused dramatically. "We're going to Hawai'i!"

Mei's jaw dropped. "What?"

"Yes! From December twenty-fifth to January first."

"No way. I already missed Thanksgiving. I can't be away for Christmas, too."

"We'll celebrate on Christmas Eve."

"I can't afford a trip!"

Ali pulled her into a hug. "This is your Christmas gift. From me, Luc, Mom, and Henry."

"I can't accept that! Plus, I have work."

"The week between Christmas and New Year's? Everyone checks out then."

"Not at Livin," Mei grumbled, though Ali had a point.

"You'll always have more work than you can finish. Anyway, it's too late! We got an incredible deal, and it's nonrefundable. Plus, vacations are good for your mental health."

Mei looked away. She couldn't argue with that.

"We'll also celebrate Alexandre's first semester!"

"Wait, what?" The blood drained from Mei's face.

"Yeah! He's coming, too."

Mei couldn't speak. Alexandre would be there. With her. In Hawai'i. She could kiss him in the ocean. Creep into his hotel room every night. Did she want that? Did he?

"Mei! Say something!" Ali jostled her shoulder.

"Wow. Um. Okay." She couldn't make sense of anything.

Ali beamed. "Start packing. We leave on Christmas Day."

CHAPTER TWENTY

Early on Christmas morning, Alexandre arrived at JFK. He found the gate for Hawaiian Airlines, rummaged in his backpack, and pulled out his laptop. In February, he was presenting the last of his zebrafish research at a conference. Better to work on his slides now, rather than in O'ahu.

Alexandre was so engrossed in editing his presentation that he jumped sometime later when Luc nudged his sneaker with his own. "Hey! Merry Christmas."

"Merry Christmas." Luc leaned down to embrace him. "How was yesterday with Mom and Dad?"

"Nice. We had the usual *dinde de Noël* and listened to Handel's *Messiah*." Alexandre had missed his mom's traditional French holiday dish of roasted turkey and chestnuts. Last Christmas, he'd eaten a sad turkey sandwich in his office while waiting for his data analysis to run on his clunky old laptop. "How was Christmas Eve with Ali's folks?"

"Also nice. Lots of appetizers, wine, and Mariah Carey."

"That sounds like Ali and Mei." Alexandre craned his neck, trying to spot them. He hadn't seen Mei since the bachelor/bachelorette. He'd called and texted several times and hadn't been surprised to receive her brief, overly upbeat responses that hinted at how not okay she was. Still, Alexandre hadn't felt right offering to drop by or joining Ali and Luc for a visit. "How's Mei doing?"

"A little better these last few weeks. She's still working all the time, but not like at Thanksgiving."

"I still can't believe that happened." Alexandre had gotten chills when Luc told him Mei had skipped out on the holiday. It sounded way too familiar.

"Right? Kind of reminds me of someone." Luc shot him a pointed look. "Speaking of, you're not going to be doing zebrafish stuff this whole trip, are you?"

"Please. My workaholic days are behind me. Wouldn't you agree?" Alexandre couldn't believe how well he'd taken to teaching. He actually enjoyed being in the classroom. Even more improbably, he'd maintained his work/life balance. He still didn't work on weekends. He was running and biking nearly every day. He'd even spent a few weekends hiking and camping.

"You have been good," Luc admitted. "Glad you've been dating, too."

Alexandre shrugged bashfully. He hadn't told Luc he'd only started dating because he'd felt foolish about his feelings for Mei. His plan had mostly worked. He'd had fun and his dates had taken his mind off Mei. For a bit.

"Alexandre! Merry Christmas!" Ali and Kaia appeared before him.

Then he spotted Mei. Her cheeks were thinner and paler. Her hair lacked its usual sheen. But even bearing the scars of the last couple of months, she was more beautiful than Alexandre remembered. Mei smiled shyly. Alexandre's heart sped up as he walked over to embrace her.

"How've you been?" Mei's familiar lemon-coconut scent teased his nose.

"Hanging in there. Taking it day by day."

"That's all you can do."

A voice crackled over the intercom. "Hawaiian Airlines passengers in zone two are now welcome to board."

"We're next!" Ali said.

Alexandre consulted his boarding pass. "I'm zone four."

"We couldn't get seats together. You two"—Ali nodded at him and Mei—"are a few rows back. Stop by if you want to help entertain Kaia for ten hours." She squeezed Kaia affectionately, and they walked to the gate.

Alexandre and Mei exchanged a smile. When their zone was called, Alexandre shouldered his pack and reached for Mei's suitcase.

"I got it," she protested.

"It's okay."

Inside the plane, tranquil ukulele music lilted through the cabin. Footage of green mountains and white sand beaches lit up the seat-back screens. Mei touched Alexandre's shoulder, sending warmth down his arm. "I can't believe we're going."

At their row, Alexandre offered Mei the window seat. She slid in while he stowed their luggage, then dropped down beside her. Their two-seater felt like an intimate nest. Mei's arm brushed against his. *We probably look like a couple going on vacation.* Alexandre nervously fiddled with his seat belt.

Mei pulled out her phone. "I'm going to deal with some work emails."

Alexandre hid a frown. He was hoping to catch up more.

As the plane taxied down the runway and rose into the air, Mei stared out the window.

"How's the view?" Alexandre asked.

"It's fine. We're still over Queens." She was back to reading on her phone before Alexandre could say anything.

Queens. She was probably thinking about Joey. Or unhappy holidays as a kid. Alexandre took out his laptop. If Mei wasn't interested in talking, he might as well work, too.

An hour in, as flight attendants began the meal service, Mei yawned and stretched.

"What are you working on?" Alexandre asked.

"A deck recapping the holiday pop-ups we held in twenty cities." She turned her laptop so he could see photos of bright yellow shipping containers outfitted as stylish lounges. They were packed with people dancing and laughing.

"That's amazing." Alexandre would never be a Livin fan, but he was impressed. The pop-ups looked like they belonged in a movie, or an architectural photo exhibit. "I can see how much time and energy went into that."

"Thanks." Mei smiled ruefully. "I know how you feel about Livin. I haven't forgotten what we spoke about, either. I just haven't been able to think about other jobs."

"You don't need to explain. You've had too much going on. I can also see how cool projects like that make it hard to leave."

"How'd your semester go?"

"Surprisingly well." Alexandre let himself savor the relief he felt every time he thought about his first semester. "It's a new challenge, taking everything I know and trying to make it interesting and useful for undergrads. My students are all bio majors, so they're into the material." He let out a short laugh. "And now that I've had some time away from it, I'm seeing that I don't miss some parts of research."

"Like what?"

"Like my job hanging on every study. I'm not trying to put a positive spin on inconclusive results or applying for grants I know I won't get. I'm also not tied to a lab with live animals. You'd think I wouldn't be feeding zebrafish twenty years into my career, but you'd be surprised. On weekends and holidays, someone had to make sure the experiments were still running and that the fish were alive."

Mei laughed. A warm glow spread through Alexandre. This was the first time he'd seen her light up since her bachelor/bachelorette.

She inclined her head toward his laptop. "So what are you working on? Lesson plans?"

Alexandre stifled a groan. "No. Believe it or not, I actually kept my work/life balance all semester. I'm not doing anything New Paltz–related on this trip." He angled his screen toward Mei. "I'm writing a research paper to present at a conference. One of my Oregon colleagues was supposed to do it, but he's stuck in Spain with visa issues. I'm filling in for him."

"Wait, it's a research paper? For Oregon? I thought you were done with that."

"I am. Sorry, I'm not explaining this well. My former colleague salvaged the last of my genetics data and got it accepted at a zebrafish conference. The findings aren't groundbreaking or all that interesting, but every publication helps the lab."

"What do you have to do for the presentation?"

"Write a paper, create slides, make a poster about the study, and present it in Cleveland the first week of February."

"A poster?" Mei chuckled. "I'm picturing elementary school science fairs with solar system dioramas."

Alexandre laughed. "I'll have my baking soda volcano ready." He clicked on his poster. "I always forget how weird it sounds to people outside of academia. But every conference has a poster hall where scientists can learn about the latest research."

"Well, if you want any branding help to make your presentation pop, I got you," Mei said before turning back to her laptop.

• • •

Alexandre worked for the next nine hours. Mei did, too. By the time the plane approached O'ahu, Alexandre was cranky, yet deliriously excited. He'd nearly finished his article, presentation, and poster.

"Ready for vacation?" he asked Mei.

"Almost." Her eyes were bloodshot with fatigue.

The captain's voice sounded over the loudspeaker. "Well, folks, there's a thunderstorm over Honolulu, which will make for a bumpy ride in. Please fasten your seat belts and remain seated. *Mahalo*."

"Thunderstorm!" Mei exclaimed.

"Hopefully it's just passing."

The plane made a rocky descent. In the terminal, they reunited with Ali, Luc, and Kaia, then took a cab to their beachfront Waikīkī resort. Rain splattered the minivan's windows. Alexandre peered out. He couldn't see anything beyond the streetlights and highway.

"We all have ocean views," Luc said once they'd gathered in his room for a quick Christmas dinner of sandwiches, chips, and cookies from the lobby convenience store. "We should be able to see the water tomorrow."

• • •

The next morning, rain poured from the sky. Alexandre checked the forecast. The storm was likely to last all day.

Alexandre had read up on O'ahu and compiled a detailed list of beaches, hiking trails, snorkeling spots, kayaking outfitters, and surfing schools to check out. None of those activities were doable in a downpour.

We'll think of something, Alexandre told himself as he rode the elevator down to the hotel's breakfast buffet. Luc and Ali would find some way to entertain Kaia. Maybe he and Mei could rent a car and drive to an art museum, then get lunch.

At the restaurant, he found everyone at a table. Alexandre ran his hand through his hair and took the seat beside Mei. She barely looked up from her phone. Alexandre frowned. He spotted Livin's logo and some kind of flowchart on her screen.

The waiter arrived with glasses of water. "Storms like this happen maybe once every four to five years. Usually showers come and go quickly."

"Just our luck," Mei said. "I guess I'll catch up on work today."

"We'll probably watch movies," Luc said. "You're all welcome to join us for a Disney sing-along."

Back in his room, Alexandre stood on his balcony, searching for any break in the clouds. All he saw was a black sky and sideways rain.

This was not how he expected to spend his vacation: alone in his hotel room.

Alexandre eyed his running shoes. The resort had a sizable fitness center; he could work out for a bit.

Then he saw his laptop. Even though his presentation no longer had much impact on his career, he still wanted to show up strong. This paper would likely be the last to bear his name. Everyone he'd worked with would be at the conference. *I'll just give everything a final polish.* Alexandre made himself comfortable at the small round table in the corner of his room.

Hours later, his phone buzzed. Everyone was going downstairs for dinner. How was the whole day gone?

Alexandre met Luc, Ali, Kaia, and Mei at the hotel's beachfront restaurant. The floor-to-ceiling glass doors remained sealed against the storm.

Beside him, Mei appeared bleary-eyed in an oversized cotton sweater, her hair pulled back in a loose bun.

"Were you working?" Alexandre asked.

"All day. You too?"

He grimaced. "Yeah."

Out of the corner of his eye, he saw his brother and Ali exchange a look.

• • •

On Monday morning, the sky was as dark as night. Rain lashed the balcony doors. After breakfast, Alexandre eyed his laptop, then got down to work.

At three, the rain slowed to a trickle. Alexandre stepped onto the balcony. Angry storm clouds floated north, leaving behind a blue sky. The ocean sparkled. Waikīkī's high-rises glistened in the sunlight. Lēʻahi's green volcanic crater rose proudly in the distance.

"Wow," Alexandre breathed.

He texted the group chat.

Who's up for the beach? Meet in the lobby!

He slipped on his flip-flops and raced downstairs. Ali, Luc, and Kaia exited another elevator a moment later. Alexandre's phone buzzed with a reply from Mei.

Ahhhh, I just need to wrap something up. Will join soon!

Alexandre met Ali's eyes as she frowned and pocketed her own phone. "Should one of us get her?"

Ali bit her lip. "Let's give her a few minutes. Maybe she'll surprise us."

The four of them strolled out of the hotel. The soft golden sand of Waikīkī Beach stretched out before them. Blue water lapped the shore. Palm trees rustled overhead. Alexandre grinned at Luc. He'd never been anywhere so tropical.

They waded ankle-deep in the cool surf. All of Waikīkī had the same idea. People streamed onto the beach, laying down towels and bounding into the ocean.

In the distance, a set of gray clouds approached from the south.

Alexandre groaned. "Great."

"Let's enjoy this while it lasts," Luc said.

And they did. Alexandre relished the sunshine on his shoulders, the warm breeze on his neck. He held Kaia's hands and lifted her high above the gentle waves. They splashed in the surf until the first raindrops sent them scurrying back to the hotel.

Mei never made it out.

• • •

That evening, Alexandre and Luc waited for their dinner order in the foyer of a takeout seafood joint. The scent of fried shrimp made Alexandre's stomach rumble.

"So Ali and I have a mission for you," Luc said.

Alexandre raised an eyebrow. "Oh yeah? What's that?"

"Get Mei away from the resort. She's beyond burnt out. She needs to be unplugged and fully occupied with other things so she can recover. Which is where you come in."

Alexandre could think of a few ways to fully occupy Mei, none of which he cared to share with his brother. He'd certainly entertained a few fantasies involving nudity and secluded waterfalls. But he'd never make a move if Mei wasn't in the right headspace.

"Go hiking," Luc was saying. "Drive around the island. The North Shore beaches are supposed to be sick."

“I can do that. What about you, Ali, and Kaia?”

Luc smiled, bemused. “You think we’d get a lot of hiking done with a three-year-old? Anyway, you need to get out, too. You’ve been consumed by zebrafish stuff since we got here.”

“It was raining! What was I supposed to do?”

“Go to a museum. Visit a brewery. Read about Hawaiian history. Work out—”

“Okay, got it.”

“I’m serious. You’ve even stopped shaving. I’m having flashbacks to the intervention.”

Alexandre ran his hand over his scruffy chin. Yeah, he’d been working. But only because of the rain. He turned back to Luc, about to retort, then softened at the concern in his brother’s eyes. “You don’t have to worry about me.”

“Good.” They sat for a minute, then a smile played at Luc’s lips. “So what are you thinking for tomorrow’s adventure with Mei?”

CHAPTER TWENTY-ONE

Only Ali and Kaia were in Ali's room when Mei arrived with a case of seltzer. She popped the tabs on two cans and handed one to her sister. "Where are the guys?"

"Still getting food." Ali set down her seltzer. "So Luc and I were chatting, and we thought you and Alexandre should go explore the island. We'll stick around here with Kaia."

"But I want to spend time with you!" Wasn't that the point of the trip? Plus, she couldn't be alone with Alexandre. The months away hadn't dulled her attraction. If anything, Alexandre looked better than she remembered. Even though it was winter, he was sun-burnished and toned, as if he'd spent a lot of time outside. He moved with more confidence and ease. Every time their eyes met, her cheeks flushed and heat flooded her body, before Joey's angry words chilled her blood. *You're ruining everything we have so you can fuck Le fucking Prof!* It was a relief to deal with Livin instead of facing Alexandre.

"We can all get breakfast and dinner and do some day trips," Ali said. "But don't stay with us at the kiddie pool all day."

Mei nodded. Her sister had a point.

"Luc's also convinced that if Alexandre never leaves the hotel, he's just going to work. Like he has been. Like *you've* been." She shot Mei an accusing look.

"Then you shouldn't have brought me! What am I supposed to do? Not work?"

"Yes. And if you won't do it for your own sake, at least do it for Alexandre. He's been so good with work/life balance. Or, he *was*, until he found out about that zebrafish conference."

"Oh yikes." Now that Ali mentioned it, Alexandre had been working this whole time, too. Was that her influence?

"He never worked on weekends. He's even been dating."

"He has?" So Alexandre was dating, just as she'd assumed months ago.

"Yeah, but he hasn't met anyone serious."

Everything would be easier if Alexandre had a girlfriend. Still, a zing of relief ran through Mei.

"You'll be doing us a huge favor if you tear him away from that zebrafish stuff."

"I can do that." Mei's mind raced. She hadn't researched anything about O'ahu. What the heck should she do with Alexandre? *Something that doesn't involve stripping off his clothing and pushing him into bed.* She drained her seltzer to cool her face.

The door swung open. Luc and Alexandre walked in, each carrying a brown paper sack. The mouth-watering scent of fried seafood filled the room.

• • •

After dinner, Mei slipped out to the balcony. She breathed in the humid air and took in Waikīkī's glittering lights. Someone rustled behind her, then Alexandre was by her side. Even with his scruffy cheeks and rumpled shirt, Mei's heart quickened.

"Looks like the rain stops tonight," he said. "Are you up for hiking tomorrow?"

"Sure!" Then Mei paused, imagining the types of hikes Alexandre typically did. "As long as it's nothing too crazy. I don't feel like falling off a cliff."

Alexandre laughed. "We won't. I was thinking of Ka'ena Point, which is the westernmost tip of O'ahu. There's a coastal trail along the north side of the island that should be pretty flat. We might even see whales and seals."

"Perfect." *Ali and Luc are right. We both need this hike.*

It almost felt like a date.

• • •

After breakfast the next morning, they drove north in a rental Prius. With the windows down, a balmy breeze filled the car. Behind the wheel, Alexandre was once again clean-shaven and wearing olive-green hiking shorts and a gray moisture-wicking T-shirt. Mei regarded him with a little smile.

He turned to her. "I'm so glad we're doing this."

For a second, Mei thought he might take her hand. But the moment evaporated as one raindrop splattered onto the windshield, then another. "Oh no!"

Alexandre flicked on the windshield wipers and glanced at his phone. "We're twenty minutes away. It's not supposed to rain on the trail."

Mei eyed the gray clouds covering the sky. "Let's keep going."

They drove on. Fog shrouded the landscape, but Mei could tell they were somewhere rural. Tall grass and leafy trees lined the road.

Alexandre pulled into a small parking lot. Outside, only a few raindrops fell. Dark clouds drifted east, revealing a calm sky. As the fog lifted and the view rendered in Technicolor, Mei gasped. Green volcanic mountains loomed before her. Blue waves crashed over the rocky coast.

According to Ka'ena Point State Park's welcome sign, they'd be hiking along a railroad route that ceased operation in 1947. The trail was a little over five miles, out and back.

Alexandre let her lead. Low-lying plants with purple and white flowers flanked the dirt trail. Wild grass covered the coastal plain. To her right, the cerulean sea stretched on to the horizon.

The trek was slow going. Three days of torrential rain had saturated the ground. Deep puddles and mud slicks overtook parts of the trail.

"Sorry it's so messy." Alexandre grimaced apologetically at Mei's dirt-caked sneakers.

"It's fine." She'd given up on keeping her sneakers, or herself, clean. Mud streaked the back of her legs.

The sun blazed in full force. Sweat ran down Mei's back. Her legs hummed with exertion. Figuring out how to cross the muddy stretches fired up her brain. Off the coast, monstrous waves slowly gathered, then crested in walls of white foam. *So this is what life feels like.* Mei snuck a glance at Alexandre. A sheen of perspiration covered his neck and forearms. His lean shoulder muscles undulated beneath his thin shirt. The view was just as appealing as the wild coastline.

When Luc had taken Alexandre skiing to awaken him to his depression, did he feel the way she did now? Was she in the same place he was then?

They stopped to admire the ocean.

"How are you feeling?" Alexandre passed her a granola bar.

"A little tired," Mei admitted. "I was working since five this morning and still have more to do."

Disappointment flashed across Alexandre's face. "Do you want to start heading back?"

Mei sipped her water. Should they call it a day? There was no sign of the nature reserve that marked the end of the trail, and they'd already seen a lot. Alexandre wouldn't be thrilled, but Mei knew he'd stop for her.

She studied the way forward. The sun illuminated the lush green mountains. Off the coast, another massive blue wave broke with a glorious splash. *I want to continue,* Mei realized. *Not just for Alexandre. For me.* She lifted her chin. "Let's keep going."

A slow smile spread across Alexandre's face. "Lead the way."

They continued down the trail. A few minutes later, they reached a larger, muddier section than they'd encountered before. Water streamed over the swampy ground. There was no other route than through.

Mei was too short to leap across. "You go first."

Alexandre scrutinized the ground, then picked out a rock barely visible in the mud. With a quick bound, he used it as a stepping stone to get to the other side. He turned around and held out his hand. "I got you."

With his help, Mei could jump onto the first rock without falling. She gripped Alexandre's hand. His steady touch filled her with wonderful heat. She flashed him a smile as he helped her to the other side.

CHAPTER TWENTY-TWO

After helping Mei across the mud, Alexandre held her hand a beat longer than necessary before gesturing for her to take the lead.

As Mei forged ahead on the slippery trail, Alexandre marveled at how she'd come back to life. The fire had returned to her eyes. Each of her steps was more confident than the last. At times, Alexandre caught her smiling to herself when she spotted a patch of wildflowers, or hopped from one rock to another to cross a muddy patch. He couldn't help but notice how good she looked in a tank top and athletic shorts, with her ponytail windswept and her cheeks flushed from the sun.

Ahead of him, Mei motioned for him to join her beside a puddle. "Look!"

Alexandre peered down. "Tadpoles!" The chubby little creatures flitted under the surface of the water. For a minute, he was back in his lab, surrounded by tanks of zebrafish. Alexandre gulped down some water to banish the thought.

They reached the nature reserve and entered through a metal gate. A short distance in, they paused to read an informational sign about seabirds.

"This is a nesting ground for albatrosses," Alexandre said.

"How appropriate."

Alexandre knew Mei was thinking about her called-off wedding. For him, would his failed tenure always hang around his neck? Last semester, he'd been so busy that the shame began receding. But with the upcoming conference, it once again lurked under his skin.

"I see one!" Mei pointed to the grassy hill in front of them, just as a large gray-and-white bird opened its wings and stepped into the breeze. It swooped close enough for them to spot the triangular markings on the underside of its wings.

"Okay, you're pretty impressive. Sorry for associating you with misery," Mei said to the albatross. "Maybe it's a sign that the things we carry don't have to weigh us down." She glanced at Alexandre and laughed self-consciously.

"I like that."

They followed the last stretch of trail over the sand, until it ended at their destination: Ka'ena Point. Ahead of them, the rocky shore dropped off into the vast blue ocean.

"We did it!" Mei jumped into the air. Alexandre pulled her into a sweaty embrace. She was momentarily still. Then she relaxed against him, her arms encircling his waist, her head against his chest. From this vantage point, they could see the cloud-shrouded mountains looming between the north and west coasts.

"After you told me about this hike, I read a little about it," Mei said. "This is a sacred spot for Native Hawaiians. They believed the recently deceased leap from this point to join their ancestors."

Alexandre imagined a parade of ghosts, young and old, walking the same trail, then bidding this world goodbye to reunite with their loved ones. He pressed his lips together. It was too easy to take life for granted. He was so lucky to be healthy and alive in this beautiful place with a woman he cared about.

They sat on a sandy ledge overlooking the waves. Alexandre handed Mei a hummus wrap. They ate in contemplative silence.

"Today was amazing," Mei said. "I was in the moment the whole time. I can't remember the last time I felt like that. These last few months have been something."

"How are you doing with all that?" Alexandre ventured.

Mei covered her eyes and laughed. "Terrible. I used all my savings to pay off the wedding. I moved into a crappy apartment. Work is a nightmare." She told him about her manager's mind games, and how he'd hired Erika, a younger, less-qualified woman, for the job he'd dangled in front of her for months.

"I didn't know it had gotten so bad," Alexandre said incredulously. "Are you planning to leave?"

"I don't want to! You saw the amazing work I do when I'm not cranking out content like a maniac. I still love my team and want to be there for the IPO."

"I get that. But the job is toxic."

"It's not the job! It's James. And Erika, even though I don't know her. Everything used to be perfect. It's not fair that I should have to leave. I was there first."

"It doesn't sound like either of them will be leaving anytime soon." *So this is what I must have sounded like when Luc begged me to leave research.* "Aren't there lots of marketing jobs in New York? You'd get hired in a second."

Mei's eyes flashed, surprising him. "Stop. Just stop. How long did it take you to leave Oregon? One year? Two?"

"Two years. Though leaving tenure track, which I'd worked for my *entire life*, is a little harder than just finding another marketing job," Alexandre snapped, then instantly felt bad. Why was he so angry?

"Stop making it sound like it's so easy! You know it's not. You haven't even fully left your old job. You've spent this whole trip working on zebrafish stuff."

Alexandre held Mei's challenging gaze. In the distance, a large seabird alighted back on the ground. He blew out a breath. "You're right. I'm being unfair, acting like it's so easy to walk away."

Mei watched a wave fizzle over the black rocks. "What helped you?"

"I don't know if I have much advice. Clearly, I haven't figured anything out."

"You're in a better place than I am."

Alexandre tried to recall those blurry weeks after Luc's intervention. "I started seeing a therapist."

"I just found a new one."

"Good. Therapy helped me see how work was an addiction. When I was sad, I worked. When I was lonely, I worked. It's probably the ultimate sign of my addiction, but I used work to avoid the fact that my tenure wasn't happening." He felt Mei's hand on his shoulder.

"That all sounds very familiar." Mei paused. "How do you break the cycle?"

"By focusing on my life outside of work. In Oregon, I forced myself to go running by blocking time on my calendar. Or I'd drive to a trail and make myself hike. Each week, my therapist made me report all the nonwork things I'd done. At first, I resented it. Over time, I realized those activities made me feel better. More like myself."

Mei smiled. "Kind of like today."

Alexandre nudged his knee against hers. "Just like today."

They stared at the horizon. The sea was a rich azure that hinted at its depths.

"I have an idea," Mei said. "We spend the rest of our trip having days like today. Hiking. Exploring. Doing whatever outdoorsy stuff people do in Hawai'i."

"And not working." Alexandre saw Mei hesitate, then nod. He squeezed her hand. "We'll keep each other strong. We'll live our Hawai'i dreams."

"You mean we'll be *Livin* our Hawai'i dreams," she said with an exaggerated eye roll.

Alexandre laughed. The fact that Mei could poke fun at her job was a good sign.

"Oh my god, look!" Mei jumped to her feet and pointed at the ocean. "I just saw something."

Alexandre stood to get a better view. The waves were choppy. Then he saw it. A humpback whale's giant fin broke the surface, then disappeared in a splash of white water.

Wow. Who needed zebrafish when he could see whales?

Screw zebrafish. Alexandre chuckled to himself. "Screw zebrafish," he said out loud.

Mei turned to him with surprise. Then she faced the water and shouted, "Screw Livin, too!"

Alexandre draped an arm around her. Together, they watched the majestic creature breach the surface of the water, sharing in the moment, before disappearing beneath the waves.

CHAPTER TWENTY-THREE

Mei awoke the next morning feeling well rested for the first time in months. She side-eyed her laptop, then snuggled tighter in her blankets. *Screw Livin.* She relished the highlight reel of yesterday's hike playing through her mind. On the trail back, she and Alexandre had helped each other across muddy patches more than they needed to. Mei could still feel the steadiness of his hands, the delicious energy flowing between them.

At the breakfast buffet, Mei surveyed the array of American and Japanese options. She filled a bowl with rice, tamagoyaki, and a piece of salted salmon, then plated a waffle and fruit. She found Alexandre at a table on the patio.

He greeted her with a hug. "Did you sleep well?"

"I did. You'll be proud of me, too. I didn't work last night or this morning."

"That's huge! I didn't, either, and I'm not going to for the rest of the trip. You've got my full attention."

Mei's cheeks warmed. She pulled a stern face. "Good, because you need to captain our ship."

Alexandre laughed. "If you say so."

They were going kayaking. Mei had never kayaked before. She wasn't a strong swimmer, either. Still, she knew she'd be safe with Alexandre, even though he'd only kayaked a few times. Mei ate a bite of her waffle.

"That looks good," Alexandre said. "I'm going to get one."

Mei watched him walk to the buffet. Yes, if she was ever going ocean kayaking, it would be with him. She imagined kayaking with Joey—him belly flopping onto the boat, sending them both flying into the water. Joey's adoring eyes and lopsided smile floated into her mind. For the first time since their last, awful conversation, instead of guilt, shame, or anger, Mei felt a hint of fondness. The beginning of closure.

Mei peeked over her shoulder. Alexandre was walking back, carrying a waffle topped with bananas and macadamia nuts. The sight of him quelled her runaway emotions.

• • •

They set off in their rental Prius. The winding Pali Highway took them through the green Ko'olau Mountains, until they reached the windward side of the island.

At the water sports outfitter, Mei and Alexandre picked up their kayak, a long, flat red plastic boat on wheels. Alexandre removed his sweatshirt and placed it in their dry bag. Mei was disappointed that he had on a long-sleeve UV shirt, though she liked how the thin material accentuated his shoulders. She felt Alexandre's appreciative gaze as she pulled off her own sweatshirt, revealing her yellow bikini top.

They wheeled the kayak to the launch point on Kailua Beach, stopping to admire the view. Soft white sand sloped into the bay. The clear, flat water shimmered in the morning sun.

Alexandre gave Mei a quick paddling tutorial, then held the boat steady in waist-deep water. Mei hopped onto the front seat. Alexandre jumped in behind her and passed her a paddle. "You set the pace. I'll match your strokes and steer."

The paddle felt heavy and awkward in Mei's hands. Her strokes were choppy, but she soon got the hang of it. From the ease with which they cut through the water, Mei could tell they were paddling in unison. She looked back and did a double take.

"We've gone pretty far!" Kailua Beach was already receding into the distance.

They paddled past green hills, palm trees, and low waterfront homes. The shoreline transformed into another expanse of white sand.

"So that's Ka'ōhao Beach," Mei said. Ali, Luc, and Kaia were meeting them there that afternoon.

"We can either land on the beach and hang out there, or paddle toward those islands." In the distance, two small, rocky islands, Nā Mokulua, rose from the sea.

"Let's keep going."

When they neared the islands, Alexandre gasped. "There's a turtle! Right in front of us. I just saw its head."

Mei set down her paddle. They watched in silence. Gentle waves rocked the kayak back and forth. Just as Mei was about to suggest they continue, a turtle's speckled head popped above the water, its glossy shell visible below the surface.

"It's beautiful," Mei breathed. "And so graceful. Kaia said that *honu* is the name for Hawaiian green sea turtles."

They bobbed along, exclaiming in whispers every time the turtle resurfaced. Once it swam out of sight, they turned the kayak around and paddled to the beach. Mei sat down in the shade of a palm tree. A moment later, Alexandre joined her, bearing trail mix and water.

As she munched on the dried fruit and nuts, Mei realized she was on the most spectacular beach she'd ever seen. Her toes dug into the powdery white sand. The breeze rustled the palm fronds overhead.

She pointed to the two islets in the distance. "I can't believe how far we went."

"And we saw a *honu*!"

What a gift. In front of her, the sky met the ocean in a dazzling blue tableau. Mei's heart ached at the beauty, even as anger flared at herself. "This trip is making me realize what a big, beautiful world this is. And how I've let my life become so small. All I do is wake up, work, and go to bed. Every single day."

Alexandre was quiet for a moment. "You weren't always like that, right? What was your life like before Livin?"

Now Mei was silent. "It's sad, but I need to think about it." How did she fill her days before Livin? One thought came to her. "I used to cook. Not just dinner every night, which I never do now, but elaborate recipes like dumplings. Or croissants. Or pies with fancy crusts. Whenever there were holidays—" Mei's mind flashed to Thanksgiving. She took a breath, forcing herself to continue, "I was the one volunteering to bring something special.

Like for your welcome home party, I probably would've made an icebox cake with ginger thins, homemade whipped cream, and berries. And a chocolate mousse. And lemon bars."

Alexandre eyed their dry bag. "You're making me wish I'd packed some pastries." He turned back to her. "I actually have a major sweet tooth. I'm a pretty good cook, but I never learned many desserts. Maybe when we're back in New York, we could do dinner. I'll bring the savory and you bring the sweet. I make a mean roasted chicken."

Was Alexandre just being polite with his vague invitation? Or was he proposing a pseudo date with an easy out in case she wasn't ready or interested? Either way, Mei's cheeks tinged pink at the idea of a future dinner with Alexandre. "That sounds like a plan."

A content smile appeared on his face, sending a little thrill through Mei.

"I'm learning so much about you," Alexandre said. "What else did you do?"

Mei picked up a stray palm frond. "I used to run. I'd do half-marathons and 10Ks to stay motivated."

Alexandre looked intrigued. "You never mentioned that."

"It's been a while." She'd run her last half-marathon in Brooklyn two months before starting at Livin. These days, she never made it to the gym.

"Want to run a race together this spring?"

Mei sipped her water. "I'd need time to train. I'm out of shape."

That mischievous smile pulled at Alexandre's lips. He arched an eyebrow. "I don't know. You look pretty good to me."

Attraction flowed from his gaze. His hazel eyes gleamed as

they roamed her bare skin. The bright morning sun highlighted the strands of gray near his temples. Mei had a sudden urge to brush the sweat off his fine nose, to lean in and taste the salt on his lips. She bumped her arm against his. "You're not so bad yourself."

Alexandre laughed, then shifted so their shoulders touched. The heat from his body pulsed through her. She could say more. So much more. But not yet.

Instead, she rested her head against Alexandre's arm. He leaned into her. Together, they sat in comfortable silence, relishing each other's warmth.

• • •

Back in her hotel room, Mei settled onto a plush easy chair with her phone. For the past few months, she'd pushed off Kathy's invitations to chat. Now that she was on vacation, they'd set a time to talk.

A video call chimed. Mei clicked the answer button. "Kathy!"

"Mei!" Her best friend looked just as excited to see her. "How are you doing?"

"It's been a rough few months, but I'm feeling a little better every day. I'm actually in Hawai'i. That's helping."

"Amazing! How is it?"

"Just incredible." Mei told Kathy about the stunning beaches and landscapes she'd seen while kayaking and hiking.

"You're with Ali and Luc? And Kaia? She did all that?"

"They're in Hawai'i, but I went hiking and kayaking with Alexandre, Luc's brother. He's here, too." Thank goodness her tan hid the flush rising to her cheeks.

"Oh right! I remember him from the bachelorette. He was really sweet."

"He is."

"I'm so glad you're having a good time. You're looking more like yourself."

"How so?"

"I don't know. Just happier. Less stressed."

Mei's smile faltered. Kathy's words made her wonder. "Did I not seem like that with Joey?"

Kathy frowned. "You did the first time I met him, but not at the bachelor/bachelorette. You seemed kind of on edge around him."

Mei hung her head. "What a disaster."

"It's okay! At the end of the day, Joey wasn't right for you. He wasn't a bad guy. He just had some growing up to do. I didn't see that before the bachelor/bachelorette, but I'm glad I did. I'm glad *you* did, too. It might not feel like it, but you saved both of you a lot of misery by breaking up with him when you did."

Mei let her best friend's words sink in. She nodded.

"Have you thought about dating again?"

Her morning with Alexandre flashed through her mind. "No. Not yet."

"Maybe you should." The corners of Kathy's mouth curved up. "I mean, you're in Hawai'i with Alexandre. He's cute and smart and seems like your type."

Mei tried to contain her smile. Of course her best friend picked up on that. "It feels kind of soon."

"Do you still have feelings for Joey?"

Mei fiddled with a loose thread on her shorts. "No. Thinking about him makes me sad, but I definitely don't want to be with him."

"That's okay. It's fine to move on."

"I don't know. I'm not sure how I feel about Alexandre. What if it all goes wrong again? Instead of just ruining our lives, I'll also put Ali, Luc, and Kaia in the middle. I need to be a thousand percent sure."

Kathy was quiet. "Remember when we chatted and you asked me how I was sure about Luis? And I said, 'When it's right, you just know it.' At the time, you said you felt that way about Joey. I don't think you were being completely honest, though."

Mei looked away.

"Not to make you feel bad!" Kathy hurried to add. "You weren't being honest with *yourself.* And maybe you're not being honest now. Do you really not know how you feel about Alexandre? You're not just using Ali and Luc as an excuse because you're scared of starting a new relationship? Or punishing yourself for Joey? Because you don't need to. You did nothing wrong."

"Maybe." Kathy might be right. It was all too much to consider, though. "I should get going. I'm meeting everyone for dinner soon."

"Enjoy the rest of your trip! I want to hear more when you get back. And, Mei?" Kathy looked at her intently. "When you know, you know."

CHAPTER TWENTY-FOUR

Early the next morning, Alexandre started the Prius and followed the directions to the destination Mei had typed into his phone. “Are you ever going to say what we’re doing today, or are you going to keep me in suspense?” Mei had only told him to wear a long-sleeve shirt and pants and prepare to get dirty.

From the passenger seat beside him, Mei rolled down the window, letting the wind sweep through her hair. “It’s nothing crazy. I just wanted to surprise you. We’re volunteering at a local nonprofit that restores wetlands. We’ll be removing invasive plants and replacing them with native ones. I know how much you love the outdoors. And I wanted to give back to O‘ahu.”

“That sounds like a perfect day.” Alexandre reached over and touched her hand. “I can’t wait to rip up those invasive plants.”

Mei laughed, curling her fingers around his before letting go.

They drove back to the windward side of the island. The green cliffs of the Ko‘olau Range towered overhead, puffy white clouds shrouding their peaks.

Mei sighed. “I’ll never get tired of those mountains. Would you be hiking them if I weren’t here?”

Alexandre shrugged. He actually had researched a few challenging Koʻolau trails before the trip. "Maybe. But I'd rather be with you."

Soon, he pulled into a gravel parking lot at what looked like a cross between a farm and a nature sanctuary. A small group mingled under a thatched hut beside a greenhouse.

Alexandre and Mei introduced themselves to Lani, the nonprofit's head of community outreach, and the other volunteers: a twenty-something couple from California, and a mom and her two teenagers from Seattle.

"Today you'll be helping us maintain these wetlands," Lani said. "They're an important part of the natural ecosystem that includes the nearby estuary, coral reefs, and *kalo* fields—or taro, as you probably know it—which is a traditional part of the Native Hawaiian diet."

Under Lani's direction, they loaded tools, work gloves, and potted native plants into wheelbarrows.

"We couldn't have asked for better scenery," Alexandre said to Mei as he pushed a wheelbarrow down a dirt path. The dramatic green mountains loomed before them.

Lani stopped beside a riot of greenery covering a stream bank. She pointed out the plants they were to weed, which was nearly everything, except for *neke*, a spiky fern, and *pāʻūohiʻiaka* and *kīpūkai*, which both had tiny flowers.

Alexandre and Mei crouched down in the spot they'd claimed. The ground was damp from the rain earlier in the week. Alexandre barely needed the tools. He extracted the plants, and their roots, with a quick tug. The scent of fresh earth filled his nose. Sweat dripped from his face onto the ground. Mei was sweaty, too. A bit of soil smudged her cheek, and wisps of hair escaped her messy bun. She smiled at him every time their eyes met. They filled bucket after bucket with plants, leaving behind fertile ground.

After everyone cleared their patches of land, Lani demonstrated how to plant the native species. They dug small holes, placed the delicate ferns in the ground, and gently covered the roots with soil.

At the end of the session, Lani thanked them. "Your work here will live on long after you leave. Maybe one day you'll come back and see how your plants have grown."

"Hopefully." Alexandre and Mei shared a smile, though Lani's words made him a little sad. Would they ever return? And if they did, would it be as a couple? Married to other people? Alexandre didn't want to dwell on the unknown. He shucked off his work gloves and dropped them in the wheelbarrow.

The young California couple, Tessa and Nate, were taking selfies. They mugged for the photos, their cheeks pressed together.

"Want me to take one of you?" Alexandre offered.

"That'd be lit!" Tessa handed him her phone. She ran back to Nate and threw her arms around him. He leaned over and kissed her cheek.

Alexandre snapped a series of photos, capturing the emerald mountains in the background.

"Want me to get one of you two?" Tessa asked.

Alexandre glanced at Mei. Her eyes lit up. "Sure."

They jogged to the same spot. Mei wrapped her arms around his waist. Alexandre draped an arm over her shoulders. He was tempted to kiss her, too.

Tessa grinned at the phone. "Adorable. You two are the cutest."

Alexandre didn't clarify that they weren't a couple. Neither did Mei.

At their car, Alexandre hugged Mei again. He relished the feel of her against him, her lemon-coconut scent mingling with sunscreen, sweat, and fresh dirt. "Today was the best. My favorite part of the trip, so far."

Mei beamed. "I'm so glad you liked it!"

Using all his willpower, Alexandre released her. They were starving, so they picked up banh mis. At a nearby state park, they found a bench on a grassy knoll overlooking the ocean.

Alexandre bit into his sandwich with a satisfying crunch. The airy baguette, pickled vegetables, rich paté, and creamy mayonnaise made the perfect bite. From their bench, he could see where they'd volunteered, a verdant area at the foot of the green mountain ridge.

"We had a nice group. The teens seemed into it. The other couple, too." Whoops. He'd referred to Tessa and Nate as "the other couple," as if he and Mei were one. Alexandre hurried on so Mei wouldn't notice his slip. "They were cute. They seemed so happy."

She let out a short laugh. "They *seemed* happy. But maybe they're all smiles on the outside and miserable on the inside." She frowned. "Sorry. I shouldn't project on other people."

"You and Joey." Obviously. Alexandre couldn't think of anything else to say.

"Yeah. Sometimes I get so angry. Not at Joey. At myself. For going along and telling myself everything would work out when I knew, deep down, that it wouldn't."

Alexandre crumpled up his sandwich wrapper. Good thing he'd finished eating before getting into a Joey discussion. "That's human nature. We all want to believe in the choices we've made, so we dig in and try to make them work."

"Well, digging in only works if you're not digging into a horrible mistake. I've learned a lot about self-delusion and the value of listening to that little voice sooner, when it says you're headed down the wrong path."

"Petit à petit."

Mei's brows knitted in confusion.

"That's an old French expression my mom used to say," Alexandre explained. *"Petit à petit, l'oiseau fait son nid.* It means, 'Little by little, the bird makes its nest.' I hadn't thought of it in ages, but I started repeating it to myself once I decided to leave Oregon. I knew that forgiving myself and rebuilding my life would take time. But I could try, *petit à petit."* Alexandre had never told that to anyone. He hoped it would bring Mei comfort.

"Petit à petit," she repeated. "I like that. I'm going to make it my mantra."

Puffy white clouds dotted the blue sky. With the sun shining down, the thunderstorms earlier in the week felt like a lifetime ago.

"Are you dating now?" Mei asked.

Alexandre startled, then composed himself. "I have been. I'm not seeing anyone, though."

Mei nodded. She didn't ask for details. Alexandre didn't share any, either. What would be the point of telling her about the Vassar drama professor? Or the local entrepreneur who made goat milk soap? Or the barista he'd had a brief fling with, leading him to avoid her café, which, unfortunately, served the best espresso in town?

"Have you dated?" he asked Mei.

"Not yet. Maybe soon. I already know next time will be different." She laughed ruefully. But when their eyes met, Mei looked away quickly, as if she'd said too much.

Next time . . . with him? Alexandre was hesitant to ask. He didn't want to sound callous, like, *Sorry you dumped your fiancé three months ago. Are you over him yet?*

His mind whirred. Should he make a move? Mei was doing better every day, but she was still healing. Alexandre certainly didn't want to be a rebound for Joey. Then there was that awkward moment after their near kiss during the hurricane. *Why do our siblings have to be married?* Alexandre stifled a sigh. That just added another degree of complication.

Still, their attraction was undeniable. His feelings for Mei were real, too.

"Next time will be different," Alexandre said. "The right person will be there when you're ready." There. That sounded like the perfect answer. Reassuring and encouraging with enough subtext.

Mei seemed to get it. A little smile played on her lips.

CHAPTER TWENTY-FIVE

The last day of the year was also the last full day of vacation, and Mei was determined to make the most of it. She and Alexandre drove to the North Shore, admiring the pastoral views as the sun dappled the rolling fields at the foot of the mountains.

They beach-hopped along the coast. At Kūkaeʻōhiki Beach, they spotted two green sea turtles nearly camouflaged among the dark rocks. At Waimea Bay Beach, they sunbathed on the vast expanse of golden sand, watching surfers paddle out, then ride the waves back in.

For lunch, they stopped at one of the North Shore's famous shrimp trucks. Mei was set on getting their specialty, butter garlic shrimp, but paused when she saw they also offered Cantonese salt-and-pepper shrimp.

"Let's split both," Alexandre said.

They sat side by side at a picnic table, laughing and getting their hands messy while peeling the fresh shrimp.

After the meal, they drove along the coastal road. At times, the ocean lay just on the other side of the asphalt. They passed narrow beaches with choppy blue waves and impossibly tall palm trees. Inland, waterfalls cascaded down craggy green cliffs. As they approached the wetlands where they'd volunteered, Mei thought about the delicate plantlings they'd placed in the ground. They'd drink in the fresh air and grow stronger each day. Mei smiled to herself. She was doing the same.

They ended their drive at Ka'ōhao Beach. Mei found a quiet spot on the white sand, under a low palm tree. She and Alexandre lay on their towels, facing each other. Mei took in the strong line of his jaw, his intelligent eyes. Her fingers itched to run through his tousled hair. *Not yet. But maybe soon.*

• • •

An hour later, Ali, Luc, and Kaia joined them. Luc and Alexandre took Kaia for a swim, leaving Mei and Ali on their towels.

"I can't believe it's New Year's Eve," Mei said.

"Right?" Ali luxuriated under the sun's rays. "We've never spent it anywhere warm. This should be our new tradition."

"Seriously. But next time, I'm paying. I owe you."

"Oh please. You don't owe us anything."

Mei nodded, though she'd try to return Ali and Luc's kindness as soon as she could. She gazed at the sun glittering on the water, then cleared her throat. "So I'm thinking that maybe—*just maybe*—it might be time for me to leave Livin."

"Really?" Ali whipped her head toward her. "How did you decide that?"

Mei took a minute to sort through her feelings. "At Livin, I like being busy. I feel accomplished every day. But being here made me remember what's really important. It's not killing myself to be the top marketing employee. It's spending time with you, Luc, and Kaia. And Alexandre." Mei hoped her tone didn't change when she said Alexandre's name. "And it's being healthy and present enough to enjoy those moments."

Shame welled up as she recalled the state she was in before this trip: Holing up in her filthy apartment. Skipping Thanksgiving. Avoiding people who cared about her so she could give everything to a company that didn't love her back.

"Livin hasn't been a healthy place for a while," Ali said. "It's time to go."

"How do you do it? Work full-time and have a kid? And make sure your sister and brother-in-law aren't burnt-out disasters?"

Ali waved off her last remark. "Have you ever heard the rocks and sand analogy?"

Mei shook her head.

"Think of filling a clear vase with rocks and sand. You'd put the largest rocks in first, then the pebbles. Then you'd pour in the sand." Ali let a handful of powdery white sand slip through her fingers. "The biggest rocks are your priorities. Everything else falls around them."

"I just have a hulking, Livin-sized rock that takes up the whole vase."

"Yeah, but it doesn't have to be that way. Your big rocks change over time. Before I was a mom, Luc and you were my biggest rocks. Now Kaia, Luc, and you are."

Mei's cheeks burned. How had she let work eclipse everything? How had she thought of Livin as a bigger rock than her sister? Joey's face drifted into her mind. Maybe if she hadn't been so consumed with work, she would have realized their incompatibility sooner, saving them months of anguish. Mei watched Alexandre pull Kaia on a pineapple-shaped float. Her heart gave a little pang.

"You have your priorities right," she said to Ali. "Mine are all screwed up."

"You'll straighten them out."

"I just need to figure out where to go next."

"Back to food marketing? Somewhere more exciting than Daisyland?"

Mei shrugged. Not a single job seemed appealing. "I have to see what's out there. And update my résumé. I'll do it in the new year."

"Tomorrow," Ali cracked.

"Ha ha." But she was laughing, too. "New year, new job."

She spotted Alexandre splashing in the water with Luc and Kaia. His eyes met hers. The corners of his mouth curled up.

Mei smiled back. *And maybe a new love, too?*

• • •

For the last dinner of the year, everyone went to an udon restaurant. Over steaming bowls of noodles in rich broth and crispy platters of shrimp and vegetable tempura, they toasted the trip and their hopes for the new year.

Afterward, they headed back to Alexandre's room. Kaia vowed to stay up until midnight but dozed off at eleven. After tucking her into the spare bed, Mei, Ali, Luc, and Alexandre tiptoed out to the balcony. Under a crescent moon, waves rippled in the ocean. Just before midnight, Luc popped open a bottle of champagne and poured four glasses.

"One minute to go," Ali said.

Mei leaned her head against her sister's. Scenes from the year flashed before her: Joey proposing in their shiny new apartment. A hurricane-drenched Alexandre running to her at Livinpalooza. Joey crying hysterically when she ended their relationship. James introducing Erika to the marketing team. Ali announcing their trip to Hawai'i. Coming back to life in this beautiful place. A year of pain. And joy. And hopefully growth.

"Ten seconds!" Luc called.

They counted down together. "Five . . . four . . . three . . . two . . . one! Happy new year!"

Fireworks lit up the sky in bursts of red, gold, green, and blue. People on balconies cheered. Ali and Luc embraced with glee.

Mei turned to Alexandre. Desire shone on his face, but his hesitation was clear. Mei knew she had to make the first move. Every nerve ending thrummed, anticipating his lips on hers.

Without taking her eyes off him, Mei wrapped her arms around his neck. A slow smile spread across his face. He pulled her close. Electricity shot through Mei. She brushed her nose against his. He brought his face to hers. As Mei's eyes closed, she noticed Ali and Luc breaking apart.

Mei jumped away from Alexandre. She ran to hug her sister.

A moment later, Kaia wandered onto the balcony, rubbing her eyes. "It's New Year's? You didn't wake me!" she wailed. Chandeliers of golden sparks rained down in the sky. "Ooh."

Everyone laughed and gathered at the railing. With Alexandre beside her, Mei barely registered the fireworks. She was all too aware of the buzzy heat emanating from him, making her whole body hum.

After the last firework faded into the night, Ali yawned. "It's way past Kaia's bedtime. And ours."

Mei grabbed the champagne. "There's still half a bottle. You sure you don't want a top-off?" Her eyes slid to Alexandre.

He raised an eyebrow. Then that mischievous smile pulled at his mouth. "I could go for one."

Mei refilled their glasses, biting her lip to contain her giddy laughter.

"We're good," Ali said. "We'll see you tomorrow."

Mei waved as they walked out of the room.

The door closed. Mei's eyes met Alexandre's. For a moment, they stood frozen. Only the sound of their shallow breathing filled the space. Then Alexandre took a step toward her. Mei leapt onto him.

Her lips found his. Her hands ran through his hair. For a second, Alexandre seemed stunned. Then he pulled her in. His tongue brushed hers. His hands roamed down her back, as steady and assured as she'd imagined. Mei snuck her hands under his shirt, her fingers tingling as they devoured his skin.

They toppled onto the bed.

Mei giggled. "This is so ridiculous."

"It is." Alexandre's lips trailed her jawline. "But I don't care."

She wrapped her legs around him, feeling him hard against her.

Too much clothing lay between them. Mei unbuttoned Alexandre's shirt and attempted to rip it off. They laughed when his arm got stuck. He sat up to untangle himself, while Mei yanked off her sundress. Her bare skin against his was more than she could bear.

She grabbed his shoulders. He ran his hands over her breasts, making her sigh and arch against him.

Joey's angry face suddenly floated before her. *You're ruining everything we have so you can fuck Le fucking Prof.*

Mei stiffened. Not this. Not now. She drew in a breath and faced down her glaring ex-fiancé. *Sorry, Joey. We had problems long before Le Prof.*

Alexandre pulled back. "You okay?"

Mei nodded.

He touched her cheek. "We can stop."

Mei took in Alexandre's concerned expression, the care in his touch. "No. I don't want to." She wrapped herself around him decisively.

Alexandre kissed her gently, slowly. Mei relaxed into him.

Their kisses deepened, driving any hesitation out of her mind. Mei undid Alexandre's shorts. She ran her hand over his erection, feeling him suck in his breath. He paused at her underwear, his eyes meeting hers. Mei helped him pull them off. A moan escaped her as his fingers slipped inside her.

Alexandre smiled at her arousal. He kissed down her neck, moving to her stomach, then in between her legs. Mei's breath caught at the feel of his tongue, then melted into the delicious sensations flowing through her.

"Do you have a condom?" she asked.

Alexandre retrieved one from the bathroom. Back in bed, he pulled her close. His hazel eyes caressed her face. "Remember during the hurricane, when you asked whether it's possible to be one hundred percent sure about anything? At the time, I said no. Now I know I was wrong. I'm one hundred percent sure about you."

Mei stroked his face. "I am, too." And she was.

Alexandre kissed her, then looked at her again. She nodded.

Mei inhaled when he entered her. When their eyes met, Mei nearly burst into giggles. They were finally naked together and it felt so right. Alexandre seemed to feel the same way. He leaned down and pressed his lips against hers.

She sensed Alexandre taking her in, noting what made her sigh with bliss or move with more urgency, as if committing it to memory. *Of course he is.* Not many of the men she'd been with had cared so much about her pleasure.

Then Alexandre kissed her deeply, bringing her solely back to him. She took his hand and guided it between her legs. Mei touched herself with him, smiling at his change in arousal.

Then she was climaxing. She gasped and panted, clutching at Alexandre. A minute later, he was breathless too, gripping her just as tightly.

They lay together nose to nose. Alexandre kissed her, filling her with radiating joy. As Mei drifted off to sleep, her head nestled against Alexandre's shoulder, him holding her close, all she could think was, *Finally.*

CHAPTER TWENTY-SIX

Alexandre's alarm rang at six a.m. on New Year's Day. He fumbled for it, disoriented by the pressure on his right arm. He looked down, and the night's events came rushing back. Alexandre might not have believed he and Mei had gotten together if she wasn't stirring against him.

"Morning." He kissed her head. "Do you still want to go to the beach?"

"Hmm." Mei rolled on top of him. "I'm tempted to spend all day in bed. But I don't want to miss our last chance at Kaʻōhao."

Alexandre smiled mischievously. "If the beach is empty, we could do everything there that we'd do here."

Mei laughed and jostled his shoulder. "I like the way you think."

He wrapped his arms around her waist, and they kissed, long and slow.

• • •

They held hands as Alexandre drove across the island. The first rays of sun tinted the green mountaintops.

Ka'ōhao Beach was deserted. They padded over the sand, found their spot under the low palm, and sat with their knees touching as they sipped coffee and ate breakfast sandwiches.

Alexandre inhaled the cool ocean air. So much had changed since they'd arrived a week ago. What would happen when they were back in New York? It was Mei's call. The thought of going back to being friends filled Alexandre with dread. Still, he had to know.

"What a trip, huh?" he said. "We stuck to our plan. We didn't let Livin or zebrafish take over our vacation." Inwardly Alexandre groaned. Ugh, work. Not exactly the stuff of romance. But it gave him an opening for the question he really wanted to ask.

"Nope. We were good." Mei set down her coffee. "Maybe we can keep that going. I need to leave Livin. My health and sanity depend on it. If I promise to leave, will you help me?"

"Sure, but you don't need to promise anything."

"I want to. We can make a pact, like we did this week: You hold me accountable, and I'll help keep you from getting sucked back into the zebrafish vortex."

"I'll always need that. The zebrafish vortex is strong."

"So's the Livin vortex. Getting out is going to be rough."

"I know the struggle. But you'll do it."

"*We'll* do it. *Petit à petit.*" Mei extended her hand.

"*Petit à petit.*" They shook on it, then Alexandre took Mei's other hand. His heart thumped with nerves. "I'm not sure what you're thinking about us—if you're open to dating, or if what happens in Hawai'i stays in Hawai'i." He forced a laugh. "I'll respect whatever you decide. I meant what I said last night, though. I really care about you. I want to see where this goes."

Mei stared out at the horizon, the pale sky growing bluer. "I want to be with you, too," she said quietly.

"But . . . ?" There seemed to be a condition to her statement.

"But maybe we go slow and keep it between us, for now. I hate having secrets, especially from Ali and Luc. I'm just not ready to tell people I'm dating again."

"I get it. I'm fine with that." He was. A tiny part of Alexandre was relieved, too. He'd be spared the weirdness of telling Luc he and Mei were seeing each other, at least for a little while. He touched Mei's cheek. "I'm just happy to be with you."

She brought her lips to his. "I am, too."

When they pulled away, Alexandre nodded toward the water. "Feel like a swim?"

"Let's go."

They waded into the surf. The cool water gave Alexandre a little shock upon entering. They bobbed out far enough to get a good view of the shoreline while keeping their feet on the sandy bottom. Alexandre gazed at the rustling palms and immaculate white sand, imprinting the image in his mind.

"Taking it all in?" Mei asked.

"I don't want to forget this view. Or this feeling."

"Of what it's like to be alive."

"Now that you mention it—" Alexandre pushed off the ocean floor, propelling himself backward, taking Mei with him. She yelped in surprise. Her arms encircled his neck. Alexandre pulled her close. He savored the softness of her lips, the salt water on his tongue. Mei's hands tugged his hair. He nipped her ear. "Now, *this* is what it's like to be alive."

They kissed hungrily as the turquoise water lapped their skin and the sun rose higher in the sky.

• • •

No one was ready to return home. A wistful feeling hung over the gate as they waited, five across in airport chairs. Maybe Alexandre was projecting, but were Luc and Ali eyeing him and Mei as if they knew something had happened between them? Alexandre smiled to himself. He wasn't going to say anything.

Like the last flight, Ali, Luc, and Kaia boarded first. Alexandre and Mei stood up a few minutes later when their zone was called. Like last time, he wheeled her bag. Unlike last time, a new closeness existed between them.

The engine rumbled. The plane gathered speed as it taxied down the runway and lifted into the sky.

Mei pulled Alexandre toward the window. "Check out the view!"

"Wow." Below them, O'ahu stood proudly in the glittering ocean. Alexandre spotted Lē'ahi's dramatic crater and the vibrant green ridges of the Ko'olau Range.

"Think we'll ever come back?" Mei asked.

"Yes." Alexandre didn't know why he was so sure. But he was.

They watched O'ahu disappear in the distance. The Pacific Ocean sparkled, as if waving goodbye.

After dinner service, the cabin lights dimmed. Mei yawned. "All the excitement from the last few days has worn me out."

"We didn't sleep much last night," Alexandre agreed. "Not that I'm complaining."

Mei poked him playfully. They settled back in their seats, legs entangled under their blankets. Mei rested her head against his arm. A few minutes later, she dozed off.

Alexandre regarded her sleeping form with affection. He was exhausted, but an unfamiliar energy ran through him. Why was he so wired?

Mei stirred and nuzzled against him. Then Alexandre realized: For the first time since leaving Oregon, he wasn't just plastering on a grin, trying to convince everyone, including himself, that he was happy. Now he was actually content. Genuinely thrilled for the life awaiting him back in New York.

A slow smile spread across his face. Alexandre brushed his lips against Mei's forehead. Then he leaned back against his headrest and closed his eyes, grateful for the fresh new year that stretched out before him.

CHAPTER TWENTY-SEVEN

Compared to Hawai'i, New York in January should have felt soul-crushingly bleak. Icy wind rattled the bare tree branches. Crusty salt covered the frozen sidewalk. But Mei floated through her chilly hometown, warmed from the inside.

Alexandre. As Mei rode the subway and braved the frigid streets, her mind flashed back to the night they'd spent together: The care in Alexandre's eyes when he looked at her. The feel of his steady, assured hands. The unbelievable bliss of falling asleep in his arms.

In her daydreamy state, Mei refilled her coffee mug in Livin's kitchen. Her phone buzzed with a text. Alexandre had sent her a photo of wintry mountains near campus.

> Not Hawai'i, but not so bad. Hope you're having a good first day back. No staying late tonight!

Now, as she worked from a communal table, her phone dinged again, this time with a selfie of Alexandre bundled up in winter gear by a gray university building.

The New Paltz biology department and some dork who teaches there.

Mei's heart swelled at the sight of Alexandre's handsome face, his nose red from the cold. Her joy evaporated as she scanned her own surroundings: her yellow "Livin It Up" coffee mug, a massive neon sign that screamed, "If you ain't here, you ain't LIVIN!"

She snapped a photo of the sign and sent it to Alexandre.

So done being brainwashed by this place.
And no, definitely not staying late tonight!

• • •

On Friday morning, the monthly rankings hit Mei's inbox. *I don't care about this*, she repeated to herself as she clicked the link to the leaderboard. Still, she held her breath as the page loaded.

Third.

Yes! Mei did a happy dance in her seat. All those hours working at the beginning of the trip let her hit her December numbers and then some. That fiery rush roared through her veins. *I'm back, baby!*

Then she remembered: She still had her pact with Alexandre. *Your workload is still ridiculous. Livin is still a treadmill to death.*

And you have a new boss.

Whom she was meeting in a half hour.

• • •

Erika had scheduled their first one-on-one in the Paris conference room. Mei took a seat at the woven bistro table and studied the photo wallpaper depicting a bustling streetscape with shoppers and cafés. She had never been to France. *Maybe Alexandre and I will go one day.*

The door opened, snapping Mei out of her reverie.

"Hi, are you Mei? I'm Erika."

"Yes, so nice to meet you!" As they shook hands, Mei noted her new boss's shiny blowout, silky blouse, and stylish trousers. *She certainly looks like a VP of marketing.* Mei tugged self-consciously at the J.Crew blazer she wore over a black T-shirt.

"I'd love to hear what you're working on." Erika smiled at her from across the table. "I've heard nothing but amazing things about you."

"Oh, ah, thanks." When was the last time anyone complimented her work? Mei sat up straighter. "I run our global brand campaigns, which includes developing the strategy and messaging, overseeing all content and creative, managing media buys, and partnering on events and experiential activations."

"Wow, you've got quite a job! The latest campaign looks great—*Livin Your Dream*? My husband and I stopped by the holiday pop-up in London. The place was packed."

"We're only going bigger. In February, we'll be projecting branded hype videos, designed by famous artists, onto landmarks like the Empire State Building and the Sydney Opera House. We'll also be launching drone art in ten cities."

"Get out! Mei, you are a wonder."

"Thanks. For the last six months, I've also been working on a major refresh to update our brand and develop inclusive marketing standards for every country. That way, people from all different backgrounds, all around the world, will know they belong at Livin."

"That sounds very worthy. I can see how you're well positioned for such a task."

Because I'm Asian or because I've been running brand marketing? Mei took a breath and continued. "I'm rolling out everything to the global marketing org at the end of the month, but we developed the current campaign according to them."

"Wonderful. Is there anything else we need to touch upon?"

"Yes. Last year, James changed my team's goals. Before, we focused on performance metrics, like how many people clicked on an ad and filled out a form. Since October, our goals have been based on quantity, like how many videos we launch. As marketers, we know that performance is more important. So I'm hoping we can revise our goals."

Erika pursed her lips. "I think it's too soon."

"I have data. We're not seeing any positive results in proportion to quantity."

"I'm sorry. Let's wait until we have six months of metrics." Erika repositioned her laptop. She seemed to be debating whether to say something. "You're a rock star, Mei. It's obvious. But James told me you've been checked out and underperforming. Why would he say that?"

Tears burned Mei's eyes, surprising her. She blinked hard to maintain her composure. "In October, I broke up with my fiancé right before our wedding, paid off the whole thing by myself, and then moved apartments. I may have been a little distracted."

"I'm so sorry. I get why work wasn't your main focus. You were going through a major crisis." Erika clucked sympathetically. "Well, now I've got your back. If you ever need support, personal days, anything, just tell me. I'm here to help."

"I appreciate that."

"Also—" Erika's eyes darted to the door. "I want you to know that throughout my career, I've been a vocal advocate for women in the workplace. Smart, talented women, like you." She leveled her gaze at Mei. "We both know that a lot of men get to the top riding on the accomplishments of women like us. I've worked with James before, and I know how to handle him. If you keep crushing it and stick with me, I'll make sure you get the credit and visibility you deserve, and that you're *very* well compensated. We women need to lift each other up."

After Erika left the room, Mei sank back in her chair. Was her new boss as bad as she'd feared? Or could Erika actually help her career?

Mei's phone buzzed. Alexandre's name appeared on the text notification. Good thing they had their pact. In Hawai'i, she was adamant about quitting. Now that familiar, fiery energy coursed steadily through her veins.

CHAPTER TWENTY-EIGHT

Alexandre set aside the presentation he was revising for his genetics class and texted Mei.

How was meeting your new boss?

He didn't have high hopes for Erika, considering Mei's loathsome former manager, James, had handpicked her. Mei's reply came a moment later.

Not what I expected. She gets how much I do for Livin and even hinted she could give me a raise, so it's tempting to stick it out more. But she won't change our goals, so I'll still be cranking out content for god knows how long.

Alexandre scrunched up his face. He knew all about false hope. Back in Oregon, he dug in whenever anything remotely positive happened, like publishing an article in a third-rate journal, or getting new filters for the zebrafish tanks.

His phone buzzed with another text from Mei.

Ugh, remind me again why I need to leave!!!

Alexandre typed his reply.

Even though Erika seems okay, James still leads marketing and that whacko, Julian, is still running the place. Nothing's going to change.

Mei wrote back a minute later.

Thank you!! I needed that. This is why we have our pact. Have I mentioned how excited I am to see you?

Alexandre smiled at Mei's reference to their weekend plans. Not that he hadn't been thinking about them. He'd suggested meeting in the city, but Mei had insisted on coming to the Hudson Valley. *I'm less likely to work if I'm not at home,* she'd said. Alexandre wasn't going to argue with that.

He checked the clock. Time to meet with his own boss.

Dr. Johnson greeted him from behind her oversized wooden desk. "Welcome back, Alexandre. Did you have fun in Hawai'i?"

"I did."

"You look like it. You have that vacation glow."

Vacation glow or love glow? Alexandre flushed as his thoughts strayed to Mei. He cleared his throat. "You mentioned you wanted to go over my evaluations. Is there anything in particular we need to discuss?"

"Yes. Overall, I'm pleased with your student feedback. I rarely see such positive comments after just one semester."

Alexandre released the breath he'd been holding. He hadn't realized he'd been nervous. "Thank you. I tried to make every class as interactive as possible, and I adapted my lesson plans based on my students' comments."

"I saw a few areas where you can improve next semester, specifically around real-world applications."

"I noticed. I take that criticism seriously." Alexandre winced. A few students wrote that he talked too much about research—three people even said he cited *his own* research way too much—and wanted to know how to use what they learned in other settings. "I'll make sure to highlight different fields, like healthcare and pharma. I can also schedule a few guest lecturers from other professions. I'll poll my classes and see what they'd like."

"That sounds like a good plan."

"It helps to have such vocal students."

"That's just as much a testament to you as to them. You gave them a safe space to open up, and they did." Dr. Johnson rifled through a sheaf of papers. "I want to read a few comments that stood out: 'I really appreciate how Professor Brodeur is open to different learning styles. I have severe anxiety, and even though I try, I have a hard time speaking up in class. I like how Professor Brodeur lets us message him questions during class and includes office hours and emails in class participation. I'm more confident in written and one-on-one interactions.'"

"I've learned that not all students feel comfortable raising their hands. Some people freeze when I call on them, even if they've done the work and know the answer. Not everyone grew up in a culture where they had to be the loudest one in the room."

"You're creating a more inclusive classroom."

"I'm trying to."

Dr. Johnson reached for another paper, then broke into a wide smile. "This one is too good not to read out loud: 'Professor Brodeur's class is lit. It hits different. I'm only taking mol bio because my parents are making me become a doctor, and somehow Professor Brodeur made it interesting with videos and improv games.'"

"I'm glad I made an impression on them. And that my class 'hits different.'" He couldn't wait to tell Mei. "Shouldn't it be 'hits differently'?"

Dr. Johnson laughed. "Your guess is as good as mine. Either way, it's high praise. After next semester, if you're performing just as well, I'd like to consider you for our admissions and planning committees. You embody so much of what I seek in educators."

"Thank you." A swell of pride rose in Alexandre's chest. "I'd like to work more closely with you on shaping your department."

"*Our* department," Dr. Johnson corrected him. "It's just as much yours as it is mine."

"That's true." Alexandre felt her words sink in. His boss was right. He wasn't an adjunct or a visiting professor. He was a full-time biology professor at SUNY New Paltz. It was time he started acting like one.

Alexandre opened his laptop to take notes. "I'm committed to being the best teacher I can possibly be. Do you have any more feedback that can help me as I'm planning for next semester?"

• • •

The following afternoon, Alexandre waited outside the train station, shifting from one foot to the other. Even though he and Mei texted all the time, Hawai'i felt like a fever dream. Would the magic from that trip exist in the real world?

Alexandre scanned the passengers exiting the platform. Then he spotted Mei in a black parka and chunky gray scarf. He trotted toward her, and they embraced tightly.

"So glad you're here."

"Me too," she said, and brought her lips to his.

Any fears Alexandre had melted away.

They drove off, past snow-dusted mountains and frosty fields. They wound their way down narrow country roads, until Alexandre turned onto a crunchy gravel driveway. Tiny white fairy lights twinkled in the trees. Up ahead, warm light spilled from a log cabin.

"What is this place?"

Alexandre smiled at the wonder in Mei's voice. "A farm brewery."

Inside, a fire crackled on a stone hearth. A host led them to a cozy wooden table. Their knees brushed as they took their seats. They perused the menu, then ordered farmhouse ales and a cheese board.

Mei's eyes sparkled as she took in her surroundings. "This place is adorable. I love it."

A warm glow filled Alexandre's chest. "I haven't been here before, but I thought you might like it."

A waitress arrived with their ales in tulip-shaped glasses. Mei held hers up. "Well, cheers to us."

They tapped their drinks together. As she sipped, Mei giggled.

"What are you laughing at?" Alexandre couldn't help but smile. Mei looked almost bashful, her eyes lowered, her cheeks pink in the firelight.

"I don't know if you remember this, but when I was at your place during the hurricane, you were telling me about hikes and restaurants you'd found nearby. At the time, I figured you'd take dates there." Her mouth twisted ruefully. "I was wishing we could go together."

Alexandre reached for her hand. He stayed quiet. Mei looked like she needed a minute to let any lingering guilt about Joey wash over her.

Her lips tipped up and she met his eyes. "Did you ever feel that way, too? Months ago?"

Alexandre sipped his beer, considering her question. "I don't think so." He saw Mei's face fall. "Not because I didn't want to! I sure as hell did. Believe me, I spent months trying not to think of you in any romantic way." A little smile bloomed on Mei's lips. Alexandre squeezed her hand reassuringly. "You felt so out of reach. I didn't want to get my hopes up about you. Or anything."

"How about now?"

Alexandre looked into Mei's big brown eyes, her own hopefulness shimmering in them. He admired the graceful shape of her mouth as she sipped her ale. Gosh, she was beautiful.

Alexandre cupped Mei's face in his hands, bringing his lips to hers. "I think you know the answer to that."

CHAPTER TWENTY-NINE

The last hints of daylight filtered through the bedroom window. Outside, a gust of wind blew, making Mei snuggle closer to Alexandre, even though they were already cocooned in his soft jersey sheets.

"What are you thinking?" He stroked her hair.

"About how happy I am."

The last twenty-four hours had flown by. After dinner at the brewery, they'd gone back to Alexandre's place. They both attempted polite small talk for about five minutes before Mei grabbed his hand and led him to his bedroom. In the morning, he'd cooked ham and Gruyère omelets for breakfast, then they'd hiked to a frozen waterfall in a nearby park. After lunch, with their time together drawing to a close, they'd ended up back in Alexandre's bed.

"How about if I drive down next weekend?" Alexandre asked. "That is, if you want me to. I don't want to be presumptuous and assume we're definitely meeting up—"

Mei laughed. "Is this about me asking if we could take it slow?"

"Yes."

She planted a kiss on his nose. "I'd love to see you next weekend." In Hawai'i, she'd been skittish about dating again. But being with Alexandre didn't feel risky. It felt just right.

Mei rubbed her foot against his. He pulled her in for a long kiss.

Finally, Mei drew back reluctantly. "I should get going."

At the train station, Alexandre waited with her on the platform. Leaving him had her feeling down, and the Sunday Scaries grew even stronger when Mei pictured her Livin inbox. Then she realized something.

"I didn't work this entire weekend. I barely even thought about Livin."

"Good! We're doing it. *Petit à petit.*"

The platform vibrated beneath their feet. A Grand Central–bound train approached. Mei stood on tiptoe and tilted her face up to kiss Alexandre. "Thanks for helping me remember what's important in life."

• • •

The next morning, Mei floated into Livin. She ordered a large latte from the barista, chose a sunny spot at a communal table, and worked until her ten a.m. meeting with her senior reports.

"Did you all have a good weekend?" Mei asked once everyone was seated in the Rio conference room.

Kaden snorted. "Not really. I just worked."

"Same," Tamiko said.

"I stopped working on the weekends so my wife isn't working full-time, raising our son, and doing everything around the house by herself. My rankings have been trash ever since," Bryce said. "It was nice working with all of you."

"We'll chat in our one-on-one," Mei said.

Bryce had been in the bottom 10 percent for the last three months. Mei had received the automated notice that she'd have to fire him at the end of January unless he turned around his performance by "demonstrating unprecedented impact in extraordinary and quantifiable ways." Mei bit her lip, thinking about how, every few weeks, Bryce updated his laptop background with a new photo of his son. *Of course he should be able to spend time with his family!* Mei gulped down the dregs of her coffee. Her weekend glow was officially gone.

"Can we talk about our goals?" Tamiko asked. "Because they're killing me. They're not good for the business, either."

"I miss when Diana was here and we could focus on results, not just quantity," Bryce added.

"I feel the same way," Mei said. "I couldn't change James's mind. When I met with Erika on Friday and told her why our goals are problematic, she wouldn't budge, either."

"What's she like?" Kaden asked.

Mei had anticipated the question. "She sees the value of our programs, including the brand refresh. I think Erika will be a strong advocate for evangelizing our work to the execs."

"Think she'll shake things up?" Tamiko asked. "Or will it be the same as it's been under James?"

Mei hesitated. "I don't see anything changing right away. Erika said we could revisit our goals, but not until we have six months of data."

Kaden rubbed their eyes. "I can't do this much longer."

Mei's heart broke as she took in her dejected teammates.

Kaden had dark circles under their eyes. Tamiko's skin looked sallow. Bryce gnawed on his cuticles. Mei's mind flashed back to kissing Alexandre goodbye at the train station. *Thanks for helping me remember what's important in life.*

"So don't," she said.

Her teammates stared at her in surprise.

Mei flushed. She hadn't planned to speak so bluntly. "I just mean that we still have our ridiculous, unsustainable workload for the foreseeable future. If it makes sense for you to pursue other opportunities, either on another Livin team or elsewhere, I'll understand and support you."

Her colleagues nodded gravely.

"What about you?" Bryce asked.

Mei was quiet for a moment. Then she gave each of her teammates a meaningful look. "I'm thinking about what makes sense for me in the long term. And you should, too."

● ● ●

Late on Friday afternoon, Mei wearily checked her goals tracker. She still had heaps of content in her queue. Could she review a few more event scripts before calling it a week? It was only five thirty.

Her phone buzzed. Alexandre had texted a photo of a coffee mug next to his laptop.

> Finishing my second latte and next week's lesson plans. Ready to start the weekend.

He was already in the city. He'd driven down after his last class and was working from a nearby café. Mei wasn't planning to meet him until seven, but she could barely concentrate knowing he was mere blocks away.

She opened a draft of Julian's South by Southwest keynote address. The words swam before her eyes. Usually scripts got Mei hyped for the actual event, but this was not what she wanted to be doing.

A half hour later, she finished commenting on the doc. Mei had just opened the latest campaign video cuts when her phone buzzed again. She clicked on a photo of a glass of red wine next to a worn paperback.

Got to the restaurant a little early. No rush. I'm having a good time reading at the bar.

Mei stared at the photo. She could practically smell Alexandre's piney scent mingling with the spicy red wine. She glanced at her teammates, who were all typing around her. Then she snapped her laptop shut. "That's it. I'm done for the week."

"Packing it in early?" Bryce's eyebrows shot up.

Ayanna gave her a once-over. "Got plans tonight?"

Mei touched her hair, which she'd actually blown out this morning. Ayanna probably also noticed she was wearing a new navy blouse with a delicate lace trim, rather than her usual T-shirt and blazer. Mei smiled. "I do."

"Good!" Kaden slammed their laptop shut. "I'm going to get out of here, too. I'm seeing a show tonight and would love to stop at home first."

"We should leave at six every Friday," Mei said.

"You don't have to convince me," Bryce said. "My wife will be thrilled."

They all rode the elevator to the ground floor, laughing and chatting. When they reached the street, the winter sky glowed dusky pink above the building tops.

Mei waved goodbye to her teammates and skipped down Park Avenue South. A few minutes later, she reached her destination, a cozy townhouse tavern. Her heart thrummed as she scanned the bar area.

Then she spotted him. Alexandre sat on a stool at the far end, his wire-rimmed glasses perched on his nose while he read his book. He glanced up. Mei gave a little wave. A smile crept across Alexandre's face as he made his way over. When he reached her, he lifted her off the ground, making her laugh.

"You're early."

Mei grinned up at him. "I couldn't wait another minute."

• • •

On Sunday morning, Mei settled against her couch, her legs resting on Alexandre's. As she sipped her coffee, she surveyed her studio.

"I still don't love this place, but it feels much nicer with you in it."

Alexandre squeezed her foot. "This place is great. From the way you talked about it, I was expecting it to be old and decrepit."

"I've fixed it up a bit." Knowing Alexandre would be spending the weekend, Mei had deep cleaned her entire apartment, arranged framed photos on her nightstand, and picked up a few succulents from the grocery store. There was nothing she could do about the water-stained ceiling or slanting floor, but her place did feel more like home.

"You know that in academia, lots of people live in student-type apartments for most of their lives? You would've been horrified at my Eugene apartment. I like it here. And I like my place better when you're there, too." Alexandre leaned over to meet her lips. "So what do you feel like doing today?"

"This." Mei leaned on his shoulder, then sighed. "I should look for jobs."

"Want to do that now?" He reached for his phone. "I can help."

Mei laughed. "Because you know so much about marketing?"

"No, but I'll search for New York marketing jobs at cool companies, and you can see if they're a fit." He raised an eyebrow. "Unless you doubt my knowledge of cool companies."

"You are so uncool! That's one of the reasons I like you so much."

"At least I have enough self-awareness not to be offended."

They were quiet as they scrolled on their phones. Mei flagged job listings for VP of marketing positions at Pure, a sustainable cleaning startup, and Sea Salt, a hip kitchen brand.

"Tempo, that running shoe company, is hiring a marketing manager," Alexandre said.

"I like the brand, but the job isn't the right level. I'm looking for VP titles."

"VP? As in vice president?" His eyes widened.

Mei couldn't hide her pleased smile. She nodded.

"Wow." He let out a dry laugh. "That sure sounds more impressive than an associate professor who's only teaching."

Mei caught the bitterness in Alexandre's voice. "Hey. You're not 'just' an associate professor who's 'only' teaching. You're a brilliant research scientist who's passing on your knowledge to lots of lucky kids. You've come so far. Plus"—she wrapped him in a hug—"you wouldn't have me in Oregon."

Alexandre buried his face in her neck. "No, I wouldn't."

She kissed his ear. "We'll stay strong together."

CHAPTER THIRTY

Alexandre released Mei and retrieved his phone to look at more job listings. She was right. He was in a good place now. In the last few weeks, he'd been truly happy. But at this moment, he felt like a colossal loser.

Mei was going to be VP of marketing at a hot company. Alexandre clicked on a job posting with that title. His eyes nearly bugged out of their sockets. The low end of the salary range was more than twice his. The high end was triple.

Beside him, Mei was scrolling through her phone, smiling to herself. Alexandre eyed her nervously. *How much longer until she realizes I'm a washed-up has-been and drops me for someone else?*

Mei looked up. A flicker of worry crossed her face. "Are you okay?"

"Yeah. Just a bit tired." Alexandre felt Mei studying him. He scratched at a faded stain on her couch.

"No, something's bothering you. What is it?"

He shrugged, unable to meet her eyes. "You're applying for all these big positions. Your career is taking off. Mine has gone in the other direction."

"That's ridiculous! You have a super-impressive job, even if it's not your old one."

Alexandre frowned. He'd heard all this before.

"You can't compare us. I'm staying in my career. You changed yours. That would be mixing the wrong data, like comparing apples to oranges. There's probably some scientific term for that, but I don't know what it is."

Alexandre's mouth twitched. He was mired in his funk, but somehow Mei was making him laugh.

"What?" she asked.

"When you construct a flawed data set, it's called 'garbage in, garbage out.' And you're right. That's exactly what I was doing." He shook his head. "My career isn't going up or down. I'm on an entirely different track from where I used to be. And from you. There's no point comparing. It's illogical. Somehow, I never saw that before."

"This is why we have each other."

Alexandre kissed her firmly, gratefully, then retrieved his coffee. "Last week, when I was meeting with Dr. Johnson, I decided it was time to start owning my job and stop treating it like a temporary gig. I need to remember that."

Mei sipped her own coffee. "You can also go to the zebrafish conference as a SUNY New Paltz professor, instead of a former UO professor."

The zebrafish conference. In two weeks, he was flying to Cleveland for it.

Alexandre stifled a sigh. "I still have to present my research on behalf of UO because I conducted it there. Plus, everyone knows me from UO—my former colleagues, my old mentor."

"Who's your old mentor? Someone from Oregon?"

"No, his name is Chris Saunders, and he's with the University of Chicago. He's a *big fish* in the genetics field."

"Ha! Were you two always *swimming in the same circles*?"

Alexandre gave Mei a playful poke. "Basically. Chris was a visiting professor my third year of grad school. We stayed in touch as I finished my PhD. He was a helpful sounding board whenever I ran into problems with my research. He even coauthored a paper with me. I fell out of touch with him during the last few years. He doesn't even know that I left research." Shame flooded Alexandre. He had essentially ghosted Chris, ignoring his former mentor's emails until they eventually stopped.

"Are you sure you'll see him?"

"Yeah. He's always at these conferences. I'm bound to run into him."

"So tell him the truth about your career change. That's exactly what I was saying, and what *you* were just saying: Go to the conference owning your new job. Present the research from UO, but the rest of the time, address yourself as Professor Alexandre Brodeur from SUNY New Paltz. You can talk up your current job and make connections for New Paltz."

The thought hadn't crossed Alexandre's mind. "That's not a bad idea."

"Wow, don't heap on the praise."

"No, you're right. As usual." He gently tackled Mei onto the couch. "How do you always know exactly what I need?"

"Because I get you."

Their lips met. Alexandre parted her legs with his knee. She pulled him up from the couch, onto her bed, and unzipped his pants.

Afterward, they lay together. Alexandre's eyes roamed her tiny apartment. The potted green succulents and framed photos of her and Ali made the tired space feel bright and cozy.

Mei spending the weekend at his place had finally motivated him to update his apartment, too. Last week, Alexandre had ordered and assembled a small wooden dining set. One afternoon, after his classes, he'd walked into town and found several framed Hudson Valley nature prints at a secondhand store. He'd hung them in the living room and bedroom, then stood back admiring the images, a quiet pride throbbing through him as he observed the symbolism of the act.

Now Mei smiled up at him, her eyes warm. "How are you feeling?"

"More ready than ever to close the door on my old life," he answered truthfully. "Here's to our pact."

"And the start of our new lives."

Together, Alexandre thought as they kissed.

CHAPTER THIRTY-ONE

On Thursday evening, Mei hit the video call button, bouncing a little as she waited for Alexandre to pick up.

"I have some news!" she exclaimed when he answered. He looked extra handsome with a fresh haircut. "I already heard back from two places I applied to: Pure, the sustainable cleaning startup, and We're the First, a nonprofit that helps first-generation college students. I have interviews with both of them next week!"

"Congratulations! You're doing it."

"*Petit à petit.*" Mei's grin faded as she remembered the other topic they needed to discuss. "So I was thinking we should strategize about tomorrow. You're still coming, right?" Her cousin, Evie, was part of a small contemporary ballet company that was performing in a showcase with several other dance troupes. Evie had invited her, Ali, and Luc. Ali and Luc had then invited Alexandre.

"Yup."

"Think we can play it cool for the night?"

"Hmm." Alexandre frowned and looked off-camera. God, he was cute when he was thinking, or just doing anything, really. "We could tell Ali and Luc we're seeing each other," he said, turning back to her.

Mei drummed her fingers on her knee. She'd gone back and forth about this all week. Whenever she thought about breaking the news to Ali and Luc, all she could think was, *You're going to take down Le Prof, too. How's that going to play out with your dear little sister and her perfect family?* When she considered keeping her and Alexandre a secret a bit longer, she'd remember, *You don't tell Ali jack shit!*

"I want to, but not tomorrow," Mei decided. "We're going to be at the show, then a bar full of people. Ali and Luc will want all the details. It's Evie's night, and I don't want to take that away from her."

"You don't think they'll pick up on it? Especially Ali?"

"Ugh, she'll definitely know! We should keep a little distance so she won't get suspicious." Anytime Mei was within a few feet of Alexandre, they inevitably ended up touching.

"That's probably a good idea. Do you still want to meet up after?"

"Of course! I'm all about our little after party."

That mischievous smile appeared on Alexandre's lips. "I am, too."

• • •

The following evening, Mei waited in the lobby of a dance studio in Hell's Kitchen. She toyed with a lock of hair as she scanned the scene. How would she ever act platonic with Alexandre?

Mei spotted Ali and Luc making their way through the crowd. "I missed you!"

"Me too." Ali gave her a tight hug. "Hawai'i feels like ages ago."

You have no idea how much has happened since then! Over Ali's shoulder, Mei glimpsed Alexandre. Her heart sped up. He arched his eyebrow, telepathically asking, *Ready for this?* Mei nearly exploded with giggles. She leaned in to give him a rigid hug.

In the theater, Mei slid into the row first. Ali, Luc, and Alexandre followed.

The room darkened. Blue lights illuminated the stage. An uptempo percussive beat filled the space as dancers emerged from the wings. Some leapt in with graceful bounds, while others ebbed and flowed on- and offstage through a series of quick-footed turns.

Evie's company performed third to a jazzy medley. Mei didn't know much about dance, but she could see that her cousin had talent. Evie's moves were languid and expansive during a slow movement, and sharp and fleet when the music picked up. At the end of the number, Mei and Ali exchanged impressed smiles while applauding wildly.

After the show, they gathered at a nearby dive bar to celebrate. Everyone cheered when Evie and her dancer friends arrived.

"You were so good!" Mei hugged her cousin.

"You remember my brother, Alexandre, right?" Luc asked, reintroducing Alexandre to Evie.

"Of course!" Evie said. "Thanks for coming."

Mei's mind flashed back to the bachelor/bachelorette, when she'd envisioned Evie and Alexandre getting together. She wanted to laugh at herself. Look at where they were now.

"Have you always been a professional dancer?" Alexandre asked.

"I wish!" Evie replied. "I've danced my whole life, but I'm not a professional. All the people in my company have full-time day jobs. We just take ballet classes and go to rehearsals after work and on weekends. It's a lot, but I love it."

"It shows," Alexandre said. "I haven't seen much dance, but I've done a lot of sports, and I can tell when someone is really good at something."

Evie beamed. Mei looked down at her beer. Alexandre had never paid her a compliment like that, but why would he? She'd dropped all her hobbies and interests for Livin.

Luc and Alexandre went to the bar for another round of drinks, leaving Mei, Ali, and Evie.

"How are you doing?" Evie asked Mei.

"Much better since the last time you saw me, and the months after." Might as well answer what Evie was really asking.

"I felt terrible for you, but it's for the best." Evie wrinkled her nose. "Joey was kind of—"

"Immature? Cringe?" Mei supplied wryly.

Evie and Ali laughed. Mei smiled, too. Talking about Joey wasn't as painful anymore.

"Are you dating again?" Evie asked.

A flush crept into Mei's cheeks. "I'm starting to think about it."

Ali looked at her with surprise.

"What about him?" Evie nodded toward Alexandre at the bar.

"Alexandre?" Ali asked.

"Yeah. He's around your age, right? And single?"

"Ha! He is." Ali turned to Mei. "Can you imagine?"

Mei gulped down her beer. Now her face was aflame. Thank goodness for the bar's dim lighting.

Ali raised her eyebrows. A sly smile tugged at her lips.

Oh god, she knows. Mei shot Evie a pointed look. "Are you asking about Alexandre for yourself?"

Her cousin laughed. "No. I just started seeing someone I met on the apps."

"What are they like these days?"

"Not fun. But they're still the best way for me to meet people, so I stick with them." Evie smiled ruefully. "I keep telling myself it'll be worth it when I find my person."

"It will." Mei's eyes slid back to Alexandre at the bar. He winked at her, a private smile passing between them. Mei's heart soared. *I found my person.*

CHAPTER THIRTY-TWO

Alexandre turned back to his brother as the bartender brought over a fresh pint.

"Not sure where you're at with dating, but this could be a good place to meet someone," Luc said. He tilted his head toward Evie's friends.

Alexandre chuckled. "True." A lot of the dancers were very pretty, and their athleticism made them even more attractive. Alexandre had watched in awe at how effortlessly they executed multiple turns and gracefully raised their legs high above their heads. Even so, there was only one woman he wanted to be with.

"I'm sure Evie can introduce you to people."

"That's okay. I'm actually seeing someone." The words tumbled out before Alexandre could stop them.

Luc's eyebrows shot up.

"It's really new," Alexandre hurried to add.

Luc clapped him on the shoulder. "That's great! How'd you meet her?"

"In person."

"Where?"

"It's so new I don't want to talk about it."

"Sounds promising!"

"It is." Alexandre sipped his beer, his eyes straying to Mei. She was talking animatedly with Ali and Evie. His heart swelled. He turned back to Luc. "I have a feeling you'll like her."

"Well, cheers to that!" Luc tapped his pint against Alexandre's. "I can't wait to meet her."

• • •

The bar turned up the music. Evie and her friends crowded the dance floor. Ali and Luc followed, beckoning Alexandre and Mei to join them.

"Want to dance?" Mei asked.

Alexandre shook his head. "I don't want you to have second thoughts about me. My dancing is the stuff of nightmares."

Mei threw back her head and laughed. "Somehow, I doubt that." Her hand discreetly brushed his back as she strutted to the dance floor.

Alexandre smiled and watched her go, then grabbed a curly fry from the plate in front of him.

"Hey, are you the biology professor?"

Alexandre looked up from his food. A toned young woman with a slicked-back ponytail and short black halter dress stood by his elbow.

"I'm a biology professor, but I don't know if I'm *the* biology professor," he said.

The woman laughed. "I'm Liz. I dance with Evie, and I'm getting my PhD at NYU. When Evie mentioned you were coming, I was hoping to chat. My research is on developing low-cost cancer screenings."

"Mine was on mobility and aging."

As Alexandre traded research stories with Liz, a familiar excitement buzzed through him. He missed this scientist-to-scientist banter. Liz reminded him of his long-lost self. She was full of the optimism that comes with nearing the end of a PhD and imagining all the possibilities ahead.

Liz took out her phone. "Let's grab dinner sometime. What's your number?"

Alexandre suddenly noticed how close Liz was standing, how much she was angled toward him. He stepped back to put more space between them. "I can give you my work email if you ever want to discuss your research." He glimpsed Mei on the dance floor. She threw him a quizzical look. Alexandre shook his head and flashed her a reassuring smile.

Understanding dawned on Liz's face. "Oh, my bad. I didn't realize that was your girlfriend. Evie didn't mention that."

"Well, she's not exactly my girlfriend. It's complicated."

Liz laughed. "Got it. I know how that goes. Well, it was nice chatting." She gave a little wave, then shimmied back to her friends.

Alexandre scanned the dance floor for Mei. She smiled with her eyes when their gazes met.

Was it really complicated between them? No, Alexandre decided. It wasn't. He and Mei might be overcomplicating their relationship by not defining it and keeping it a secret.

But in his heart, Alexandre knew how he felt about her, and his feelings weren't complicated at all.

CHAPTER THIRTY-THREE

Drinks were flowing and the dance floor was still packed when Mei, Alexandre, Ali, and Luc called it a night. They said goodbye to Evie and walked outside.

"Do you want a ride?" Alexandre asked Mei, just as they'd planned.

Mei embraced Luc, then Ali. "Get home safely."

"You too." Ali hugged her back, glancing from her to Alexandre, a question in her eyes, a smirk on her lips.

After Ali and Luc left, Mei grabbed Alexandre's hand, and they ran the two blocks to his car. Once inside, she relished his cold cheeks against hers, thawing as they kissed.

Back at her place, they shucked off their winter layers and hopped into bed.

Mei ran her hand over Alexandre's chest. "I was looking forward to this all night."

He tangled his fingers in her hair. "I was, too."

"I don't know," she teased. "You could've gone home with one of the dancers. That girl was hitting on you, right?" Mei had seen one of Evie's friends approach Alexandre. Possessiveness had overcome her, but when Alexandre had looked at her and smiled,

Mei knew she had nothing to worry about. *He's mine*, she'd thought with certainty.

Alexandre chuckled. "Yeah, I didn't think so at first. She's a PhD candidate at NYU, so she was telling me about her research."

"Is it similar to what you were doing?"

"No, but it was interesting. She's working on cost-efficient cancer screenings for underserved populations. Even though she's still a student, she's pretty accomplished."

Mei stiffened. Was she accomplished, too?

"What's wrong?" He touched her lips. "You're frowning."

"I'm not a talented dancer like Evie and her friends. I'm not doing lifesaving research, either." She forced a laugh. "I guess I'm just a boring old normie."

"How can you say that? This may come as a shock, but most people don't run global campaigns for a famous company. Millions of people have seen your work, and thanks to you, they've seen themselves reflected in it, too."

A little smile tugged at Mei's lips. She nodded begrudgingly.

"Need I also remind you that last week, I was feeling like I wasn't good enough for you?"

"Which is so ridiculous!" Mei rolled on top of him. "You're perfect for me."

"And you for me."

Mei grinned through their kiss.

"So what do you think about telling people about us?" Alexandre whispered. "Evie's friend asked if you were my girlfriend. I wanted to say yes. Luc also asked if I was dating. I said I was, but didn't give any details. It would be nice to tell everyone the truth."

Alexandre's kind eyes searched hers. Mei blew out a breath. They'd already shared so many fears and insecurities. What was one more?

"I'm afraid of ruining everything."

"With us? How?"

"By doing something that would make you hate me forever, which would destroy everything for Ali, Luc, and Kaia, too."

"How could you possibly think that? I could never hate you, no matter what happens. If we ever broke up, we'd figure it out. We're adults. So are Ali and Luc." He shook his head. "But I don't think we need to worry about that."

Alexandre clearly couldn't imagine them not working out. Mei bit back her smile. "Okay. Let's tell them. Maybe when you're back from the conference?" That would give her two weeks to work up her courage.

Alexandre's eyes shone with anticipation. "Let's do it."

Despite her apprehension, an unexpected thrill ran through Mei. Telling Ali and Luc was the first step to her and Alexandre being out in the world as a couple. Mei caressed his cheek, tracing his fine jaw. He kissed her tenderly, making her shiver. *The beginning of us.*

• • •

The following Friday evening, Mei took a seat at Alexandre's new dining table and dug into the roasted chicken, orzo, and vegetables he'd cooked for her.

He passed her a glass of cider. "Congrats on your interviews!"

"Thanks!" Mei clinked her cup against his. "I'm exhausted, but

I feel great." She'd called in sick to Livin and interviewed with Pure in the morning and We're the First in the afternoon.

"I want to hear everything. How was Pure?"

"Kind of like a much smaller Livin." She'd met with Whitney Allen, the CEO of the sustainable cleaning company, at their Chelsea office. "They only have a hundred employees, and their marketing budget is a fraction of what I have now."

"Not every startup has billions of dollars to throw around."

"Ha! True. Whitney said they're rolling out three new products, partnering with a big nonprofit, and expanding to Canada and the U.K. I'd report directly to her and oversee the entire marketing strategy and team."

"That's exciting! How was We're the First?"

"Different. In a good way." The nonprofit had a small office in Midtown East that was, admittedly, cramped and dated. "Paz Bautista, the director, was also a first-gen student. We talked about the challenges we'd faced, and that the organization's students face, like understanding that private colleges can be an option with enough financial aid." She polished off her orzo. "I'd be raising the organization's profile among first-gen students still in high school by attending college fairs, holding events, and running social media campaigns."

"You'd be joining me in the academic world."

"Yeah! I love the work they're doing. Pure's mission resonates with me, too. They're a Black- and women-owned business. Whitney said Pure is her way of fighting climate change by making concentrated, plastic-free products that cut down on waste. Unlike some companies that just pretend to save the world." She rolled her eyes.

Alexandre served her a second helping. "Did you discuss comp?"

"I did. I'd have to negotiate, but my base at Pure would be a little more than I'm making now." Mei frowned. "I'd have to take a major pay cut at We're the First. The most they could offer is half my salary."

"Oof."

"Yeah." She'd barely be able to live on it. Saving would be out of the question. "I don't think I can afford it." Mei's stomach tightened. "Does that make me a terrible person?"

"No. You can't take a job that's going to cause you financial stress."

"Maybe I can volunteer for them, or do some pro bono marketing."

"If you have time! You're trying to break the burnout cycle, not overload yourself before you even get a new job. Did you ask about Pure's work/life balance?"

"I did. Whitney said it's a priority. They have a flexible policy where you set your own hours and days in the office. People tend to work forty to forty-five hours a week, not sixty or seventy."

"That sounds perfect."

"Right? I'd have so much free time."

"Time to get the rest of your life back." He shot her a devilish grin. "And time to spend with me."

"Definitely." Mei leaned in to kiss him.

"So you'd take the job?"

Mei chewed her lip. Would she? The thought of leaving Livin made her nauseous. But really, what was left for her there? Fourteen-hour days of chipping away at pointless goals only to have them reset every month? Managers she didn't trust? Being overlooked and underappreciated by the execs? Sure, she loved her teammates. But Mei was pretty sure they were job hunting, too. She'd spied Bryce's résumé on his laptop when she'd walked by the other day. Tamiko had updated her LinkedIn profile with a snazzy new headshot and all her Livin responsibilities.

Pure would never be a major global brand like Livin. Maybe that was okay. She'd have a smart, supportive manager. Mei had also met the senior members of Pure's marketing team; they were all kind, intelligent, and brimming with enthusiasm for the company. *Like how I used to be with Livin.*

At Pure, she'd have work/life balance.

And she'd be a VP, a position that still eluded her at Livin.

Mei nodded. "If they offer me the job, I'll take it."

"Yes!" Alexandre reached around the table to pull her into a hug.

Mei laughed, squeezing him back. "Whitney said I should hear from her next week. That seems like a good sign."

CHAPTER THIRTY-FOUR

A chilly wind whipped off Lake Erie. Alexandre clutched his jacket tighter and stepped up his pace. Ahead, the glassy Cleveland convention center beckoned with warm light.

"Welcome to the 18th Annual International Zebrafish Researchers Symposium!" proclaimed a banner at the entrance.

Alexandre smiled ruefully at the sign. He still wasn't thrilled about being there. Just when he was committing to his new life, he was being thrown back into his old one.

At the check-in table, Alexandre received his name tag and a pom-pom winter hat with knitted zebrafish on the rim. He snapped a selfie in the hat and sent the photo to Mei.

Now I'm ready for this.

Mei's reply sounded on his phone.

Ready to make a splash at your LAST zebrafish conference ever! Peace, Danio rerio! ✌

Alexandre laughed at Mei's use of the scientific name for zebrafish. Spirits buoyed, he pocketed his phone and walked to the auditorium for the welcome session.

• • •

Alexandre fell into his conference routine with ease. He attended the keynote and specialized tracks in the morning, networked during poster sessions, and caught up with former colleagues over coffee.

As he'd planned, and despite his name tag saying "University of Oregon," Alexandre referred to himself as a SUNY New Paltz professor. At first, he was hesitant and—he hated to admit—embarrassed. But as the day went on, he found himself standing up straighter and speaking with pride.

"You had the right idea, getting out," said Ethan, one of Alexandre's past collaborators from Yale. "The grind is getting old. I still haven't made tenure and don't see it happening anytime soon. Between you and me, I've taken a few meetings with pharma recruiters."

"I'm transitioning to teaching, too," said Michelle, another of Alexandre's former contacts. She'd been a research scientist at Rutgers for years. "I'm starting at Williams this fall. I've always wanted to live in the Berkshires."

All that shame and despair for nothing, Alexandre thought as he waited in line for lunch.

• • •

On Wednesday morning, halfway through the mobility breakout session, Alexandre strode onto the low stage and faced the audience.

"I'm Dr. Alexandre Brodeur from the University of Oregon." Saying the name of his former employer jarred him, though he didn't let on. "Today I'm presenting a comparative study on the influence of five common mutations on midlife adult zebrafish."

Fifteen minutes always passed quickly, though Alexandre had learned to pace his talk so he could get through the methodology, results, and conclusion.

During the five-minute Q&A, Alexandre tried not to roll his eyes while answering the egomaniacal questions that were typical at every conference: "No, I did not read your *Science* article that came out this morning." "I'm not familiar with the Ebola research you published five years ago, but from what you describe, it's not quite relevant to mobility and aging."

My students ask better questions, Alexandre thought as he left the stage.

• • •

Alexandre reclined against the wooden headboard of his hotel bed and smiled when Mei appeared on his phone. Her eyes looked tired but brightened when she saw him.

"You called at the right time," she said. "I'm in between sprints."

Alexandre frowned. "Is Sprint Week a startup thing or just a Livin thing?"

"Who knows?" A few of Livin's marketing teams missed their

January goals, so Erika was making Mei and her colleagues do sprints every night for a week. They had to log on from eight to nine, then ten to eleven, to crank out as much work as they could. "It's brutal."

"Hopefully you'll be gone soon."

"Well, actually . . ." A grin crept across Mei's face. "Pure made me an offer today."

"Congratulations! Are you happy with it?"

"Yes. The salary is a bump up from what I'm making, and I already asked for more. They came back to me two hours later and said they could do it."

"Are you going to take it?" Alexandre held his breath.

Mei nodded. "I'm giving my notice tomorrow."

"YES!" Alexandre leapt up from the bed.

Mei laughed at his reaction. "I couldn't have done it without you."

"You deserve all the credit. You got the interview and wowed them with your talent." He sighed wistfully. "I wish I were there with you."

"I wish you were, too. How's the conference?"

"Kind of like a high school reunion. Being here reminds me of who I used to be, with people from that part of my life. I'll be happier when I'm home." Alexandre took in the graceful curve of Mei's lips, the slight flush in her cheeks. "I can't wait to see you," he said quietly. Alexandre hoped Mei could see the tenderness in his eyes, the feelings he couldn't say just yet. Not over a video call from a budget hotel in Cleveland.

Affection flowed from Mei's gaze, warming Alexandre to his core. "Me too," she said.

• • •

Alexandre waited by the conference center entrance, occasionally waving to a passing colleague. With the symposium winding down, people were beginning to depart. Alexandre adjusted his backpack on his shoulder. He was heading to the airport after this last coffee meeting.

He'd run into Chris Saunders a few times during the conference. His old mentor had been hurrying from one engagement to another, so each encounter had been brief and cordial—just enough time for Alexandre to share that he was now at SUNY New Paltz, and for Chris to say that he'd left UChicago for the University of North Dakota. Alexandre was shocked. Chris had been tenured at UChicago for as long as he'd known him. So when Alexandre had woken up to an email from Chris this morning, asking if they could meet for coffee, he assumed Chris would tell him the whole story.

Alexandre spotted his former mentor's bald head, bushy white beard, and circular glasses. He walked over, and they exchanged a hearty handshake.

"So you're now at the University of North Dakota?" Alexandre asked once they were seated at a café a few blocks away.

"One year, as of May," Chris said. "You're now at SUNY New Paltz?"

"Since the fall."

"They have a research program?" Chris's tone was curious, not condescending, which Alexandre appreciated.

"No, I'm teaching now." Alexandre caught himself before saying "just teaching," a reflex that filled him with self-loathing.

"Got it." Chris cocked his head. "So you're not doing research now. But do you have any interest in picking up where you left off? Starting fresh at a new lab?"

A sick feeling unspooled in Alexandre's stomach. He'd known, deep down, that this was why Chris wanted to meet. He just hadn't let himself imagine how the conversation might play out. "Why? Are you hiring?"

"I am. What do you think about North Dakota?"

"I, um, well, I've never been there." *Or ever really thought about it.*

Chris laughed. "Sorry. Let me back up. You're probably wondering why I left UChicago. World-class university. Tenure. I was set for life."

Well, how nice for you. Alexandre swallowed his resentment and nodded.

"I still have a good ten, fifteen years before retiring, though. I didn't have the university's support for the kind of research I wanted to do. They blocked me at every turn. In the end, I had a choice: ride out my time there knowing I'd never reach my full potential. Or pursue my dream elsewhere."

Alexandre smiled wryly. "I get that. I didn't switch to teaching for those exact reasons, but there are some parallels."

"I had a hunch. It's a common predicament, as you know. Anyway, I put out feelers. I learned that UND is building up their biology department. They want to make it competitive with the top programs. That'll take time, of course. But they needed someone to run with that vision."

Alexandre raised his eyebrows. "That's huge. I can't think of a better person than you."

"Thank you." Chris smiled. "Our new lab opens in May: a six-thousand-tank facility with robotic feeding and cleaning systems. State-of-the-art equipment. I've also secured funding for the next few years."

"Wow." Chris had just described every scientist's dream. "And you're hiring."

"I am." Chris sat back, satisfied. "I'm looking for a few tenure-track professors, like yourself, to help me establish UND as a research powerhouse. I want your work on genetics, mobility, and aging to be a cornerstone of this department."

"I'm flattered you thought of me." Alexandre barely found his voice.

"You know I've always been a fan of your work. I'm sorry I haven't been in touch these last few years. It's been a real whirlwind with job hunting, wrapping up my life in Chicago, and relocating to North Dakota while diving right into my new position."

"I was doing the same with moving to New York." All this time, Alexandre assumed he'd fallen out of contact with Chris, when his mentor was undergoing a similar life transition.

"I imagine you're pretty settled at New Paltz now." Chris leaned forward in his seat. "But is there any chance you'd be interested in applying to UND?"

"Where, exactly, is UND?" Alexandre choked out.

Chris laughed. "Grand Forks. Right on the state line with Minnesota. Eighty miles north of Fargo, eighty miles south of the Canadian border. Nice little city. A beautiful greenway along the Red River."

Alexandre sipped his coffee. Chris was offering him a chance to fulfill the dream he'd chased his entire life. The dream that still lingered in the depths of his mind. At UND, he'd be set up for success in a way he'd never been, with funding, a new lab, and his mentor, who'd always seen the best in him. He could make tenure in five years. Seven, max. He could go back to work/life balance after that. Hopefully.

Alexandre thought of Dr. Johnson and his New Paltz students. Could he leave them already? Alexandre's heart sank further, picturing Luc, Ali, and Kaia. He'd be back to seeing them once a year, if that. Weeklong vacations to places like Hawaiʻi would be out of the question. Not with tenure on the line, and his career dependent on every experiment, publication, grant, and conference—plus, thousands of live zebrafish.

Mei's face appeared in his mind. He could kiss any future with her goodbye if he took the UND job. Alexandre would never be able to afford frequent flights to New York, and he doubted Mei would move to Grand Forks. In the unlikely event she did, she'd be miserable, away from her sister, all the career opportunities in New York, and the city's energy that was so vital to her spirit. All the while, he'd never see her. He'd always be working.

Then there was their pact. Mei was quitting Livin today. How would she feel if he came home and told her he was pursuing a tenure-track research job? In *North Dakota*.

"It's a lot to think about," Chris said.

Alexandre set down his coffee. A rush of anger surged through him, surprising Alexandre with its ferocity. Why wasn't this UND job available when he desperately needed a lifeline? When it came to his research career, why was he always at the wrong place at the wrong time, making decisions that never turned out well?

I'm done. Alexandre huffed. He'd come to this conference to slam the door shut on his old life, and now he was going to do exactly that.

He turned back to his old mentor's kind face. "I really appreciate you thinking of me, Chris. But I'm not interested in the job."

CHAPTER THIRTY-FIVE

Mei peered up from her laptop and smiled at the "Livin the Good Life" graffiti mural spanning an entire wall. Now that she was about to meet Erika and give her notice, Mei was starting to view her time at Livin through a rosy hue.

Outside the Amsterdam conference room, Mei took a deep breath. She mentally rehearsed the resignation speech she'd prepared. She opened the door, then blinked in surprise. Erika was seated at the table, looking pristine as usual, in a burgundy silk blouse. James sat beside her in his typical white shirt and blue slacks, his face scrunched up in distaste at the floor-to-ceiling windmill and potted tulips.

"Hi, Erika. Good to see you, James." Mei forced a smile. She hadn't met with James in months. Why hadn't Erika told her he was joining their one-on-one?

"You're probably wondering why James is here," Erika said. "What we're about to tell you is confidential. It's about the future of Livin."

Mei's eyes widened. What was this all about?

"We've decided to let you and a select few of your colleagues in on these plans," James said. "With our IPO timing more concrete—"

"—in September," Erika supplied.

"Our financials will be subject to tight scrutiny," James said. "Right now, we're too heavy on human capital. Investors know that people don't scale. Technology does. We need to rightsize our workforce and replace manpower with tech-forward solutions."

Mei's mouth went dry. "Layoffs."

"Next week," James confirmed.

"How many people?"

"It'll vary by department, but we're cutting marketing by thirty percent," Erika said.

Mei did the math. "Forty-five marketers." Forty-five of her friends and teammates. "And how many overall?"

"Three thousand."

Mei narrowed her eyes. "That's why we're doing sprints this week. So you can wring the most out of people before firing them."

"Productivity takes a hit after layoffs." James shrugged. "We need to set ourselves up for success."

"Sprint Week is going so well, though!" Erika said. "We should keep doing them after the layoffs."

Mei glared at her. "Who's getting laid off from my team?"

James consulted his laptop. "The two guys in New York—Bryce and Kaden."

"Kaden uses they/them pronouns," Mei shot back.

"From your regional reports, Yiwen from APAC, Anne-Marie from EMEA, and Xochitl from LATAM."

"That's half my team!" At least Bryce was job hunting. Hopefully everyone else was, too. "How do you expect me to run campaigns without brand managers and strategists?"

"Generative AI has really improved!" Erika said. "The board would love to see us use it to streamline costs."

"Yeah, AI can spit out content and strategies, but you still need *real people* to make sure they're on-brand, high-quality, and accurate!"

James scowled at Erika. "I knew this was a mistake," he grumbled.

"What's a mistake?" Mei asked.

"Keeping you. I was in favor of cutting you, based on your tepid performance last fall. But Erika insisted."

"Mei, you're one of our biggest talents," Erika said. "We need you to make sure the Livin brand stays consistently amazing through the layoffs and automation. It'll be a challenge, for sure, but I know you're up for it. If anyone can do it, it's you."

Mei hated herself for perking up at the praise.

"This is your chance to step into a real leadership role and shape the future of Livin. Not to mention our team culture." She shot James a look to jump in.

"We're also planning to reward people who stay, if all goes well," he said.

Mei's heart pounded with dread. "How?"

"Raises. Bonuses. Additional options."

"How much are we talking about?"

"Let's just say that you'll actually know what it's like to be a rich girl."

Mei didn't even react to James's snide remark. She was too

focused on the dollar signs flashing before her. She saw her bank account balance skyrocket with tens, then hundreds of thousands of dollars, replenishing the hard-earned savings she'd lost last fall.

"We'll also do promotions," Erika added. "You'll be our VP of brand marketing."

"What will you be?" Mei asked.

Erika smoothed her hair. "Senior VP of marketing."

"In a month or two, after the dust settles," James said. "We need investors to think we're saving money."

Mei's mind whirred. Livin was a much-larger, higher-valued company than Pure would ever be. After her promotion, her salary would be substantially higher than anything Pure could offer. She'd get another major windfall from all her options after the IPO, and now she knew when it would be. September. Seven months away.

Still, those months would be brutal. Mei had survived layoffs at previous jobs, and the aftermath was always chaotic. Morale plummeted. Her workload increased exponentially because she had fewer teammates. Many employees who didn't get laid off ended up leaving anyway.

"What would happen if I didn't want to be part of this?" Mei asked hesitantly.

"Then you'd just leave," James said. "Since we weren't planning to fire you, you wouldn't get a severance package." He fixed her with a pointed look. "Is that what you want?"

"No! I was just wondering!"

"Mei, I hope you see the extraordinary opportunity we're giving you," Erika said. "We were even thinking"—she glanced at James, who nodded—"that you could join us onstage at Livin Forum to show off your latest campaign with the new inclusive imagery."

Mei's breath caught. Livin Forum was the company's annual strategy meeting. It was like Livinpalooza, except it was actually work-related. Every employee from around the world, and many investors and board members, flew in for a week of talks, events, and team-building activities. This year's Livin Forum was in Los Angeles at the end of the month. Mei grew starry-eyed as she imagined herself onstage in front of twelve thousand people.

Well, nine thousand, after the layoffs.

Erika was right. This was an amazing opportunity. She would be VP of brand marketing at the world's hottest unicorn. She could lead the marketing team through the layoffs, then rebuild with a stronger, healthier, more inclusive culture. She didn't love the idea of replacing people with AI, but there were, admittedly, some tasks she wouldn't mind automating, like repurposing a keynote script as a blog post.

And after all the systems were in place, she'd get a massive payday from the IPO.

She'd never have to worry about money again.

Pure was so dinky in comparison. Why on earth had she wanted to work there?

Mei's heart clenched. *Alexandre.* Their pact. He'd actually leapt in the air last night when she said she was quitting.

And it wasn't just him. She'd told Ali and Luc she was leaving, too. They were taking her out to lunch on Sunday to celebrate her new job—and for her and Alexandre to tell them about their relationship.

Everyone will still be proud of me, Mei told herself. *I'll explain everything.*

She lifted her chin. "Thanks for bringing me in on the plan. I'm happy to partner with you on anything you need."

James cracked a smile.

Erika's eyes gleamed. "Perfect. We have loads to do. I'm blocking the next hour for us."

• • •

Mei emerged from the Amsterdam room, her brain teeming with details. The layoffs were next Wednesday. On Valentine's Day. Bile had risen to Mei's mouth when Erika told her, with a little cackle, that the execs had dubbed the layoffs "Operation My Bloody Valentine."

Back in the common room, the final events of Sprint Week were about to begin. The marketing team was going to sprint from five to six, break for dinner, do a final sprint from seven to eight, then celebrate.

Buoyant dance music pounded through the speakers. People filled tumblers with beer. The air crackled with excitement, even though everyone was spending Friday night working.

Mei poured herself a beer from the tap. Normally, she tried not to drink at Livin events, but today called for an alcoholic beverage.

She checked her phone. Alexandre had texted an hour ago.

Just boarded! Should be landing around seven. I have the wildest story to tell you tomorrow. Talk about a crazy end to the conference.

But more importantly: How did it feel to quit? 😀

Mei inhaled through her nose. There was no way she could tell Alexandre her news over text. At least it sounded like he had something big to share, too. Mei typed back:

I'll tell you everything tomorrow!

His reply came a moment later.

Can't wait to hear! I'm so proud of you, Mei. We're doing it. YOU DID IT!

Mei shoved her phone into her pocket. She made her way through the tables of marketers until she found her team. Kaden, Bryce, and Tamiko were chatting with the good-natured air of people who'd resigned themselves to Sprint Week but would rather be elsewhere.

Mei took a seat beside them, swallowing her guilt about the impending layoffs. "Ready to wrap this up?"

Tamiko groaned. "Beyond ready."

"Are these Sprint Weeks going to be a regular thing?" Kaden asked.

"I think so," Mei said.

Her team rolled their eyes.

"Attention, marketers!" Erika called into a mic. "Are you ready to sprint?"

For the next hour, Mei forced herself to work.

During the dinner break, Kaden turned to Mei. "So much for leaving early on Fridays."

Mei paused, her samosa burger halfway to her mouth. "What do you mean?"

"Remember a few weeks ago, you said we should all leave at six on Fridays? And we did?"

Mei nodded. Uneasiness seeped through her.

"We never did that again, and it looks like we'll have fewer chances to, with these Sprint Weeks."

Mei ran through the last few weeks in her head. She'd been out last Friday for job interviews. The week before was Evie's dance performance, so she'd stayed late until it began. She should have set a better example for her team.

"I'm sorry," Mei said.

She surveyed the room. People packed the space. Erika wouldn't notice if someone was missing. Well, not until she tabulated the finished work. Unless Mei reallocated a few pieces from one sprint to another.

Mei caught her teammates' eyes, then lowered her voice. "If any of you want to cut out early, I'll cover for you."

Kaden, Bryce, and Tamiko exchanged surprised looks. They quietly considered her offer.

"I should get home, but I'll stay for the last sprint," Bryce said.

Mei couldn't think of anything to say. Bryce had done the unthinkable and climbed out of the bottom three percent. His wife and son had stayed with her parents every weekend in January so he could work uninterrupted. He'd saved himself from being fired for his performance, and now he was getting laid off anyway.

"I'll stay, too," Kaden said.

"We're all in this together," Tamiko agreed.

"We are." Mei looked away. The crowd at the beer taps was several people deep. Drinks sloshed onto the floor. How good was the work everyone was producing tonight?

"All right, marketers!" Erika's voice trilled through the speakers. "Let's get our final sprint on!"

• • •

Mei cracked her eyes open and squinted. Why was the sun so bright? She fumbled for her phone, then bolted upright. It was past ten. How had she slept so late? Mei winced, remembering the three beers she'd downed at last night's Sprint Week party.

Alexandre would be here soon. Mei clicked on her text icon, surprised at the number of unread messages.

They were all in her group chat with Alexandre, Ali, and Luc.

Ali: Morning! Any chance we can do lunch today? Kaia's friends are having a playdate tomorrow and she wants to go.

Alexandre: Sure, I'm dying to tell you guys what happened at the conference yesterday. Mei, lunch today works for you, right?

On and on it went. When Mei didn't chime in, they assumed she was still sleeping after Sprint Week. In the meantime, they were all getting ready to drive down and meet for dim sum at noon. The thread wrapped up with a text from Alexandre:

We have so much to celebrate!

Mei groaned. Her news was still kind of worth celebrating, even if it wasn't what everyone was expecting. She sent a quick reply, then dashed into the shower.

• • •

Mei found Alexandre waiting outside the Upper West Side outpost of a popular dim sum parlor. His face was the picture of joy as he swept her into a tight embrace.

"I'd kiss you, but Luc just texted that they're walking over from the car," he whispered.

Mei let out a strangled chuckle. Alexandre looked extra handsome in his black winter jacket. He buzzed with restless energy. Then he looked at her closely.

"Is everything okay?" His brow creased with concern.

"It's just been an emotional week."

"For sure." Alexandre rubbed her shoulder. "We'll have a relaxing weekend."

Ali, Luc, and Kaia arrived. Soon they were seated. A sumptuous spread of small plates lay before them: har gow, shumai, beef cheung fun, char siu baos, and shrimp and snow pea leaf dumplings.

"So?" Ali grinned across the table. "Sounds like you two have a lot to share."

If only we just had to tell them about us! Mei gestured to Alexandre beside her. "You go first. What happened at the conference?"

"So yesterday, right before I left, I met with Chris Saunders. My old mentor," he explained to Ali and Luc as he dipped a shumai in chili oil. "He recently left the University of Chicago to build up the biology department at the University of North Dakota. He secured a ton of funding and is opening a new zebrafish lab. And he's hiring. He offered me the chance to work with him, restart my research, and get back on tenure track."

Mei's jaw dropped. "Whoa."

Luc's eyes widened, then narrowed. "Are you going to do it?"

Mei's breathing went shallow. Either way, she was screwed. If Alexandre pursued the job, he was moving to North Dakota. If he rejected the offer, that made her news so much worse.

"Nope." Alexandre grinned triumphantly. "I turned it down on the spot."

"Yes!" Luc reached across the table and clapped Alexandre's shoulder.

"Good for you!" Ali cried.

"Amazing!" Mei choked out.

"I'm so proud of you," Luc said. "You chose yourself, your health, and the new life you've worked so hard to build."

Mei's hands shook as she took a tiny sip of tea.

"I'm proud of myself, too. I couldn't wait to tell all of you. Especially you." Alexandre smiled affectionately at Mei. "I couldn't have done this without you."

She stared at her lap. "I didn't do anything."

"How can you say that? Whenever I was down about my job, you cheered me up and reminded me why I chose it. You helped me stay strong against my doubts and fears." He passed the shumai to Ali and Luc. "In Hawai'i, we made a pact to help each other with work/life balance. Mei made sure I didn't go back to research, and I encouraged her to get out of Livin."

"Look at you two now!" Ali said. "You've done it!"

Mei kept a smile plastered to her face. A cold sweat ran down her back.

"I'm talking way too much," Alexandre said to her. "I want to hear all about yesterday."

His elated smile made Mei want to die. "So, ah, um—"

"Mei! So funny seeing you here!" a familiar voice interrupted.

No way. Mei glanced up to see her boss, clad in a pink cashmere sweater and expensive-looking jeans. "Erika! What are you doing here?"

"Having lunch with Dean. My husband." Erika inclined her head toward a tall Asian man sitting at a window table. "We live a few blocks away. We're regulars here."

Mei swallowed her surprise. She'd always pictured Erika's husband as a rich, preppy white guy.

Erika was introducing herself to Alexandre, Ali, Luc, and Kaia. "Mei works for me at Livin. She's one of our all-stars. We're going to take Livin's marketing to new heights. We just had a big strategy session yesterday to map out the next few months."

Ali and Luc were still smiling at Erika, but Mei saw the confusion on their faces. Alexandre's eyes bored into her.

Erika winked at Mei. "Didn't I tell you that if you stuck with me, you'd come out on top? Our soon-to-be VP. Anyway, I gotta get back to Dean. More fun on Monday, Mei!"

Everyone watched Erika strut off.

Mei drew a shuddering breath. Avoiding everyone's eyes, she pointed to a steamer basket. "Anyone want the last har gow?"

"So . . . you didn't quit?" Ali asked.

"No."

"You were so excited about Pure."

"I was. But before I could give Erika my notice, she and James shared some news. This is all confidential." Mei lowered her voice and relayed the plans for the IPO and layoffs. Ali and Luc listened, visibly concerned. They both recoiled when she mentioned "Operation My Bloody Valentine." Mei still couldn't look at Alexandre. She was aware of his leg no longer pressing against hers. A stony vibe emanated from him.

"The next month will be rough, but we'll get through it. I'll be in a bigger leadership role." Why had her voice taken on a pleading tone? Where was the conviction she'd felt yesterday? "I'll make the culture healthier."

"Do you really think that'll happen?" Ali asked.

"I do."

"Man, those layoffs." Luc shook his head. "You were already so slammed. Now you'll have to do everything, plus all the work your teammates did."

"But we'll have more tech-driven solutions."

Alexandre still hadn't said anything. Mei finally made herself look at him. The expression on his face made her heart seize. Hurt, betrayal, sadness, and anger shone in his eyes.

Yell. Scream. Say something. Anything was better than sitting here awash in his silence.

CHAPTER THIRTY-SIX

Alexandre stared at Mei. No matter how many times he repeated it to himself, he couldn't believe it. Mei was staying at Livin.

Her eyes begged him to say something.

"You didn't even tell me," was all Alexandre could get out.

"You were traveling! I wasn't going to tell you over text."

"Maybe you didn't want to tell me at all."

Hurt flickered on Mei's face. Alexandre almost reached for her hand. Then her eyes flashed defiantly.

"You're right. I didn't want to tell you. Or you." She thrust her chin toward Ali and Luc. "But can't you see what an incredible opportunity this is? I'm finally going to get promoted to VP. And I'll present at Livin Forum. That's a big deal!"

Alexandre sighed. "Are you sure about that? The people making those promises are the assholes who screwed you out of that very same promotion just a few months ago." Out of the corner of his eye, Alexandre saw Ali frown at his sharp tone. "Also, not every job is worth taking. I just turned down my own *incredible opportunity* because even though it seems perfect, it's going to be hell. Like staying at Livin!"

"Well, you've had way more opportunities than I've had," Mei shot back. "I never get chances like this."

The still-lucid part of Alexandre's brain knew Mei was right. Throughout his life, he'd had more than her in every realm: money, privilege, education, family support. He was a straight white man in a world built for him. The fact that Mei was so successful was a testament to her strength, resilience, and intelligence.

The gracious move would've been to say so. But Alexandre couldn't stop the words flying out of his mouth.

"What did you say back in Hawai'i? About learning from self-delusion and knowing to stop when you're headed down the wrong path? What happened to that? The last time didn't work out so well, did it? Are you just going to keep making empty promises to me, and yourself, and everyone else, while you dig deeper into that shitshow company you're so devoted to?"

Mei flinched. She narrowed her eyes. "Speaking of self-delusion, are *you* being honest with yourself? You act like I wronged you by not quitting. But maybe you're just pissed because I know what I want and *you don't*."

Alexandre sat stricken. The anger in Mei's eyes extinguished. She looked at him with sorrow.

Ali and Luc exchanged a glance.

"I'll get the check." Luc hurried to the counter.

Ali helped Kaia into her coat. "We'll get going and let you two talk."

Mei grabbed her jacket. "I'll walk out with you."

In front of the restaurant, Alexandre stood off to the side while the sisters talked. At one point, Ali scowled at him. Great. He and Ali had always gotten along spectacularly. Now he was a jerk who'd been mean to her sister.

"I'm sorry for the scene in there," Alexandre said when Ali came over to say goodbye.

"It's okay. I know you're upset." Ali smiled tightly, then turned her attention to Kaia.

Luc clasped his shoulder. "I don't know what's going on with you and Mei," he said quietly, "but I know you'll figure it out."

After they left, Alexandre walked over to Mei. "Want to chat?"

She shrugged. "There's a spot a couple blocks away."

They trudged in silence to a little park outside the American Museum of Natural History. Alexandre registered the gaping distance between him and Mei as they sat down on a bench.

"Look," she said, "I get why you're upset. I'm sorry I didn't tell you about Livin. I knew you wouldn't understand, and you don't."

Alexandre laughed mirthlessly. "I do and I don't."

Mei acknowledged his remark with a wry huff. She watched a squirrel dig in the scraggly grass. "I'm not changing my mind. Where does that leave us?"

Alexandre searched her face for any hope or affection. All he saw was anger. Weariness.

His own exhaustion hit him. He rubbed his eyes. "I don't know. I can't think right now."

His heart broke a little as Mei nodded. "Yeah. I need some time, too."

"I guess I'll get going."

Mei didn't move to hug him. Alexandre didn't reach for her, either.

• • •

Back at his apartment, Alexandre tried to lose himself in unpacking and laundry. All the while, Mei's words echoed through his mind. *Are* you *being honest with yourself?*

As upset as he was, Alexandre missed Mei. He grappled with his phone every time it buzzed, hoping to see her name on the screen. It never appeared.

When he woke up on Sunday morning, Alexandre's head was clearer, but his heart still ached. He laced up his sneakers and went for a run. *What do you really want?* Alexandre asked himself with every step. Mei immediately came to mind. But it was the spirited, optimistic Mei he thought he knew, not the stony-eyed woman who put Livin above everything.

Afterward, Alexandre stood in his entryway. For the first time since leaving Oregon, Alexandre missed his lab. He missed the zenlike zebrafish facility with row after row of clear tanks, quietly gurgling with flowing water. He missed losing himself in endless columns of data. And he missed the fire that fueled him when he was on the verge of a major discovery.

Who was he kidding? He'd been so wrong about Mei. Was he just fooling himself about his new job, too?

There was only one way to find out.

Alexandre opened his laptop and drafted an email.

Hi Chris,

It was great catching up with you at the conference. Thanks again for reaching out to me with the UND opportunity. Now that I've had time to think about it, I realize I was a bit hasty. Could we set up a time to talk this week?

Alexandre

CHAPTER THIRTY-SEVEN

Mei lay on her couch, staring at the ceiling. She couldn't stop seeing the hurt in Alexandre's eyes, or hearing his angry words. Why had Erika, of all people, been the one to tell him she was staying at Livin? Mei buried her face in a pillow and screamed.

Still, no matter how many times she parsed through the ugly scene, Mei couldn't think of anything she would have done differently.

She eyed her phone. Alexandre hadn't called or texted. Even though she was still angry, she longed for him to reach out. *I'm sorry*, he'd say. *I understand why you're staying at Livin. I'll support you and your decision.*

Mei reached for her laptop. Enough self-pity. Her to-do list was longer than ever. She had to turn down Pure's job offer and prepare for the layoffs. Mei tamped down the guilt starting to rise in her chest. *I won't make anyone work this week. I'll take on their work as my own.*

At least she'd let her teammates go with dignity.

• • •

On Monday morning, Mei arrived at Livin a few minutes before eight. She grabbed an everything bagel with tofu cream cheese and found a spot at a long communal table. As she worked, colleagues trickled in. By nine, the room was packed.

A strange energy filled the space, until Mei could no longer concentrate. Even by Livin's standards, the vibe felt unusually fevered.

"I can't believe it," one of the designers said to an art director as they walked by. "I thought Livin was different."

The art director snorted. "All these fucking companies just look out for themselves."

"Happy layoff week," a guy from the sales team quipped as he approached two of his teammates.

"I'm gonna save all my clients' info this morning before I lose access," one of the teammates replied.

So people knew about the layoffs. How? Mei glanced to her left, where three account managers were huddled together.

". . . in *Bloomberg* first, then *The New York Times*," one of them said.

Mei typed "Livin" into her browser. A stream of headlines appeared. "LIVIN TO LAY OFF 3,000 EMPLOYEES." "LIVIN WILL CUT THOUSANDS OF JOBS." "A LIVIN NIGHTMARE: HOT STARTUP ANNOUNCES MASS LAYOFFS."

She perused the stories. They didn't contain much besides Livin's plan to downsize. The head of Livin's public affairs team confirmed the layoffs with generic remarks about "rightsizing the company and relentlessly focusing on cutting-edge technology to continue our unprecedented growth."

All around her, people chattered about the layoffs.

• • •

In Mei's meeting with Kaden, Bryce, and Tamiko, they just wanted to talk about the layoffs.

"I've had it with this place." Kaden rolled their eyes at their surroundings. They were in the Munich room, which had an Oktoberfest theme, complete with working taps, giant beer steins, and a mini food cart with oversized pretzels.

"Is this a safe space?" Tamiko asked Mei.

"Always. Nothing anyone says leaves this room."

"Good." Tamiko's eyes flashed. "I hope they lay me off! I've been interviewing and I might have a job offer soon. If I get canned, I'll get my severance and my new salary."

"I'm hoping for that, too!" Kaden exclaimed. "I think I might also get an offer."

"From where?" Bryce asked.

"We're the First. It's this amazing nonprofit that helps first-generation college students. I'd be their head of marketing and communications." Kaden grinned. "It would be so nice to work somewhere that aligns with my values. I can't keep looking the other way here."

Mei swallowed her shock. Had she made a mistake by turning down that job? *No, the salary didn't work.*

"I hope you get it," Mei said truthfully. "We're the First would be lucky to have you."

"Where are you interviewing?" Kaden asked Tamiko.

"A few places in the ed tech space."

"Maybe we can do a partnership!"

"Can I get in on this, too?" Bryce asked.

Mei watched her teammates talk excitedly. An unsettling feeling welled up inside her.

"I've been thinking about what I want in a job," Bryce was saying. "Yeah, it's exciting to work at a hot company. But not when I have to give up everything else. I'm never letting a job come between me and my family again."

"Hear, hear!" Tamiko high-fived Kaden and Bryce. "We've been working ourselves to death for a company that treats us like shit."

"We all deserve better," Bryce said.

"You do," Mei agreed.

All eyes turned to her.

"*You* do, too," Bryce said. "You're the best manager."

"You really are! I hope you go somewhere that appreciates you," Tamiko chimed in.

"Yeah, you're not planning to stay *here*, are you?" Kaden asked.

"Well, I, um," Mei stammered. Tamiko's eyes turned pitying. Kaden's mouth twisted. Bryce smiled sympathetically.

"You probably know more than you can share," Tamiko said.

"We won't put you on the spot," Bryce added.

Mei lowered her head. She didn't deserve her team's grace. "I can't wait to see where you all go from here."

She adjourned the meeting. In the hallway, she ran into Ayanna.

"Got a minute to chat?" Mei asked.

"I was just coming to find you."

They ducked into the New Orleans room.

Mei flopped down in a Café Du Monde–style chair. "Can you believe this?"

"The layoffs? Replacing everyone with AI? Sure can!"

"At least we'll have each other." Mei had taken solace in knowing that Livin was also keeping Ayanna.

"For the next few days. Then I'm out, too. I just gave my notice."

"Stop. Where are you going? Or are you just quitting?"

"I'll be running brand strategy for a new product line at Trillion." The global tech behemoth was known for its sleek devices, edgy branding, and soaring stock prices. "My new manager is one of the few Black women at such a senior level—obviously they have some work to do in that area, too. She's a visionary with big ideas, while knowing how to set up teams for success. Unlike some people."

"I know. James is the worst."

"And Erika. Don't get me started. She's a snake."

"Is she?"

"Don't tell me she's fooled you. She'll be charming to your face, then undercut you when you're not around."

"Yikes." Would Erika do that to her?

"Are *you* staying?"

"I was planning to," Mei said weakly. "I just turned down a job at Pure. VP of marketing."

"What?" Ayanna stared at her. "Pure's hot. Their CEO, Whitney Allen, is a total boss. I've seen her speak at conferences."

Mei winced, recalling Whitney's reply to her email. She'd been disappointed but gracious about Mei not taking the job.

"Why would you choose Livin over Pure?"

"The IPO. The career opportunity."

"Who knows if the IPO will ever happen! Some companies

talk about it for years and never go public. And what, specifically, is here for you, careerwise?"

"Erika said she'll promote me to VP." Mei didn't even sound convincing to herself.

Ayanna shook her head sorrowfully. "Do you really believe that? Also, I've got news for you: You could already be a VP. At Pure!"

Mei let out an exasperated sigh. "I'm also presenting at Livin Forum."

"Livin Forum is an *internal* event! You'll just be presenting to Livin employees. You should be in the spotlight at *external* events, where your industry peers can soak in your brilliance and recruit you for better jobs!"

Mei paused. She hadn't even thought of that.

Ayanna fixed Mei with a steely look. "You're not helping yourself by staying. Your career and mental health will just suffer. Leave as soon as you can."

• • •

Tuesday passed in a fog. Tamiko received a job offer and gave her notice—whether or not she was getting laid off, tomorrow would be her last day. Mei couldn't blame her. She congratulated Tamiko, then went to the bathroom and splashed water on her face. *Now I'll have NO teammates in New York.*

On Wednesday morning, Mei arrived at Livin. The place was eerily quiet. Only a few employees were scattered at the communal tables. Even the sound system, which always thumped with upbeat dance tracks, was playing soft jazz.

The layoff emails had gone out at six a.m. Everyone must have stayed home.

Mei opened her laptop. The digital Livin world was just as subdued. No Slack messages popped up. No emails came in. Hopefully, Julian would address the company, and James would reach out to the marketing team.

Mei texted Bryce, Kaden, Tamiko, and her other reports to let them know she was available if they wanted to talk. Then she got down to work.

As the hours passed, her Slack and inbox stayed silent. The office remained a ghost town. Mei's phone buzzed with texts from Ali, Luc, Kathy, her mom, and Henry; they'd all seen the news. Mei reassured them she was fine.

Late in the day, after she'd scrounged a few vegan granola bars from the kitchen and given up on Julian and James addressing the remaining employees, Mei noticed an unread text on her phone.

Alexandre: Hi Mei. Just wanted to let you know that I'm thinking of you and hoping you're doing okay.

Mei stared at her phone. Why didn't Alexandre call her? Or offer to chat? She could ring him now. But what would she say? *You were right. Livin is a shitshow. I shouldn't have stayed. Oh, and happy Valentine's Day.*

Even before their blowup, they hadn't made any plans. Mei hadn't minded; their relationship was so new, and she'd always considered Valentine's Day an artificial holiday. But Alexandre had casually mentioned he would cook her chocolate and raspberry crêpes the next time they were together.

So much for that.

Mei clicked on her goals tracker, duly noting how all her teammates' responsibilities had already been reassigned to her. The ironic bright spot in this truly terrible day was that she'd been able to work uninterrupted, making today surprisingly productive. Mei heaved a sigh and opened a new video script. There was nothing left to do but keep chipping away at her content queue.

• • •

With everything happening at Livin, Mei almost forgot about Lunar New Year. *What an auspicious beginning*, she thought sarcastically on Saturday afternoon as she waited on the corner of Mulberry and Bayard in Chinatown. Mei waved at Ali, Luc, and Kaia coming down the sidewalk, even as her heart ached at the absence of Alexandre's lean figure and bright eyes.

"*Gung hay fat choy*!" Mei handed Kaia a red envelope she'd stuffed with a few twenties. "I can't wait to collect my *hongbaos* tonight," she teased Ali. The upside to being single at thirty-six meant she still received red envelopes, while Ali and Luc did not.

Ali looped her arm through Mei's. "You can use your *hongbaos* to treat me to a snack. We're going to chat before the lion dances."

At an old-school Chinese bakery, they selected egg tarts and melon cakes from the plastic-domed display cases. They sat across from each other at a table, each with a steaming cup of coffee.

Mei eyed her sister. "Dare I ask what you want to talk about?"

"Where to start? There's Livin, and there's Alexandre. I haven't wanted to pry, but what the heck is going on with you two? And how are you, after this week?"

"Not good. I basically have no team. All my direct reports in New York are gone, as are half of my regional reports. Ayanna, my best work friend, quit."

Ali's eyes widened. "Oh wow. Think you can go back and accept that Pure job?"

"I don't know!" Mei exploded. "I don't want to talk about Livin."

"I get it. What about Alexandre? Are you two dating? Luc and I still haven't figured out whether you got together in Hawai'i and have been seeing each other this whole time, or what."

Mei covered her eyes. "We were dating."

"Ahhhhhhhhhhhhhhh, Mei!" Ali burst out laughing. "Oh god, just the thought of you two sleeping together!"

Mei's face was redder than a *hongbao*. "This is why I didn't tell you!"

"Sorry." Ali coughed to compose herself. "But wait. You *were* dating? Past tense? Because of what happened at dim sum?"

"We haven't spoken since."

Ali blew on her coffee. "I was mad at him, too. But—I'm not taking his side—I can see why he got upset, even though he didn't handle it well. Why don't you talk to him?"

Mei fiddled with her egg tart's crinkly wrapper. *Because I'm afraid he's right. Because I love him and I'm afraid I've lost him.*

"You can't avoid him forever."

"Or can I?"

"Seriously, Mei. Is that what you actually want?"

Alexandre's kind face appeared in her mind. Mei sniffled as her eyes welled up.

Ali smiled sympathetically. She touched Mei's arm. "What about Livin?"

"I think I want to stay."

"So talk to Alexandre. You two will work it out."

"You think so?"

"Yes."

Mei finally bit into her egg tart, the flaky pastry rich on her tongue. "It's not too weird, though? Me and Alexandre?"

"It's a little weird." Ali giggled. "Okay, it's super weird. But Luc and I just want you two to be happy. And you and Alexandre are clearly happy together."

• • •

Mei meant to speak to Alexandre. She really did. But on Sunday morning, Erika called an emergency meeting. Livin Forum was a week away, and they needed to prepare their presentation. Plus, marketing morale was abysmal. Erika tasked Mei with planning a slate of team-building events for the coming week in New York, and the following week in Los Angeles. Mei immediately dove in to scripting their presentation; hiring a massage therapist, yoga coach, and meditation guru for daily wellness sessions; planning a trapeze artistry offsite; and organizing a swank rooftop happy hour for the first night of Livin Forum—all while tackling her gargantuan goals.

By the time the weekend rolled around, Mei saw the error of her ways: She still hadn't spoken to Alexandre. Now she had to face him at Kaia's "unicorn, sparkles, rainbow, glitter" fourth birthday party.

Kaia had made it clear that everyone had to dress up. "Including adults," she'd declared at Lunar New Year. So Mei pulled on white leggings and a soft white sweatshirt. She ran glitter gel through her hair and clipped on colorful extensions to create a flowing black-and-rainbow mane. On the train to Ali and Luc's, Mei followed a dramatic eye makeup tutorial. In the parking lot, she donned her unicorn headband and galloped to her stepdad's car.

Henry burst out laughing. "You look great! Kaia will be thrilled."

"I hope so." Mei climbed into the passenger seat and noted Henry's down jacket. "Are you wearing your outfit?"

"Yup. It's just not as elaborate as yours."

They arrived at Ali and Luc's house. Upon entering, Mei saw Henry was just wearing a striped rainbow shirt under a navy sport coat.

"Wow, your costume!" Kaia danced around Mei in a pastel pink shirt, sparkly tulle skirt, and glittery unicorn headband.

"I love it!" Ali laughed. She wore a white sweater with iridescent rainbow threads. Luc had on a silver button-down and a unicorn headband. Her mom donned a rainbow sweater.

Mei turned scarlet as she followed Ali to the kitchen. "I thought everyone was dressing up."

"We are dressed up! Just not as much as you. Well, you and one other person."

Mei's heart clenched when she entered the kitchen. Alexandre stood before her, plating a tray of sprinkle cupcakes. He was a head-to-toe rainbow in a sparkly tie-dyed sweatshirt and joggers, and a matching eye mask. His tousled hair shimmered with glitter.

Mei tried to smother a laugh. "Wow. Nice outfit."

Alexandre jumped at the sight of her. "You look incredible."

Familiar heat flooded Mei. She could still make out his strong, lean shoulders beneath that crazy sweatshirt. She wanted to run her hands through his glittery hair and press her unicorn body against his. Behind her, Mei heard Ali snicker.

"You two will be the hit of the party!"

"The center of attention. Our favorite place," Mei deadpanned.

Alexandre gave her a commiserating smile, sending a hopeful thrill through her.

They carried the cupcake platters to the living room. Mei set up a beverage station and filled two glittery pink cups with rosé. She handed one to Alexandre. "I think we could use this."

"Cheers." He held his cup against hers, never breaking eye contact.

The front door opened, and Clarisse and Jean-Germain waltzed in, looking like they'd come straight from the Metropolitan Museum of Art gift shop. They wore matching black shirts with an image of *The Unicorn Rests in a Garden* tapestry. *They're such professors,* Mei thought, trying to keep a straight face as she greeted Alexandre's parents.

Twenty minutes later, it was time for guests to arrive. The doorbell chimed. Mei's eyes slid to Alexandre. Without a word, they bolted to the kitchen.

"Can we just hide out here?" Mei folded up the empty cupcake box.

"Right? I don't feel like mingling with random parents and kids looking like this."

"Maybe no one will miss us." They smiled at each other. How Mei had missed those hazel eyes. "Hey, I wanted to—"

"There you are!" Ali burst into the kitchen. "The birthday girl was wondering where you went." She grabbed a wicker basket that jangled. "The Rainbow Rockers are about to go on."

Mei blinked. "Who?"

"Suzy Sparkles and the Rainbow Rockers. A local music group that does birthday parties. It would be fun if you two danced with the kids and handed out instruments. Your costumes are just too good!"

Mei stared at her in disbelief. Beside her, Alexandre gritted his teeth. He wasn't going to say no, either.

"Fine," Mei said. "Let's get this party started."

"You're the best!" Ali handed her the basket of egg shakers, tambourines, and maracas.

Applause erupted when they entered the living room. Parents whipped out their phones and started recording videos.

Mei turned red. "We're not the entertainers."

"We are now," Alexandre mumbled. He broke into a genuine grin when Kaia ran over to him.

Mei handed out egg shakers while dancing to a Kidz Bop cover of "Celebration." A few minutes later, cheers rang out. A beaming redhead in a flouncy rainbow dress walked in, followed by two guys in rainbow suits, carrying a guitar and bongos.

"I'm Suzy Sparkles and we're the Rainbow Rockers!" the redhead cried. "Let's wish Kaia a very happy birthday!"

They launched into "Shake It Off."

Maybe it was the music, the occasion, or just that she actually felt happy, but Mei kept dancing. She jumped around with Kaia. Her shoulders bumped Alexandre, making them both laugh. Mei grabbed his hand. He twirled her under his arm, gathering her close for a wonderful second, before breaking apart to give out tambourines.

Afterward, everyone had pizza, sang "Happy Birthday," and ate cupcakes. As the party wound down, parents began gathering their children.

Mei's heart thudded. She touched Alexandre's arm. "Can we talk?"

He nodded. They slipped down the hallway into the kitchen.

It was empty. Mei stood by the counter so she had a view of the door. "I know we left things badly. I'm sorry I didn't tell you about Livin, and that you found out the way you did."

"Mei." Alexandre took a step toward her. "I feel awful. I'm sorry I hurt you, and I'm sorry I didn't reach out. We should've talked through everything."

Mei reached up and removed Alexandre's eye mask. Her breath caught at the sight of his handsome face, now in full view. She brushed back a rogue lock of his hair.

"I missed you," she whispered.

"I missed you, too," Alexandre said, his voice rough. He took her in his arms. His heart was pounding just as much as hers.

Mei's eyes flitted to the door. The din of the party had lessened. She stood on tiptoe so her lips skated along his ear. Alexandre inhaled sharply.

"We'll figure everything out," Mei said. "Can we talk more tonight? At your place?"

Alexandre went rigid. His arms dropped, releasing her.

Mei's stomach plummeted. "I'm sorry," she mumbled. "I misunderstood."

"Mei, no." Alexandre took her hand. "I want to be with you. That's all I've wanted for months. You. It's just—" Alexandre looked away and blew out a breath. When he turned back to her, dread clouded his eyes. "I have an early flight tomorrow. To North Dakota."

Mei staggered back. "You're flying there? For that research job?"

"For that research job," Alexandre confirmed, his voice tight.

"Wow." Pain squeezed Mei's chest. She couldn't extract a single clear thought. "North Dakota." Out of the corner of her eye, she saw Luc stroll into the kitchen.

He froze. "North Dakota? What about North Dakota?"

CHAPTER THIRTY-EIGHT

Alexandre glanced from Luc to Mei. His brother eyed him warily. Mei looked stricken. *And it's only going to get worse.* Alexandre faced Luc.

"I'm flying to North Dakota for a week to interview for the job. I just want to learn more about it."

Luc narrowed his eyes. "You weren't even going to tell me."

"I was. Today." Alexandre hated how defensive he sounded.

Luc snorted. "Sure. You weren't going to tell anyone until you'd signed the contract."

Alexandre's face burned. "That's not true." He'd planned to tell Luc about his trip. He really had. But ever since he'd emailed Chris, every second of his days had been full of teaching, catching up on the latest genetics findings, and preparing his interview presentation. Alexandre had fallen back into the rhythm he knew so well, working fourteen-hour days and barely sleeping at night.

His eyes met Mei's. The shock on her face made him look away. *Wonderful. Now I'm the ultimate hypocrite.*

Suddenly, Alexandre was angry. And exhausted. And frustrated. Now he understood why Mei was staying at Livin. This was his life. His career. And ultimately, his decision.

"I'd be an idiot to pass this up," he snapped. "This is a once-in-a-lifetime chance."

"What's a once-in-a-lifetime chance?"

Alexandre closed his eyes. *Of course.* When he opened them, his parents were looking at him expectantly in their ridiculous unicorn tapestry shirts. He had not planned to tell them about the job unless he took it.

"The University of North Dakota is building up their biology department," Alexandre said wearily. "My old mentor, Chris Saunders, is the department chair. He invited me to interview. I'm spending the week there, starting tomorrow."

Clarisse gasped, a hand fluttering to her mouth.

Jean-Germain threw his arms around him. "A second chance! That's incredible!"

His mother piled on. "Why didn't you tell us? This is major news!"

"What's major news?" Ali walked into the kitchen with Kaia, Vivian, and Henry.

Alexandre sighed. "I'm flying to North Dakota tomorrow for that job."

"Oh." Ali glanced at Luc, who was glaring at him, and Mei, who still appeared stunned.

Vivian's and Henry's brows furrowed as they tried to read the room.

"Hey, Kaia, want to play with your presents?" Vivian took her granddaughter's hand and led her out of the room. Henry followed.

"Is the lab well funded?" Clarisse asked.

"Yes," Alexandre said.

"How are the facilities?" Jean-Germain demanded.

"Brand-new. They're opening a huge zebrafish facility with robotic feeding systems." Pride snuck into his words.

"Yeah, you'll have new fish tanks, but that doesn't mean you won't work yourself to death!" Luc ripped off his unicorn headband and tossed it on the counter. "High-risk, high-reward research is always going to be high-risk, *no* reward. Especially when you're starting from nothing."

"It might be wonderful." Clarisse shot Luc a look. "Different lab, different circumstances. Plus"—she turned to Alexandre—"you'll have had a year off. You'll be recharged."

Alexandre bristled. "Well, I'll have had a 'year off' from research, but I'm still teaching full-time."

"Ah, teaching." Jean-Germain waved a hand. "It was a good plan B. Now you can get back to plan A."

"But you like teaching." Luc's eyes bored into Alexandre. "You're happy in New York."

"I am."

"This is your *life's work*!" Clarisse cried. "What's more important than that?"

"Opportunities like this never come along," Jean-Germain added. "This is another shot at everything you've always wanted."

"I might not even get the job," Alexandre mumbled.

"They'd be fools not to take you! Fools!" Jean-Germain said.

"You'll get it. And take it." Luc's shoulders drooped.

Alexandre gazed at the three people he'd become closest to in the last few months. Luc shook his head in disgust. Ali offered a sympathetic smile. Mei wouldn't meet his eyes. Doubt coursed through Alexandre. When he and Mei weren't speaking, it had been so easy to lose himself preparing for the interview. Now that she was in front of him, Alexandre could feel, on a cellular level, what he'd be giving up by going to North Dakota.

Kaia's laughter echoed from down the hallway. *It's still her birthday,* Alexandre realized. Wow, he'd made a mess of the day.

"I think I'll head home now," he said. "My flight's really early."

"Fine. Go." Luc stalked out of the room.

Ali patted his shoulder. "We'll see you when you get back." She left the kitchen, too.

"You should rest up," Clarisse said. "And wash that glitter out of your hair before the interview."

"I will." Alexandre looked from his mom to his dad. "I'll walk myself out. Can I have a minute here?"

Amazingly, his parents understood. They glanced at Mei, said hasty goodbyes, and retreated from the kitchen.

Alexandre stepped closer to Mei. "I'm sorry." He reached for her hand, then reconsidered. "I wish I'd told everyone sooner. I wish I'd told you. Now I get why you didn't tell me about Livin."

Mei smiled crookedly. "Well, we are two of a kind."

Alexandre cracked a little smile. "Can we still talk when I get back?"

"I guess? I'm actually flying to LA on Monday for Livin Forum."

"Well, let me know if you need an accomplice for breaking out of there." His joke rang hollow, as did Mei's chuckle.

"I'm going to be presenting."

"You are?" So Erika had kept her promise. "You'll be amazing."

"Thanks. Good luck with your interview."

Alexandre didn't know what to do, so he opened his arms. Mei stepped in. Her touch was warm and familiar, but distant, a protective wall surrounding her. Alexandre pulled away, his heart breaking.

It was, he realized, a hug goodbye.

• • •

As Alexandre's plane descended over North Dakota, he peered listlessly out the window. Grand Forks lay below, a collection of short buildings along an icy river. *It's probably pretty in the summer*, Alexandre reasoned, picturing green fields and leafy trees. But right now, the frigid landscape was as gray as his spirit.

Outside the terminal, frosty wind punched him in the face. Alexandre hurried to his rental car and drove to the budget chain motel where he was staying. He cranked up the heat when he got inside, then checked his phone. Nothing from Luc or Mei. Just his parents, who rarely texted.

Clarisse: Good luck! Let us know if we can help.
Jean-Germain: Knock 'em dead. We're so proud of you.

• • •

On Monday morning, Alexandre's head felt a little clearer after a decent night's sleep and a steaming-hot shower. *Maybe everything will be terrible*, he thought as he mussed his hair with a touch of pomade. Low department morale, subpar facilities despite promises otherwise—that would make his decision easy.

At the biology department, Chris greeted him heartily. "Welcome to UND! I can't tell you how thrilled I am to have you here."

Alexandre's mood lifted as Chris introduced him to the faculty and staff, talking up his research background and their past collaborations. Every person enthusiastically asked about his life and work.

Outside, the campus teemed with youthful energy. Though SUNY New Paltz was on spring break, UND wouldn't be for another week. Chris shared bits of the university's history as they strolled. Finally, they arrived at a low brick building.

"I know you're dying to see this. We won't open for another two months, but you'll get the idea." With a flourish, Chris flipped on the lights.

Rows of plastic-enshrouded fish tanks filled the space. The workstations gleamed.

"Here's the injection room, the quarantine, microscopy rooms, and the nursery," Chris said as he walked Alexandre through the space.

Alexandre nodded in awe. This was the most high-end zebrafish facility he'd ever seen.

• • •

Early on Tuesday morning, Alexandre stood before UND's biology faculty. An overhead projector displayed the title slide of his presentation. A few nerves knotted his stomach but disappeared as he talked through his research methods and results. Chris nodded with satisfaction at several points. Others did, too. Afterward, Alexandre invited everyone to share questions and comments.

"That's interesting data," said Jamal Ferguson, an associate professor. "I've been studying some of those mutations on food foraging in turbid water, and I've seen similar trends. There's a lot we can explore together," he added with a friendly smile.

"I haven't looked at those mutations, but now you've got me thinking," said Samantha Wilkerson, another associate professor. "I study reproductive disorders. Are you planning to continue with those mutations or branch out to others?"

Alexandre relished every question. He especially enjoyed speaking with Jamal and Samantha, who'd be his tenure-track peers. Soon, the hour was up, and he and Samantha were the last ones in the room.

"Want to get coffee?" she asked.

"Coffee always sounds good." Alexandre registered that Samantha was the kind of woman he'd once gravitated to: She had an outdoorsy look and was nearly his height, with long auburn hair and a smattering of freckles.

He and Samantha—or "Sam," as she corrected him—ordered lattes at a nearby café and sat down at a table.

"We don't get many new people." Sam smiled over her mug. "It's just been me and Jamal for so long."

"Where were you before?"

"I did my PhD at the University of Washington. I'm originally from Seattle."

"I just came from Oregon. But you knew that."

"I was excited to meet you because of that! And your work, of course. I'm happy here, but I miss the Pacific Northwest."

"I loved the outdoor scene there."

"Oh yeah?" Sam lit up. "I'm always looking for people who like outdoor activities. I've wanted to do a ski trip, but I haven't found enough people."

"If I end up here, I'd be game."

"Then we have to hire you! Chris has been talking you up nonstop. I think you're a shoo-in."

The thought made Alexandre shift uncomfortably in his seat.

They chatted some more, then Sam had to get ready for a class.

"Would moving here be a big deal?" she asked.

Alexandre set down his empty mug. Somehow, he hadn't even asked himself that.

"It would." He adjusted the cup on the table. "I grew up in New York, then spent most of my adult life in Eugene. I never thought about living in North Dakota, so I'm still getting used to the idea."

"What about your family? They'd move here, too, right?" Sam's tone barely changed, but she lowered her eyes.

Oh. Alexandre flushed. "It would just be me."

A little smile appeared on Sam's lips. "I see."

• • •

On Wednesday afternoon, Alexandre met with Chris and three other professors. For one hour, he answered their questions and detailed his vision for the lab. He spoke of experiments he'd run, grants he'd apply for, and collaborations he'd pursue within UND and with other universities. At the end of the interview, the professors were visibly pleased.

"I hope we'll see a lot more of you soon," said the associate chair as she shook Alexandre's hand.

Alexandre took himself out to dinner to celebrate. He sat at the bar of a nearby restaurant and ordered a beer and a walleye sandwich, savoring the perfect combination of local fried fish, tangy tartar sauce, and crisp lettuce.

He checked his phone. Still nothing from Luc or Mei.

Well, maybe I don't need them. Alexandre picked up his sandwich. Maybe in a year or two, he'd be a regular at this joint, coming here to celebrate every time he published a big paper or secured a substantial grant.

Then Alexandre frowned, thinking of everything he'd need to do to get to that point: Recruiting and hiring a lab team. Supervising grad students and postdocs. Applying for national grants, with their impossibly high rejection rates. Managing more populations of zebrafish than he'd ever had in a single lab, while using new equipment he'd never handled.

He'd be back to working late nights and long weekends. His career would once again hang on every experiment as he anxiously waited for it to run to conclusion.

And he'd be here. In Grand Forks. Thousands of miles away from his loved ones.

Alexandre took a long sip of beer to tamp down his mounting dread.

• • •

Alexandre spent Thursday having one-on-one meetings to learn about the biology faculty's research. He was back in his element, asking questions and reviewing data. The technical conversations fired up his brain, making him second-guess the doubts he'd had at the bar. *Maybe I do belong here.*

That evening, Alexandre went for drinks with Sam, Jamal,

and a few others from the department. For hours, they bantered like old friends.

Somehow, Sam always ended up next to him, first at the bar, then at the table, her long legs angled toward him.

• • •

On Friday morning, Alexandre made the rounds saying goodbye.

"You're leaving already?" Sam asked when he rapped on her office door. She got up from her desk and grabbed her phone. "Let's stay in touch."

They exchanged contact information, then Sam smiled. "Is it weird if I hug you goodbye?"

"No, it was great to meet you." Alexandre leaned in for the friendly hug that was customary with colleagues. But Sam's arms were tighter around his neck than he'd expected. Her cheek brushed against his. Her hug took him back to another embrace he'd tried so hard not to think about. Another woman pressed against him, her breath tickling his ear. Alexandre stiffened. He released Sam.

"Well, maybe I'll see you soon."

Sam's smile was confused, then confident. "I hope so." She winked. "I have a good feeling about you."

• • •

"Come in, come in," Chris said when Alexandre appeared in his doorway. He motioned for Alexandre to have a seat. "This has been quite a week. We'll make our decision in the coming days, but you should leave here feeling great. You made a strong impression on everyone, as I knew you would."

Alexandre flushed. "Thank you. I enjoyed my time here. I can see myself fitting in while bringing my own ideas and expertise."

"We'd be lucky to have you. Oh." Chris slapped his palm to his forehead. "We didn't talk about teaching. I know that's what you're doing now, but I assume you won't want to spend a lot of time in the classroom here. Nor should you. I'll give you a light course load and our best TAs."

Alexandre's hands felt icy. He nodded.

Chris peered at him intently from behind his glasses. "We have a reputation to build. First, we'll establish UND as the genetics powerhouse of the Midwest. Then we'll climb the national rankings. I'll be counting on you for big wins. That's one of the main reasons I'm recruiting you."

"Because of my past wins?"

"Because of your *work ethic*. You are one of the most dedicated scientists I know. Even from your grad school days, you were in the lab, emailing me at three a.m. on weekends and holidays, thinking through your research while others weren't. That's the kind of tireless devotion I want on my team, and why I immediately thought of you for this job."

Alexandre swallowed hard. "I won't let you down, Chris."

"Good." Chris's eyes glinted. "Alexandre, it's been a pleasure. I'll be in touch very soon."

CHAPTER THIRTY-NINE

"Attention, passengers. You are now free to use approved electronic devices," a flight attendant announced to the 8:59 flight from JFK to LAX.

As if on autopilot, Mei woke up her laptop. Around her, people did the same. Nearly everyone on board was a colleague en route to Livin Forum.

Mei stared at the script she'd written for her presentation. She, James, and Erika had rehearsed and revised it several times. Mei just had to incorporate their edits into the final version, but her brain refused to work.

Alexandre was going to get the North Dakota job. And take it. Was there any point in pursuing a future with him?

She'd fallen for Alexandre the biology professor, who strove to help his students and had an active life outside of work.

If she were being completely honest, Mei didn't know how she'd feel about Alexandre the research scientist. Mei couldn't see him taking the job without falling back into his old ways. With the pressure of tenure track, could Alexandre sustain a long-distance relationship? If she visited him in North Dakota—or moved there—would he spend time with her? Mei envisioned herself waiting around for hours while he crammed in as much lab time as possible.

He'd always be preoccupied with work.

Just like she was.

Mei inhaled shakily. She scrolled through her presentation. Her title, "Onward and Upward," had a double meaning: Livin's marketing team would continue to push the boundaries—even in the wake of the layoffs. First, James would highlight the marketing team's recent wins. Then Erika would get the crowd pumped about the latest campaign. She'd welcome Mei, who'd speak about the holiday pop-ups, building projections, and drone art, as images, press clips, and social media posts appeared on the big screens. Then Mei would introduce the brand refresh with the inclusive imagery. She'd close the presentation by unveiling their new brand campaign hype video, which featured a soaring pop track and a montage of Livin members and locations from around the world.

I'll finally get my moment in the spotlight. But what have I sacrificed for it?

Mei clicked on the goals tracker. Her workload was hilarious. Even if she worked every second of every day, her March numbers were impossible.

The flight map on her seat-back screen showed they were approaching the Midwest. Mei spotted North Dakota, making her eyes tear up. So much for their pact.

With a deep breath, she refocused on her laptop. Still, one question nagged Mei all the way to California: If she hadn't been so consumed with Livin, would Alexandre be in North Dakota?

• • •

The hazy Los Angeles sunshine and rangy palm trees were a welcome change from New York's gray winter, but they didn't help Mei's mood. She faked a smile while making small talk at the roof deck happy hour she'd planned for the marketing team. Everywhere she looked, she saw loss. No Ayanna. No Kaden, Bryce, or Tamiko. No texts or funny photos from Alexandre. *I chose this,* Mei thought numbly. *This was my decision.*

Early the next morning, all nine thousand Livin employees filled the LA Convention Center's stadium-sized auditorium. Excited chatter rippled through the space, though Mei couldn't help but think of the missing three thousand employees who had just been laid off over email. As strobe lights flashed and electronic music played, Julian loped onto the massive stage. As usual, his golden mane flowed and his green eyes glowed. The yellow T-shirt under his expensive sport coat read "Livin Proof."

"My friends. My Livin family." Julian lifted his face to the crowd. "Welcome to Livin Forum! Who's ready for a good time?"

Mei clapped along. Good time. Sure.

Onstage, Julian solemnly opined about how Livin employees had the unique power to help people fulfill their destinies. He bowed his head in reverence. His voice caught. He wiped away a tear.

Mei heard sniffles around her. Usually, she was reaching for tissues, too. Not this time. Was the man before her really a visionary? Or was he an actor? A con man? A billionaire laughing all the way to the bank?

For the rest of the morning, Mei allowed herself to see the hypocrisy she'd tried to will away: The all-white, all-male speakers talking about inclusion and belonging. The overflowing trash cans, despite the vegan menus. The exorbitance of flying in nine thousand people from around the world after laying off three thousand employees.

Kaden's words rang through her mind. *I can't keep looking the other way here.*

That evening, Mei stood on that giant stage as she, James, and Erika ran through their presentation. She blinked under the spotlights and tried to summon the feeling of all eyes on her, the roar of nine thousand people clapping and cheering.

The tech team played her campaign video. The uplifting music made her shiver. The sight of her work—the hard-won vision she'd crafted over the last year—on the colossal screens filled her with a strange mix of satisfaction and sadness.

At least I'll have this, Mei thought, a lump rising in her throat.

• • •

At six thirty on Thursday morning, Mei awoke to a string of texts from Erika.

Can you meet me now at the coffee shop downstairs? It's urgent.

Mei threw on a sweatshirt and frantically brushed her teeth. When she reached the lobby café, she spotted Erika waving from a table.

"What's this all about?" At least Erika didn't have bad news.

Her manager gleefully bounced in her seat. Somehow, even at this early hour, her hair was perfectly blown out.

"So I'm making a small change to our presentation. You've got to see this." Erika thrust her laptop at Mei and hit play on a video.

A cool bass pulsed from the speakers. Words flashed on the screen: "Would you rather be LIVIN? Or DYIN?"

Mei pressed her lips together. Did they really need to evoke death?

On-screen, the video flashed through a series of contrasts.

Livin. A radiant blonde moving into a colorful Livin apartment.

Dyin. An overweight woman eating dinner in a drab kitchen.

Livin. A sunlit couple embracing outside a rustic cabin.

Dyin. A bespectacled Asian man bathed in the blue light of a computer.

Livin. A vibrant group of twenty-somethings toasting cocktails in a sleek lounge.

Dyin. An overworked Black woman sighing in her cubicle while her laughing coworkers file out around her.

A smooth voice asked: "You only have one life. Would you rather be LIVIN? Or DYIN? We thought so."

The screen cut to black.

Mei blinked at the laptop.

"What do you think?" Across the table, Erika beamed at her.

"What *is* that?"

"Our new campaign video that we're going to unveil during our presentation!"

"When did you make this? And how? Did our agency do it? Why didn't you tell me?" Erika knew campaigns were her remit and that she managed their creative agency.

Erika laughed. "So this was a top-secret project I pitched to James. Remember how I said we could use AI to replace the people we laid off? This was a test. I worked with a generative AI agency to see if their technology could create a brand video as good as or better than humans at a fraction of the time and cost. If so, we'd feature it at Livin Forum to show where we're headed as a department. And we will! Onward and upward, right? I love the video and so does James."

Mei stared at her boss. "Yeah, the production value is high. But it's not in line with our updated brand or our inclusive marketing standards."

"How can you say that? We worked off the new style guide. The video has lots of diverse people!"

"All the 'diverse people' are in the Dyin parts! Everyone in the Livin parts was white, straight, young, and stick thin, except for that token Black model. There are also so many stereotypes."

"Like what?" Erika looked genuinely confused.

"Like a sad larger woman eating a double cheeseburger. And a nerdy Asian guy alone on his computer. And a Black woman who has to work twice as hard as her coworkers—all while implying their lives aren't worth living."

Erika frowned. "I hear what you're saying, but I think you're reading too much into it. I don't think your average person would feel that way."

"I disagree. Can your agency cut a new version? Especially since they did it *at a fraction of the time and cost*?"

"No. Julian has already approved this. James and I rewrote our script and gave the video to the tech team. It's all ready to go."

An incredulous huff escaped Mei's lips.

"It'll be fine, Mei." Erika softened, even as her voice remained firm. "Look, I know I kind of sprung this on you. But didn't I tell you that if you stuck with me, I'd take you to the top? You'll still be onstage at Livin Forum. Your first time, right?"

Mei nodded begrudgingly.

"What did I say when I started?" Erika continued. "We know what kind of people run this place. What kind of *men*. We smart women need to stick together. This is my first Livin Forum, too. I need to make a strong impression. I have your back. Now I need to know that you have mine."

Despite the nausea rising in Mei's throat, she nodded again.

"So we're good to go with this video? I promise to loop you in earlier next time."

Mei hesitated. "Yes." Her voice sounded far away, even to her.

"Perfect." Erika smiled. "I'll see you backstage."

• • •

"You've got gorgeous tresses," said the stylist in the hair and makeup room. She finger-combed Mei's locks and reached for a curling iron.

"Thanks," Mei mumbled. Her stomach roiled with dread. Disappointment. Shame.

As if sensing her emotions, the hairstylist clucked with concern. "Are the nerves getting to you?"

"A little."

In less than an hour, she'd be onstage when Erika unveiled that campaign video. In doing so, she'd be endorsing a shoddy video filled with stereotypes and microaggressions, negating all the work she'd done to make Livin a more inclusive company. She'd be supporting AI as a replacement for her former teammates—her talented, creative, *human* teammates.

And she'd be aligning herself with Julian, James, and Erika in a very public way.

Maybe it was good that Ayanna, Kaden, Bryce, and Tamiko weren't there to witness it.

The stylist gave Mei's hair a satisfied fluff. A makeup artist took her place and examined Mei's complexion.

Mei peeked at Erika, one chair over. Her boss's eyes were closed, a relaxed little smile on her face as another makeup artist brushed eyeshadow on her lids. *She's a snake. She'll be charming to your face, then undercut you when you're not around.* Now Ayanna's words made sense. For all of Erika's talk about supporting other women, she had no problem stepping on Mei when she needed to.

Out of nowhere, Mei heard Alexandre's words from months ago. *Don't you think you're worthy of more? Of a job that's not a treadmill to death? With leaders who respect you?*

Tears sprang to her eyes.

"Sorry! Is the eyeliner bothering you?" the makeup artist asked.

"No, I'm okay." Mei reached for a tissue and carefully dabbed her eyes.

"Let me touch you up." He reapplied the eyeliner and mascara, then stepped aside. "You're all set."

Mei stared at herself in the mirror. Her hair cascaded down her shoulders in shiny waves. Liquid eyeliner and smokey eyeshadow gave her a fierce look. She was the picture of a boss lady. A leader. She looked as polished and confident as Erika always did.

"You like?" the makeup artist asked, clearly pleased with her reaction.

She raised her chin. "I love it."

"Go get 'em, sis."

Mei flashed him a grateful smile. She strode out of the room, heart pounding, head high.

She found James and Erika in the green room. They both did a double take when she entered.

"Mei! You look amazing!" Erika said.

James lifted an eyebrow. "Nice shirt."

Mei fingered the lace trim on her navy blouse. It was the one she'd worn to go out to dinner with Alexandre the first time he visited her in New York. She squared her shoulders. "I need to talk to you two—"

"James Smith, Erika Fairchild, and Mei Li, come with me. You're on in five," a stage manager called.

James and Erika walked toward the door. Mei hesitated. Had she missed her chance? She drew a breath, then hurried after them.

From the wings, Mei glimpsed Julian onstage. His amplified voice filled the space ". . . our community is the heart and soul of Livin. That's why we lead with empathy and act with integrity. Everything we do is in service of building trust with our members—and one another."

James nodded along coolly. Erika clasped her hands with a little shimmy.

Mei stared out at Julian. Then she faced her managers. "I'm not going on."

Erika's mouth fell open. "What?"

Beside her, James rolled his eyes.

"I'm not presenting. That video goes against everything I believe in and everything I've worked for. I don't want to be onstage when you show it."

Erika gaped at her. "I don't know what to say. Did I not give you this opportunity? I'm planning to promote you. Don't you want that VP title? More money? It's all coming your way."

Money. Mei froze. Could she stick it out a few more months? Just suck it up and present that damn video?

James leveled a cold gaze at her. "If you refuse to go on, think about what message you're sending to the execs. Sure, Erika and I can present without you. But if you walk away from this, you can kiss any future at this company goodbye."

Thundering applause rang out. Julian had concluded his speech.

"And now," he announced from the center of the stage, "let's hear from our marketing team! They're about to show us the extraordinary heights we're soaring to this year. Onward and upward!"

"Mei." Erika grabbed her arm. "Why are you doing this? I thought we were in this together. What more could you possibly want?"

A company that's not a treadmill to death, with leaders who respect me.

Alexandre. Mei could see his face so clearly, it took her breath away. *I'm worthy of more. So much more.* Finally, she knew it.

Mei drew herself up, feeling taller than ever in her five-one frame. She looked from James to Erika. "As your video said, 'You only have one life.' And I'd rather be *living.* Have fun onstage. I'll send you my resignation letter this afternoon."

CHAPTER FORTY

After his Wednesday genetics class, Alexandre found a message from Chris in his inbox.

Dear Alexandre,

I hope this finds you well. On behalf of the University of North Dakota Biology Department, I am pleased to offer you a full-time position as an associate professor.

An attached contract outlined the terms of the role.

Alexandre read the email three times and let out a whoop. He did it! The biology faculty had unanimously voted to hire him.

Then he sank back in his chair, his elation fading at what he was about to do.

Afterward, he texted Luc.

Hey, I know you're still pissed. I get it. I'm sorry.
Any chance we could meet up tomorrow?

Luc responded an hour later.

Hey. Yeah. Let's.

• • •

The following afternoon, Alexandre sat with a brown ale at the bar of a local brewery. He saw Luc walk in and stood to greet him.

"I'll get the double IPA," Luc said. "I'll probably need it for what you're about to tell me."

Alexandre winced. "Sorry."

Luc settled onto the stool next to him. "You took the job, didn't you?"

"I did. I'm telling my boss tomorrow." Once Luc had his beer in hand, Alexandre recounted his time at UND, from the enthusiastic faculty to the new zebrafish facility.

When he finished, Luc shook his head. "I still think you're making a mistake."

"This is a once-in-a-lifetime—"

"Enough. I'm sick of hearing about this 'once-in-a-lifetime' chance. Just because this job appeared doesn't mean you should take it. Ali could be working for a bigger PT practice or opening her own. I could be making loads more as an engineering manager at a big tech company."

"Do you ever wish you were? Honestly."

Luc turned his glass in his hand. "I miss the salary and stock options. I'll always be grateful that tech set us up financially. But I don't miss the actual job, commute, or insane workload. Ali was taking care of Kaia and doing everything around the house while also working full-time. None of us were happy." He sipped his beer. "When I was younger and unmarried, my top priority was making and saving money. Now time with Ali and Kaia is more important. Speaking of, after all the life you've lived and everything you've experienced, do you really want the same thing now as you did twenty years ago?"

Alexandre caught the skepticism in Luc's voice. "Well, I'd be set up for success—"

Luc's withering look cut him off. Now Alexandre stared at his pint. It was a fair question. Did he, at forty-two, want the same thing he did at twenty-two?

Instinctively, the answer was yes. He did.

But did he have the relentless drive, infinite energy, and unyielding optimism he'd had years ago, before he'd learned he couldn't bend life to his will by hard work alone? Alexandre gulped his beer.

"Will you be teaching?" Luc asked.

"Not really." He didn't have to look up to feel Luc's disdain.

"What about Mei?"

Alexandre startled. "What about her?"

"She didn't factor into your decision? You obviously care about her, and she cares for you."

"I do care about her. A lot." Alexandre's face was on fire. "Sorry. I know this is awkward."

Luc smiled dryly. "I've had some time to get used to it."

"How'd you know something was going on between us?"

"I have eyes, you know. The two of you aren't exactly slick when it comes to hiding your feelings. Plus, Mei told Ali you were seeing each other."

"She did? What did she say?" His heart ached just thinking about Mei.

"Not much beyond that. What happened?"

"We blew it. Or maybe I did." Alexandre tapped his coaster

on the bar. How had they unraveled so spectacularly? "In Hawai'i, we made that pact. I was going to encourage Mei to get out of Livin, and she was going to help keep me from getting sucked back into research. I guess we both failed."

Luc gave him the side-eye. "Well, *she* didn't fail."

"She didn't?"

"Nope." Luc smiled triumphantly. "She quit."

"No way." Alexandre recalled the quiet pride in Mei's eyes when she told him she was presenting at Livin Forum. Now she was giving that up?

"Yup. Her last day is tomorrow. We're so proud of her."

"Does she have a new job?"

"Not yet. Either way, she's brave enough to do what's best for her, even though it's scary. Unlike some people." Luc checked his phone. "I have to head out. It's almost time to get Kaia from school."

Alexandre nodded. What made Mei quit? He had so many questions. When Alexandre glanced up, his throat caught. Luc was frowning with resignation.

"I've loved having you back here. So have Ali, Kaia, and Mei, even with whatever's going on with you. But never mind us. *You've* been happier than I've ever seen you. I just wish you could see that." Luc looked away. "I don't agree with your choice, but I'll always be here for you. Even if you're in North Dakota."

Alexandre swallowed hard. "Thanks, Luc."

After Luc left, Alexandre stayed at the bar, dazed. His brother's implicit question lingered: *What kind of life do you want?*

CHAPTER FORTY-ONE

Mei and Erika agreed that the Friday after Livin Forum would be her last day. So once she was back in New York, Mei prepared for her exit. She saved work samples, wrapped up her major projects, and wrote a transition document. The goals tracker no longer held a death grip on her. Mei could mark off items without her heart racing.

In her final days, more than a dozen colleagues reached out to express their dismay at James and Erika's Livin Forum presentation.

"I couldn't believe they were bragging about replacing the brand team with AI," said Steve, a program manager who'd joined Livin from the music industry. "I need to start looking. They're going to replace me soon, too."

"You'd think that after all their talk about inclusivity and belonging, they'd see that their video was whack," said Layla, a marketing ops manager.

"It probably doesn't feel like it now, but your work has made a huge difference," said Ash, a creative director who'd been a key partner in making the Livin brand more inclusive. "Your legacy will live on."

Mei thanked each person gratefully. When folks asked why

she was leaving, she was honest: She told them she didn't agree with Julian's leadership, nor the direction James and Erika were taking the marketing department. She was going to take some time to focus on her mental health, then find a new job aligned with her values.

• • •

On Friday morning, Mei walked into Livin's headquarters. Sunlight bathed the open space. The colorful couches appeared more vibrant than ever. Mei gazed at the massive street art mural: "Livin the Dream."

For so long, this had been it. Now she was off to chase other dreams.

Erika had been cool to her all week, so Mei wasn't expecting any kind of send-off. Sure enough, Erika pinged her on Slack a few minutes later.

Happy last day! Hope you can shut down early and head out!

That's all? Mei assumed they'd have a quick sync before she left.

Thanks, Erika. Do you want to meet for a few minutes?

Erika wrote back a second later.

No need! Just email me your transition doc before you go. Best wishes!

Mei stared at the message. After nearly three years, she was expected to show herself out the door? What kind of manager didn't take a moment to say goodbye? Then it dawned on her. Erika would no longer benefit from Mei's work. She no longer had any use for her.

Mei took a calming breath. She could just leave early. What was keeping her there?

She texted Ali. Her sister had mentioned something about taking the day off because Kaia's school was closed for teacher training.

Are you and Kaia around today? Can I come up for lunch?

Ali replied immediately.

ABSOLUTELY!

Mei sent Erika her transition doc, emailed her colleagues a goodbye note, and turned in her laptop. Then, with one last glance at the "Livin the Dream" sign, Mei strode out of Livin headquarters for the final time.

She rode the train north. At her stop, Ali, Luc, and Kaia ran over to greet her. Mei grinned wildly, even as tears pooled in her eyes—all the emotions from the last few days, weeks, months, pouring out.

They drove to a nearby Chinese restaurant and got seated at a sunny table.

"I'm so glad you're done with that place," Ali said. "You deserve so much better."

"I do," Mei agreed. Now she knew that for sure.

"I'm happy you're taking time off," Luc said.

"I need to process all this and recover. Thank god for therapy." Besides rent, paying for health insurance and weekly sessions with Violet were going to be Mei's biggest expenses. She'd never skimp on therapy, though. In their last session, Mei told Violet she wanted to start digging into her workaholic tendencies—what she used them to hide from, and why.

"Good," Ali said. "Keep going. Let us know if you need help with money, fun weekend plans, anything."

"I should be okay, moneywise." Ironically, her apartment—the one she'd initially despised—and its cheap rent, was the reason she'd replenished her savings enough to quit Livin without another job. "Now I can come up and spend more time with you."

"We'd love that."

A waiter came over bearing plates of plump dumplings and thick noodles stir-fried with vegetables.

Mei looked from Ali to Luc to Kaia. "I couldn't have done this without you. Thanks for being there for me." She dabbed her eyes as tears welled up again.

Ali hugged her. "We'll always look out for each other. You've taken care of me, too, especially when we were kids. Now it's my turn."

They tucked into the food and chatted about hikes they could do the next time Mei visited. Hiking reminded Mei of Alexandre, sending a wave of sadness through her.

"How's Alexandre these days?" she asked. "How was North Dakota?"

Ali and Luc shared a look.

Mei's stomach dropped. "He took the job, didn't he?"

Luc rolled his eyes. "He's telling his boss this afternoon."

Mei checked her phone. 12:43. Alexandre had a standing biweekly with Dr. Johnson on Fridays at two.

She dipped a dumpling in chili oil. Thoughts swirled through her mind.

When you know, you know.

You only have one life.

I'd rather be living.

All the chatter resolved into one person, his hair slightly mussed, his intelligent eyes bright with urgency. *You deserve all the love and happiness in the world. You're worthy of everything.*

Mei glanced at her phone again. 12:48.

"Any chance you feel like driving up to New Paltz?"

A smile spread across Ali's face.

Luc's eyes glinted. "Let's go."

• • •

"We're about forty minutes away?" Mei asked when they got in the car. She pulled up the New Paltz biology page on her phone and searched for Alexandre's office.

"Yup." Luc merged onto the highway. "We should arrive right before Alexandre's meeting."

"What are you going to do when you get there?" Ali asked from the front passenger seat.

"I'm not sure." What was she thinking, rushing up to New Paltz? Was she going to throw herself at Alexandre's feet while confessing her love? Beg him to stay?

"Are you doing something important?" Kaia asked from her car seat beside her.

"Yes," Mei said. "Your uncle Alexandre and I made a pact—a promise to each other. And I'm going to keep it."

"Want my lucky cat?" Kaia held out a stuffed white cat with one paw raised.

Mei carefully tucked the feline into her pocket. "Thanks, Kaia. I can use all the luck I can get."

Luc pulled into the SUNY New Paltz visitors lot. "One forty-one. Right on time." He turned in his seat to hug her. "Good luck, Mei. If anyone can talk some sense into my bonehead brother, it's you."

Mei kissed Kaia on the cheek, then jumped out of the car.

Ali ran around to her. Mei pulled her into a tight embrace. Her sister was her greatest gift. No matter what came next for her, in love and in life, Mei would be okay as long as she had Ali.

"Remember what I said about you always going after what you want?" Ali asked.

Mei nodded.

"Now go get your guy."

Mei laughed. "I can't believe I'm doing this."

Ali grinned and gave her a final squeeze. "I can. Love you."

"Love you, too."

CHAPTER FORTY-TWO

Alexandre sat at his desk reading the resignation email he'd drafted. He frowned and edited a few sentences to get the sentiment right. The gravity of the moment weighed upon him. Once he sent the email, there was no going back. He was effectively burning a bridge.

He checked the time. 1:40. Twenty minutes until his meeting with Dr. Johnson.

Twenty minutes to make his decision official.

Alexandre ran his hand over his face.

For so long he'd been torn between two lives. Two dreams.

A parade of images ran through his head: The sun-dappled gray mountains he saw every morning from campus. Dr. Johnson speaking proudly about her vision for the biology department. The students who flocked to his office hours. UND's gleaming zebrafish facility. His passionate future colleagues. The zealous look in Chris's eyes when he spoke of his plans for the genetics department.

Alexandre pictured Luc, Ali, and Kaia.

And Mei, her big brown eyes and long brown hair cascading

over her shoulders. Alexandre could practically smell her lemon-coconut scent.

Alexandre wanted her. He wanted it all. This life in New York, and this second chance in North Dakota.

Too bad that was impossible.

Dr. Johnson rapped on his door. Alexandre jumped.

"Sorry, Alexandre. Didn't mean to startle you. My last meeting ended early. We can chat now, if that works."

"I just need to send an email, but I'll catch up to you in the hallway."

Alexandre turned back to his resignation letter.

North Dakota.

New York.

Research.

Teaching.

Two futures.

One choice.

Alexandre drew a breath. In the end, there was no question at all.

He hit send, then walked out to give Dr. Johnson his news.

CHAPTER FORTY-THREE

Mei hurried across the campus, past groups of students gathering in the chilly March air. She'd memorized the path from the parking lot to Alexandre's office but frantically scanned each building to make sure she didn't miss her destination.

The science building loomed ahead. Mei broke into a run and checked her phone. 1:51. Just in time. She strode down the hallway, noting each office number until she reached Alexandre's.

It was empty. Mei stepped inside and glanced around, as if her presence would somehow conjure Alexandre. She peered outside. Still no sign of him. Maybe he was in another office.

Feeling a bit like a creeper, Mei walked the hallway, casually eyeballing each room.

"Can I help you?" a woman about her age asked when Mei peeked into her office.

Mei reddened. "I'm looking for Ale—, um, Professor Brodeur."

"His office is down the hall. I think he's with Dr. Johnson, though. They walked by a few minutes ago."

Mei's heart plummeted. She thanked the professor and slunk back to Alexandre's office. Inside, she lowered herself into the wooden chair next to his desk. There was nothing left to do but wait.

A clock on the wall ticked off the passing minutes. Mei stared at it until tears blurred her vision. How had she let Alexandre slip away?

She fumbled in her pocket for a tissue. Her hand brushed something soft. Mei pulled out Kaia's lucky cat. She stared at its smiling face. Sure, she needed luck now, more than ever. But so much of life came down to the decisions you made—how you handled the situations you found yourself in. Mei squeezed the lucky cat, then placed it back in her pocket. *I'll make my own luck.*

Footsteps sounded in the hall, then stopped abruptly.

"Mei?"

She turned. Alexandre stood in the doorway, looking spooked. Mei's heart hammered at the sight of him.

"Hi." She took a step toward him. Alexandre's piney scent filled her nose, tying her stomach in knots. His hazel eyes searched hers. His face mirrored her emotions. All the sadness and regret. "You're probably wondering what I'm doing here."

"I am." Alexandre let out an incredulous little laugh. "Sorry, I'm kind of in shock. I'm glad you're here, though. I need to tell you something." He shut the door and gently led her back to her seat. He sat down in his own chair, so close their knees nearly touched. "Mei, I—"

She held up a hand. "I want to hear everything you have to say. But if I don't speak now, I'm going to throw up, faint, or explode, and I don't think either of us wants that. Especially in your office."

The corners of Alexandre's mouth curved up. He nodded at her to continue.

"Last year, when you moved back, I thought I finally had it all: an amazing job, financial security, and a beautiful apartment. Everything came from my hard work—or so I thought. Work was a drug for me, like it was for you. It made me feel invincible, even as it hollowed me out from the inside. Worse, work let me avoid the problems between me and Joey—and my feelings for you." A flush rose to her cheeks, but she pressed on. "I've learned that being strong isn't about doing superhuman amounts of work. It's about facing reality, especially when it's messy and uncomfortable. I thought that getting promoted and speaking at Livin Forum was my dream. But when I got there, I saw how much more I'd lose if I stayed. So I quit. Today was my last day."

"I heard!"

"I don't have another job. I don't have that much money saved. I'll need a lot of time and therapy to heal. But I do know one thing: I haven't given up on you, or us. I care about you in a way that makes me believe anything is possible. Even if you're moving to North Dakota."

Mei looked into Alexandre's intelligent eyes. She drank in the angle of his jaw, the curve of his lips. The faint lines around his eyes, and the rogue strands of gray near his temples. Alexandre's gaze caressed her face. Mei knew he could see the dark circles starting to fade below her eyes, the healthy color finally returning to her cheeks.

"About North Dakota," Alexandre began. "I went there hoping it would be terrible. Instead, I was faced with every scientist's dream. So when I got the offer, I accepted."

Tears gathered in Mei's eyes.

"Then I turned it down."

Mei blinked in disbelief. "Really?"

"Yes." Alexandre wiped away her tears. "Just now. I sent UND my resignation letter."

"Why? How?"

Alexandre took her hand. "*You* made me see the error of my ways. When Luc told me you'd quit Livin, I was floored. Then I saw that you were choosing yourself. That made me think hard about my situation. At SUNY New Paltz, I already have a job that challenges me, while giving me growth opportunities and work/life balance. Plus, I get to live near the people I care about. I was so hung up on UND being a once-in-a-lifetime opportunity that I didn't see that I already had a once-in-a-lifetime job."

"You remembered what's important in life." Mei's lips tipped up into a smile.

"Finally. I met with Dr. Johnson just now to tell her I'll be renewing my contract here." Alexandre smiled, then his expression turned somber. "I realized that I still have a lot of work to do on myself. I nearly lost everything to research, again. I lost *you*, Mei. I wasn't there when you needed me the most. I'm so sorry. I hope you can forgive me."

Mei let out a sad little chuckle as she recalled her state of mind during that disastrous dim sum. "Well, I wasn't exactly honest with you. I hope you can forgive me, too."

"I can. Always. I'll do better for you, too. I emailed a few therapists to find one who can help me with chronic workaholism."

Mei squeezed his hand. "We'll do it together. *Petit à petit.*"

"*Petit à petit.*" Alexandre traced his fingers along her cheek. "I believe in us, too. I'm more sure about you than anything in the world."

Mei leaned in and closed the space between them. Those lips she'd longed for were finally right where she wanted them. As Alexandre pulled her close and ran his fingers through her hair, Mei's heart exploded with the warmth of a thousand dazzling suns.

This was love. The kind of love she'd never let herself dream of. A love she never thought she'd find, but one she now knew was possible.

A love she was worthy of.

Footsteps and laughter rang out from the hallway, making them jump.

"Good thing you closed that door," Mei said. "What if Dr. Johnson or one of your students busted in on us? Kissing in your office is a pretty high-risk, high-reward move."

Alexandre laughed, filling Mei with sunshine. "That's a risk I'm more than willing to take."

He drew her in, so close Mei felt his heart beating in time with hers. She smiled as their lips met. "I feel the exact same way."

EPILOGUE

Ten Months Later

The first hint of sunshine danced through the rustling palm trees. A gentle ocean breeze blew through the open windows, ruffling Mei's hair. She smiled sleepily. Beside her, Alexandre stirred.

"Morning." Mei reached up to brush back his sleep-tousled hair. Alexandre kissed her drowsily and wrapped an arm around her. Mei grinned as she snuggled against him, relishing his steady, assured touch. That golden current still glowed between them, electrifying, intimate, and soothing.

"What time is it?" Alexandre murmured.

Mei glanced at the small silver clock on the nightstand of their Ka'ōhao Beach rental. "Six thirty. We should get going. We don't want to be late." She pressed her lips against Alexandre's for another lingering moment, then pushed back the covers.

They roused themselves from bed and padded through the airy cottage. Mei showered, then pawed through her clothing to select an outfit. Noticeably absent from her luggage: her laptop. Neither she nor Alexandre had brought one on this trip.

After quitting Livin, Mei had taken three months off to sleep in, rediscover her hobbies, go to therapy, reconnect with friends, and spend time with Ali, Luc, Kaia, and, of course, Alexandre.

When her bank account balance began to make her nervous, she reached out to Diana, Ayanna, Kaden, Bryce, and Tamiko for contract marketing assignments. Her former colleagues were thrilled to work with her again. Mei liked how freelancing let her choose her projects while distancing her from the office politics and all-consuming nature of a full-time gig. Before long, she'd signed lucrative annual retainers with Diana's and Ayanna's companies. That financial security let her take on projects she was passionate about but paid less well, like working with Kaden on We're the First, or with new clients, like Hearts Across Chinatown, a nonprofit supporting local businesses.

Mei always had projects coming her way—more than she could ever accomplish. Last year, she would have said yes to everything. Now she said no. It wasn't easy. Guilt, fear, and regret racked her every time she turned down an assignment. But those ugly feelings lessened each time. *Petit à petit.* She knew better now.

In the kitchen, Alexandre mixed waffle batter. Mei squeezed his shoulder, then started chopping the pineapples and bananas they'd purchased from the farmer's market. They moved with an innate rhythm, passing utensils and washing each other's dishes. Mei glowed, remembering how they'd always had that ease, from the first time she'd stayed at his apartment after Livinpalooza.

Over the summer, Alexandre had moved to a more permanent place. He'd found a cottage, twenty minutes from the university, on what was once a working farm. The airy, minimalist space had white walls and reclaimed wood floors. It wasn't much larger than a studio apartment with a full kitchen, but it was the perfect size for two. Mei and Alexandre grilled outside and went running on nearby trails as the seasons changed from wildflowers covering the meadows to snow dusting the pines.

In October, after weeks of debating, Mei had moved out of Astoria. Her apartment had grown on her, but she missed the Upper West Side. Right before her lease expired, she found a cozy studio on West Sixty-Fourth Street. Queens would always be in her blood. And two places wouldn't make sense forever. But for now, Mei was living her dream with Alexandre, splitting their time between Manhattan and the Hudson Valley.

Once breakfast was ready, they carried everything out to the patio. The wooden table bore freshly brewed Kona coffee, waffles with fruit and honey, and scrambled eggs.

"It's snowing in New York." Alexandre pocketed his phone. "Ali requested sunny photos so she can live vicariously through us."

Mei pressed her cheek against Alexandre's and snapped a selfie, green palm fronds thick behind them. She sent Ali the photo.

Miss you!

Her sister replied a minute later.

You both look so relaxed and happy! Enjoy the sunshine! Also, your breakfast looks amazing, now that my appetite's back.

Mei's heart soared. Ali was four months pregnant and getting over a queasy first trimester. This time, she and Luc were expecting a boy.

After breakfast, Mei and Alexandre hopped into their rental Prius. They drove north until they reached a familiar parking lot: the nonprofit where they'd volunteered a year ago. Mei stepped out of the car, breathing in the loamy air and marveling at the green mountains towering overhead.

She pulled Alexandre into a side hug. "Ready to get dirty?"

His eyes twinkled as that mischievous smile spread across his face. "Always."

Lani greeted them warmly. "Welcome back! We love when volunteers return."

Soon, they were knee-deep in a muddy taro patch. The sun rose higher in the sky. Sweat ran down Mei's face. Working in the wet ground wasn't easy, but she was healthier and stronger than ever. So was Alexandre. Mei smiled to herself, admiring how his sweaty shirt clung to his lean torso. That view would never get old.

Two hours later, they stood on the bank of the streambed they'd replanted a year ago. A tangle of rich greenery lay before them. The delicate plantlings they'd placed in the ground had taken hold, burrowing their roots and growing hearty with nutrients from the soil.

Mei leaned against Alexandre's shoulder. "Last year, you were so sure we'd be back. How'd you know?"

He shrugged and kissed the top of her head. "I had a feeling."

Mei smiled into his chest. She had a feeling about a few things, too: how she wanted this life, with this man. And how he wanted that, just as much as she did.

Mei wrapped her arms around Alexandre's neck and stood on

tiptoe. He pulled her close, bringing his lips to hers. Mei tasted salt, sweat, and certainty. Alexandre's piney, sunscreen scent filled her nose, making her heady with joy. Arms around each other, they turned to gaze at the rainbow stretching over the green mountains, the sunshine flooding the lush fields. *How lucky we are.*

ACKNOWLEDGMENTS

Writing *Double Happiness* was a true joy. I'm so thankful for all the talented people who were part of my journey.

To my *Double Happiness* dream team, Clare Mao and Lashanda Anakwah: How did I end up with two extraordinarily smart, kind, funny, talented, and all-around wonderful fellow native New Yorkers as my agent and editor? I still can't believe how lucky I am.

Clare, you are the best partner. Thank you for your guidance every step of the way, from giving me tough but insightful editorial notes, to answering all my questions about publishing. From one Queens girl and Townsend Harris alum to another: I'm so glad we found each other.

Lashanda, in your first editorial note, you said your goal was to help shape *Double Happiness* into the best possible version of itself—and I think we did it. Thank you for pushing me to write a smarter, sharper novel, while always trusting my vision. I've grown so much from working with you. *Double Happiness* would not be the book it is today without your wisdom and editorial brilliance.

Phoebe Robinson, thank you for believing in me and my story. You've created an incredible space in the literary world, and I'm truly honored to be a Tiny Reparations author.

Also at Tiny Rep, thank you to Jamie Knapp, Diamond Bridges, Melissa Solis, Dora Mak, Alice Dalrymple, and Amy Ryan for your talents in bringing *Double Happiness* into the world. Joan Wong, Alissa Theodor, and Lorie Pagnozzi: Your cover and book design beautifully capture the essence of my story. Joan, I'm still in awe of how perfectly you rendered Mei.

I'm indebted to the talented teachers who taught me the art and business of fiction. Bryn Donovan, is it crazy to admit that when I was taking your class, I had a premonition that if I ever published *Double Happiness,* I'd be thanking you near the top of my acknowledgments? From the beginning, you understood my story—and that was the greatest gift. Your belief in my abilities, and my novel, boosted my confidence whenever I doubted myself. Your editorial notes and craft tips were so helpful, I carried them with me through each draft. Thank you for being a generous teacher and mentor.

Jennifer Close, thank you for giving me a supportive space to share my long, messy early draft (110,000 words, eek!). Your belief in my voice encouraged me to keep revising and start querying.

Vu Tran, your workshop on character provided much-needed inspiration when I was stuck. Thank you to Emily Adrian for helping me hone my dialogue, and to Thien-Kim Lam for offering an inclusive, inspiring romance workshop. Zulema Renee Summerfield and Kayla Rae Whitaker, I took your respective classes when I was new to fiction and had no idea what I was doing. Thank you for seeing the potential in my work and kindly encouraging me to keep writing.

Emma Brodie, your class truly helped me understand the art of querying. Elaine Hsieh Chou, your words of encouragement at the end of your flash fiction class gave me the push I needed to keep querying after many rejections.

I'm grateful to all the friends, acquaintances, and colleagues who shared their time and expertise. Anjie Zheng, my other fellow Queens girl and Townsend Harris alum: Thank you for pointing me in Clare's direction and introducing me to Kundiman classes and a wider community of Asian American writers and readers. I would never be here without you.

Huge thanks to my novel workshop mates: Liz P. G. Hirsch, Leah Kalinosky, Michael Londra, and Nicole Vecchiotti for being my first readers. Susan Lee, you are the most insightful reader and I always kept your notes in mind. I miss having you in the neighborhood!

Crystal Hana Kim, your feedback on an early excerpt helped me nail the perspective. Thanks to Celia Shatzman for your comments on the finer details. Kate Lee and Brendan Flaherty, your respective knowledge of the publishing business helped me immensely.

Lisa Andriolo, your bighearted answers to my questions about Eugene, Oregon, were key to my developing Alexandre's backstory. Thank you to Nathan Gioacchini for helping me understand the academic path of biologists. Meghna Majmudar, your insight into the current state of workplace DEI was so helpful. Yumeng Zhao, thank you for consulting on elements related to the Chinese language. Mei and Alexandre's volunteering experiences in Hawaiʻi were inspired by a trip to Kākoʻo ʻŌiwi, a wonderful Oʻahu nonprofit; thank you to Melissa Mau. Any inaccuracies on any of these topics are mine.

Endless appreciation to two of my oldest and dearest friends:

Karen Andriolo, thank you for your librarian expertise and for being a wonderful reader. Derek Guillemette, you've been a helpful sounding board on every random book topic that comes up during our coffee walks.

Laura Lee, a million thanks for everything.

A big shout-out to my former colleagues—and an extra-big shout-out to Frankie Goldstone and Marnie Williams—who cheered me on when I said I was taking a break from tech marketing to write a romance. I remember each of your kind words.

To the Asian American authors who came before: Seeing your names on book covers made me believe there might be a place for me in the publishing world.

My uncle, Alvin Eng, is the fellow writer in my family, and has encouraged me to keep at it ever since I was a kid. Alvin, your perseverance and success inspire me.

To my family: the Engs, Restifs, SooHoos, Moores, Burgers, and Zimmers, thank you for your encouragement during the many years I spent writing this book.

To Meme and E, so much love and appreciation for looking after little Lily and giving me precious time to write.

To Lily, for filling my life with love. I'm in awe of you and so proud of you every day. Thank you for reminding me to be proud of myself, too.

Mallory, you are forever my inspiration. Who would've guessed our long-running inside joke would become a novel? I write every word with you in mind, as if I'm speaking to you. You are the world's best sister, my most supportive reader, my real-life Ali, and my other half. Love you so much.

And Christophe. Your unconditional love is the only reason I was able to write a love story. You believed in my ability to write a novel before you'd read a word of my fiction. Your academia tales and wise life advice shaped every part of this story. Thank you for reading countless drafts, instantly understanding my intentions, laughing at my humor, offering the most intelligent suggestions, and always being up for research trips. You are the best partner in every area of life, and I'm so lucky. I love you.

ABOUT THE AUTHOR

Heather Eng is a third-generation Chinese American who grew up in Queens, New York. A lifelong writer, she graduated from Boston University with a journalism degree and worked as a newspaper journalist, a web editor, and a senior marketing leader in the tech industry. Heather lives in Manhattan with her husband and daughter. *Double Happiness* is her first novel.